To calm himself by movi███████████████████
the opened target made h████ ██ a baffoon,
Follett rose from his chair. He fingered the duplicate
target on its display stand. It was a missile nose
cone, sectioned to split along the centerline and to
display the dummy nuclear trigger within. Lead
segments were individually pinned to the inner
surface of a sphere the size of a soccer ball. In the
original, mirror-polished wedges of plutonium would
be held in place by the explosive lining itself.
Follett and his aides had considered using a filling
of flash powder or the like. In the end they had
decided not to do anything that might have put
their demonstration on a level with all those others
which were intended only to maintain modest
program funding. The DIA was going for the throat
on this one. Nothing that would cheapen the effect
could be permitted.

DAVID DRAKE
SKYRIPPER

TOR

A TOM DOHERTY ASSOCIATES BOOK

This is a work of fiction. All the characters and events portrayed in this book are fictional, and any resemblance to real people or incidents is purely coincidental.

SKYRIPPER

First Tor printing: April 1983
Second printing: February 1986

A TOR Book

Published by Tom Doherty Associates
49 West 24 Street
New York, N.Y. 10010

Cover art by Vincent DiFate

ISBN: 0-812-53618-5
CAN. ED.: 0-812-53619-3

Printed in the United States

0 9 8 7 6 5 4 3 2 1

DEDICATION

To Mr. August Derleth, who spent more effort on helping young writers than we were objectively worth at the time.

ACKNOWLEDGMENT

Friends are people who come through when you need them. Many of my friends came through for me while I was writing this novel. I regret that I cannot for their own sakes acknowledge them by name; but that does not mean that I have forgotten or will ever forget their help.

PROLOGUE

The sound of the weapon firing was as brief and vicious as the first crack of nearby lightning. There was nothing more, no thunder rolling, deafening. Banks of fluorescent lights staggered on all over the laboratory compound as the TVA grid took over again from the emergency generator. The yellow glow-lamps that had remained on during testing tripped out when the generator driving them did.

The Secretary of State frowned in a combination of surprise and mild irritation. He had seen laser weapons tested in the past. A pale beam would lick out of the ungainly apparatus. Relays might hammer, pulsing the available power into microsecond bullets of energy that were hot enough to do realistic damage downrange. The target was ordinarily a thin sheet of titanium whose thermal conductivity was so low that it concentrated every erg it received on the point of impact. Vaporized metal would curl away like smoke from a cigarette—incidentally and inevitably scattering the beam which still attacked the target surface. At last a hole would open in the sheet, expanding as the operator shifted the beam to nibble away at the edges.

In addition, if the laser were chemically fueled, there would be the roar and rush of fluorine and heavy hydrogen combining into an expensive form of hydrofluoric acid. The waste product cheerfully dissolved glass, platinum, and virtually

everything· else. Cleaning up after a test was
similar to dealing with a spill of Cobalt 60, but
presumably it would be all right to dump the crap
straight into the upper atmosphere during service
use.

All in all, a laser demonstration could be expected to be a spectacular show. It was that, even
more than his frequent assertions that a strong
defense was a necessary concomittant to a strong
diplomacy, which had led the Secretary of State to
accept the invitation to a Top Secret briefing by
the Defense Intelligence Agency.

And this had not been spectacular in the least.

The Secretary turned away from the heavy lead-
glass window of the observation room. He and his
aide wore civilian clothes, but his aide would
return to active duty as a lieutenant commander
when he left the Secretary's personal service. The
other three men were in dress uniforms, imposing
with gold braid and medal ribbons. Still, there
was no question as to where the power lay during
this administration. "All right," said the Secretary
of State, "what went wrong, Follett?"

The lieutenant general in Air Force blue was
Director of the Defense Intelligence Agency. He
understood his duties perfectly. His two top
aides—a rear admiral and an army Brigadier
general—were less experienced in testifying to
hostile Congressional committees and like affairs.
General Follett gave them a sweeping glance of
reminder before he said, "Nothing at all went
wrong, Mr. Secretary. That is—" he nodded to the
observation window. Mechanical arms could
be seen dollying toward the target— "This was
a normal test. That's all that happens. Overt-
ly."

He paused, coughing to clear his throat and to
settle the wash of fear that had leapt up when he
committed himself. Normally, high-ranking observers would have been in the control room with

the scientists conducting the test. If anything had gone wrong under those circumstances, General Follett would have known before he had to make a fool of himself. This time the observers had to be rigidly separated from the scientists: top secret matters much more sensitive than the hardware were about to be discussed.

To calm himself by moving and to fill time before the opened target made him a hero or a buffoon, Follett rose from his chair. He fingered the duplicate target on its display stand. It was a missile nose cone, sectioned to split along the centerline and to display the dummy nuclear trigger within. Lead segments were individually pinned to the inner surface of a sphere the size of a soccer ball. In the original, mirror-polished wedges of plutonium would be held in place by the explosive lining itself. Follett and his aides had considered using a filling of flash powder or the like. In the end they had decided not to do anything that might have put their demonstration on a level with all those others which were intended only to maintain modest program funding. The DIA was going for the throat on this one. Nothing that would cheapen the effect could be permitted.

Metal squealed in the test chamber, audible even through the thick walls. It was the first sign that the weapon had functioned properly. The mechanical arms prizing apart the halves of the target had popped a fresh weld.

All five of the men in the observation room were staring intently through the window now. General Follett had remained standing; the others leaned forward in their chairs. The arms, controlled by the technicians invisible in the room next door, slowly rotated the dummy warhead. Floodlights especially rigged for this demonstration flashed on to illuminate the interior.

"I'll be damned," said the Secretary of State.

The three uniformed men shifted stance minusculy. It had worked. At least—the hardware had worked.

The lead blocks which had been in the path of the momentary beam had slumped and twisted. Their surfaces were no longer dully metallic but rather a furry white where the lead had recrystallized after melting. Other segments only a finger's breadth away were unchanged from their original appearance.

"If this had been a live trigger and not a test unit," the general said, "the implosion charge would almost certainly have been set off by the beam. Even if it had not exploded, the elements of the fission trigger have obviously—" he waved toward the window— "been damaged to the extent that the device would melt down rather than detonate when the warhead reached its target. And if the particle beam had struck the booster stage of a missile rather than the nose cone proper, the fuel and oxidizer tanks—no matter how they were hardened and protected—would have been flash-heated to the point of catastrophic explosion."

"Particle beam," repeated the Secretary, staring at the damaged target. He turned slowly toward the military men. All of them now were standing. "All right, I'm not a bad person to impress . . . but I don't have a thing to do with the funding of this project, you know. And I don't have a thing to do with you or the DoD, either—not in any way that matters to you.

"So why did the Defense Intelligence Agency drag me out to Oak Ridge to see—" he waved— "this?"

Follett sucked in his gut. In round tones that masked his nervousness he said, "As you have seen, Mr. Secretary, particle beam technology has the potential of developing into the most important defensive tool in our nation's arsenal."

He paused. "In the arsenal of *any* nation. What concerns us—here in this room—is that evidence suggests that the Soviets have already developed the—principle—to a stage well beyond what you have seen here. If our information is correct, a Russian scientist has made a breakthrough as important as the one that gave the Soviets their initial lead in hydrogen bombs."

The Secretary's aide straightened in surprise. The Secretary himself was more direct. "What the Hell do you mean by that?" he snapped, his heavy eyebrows closing together. "*We* had the H-bomb first. Have you forgotten Bikini?"

General Follett dipped his chin, knowing the chance he was taking to make his point. "We— American scientists—detonated the first thermonuclear device on Bikini Atoll, that is correct," he said. "The device used tritium and deuterium to fuel the reaction. These isotopes were in such short supply that no significant—no military—use could have been made of the principle. Furthermore—" the Secretary of State's look was fading from irritation to puzzlement, but Follett avoided making eye contact— "the tritium had to be chilled. The entire apparatus would have filled two railroad boxcars. It could not have been *transported* by air, much less delivered in the military sense of the term. Unlike the bomb the Russians exploded nine months later, using lithium hydride instead of heavy hydrogen as the major fuel element."

"Fortunately," broke in Rear Admiral Haynes, "by analyzing fallout from the blast, we were able to duplicate the Soviets' research before their advantage became decisive. Our own personnel— scientists—had determined to their satisfaction that lithium hydride would not sustain a thermonuclear reaction. Fortunately, they were not wholly incapable of learning from their opponents. I assure you, the Soviets gained nothing from Klaus Fuchs and his like to equal what we learned from Soviet above-ground testing."

"All right, get to the point," said the Secretary, straightening again in his chair. The men in uniform had five minutes, a fact the politician made adequately clear by glancing at his thin, gold watch.

"The problem with particle beam weapons," said Follett, plunging toward the invisible deadline, "and with all energy weapons, is the energy source. It's all very well to tie into the commercial power grid when we're testing devices here in Tennessee or Nevada. For the weapons to be really effective, however, they need to be based in space, in orbit over the sites from which hostile missiles may be launched. For that . . . well, all manner of solutions have been suggested. But the simple solution, and a solution that might work for the microseconds which are all a particle beam—" he tapped the dummy nose cone— "requires, would be to detonate a thermonuclear device and focus portions of its energy output into, ah, beams."

"How are you going to focus something that's vaporizing everything around it the moment it gets there?" asked the Secretary. The demonstration he had just seen was real. If the reason behind it turned out to be nonsense, he was out the door and gone, though. "Look, Follett, we have a Science Committee at State, too. If you people want to go jaw them about this stuff, that's fine, but *I'm* on a tight schedule."

"Many of the best minds in the field agree, Mr. Secretary," the general said soothingly, "that such a proposal is impossible, even in theory. It would appear, however, that on the other side of the line there's a Professor Evgeny Vlasov, who has developed a—theoretical, at least—method of drawing several dozen simultaneous, magnetically focused, bursts from a single thermonuclear device."

"Oh, for Christ's sake, call it an H-bomb like a human being!" snapped the Secretary of State. He was not looking at the military men, though. His bushy stare was directed at some indefinite bank of instruments while his fingers drummed the side of the chair seat. His mind was neither place, turning over possibilities. He looked up at Follett. "If that were true," he said carefully, "any missiles we attempted to send over the Pole would detonate a few yards out of their silos. That's what you're trying to tell me?"

Redstone, the Brigadier general, spoke for the first time since the demonstration. "Yeah, with normal allowance for error, of course. 95% of anything we launched, say. And we guess a bolt that can do that—" he thumbed toward the twisted warhead in the test chamber— "would pretty well scramble a B-52, too. Or the White House, if somebody wanted to get cute."

"All right," the civilian repeated. "Since I don't suppose you brought me here to propose we surrender now to the Sovs, what *do* you have in mind?"

"We would like," said General Follett, staring at his wedding band rather than the Secretary of State, "your support for a plan to secure Professor Vlasov's defection to the United States."

"Oh," said the Secretary. "Oh . . .," and he settled back in his chair, relaxing now that he had enough information at last to guess why he was being manipulated. A smile quirked the corners of his mouth. "Does the JCS know you've got something in mind?" he asked in amusement. "You people at the DIA, that is."

Follett's tongue touched his lips, but he managed to control his reflexive glance toward the Secretary's aide. He knew that Lieutenant Commander Platt was secretly reporting to the Joint Chiefs of Staff on all of the Secretary of State's activities. The DIA further suspected that

Platt was also leaking information to the Office of Naval Intelligence. By charter, the ONI was supposed to be under the control of the Defense Intelligence Agency. In practice, it—and the other service intelligence staffs—were as parochial as the KGB and very nearly as hostile to one another. The presence of a known double agent at the secret meeting had complicated Follett's task enormously, but there had been no alternative. If the DIA had burned Platt, exposing him to the Secretary, his replacement might very well have been controlled by the CIA.

"I have briefed the Chairman, yes," Follett said, "on our intention to approach you, sir, and the necessity for it." With an appearance of steely candor, he added. "The Defense Intelligence Agency is only the information collection and assessment arm of the Department of Defense. My colleagues and I are as much controlled by the Joint Chiefs as are the lowliest recruits in training."

"Go on," said the Secretary in irritation. "I'm waiting for a concrete proposal." He could not know, of course, that Follett's bit of fluff was meant not for him but for his aide.

"Yes sir," said the general, nodding quickly and continuing to meet the civilian's eyes. "Well. One of our agents made contact with Professor Vlasov. This was fortuitous, rather than a major priority of the Agency—" perhaps he shouldn't have admitted that— "because the Professor appeared from all the information we had available to us to be at least as politically reliable as a member of the Politburo." Follett cleared his throat. "The Professor not only had all the perquisites available to a scientist of genius—which he is—within the Soviet Union, his love for his motherland is of exceptional and tested quality. He has only one arm, you see. He lost the other in 1943 during the Siege of Leningrad when the satchel charge he had been throwing into a German blockhouse exploded prematurely. He had refused several offers of evacuation previous to that occurrence, since it was evident even then to the Party leadership that Vlasov's endeavors would be more valuable to the State in the laboratory than on the front line."

"How did you get an agent into the Soviet Union, Follett?" demanded the Secretary as if he had not been listening to the remainder of the general's discourse.

Admiral Wayne coughed behind his hand. Follett warned him with a quick gesture. "Ah, Mr Secretary," he said. "I'm afraid we can't go into sources and methods at this time. . . ."

"Look, General," the civilian went on, "either your agent is playing you for a fool—or the KGB is." He paused. "Or maybe everything you've just told me about Vlasov is a lie? Why would a man like that want to defect? Did somebody catch his son in Dzerzhinsky Square with a firebomb? Have we turned up photos of him with the Premier's wife? Because there's not a whole lot else that would make somebody like that decide to fly the coop, is there?"

One of Follett's subordinates cleared his throat nervously. There was an answer to that question, but it was an answer they had hoped to be able to finesse giving. They had even considered concocting a lie, but there were no lies they could think of which fit Vlasov's background and were significantly more reasonable than the story their agent had told them for true. "Well, Mr. Secretary," the general said, "it appears that Professor Vlasov has been experiencing difficulties of a, ah—" Follett locked his hands behind his back to stop himself from twiddling his fingers in front of the others— "problems of a psychiatric nature."

The Secretary of State blinked. Follett bulled

onward, saying, "Ah, the Professor believes he is being persecuted by, well, aliens . . . And he appears to believe that we in the West will be better able to protect him from them."

The civilian hooted and slapped his thigh. "Say, that's *great*!" he roared. "And I suppose you want me to set up a Little Green Man Patrol in State? Jesus, that's great! Chuckie—" he prodded his embarrassed aide in the ribs— "how'd you like to head up the National Space Patrol?"

"I assure you, Mr. Secretary," the DIA chief said stiffly, "that we would not have developed this mission—even to the present extent—were we not. . . . Well, our agent assures us that Professor Vlasov was entirely lucid during lengthy discussions of nuclear physics. He may well have cracked under the strain of his work or of life within a police state—but he has not become stupid as a result; nor has he lost his expertise."

The uniformed men stiffened when the Secretary stood up, but the politician was walking toward the duplicate nose cone rather than the door. "All right," the civilian said, "I can see that. Does he speak English?"

"Ah—" Follett said.

Rear Admiral Wayne cleared his throat and replied, "No Sir, he does not, though we gather he may be able to parse his own way through technical material. His French is fluent—his mother was a Breton—and it was in French that our agent contacted the Professor."

That was more than Follett had wanted the Joint Chiefs—or the State Department, for that matter —to know about their agent, a Vietnamese physicist named Hoang Tanh. The Secretary, at least, ignored the slip. "Well, if he can't talk to them directly," the civilian said, "we can make sure the story we give the media is *our* story and not his own. All right." The Secretary's fingers traced the sharp edges of the blocks which simulated the plutonium core. His nails left a hint of a line across the lead oxide. With the unhurried certainty of a record changer cocking, he turned to the general again. "All right," he repeated, "what *do* you want from State, Follett?"

Brigadier General Redstone took over as planned. "Sir," he said, a mental heel click though his feet remained splayed on the concrete floor. "Mr Secretary, you'll appreciate that however bad Professor, ah . . . the Professor may want to get out of Russia, it's flat out impossible for a scientist like that to do it. Some Jew doctor, sure, if he's willing to sweat for a couple years. But, ah, Vlasov, they *know* he's worth more to us than he is to them. They've *got* his math already. Any hint that he plans a bunk and *zip*! He gets it where the chicken got the axe."

General Redstone had the intense glare of a preacher warming to his subject. He cocked his upper body forward, bringing his face a few inches closer to that of the Secretary of State. The civilian edged backward reflexively. "Now, the Professor *will* be getting out from behind the Iron Curtain in a couple weeks," Redstone continued, "a conference in Algiers. That's his chance and our chance—and it's the only chance we're going to get. If Vlasov's as crazy as the reports say—" Follett and the admiral winced, but Redstone plowed on obliviously— "then the Sovs aren't going to leave him loose very long, even if they don't know we've contacted him."

"The conference on nuclear power?" said the Secretary's aide, speaking almost for the first time that evening. "The one in Algeria? We're boycotting it because it threatens still wider proliferation of nuclear weapons in the non-advanced world."

"That's right," agreed the soldier, "and there you've put your finger on the fucking rub. On both of them, I ought to say."

You ought to have said something else entirely, thought Follet; but the Secretary appeared to have been caught up in Redstone's enthusiasm, so the DIA chief did not interrupt. Not the sort of candor you ran into a lot in Foggy Bottom, he supposed. Or the Pentagon, come to think.

"Because the Algerians are just as red as the Chinks and the Russkies," the brigadier was continuing, "what with them and the Libyans carrying on a war against us in the Western Sahara—"

Here Follett had to interrupt. "Against our ally, the King of Morocco," he corrected.

"Right," Redstone went on. "That's the sort of people we'd be dealing with. They'll take our dollars for natural gas quick enough, but they're not about to help a top scientist escape from one of their Communist buddies. And the other thing is—" Redstone paused to take a deep breath, fixing the Secretary with his eyes during the pause— "we don't have a delegation to the goddam conference to plant a team in. The Canadians do, but they won't play ball—all that new flap with *their* security force scared them shitless."

"Ah, Red," Follett said, "I don't think the Secretary is—"

"Oh, right, right," the brigadier said. "Well, if it weren't for the agent who made the touch to begin with, we still wouldn't have a snowball's chance of extracting the Professor. But he's there in place. And if you can keep the lid on at the UN—and the White House—if there's a flap, we'll get Vlasov out."

The civilian gave Redstone a scowl of dawning concern. "What sort of flap?" he demanded. "You don't have some wild-hare notion about going in with a battalion of Marines, do you?"

"Huh?" said Redstone. "Oh, Hell, no. Not Marines—"

"Let me take over here, General," Follett said loudly. Brigadier General Redstone had wanted to use elements of the 82nd Airborne Division for the snatch; Follett was sure that he was about to blurt that fact. To anyone outside the military community, that would have appeared to be a distinction without a difference.

"Mr Secretary," Follett continued, "we will —our agents will be operating in what must for the purpose be considered a hostile country. And Professor Vlasov, despite his desire to flee to freedom, will be escorted by KGB personnel who will stop at nothing to prevent him from doing so. It may well be necessary to take—" the general drew a deep breath; his Air Force background permitted him to be queasy when discussing murder from less than 40,000 feet up— "direct action to save the Professor's life. Furthermore, while the operation will be under the control of a DIA operative, the—heavy work—will be carried out by local agents. It is simply a fact of life that one cannot expect perfect . . . discretion from, ah, freedom fighters in a situation of this sort."

The Secretary of State turned away with a look of distaste. "You mean," he said, "that it's going to be World War III in downtown Algiers if you go ahead with this."

"No, Mr Secretary," said Rear Admiral Wayne. "It's going to be World War III if we don't go ahead with this. And we're going to lose."

The civilian grimaced, but he did not respond at once. Finally he said, "General Follett, isn't the Central Intelligence Agency better suited to carry out this, ah, program with a minimum of, of publicity?"

Follett sucked in his gut again. "Sir," he said, "without a contact agent to keep Professor Vlasov informed of the plans, there would be absolutely no way of achieving his successful defection. Only we in the Defense Intelligence Agency have such an agent—or could have one in the time available."

"Well, you could tell the CIA about your prize agent, couldn't you?" the Secretary snapped. "Does he only talk Army jargon or something?"

"Sir," Follett said, standing as if he were about to salute the flag, "the Central Intelligence Agency is not responsible for the safety of our agent. *We* are. This is a man who has trusted us, who has provided valuable intelligence for many years out of his love of free society. I'm sorry, sir, I cannot permit him to be compromised by divulging his identity to parties who would throw away his life without hesitation if it suited their purposes."

"We can handle this, Mr Secretary," added General Redstone. "Remember, it was us and not those state-department rejects at Langley who bribed the Russky to defect with his MiG-25."

"Jesus," said the Secretary of State. He was staring out the observation window at the melted target. "All right," he said, turning. "General Follett, you have my support for this project—"

"Project Skyripper," Redstone interrupted unhelpfully with a grin.

"My support for this project," the Secretary repeated, "let the chips fall where they may. And yes, I'll take care of the President. . . . But General—" he scowled at the trio of uniforms— "all of you! You'd better get him out. If you've made me a party to another Bay of Pigs, believe me—you won't have careers. You won't have heads."

The Secretary spun on his heel. "Come on, Chuckie," he snapped, "we're getting out of here. And I only pray I shouldn't have left an hour ago."

The door banged behind the two men from State.

"Well, that's settled," said Follett in relief.

"Whether it was or not, I think we had to go ahead with the operation," said Rear Admiral

Wayne somberly. "You know how much I dislike the methods we have to use on this one, but the alternative is—" he shook his head— "just what the Secretary said it was. Surrender to the Russians now. I just hope that this man Kelly doesn't let us down."

General Redstone was rubbing his hands together. "Tom Kelly?" he said. "Oh, he'll come through. And what a punch in the eye for those bastards down in Langley!"

I

"Mr. Kelly?" called the lieutenant in dress greens. "Mr. Kelly? Over here—I'm here to pick you up."

Tom Kelly scowled across the security barrier at the green uniform, showing more distaste than he actually felt for the man inside the cloth. Of course, he didn't know the lieutenant from Adam; and he knew the uniform very well indeed. "In a second," he called back in English. Moving to the side so as not to block the flow of disembarking passengers, Kelly relaxed and watched the show that Orly Airport and the Russian Embassy were combining to stage.

Six men as soft and pasty-looking as maximum-security prisoners were being passed through the magnetic detector arch. None of them had hand luggage to be fluoroscoped. It was enough of a break in routine that the women and lone gendarme in charge of the barrier were more alert than usual. That was nothing compared to the attentiveness of the four bulky men escorting the others, however.

Two of the escorts had stepped around the barrier ahead of their charges. They had displayed diplomatic passports and a note to avoid the detector. Otherwise the alarm would have clanged at the pistols they wore holstered under dark suits. The suits were in themselves so ill-fitting as to be virtually a uniform for low-ranking Russians. The escorts watched the six pale men with angry determination. In general, the passengers bustling

22

through the barrier in either direction ignored the scene, lost in their own meetings and farewells. If the crowd seemed to be edging someone too close to the men under escort, one of the guards would interpose with as little ceremony as a linebacker going for the ball. Squawks of protest from buffeted travellers were ignored with flat-eyed disdain.

The last of the six charges passed through the arch. The steel zipper in one's trouser fly had set off the alarm; there had been no other incident. The two escorts in the rear shouldered past the barrier in turn, waving passports without bothering to speak to or even look at the attendants.

The whole group tramped down the hallway toward the Aeroflot gates. Even a note from the Russian Ambassador would not have gotten armed men around the security check had they not been travelling on their own national airline. The charges shambled in a column of twos, with their escorts half a pace out at each corner. One of the latter gave Kelly a hard look as he passed. The American smiled back and nodded. Not a real bright thing to do, but he wasn't a surveillance agent. The Lord knew he wasn't that.

Tom Kelly was five-foot nine and stocky. In bad light he could have been any age; in the combination of sunlight and the fluorescents over the security barrier, he looked all of his 38 years. His face was broad and tan and deeply wrinkled. Black hair was beginning to thin over his pate. Though he was clean-shaven, an overnight growth of whiskers gave him a seedy look that his rumpled blazer did nothing to dispel. Sighing, he picked up his AWOL bag and his radio, then walked to the impatient lieutenant across the barrier.

"The general is, ah, anxious to see you, sir," the lieutenant said. "If you don't mind, we'll leave your luggage to be claimed later. There's need for haste."

"Here, carry my clothes, then," Kelly said, thrusting his AWOL bag at the officer. "Well, don't look so surprised. For Christ's sake, I was just over in Basel. Train would have made a lot more sense than buying me a ticket on Swissair."

"Er," said the lieutenant. "Well, we have a car and driver waiting at the front entrance." He began striding off through the concourse, glancing back over his shoulder at Kelly. The civilian paced him, moving with an ease surprising in a man so squat. He held his short-wave receiver out in front of him nonchalantly enough to belie its twelve-pound weight.

The car was there, all right, though the driver with Spec 5 chevrons on his greens was arguing with a pair of airport security men and a gendarme. "That's all right," the lieutenant called in English. He tossed Kelly's bag on the hood of the sedan and fumbled out—for Christ's sake!—his own black passport which he waved in the policeman's face. Must be great to work in an airport the dips use a lot, Kelly thought. He opened the door of the sedan and flipped the seat down.

The lieutenant swung back to the car, but he hesitated when he saw that Kelly was gesturing him into the back seat. "Go ahead," the civilian said. He peered at the lieutenant's name-plate. "Morley. I figure if I rate a chauffeured limousine—" it was an AMC Concord, olive drab, with motor pool registration numbers stencilled on the doors— "I can choose where I sit in it."

Lieutenant Morley ducked into the back. Kelly retrieved his AWOL bag from the hood and handed it ceremoniously in to the lieutenant. Only then did he set his radio on the seat beside the driver and get in himself. "The Embassy, as fast as you can make it," Morley muttered.

"Which is probably less fast than a local taxi would get us there," Kelly said, watching traffic as the driver eased into the stream of vehicles. "But then, it's still probably a lot faster than we really need to get there. Unless the Army has changed one Hell of a lot in the past few years."

The lieutenant did not respond. The pink enamel of his Military Intelligence lapel insignia clashed with the green uniform. The insignia was a dagger, covered by a rose to 'symbolize the *sub rosa* mission of the organization.' Christ, if brains were dynamite, there still wouldn't be any need to tiptoe in the Military Heraldry Office.

Or in any MI unit Tom Kelly had ever been around. "Do you know what you were seeing in the airport?" he said aloud, leaning his back against the door to be able to watch Morley's expression. "The KGB types and all?"

"What?" the lieutenant said, sitting up abruptly enough to skew his saucer hat on the car's headliner.

Kelly rocked also as the sedan shifted to the right, around a wheezing stake-bed truck. For as long as it took to pass the truck, they were in a slot between a pair of buses who were moving as fast as traffic on the A6 permitted. Kelly could see no higher than the bumper of the second bus when he glanced into the rear-view mirror. "Right, KGB," he continued. "Four of them, big fellows guarding those other—" the car snapped left again, barely clearing the truck's radiator, but without danger since they were accelerating away— "Russians."

"Phillips, my God!" Morley said to the driver. Then he swallowed angrily and took off his hat. "I didn't. . .," he said to the civilian. "That is—I saw them, but I didn't know that's who they were. Good God, do you mean those hunched up little men were prisoners? What *was* that?"

Kelly smiled, leaning a trifle away from the door. The sedan was riding hard, transmitting the road shocks through the frame unpleasantly. "Oh, no," he said, "they were all free citizens of Mother Russia. Thing is, they were the embassy's code and communications staff, the folks who've been handling and encrypting all the message traffic for the past couple years."

The sedan braked heavily in the congestion of the approaching Boulevard Peripherique. Kelly braced his foot on the firewall and laid his left hand on the top of his radio to anchor it. "They come in the same way, under escort from the moment they leave the plane to the time the embassy gate shuts behind them. They spend the next two years in the embassy compound, working shift and shift—and generally stay in the same building that whole time besides. And when their tour's up, they're guarded back to the door of the plane. What they see of Paris is right out there—" he waved at the building fronts of the Citie Internationale they were passing. The sedan was accelerating at its sluggish best.

"You don't have to kill us, you know, Phillips," the lieutenant protested.

"No sir," agreed the driver. He crossed the Boulevard Brune on what the cross traffic thought was a green light for them. Brakes and horns protested.

Morley swallowed again but did not comment. The green shade of the Parc de Monsouris swept past the windows at speed. "You know," the lieutenant said at last, "that's really what sets the Free World off from the Reds. It's not economics, the way they like to pretend; it's the way each side treats human beings. What you've just described is quite simply inhuman."

Kelly shrugged. "Well, you do what you've got to do," he said. "They don't have many code clerks defect, for damn sure." He paused. The tires were drumming heavily over the pavement of the Boulevard Raspail. "Besides," he continued, "I saw a lot

of Cambodia about the same way. Something
short of a leisurely tour, you might say. And Laos,
for that matter."

"You were in Laos?" Morley asked. He was
keeping his eyes fixed on the civilian, apparently
so that he would not have to be visually aware of
what the sedan was doing.

"Off and on," Kelly agreed. "Hunting elephants,
of all things."

"*Oh*," the lieutenant said. "Oh." He laughed
awkwardly. "You see, I thought you meant while
you were, ah, in service."

The civilian smiled back. "Right the first time,"
he said. "We were machine-gunning them from
slicks—ah, from UH1 helicopters—"

"I know what a slick is," Morley objected stiffly.

"Good, good—shooting them from slicks at
night, using starlight scopes. Somebody'd decided
that the dinks were using the elephants to pack
supplies down the Ho Chi Minh trail. We were
supposed to be destroying hostile transport by
blasting Dumbos."

The lieutenant's lips worked. "That's—that's
. . . . I mean, elephants are an endangered
species, and to just massacre them from the
air. . . ."

"Don't expect *me* to argue with you," Kelly said
with another shrug. "But we were getting some
secondary explosions when we hit the beggars,
too. So I suppose the folks in Washington were
right, at least on the Intelligence side."

As they swung from the Quai Anatole France onto
the approaches of the Pont de la Concorde, the sedan
took the line in front of a Mercedes. Metal rang
as the cars stopped. Traffic began to move again,
and Phillips eased the sedan along with it. A
plump man in a three-piece suit rolled down the
passenger window of the Mercedes and began
shouting curses in French. Kelly rolled down his
own window and leaned out. He did not speak. The

Mercedes window closed again. Its liveried
chauffeur braked to permit a Fiat to slip between
the two bigger cars.

Morley scowled into his clenched hands, but he
said nothing aloud.

Kelly, on the outside of the sedan as it rounded
the Place de la Concorde, could see only the base
of the obelisk in the center. Perversely, he
watched that none the less, rather than the Neo-
Classical magnificence of Louix XV's own time for
which the obelisk was to be only the neutral hub.
220 tons of polished and incised granite, 75 feet
high even without its 18th Century base, the
obelisk was Kelly's own answer to Shelley's
'Ozymandias.' Indeed, look on that work and
despair. Like its slightly smaller sister—Cleopatra's Needle—and the both of them well over
a millenium old before Cleopatra was con-
ceived—it had remained effectively unchanged
as empire followed empire, as monarchs and
nations fought and built and died. The stone remained, though no one knew the name of the men
who had fashioned it, and few enough that of the
Pharaoh—Thutmose III—who had commissioned
its erection. Men, even men whom their age
thought great, would pass utterly away. But with
determination, a man might leave behind him an
achievement that could be his personal—though
anonymous—beacon to history.

In front of the American Embassy on the Rue
Gabriel strolled a pair of French police carrying
submachine guns. Kelly touched his tongue to his
lips, a sign of momentary tension to anyone who
knew him well enough. He had carried a gun like
that, an MAT 49, in the field for several months,
after he took it from an NVA officer killed by
Claymore mines. In the field, in War Zone
C ... Khu Vuc C ... and that gun had been
rebarreled to chamber East Bloc 7.62 mm ammo,

but the sight of the gendarmes took him back regardless.

And it seemed that the Pentagon wanted him back in those jungles of his mind. It was the only reason he could imagine for a terse summons five years after they had decided Tom Kelly was too erratic to keep on the government payroll.

At the embassy gate, the driver brought his sedan to a halt that did not squeal the tires but did rock both passengers forward from deceleration stresses. A uniformed Marine saluted from the guard post to the right. The gate slid back, allowing the sedan to accelerate through. Across the driveway, the statue of Franklin scowled. Kelly wondered whether his own expression mimicked the statue's—and the thought broke his heavy face into a genuine smile.

The car stopped in front of the entrance. "As ordered, sir," Phillips said. He opened his door.

Kelly got out without waiting for the driver to walk around the car. They met at the front fender while Lieutenant Morley straggled out of the back seat. The civilian kicked the tire and smiled. "Keep about forty pounds in there?" he asked.

The driver smiled back. "Thirty-six all round, sir," he said. "She's still a cow, but it helps a bit on the corners."

"Mr. Kelly, if you'll come with me," the lieutenant said at Kelly's elbow.

"Sure I will—if you'll get off my back for a minute," the civilian said. He pointed toward the building's steps. "There—go stand there for a minute, will you, Lieutenant?"

"But—" Morley began. He thought better of whatever he had planned to say. Nodding, he stepped a few paces away from the other men.

"Look," Kelly said quietly, "I apologize for what I said. I was wrong, and there wasn't any call to say it anyway." He consciously raised his eyes to meet the driver's.

The driver grinned. "No sweat, sir," he said.
"Just remember there's a few of us around who
still give a shit about the way our work gets done."
The grin faded, then flashed back again full
strength. "You know, he'll probably have my
stripes for that—but I'd do it again."

Kelly stuck out his left hand—he held the radio
in his right—and shook awkwardly with the
enlisted man. "Maybe so, maybe not," he said.
After ducking back into the sedan to get the AWOL
bag which Morley had left on the seat, Kelly
rejoined the lieutenant.

II

"Do you have any notion of what they want me for?" Kelly asked as they strode down a linoleum hallway. His crepe soles squelched in marked contrast to the clack of the soldier's low quarters.

"Not here!" the lieutenant muttered.

"I didn't ask *what*," Kelly said. "I asked *whether*."

"Here we are," Morley said, turning into the suite at the end of the hallway. "Oanh," he said to the Oriental secretary at the front desk, "General Pedler wants to see Mr. Kelly here as soon as possible."

The secretary nodded and touched an intercom button, speaking softly. In Vietnamese, Kelly said, "Good morning, Madame Oanh. Is it well with you?"

"Oh my God!" said the girl, jumping upright in her seat. Her accent was distinctly Northern. Though she was too young to have been part of the original resettlement in 1954, Oanh could of course have been born in a village of such refugees. They had tended to stay aloof from the original population of what became South Viet-Nam. At any rate, she was clutching at a crucifix. "Oh, I'm so sorry, you startled me," she rattled on. "It's so good to—I mean, my husband doesn't speak Vietnamese, and he—we're afraid of how it would look, with his job, you know, if I spent time with. . . ." Her voice trailed off. The intercom was answering her.

"I suppose there are a lot of members of the

community here in Paris who aren't—exiles the
way you are," Kelly sympathized. "Your husband
is—"

The intercom crackled again. The woman stood
up. "Oh, you must go in now, sir. Perhaps when
you come back. . . ." She scurried over to the inner
door, clad in a prim white blouse and a navy skirt.
How much more attractive she would have been in
an ao dai, thought Tom Kelly; though as a well
brought up Catholic girl, she might never have
worn the flowing, paneled dress in her life.

An Air Force major general was standing behind a
desk of massive teak. It clashed with the curves
and delicacy, both real and reproduction, with
which most of the embassy was furnished. On the
other hand, the desk looked a great deal more
comfortable under its mass of strewn papers than
its Directoire equivalent would have been; and it
matched Wallace Pedler's own bearlike solidity
very well.

"Kelly?" the Defense Attache demanded. "Come
on in. Oanh, where the Hell is Mark, I told you to
buzz him, didn't I?" The secretary bobbed her
head twice and disappeared back to her console.
"And what in Hell are those?" Pedler continued,
staring at the bag and radio Kelly was carrying.

"My clothes," said the squat civilian, sitting
down carefully on a cushioned chair, "and my
radio. Want to listen to Radio Moscow? Take me a
moment to rig the antenna. . . ." He took a coil of
light wire, perhaps fifteen feet of it, from a coat
pocket and began unwinding it as if oblivious to
the general's burgeoning amazement.

There was a bustle at the door. A naval captain,
no doubt the Naval Attache and the second-
ranking officer in a post this size, stepped past
Lieutenant Morley. He was carrying a set of file
folders, their contents attached to the manila
covers by hole clips. "Glad you could make it,
Mark," General Pedler said caustically. "Mr.

Kelly, Captain Laidlaw. Morley, what the Hell are
you doing here? Close the door behind you."

Kelly had clipped one end of the antenna wire
onto the receiver—length for length, a piece of
supple copper worked just as well as a steel whip,
and it was easier to transport without poking anything. Now the civilian took the six-foot power
cord out of the other coat pocket and began
looking for a wall socket.

"What is that?" asked Captain Laidlaw, poised
over a chair at the corner of the general's desk.
"Some sort of debugging device?"

"No, just a radio," said Kelly. "The general
wanted to hear—" there was a socket directly
behind his own chair— "Radio Moscow."

"Put that goddamned thing down!" the Defense
Attache snapped. "Mark, sit down." Pedler seated
himself, breathing heavily and looking at his
hands. The uncurtained window behind him
looked along the Boissy d'Anglais. One of the
roofs, a block or so away, might be that of the
ETAP, one of the finest luxury hotels in Paris. Presumably Kelly would be put up in one of the block
of rooms there which the embassy kept rented at
all times for Temporary Duty personnel and high-
ranking transients.

Kelly would be put up there if he decided to
stay, at least.

"We—ah," General Pedler began. "Ah, Captain
Laidlaw here will brief you on the situation."

Laidlaw smiled brightly over his crossed knees.
"Well, Mr. Kelly," he said, "what have you been
doing since you left the Army?"

The civilian took out a multi-blade jackknife and
began cleaning his nails with the awl. Without
looking up from his fingers he said, "That's my file
there, isn't it?"

"Ah—"

"Isn't it current? Doesn't it say I've been selling
office equipment for Olivetti?" Kelly glared at

Laidlaw. The captain's eyes seemed focused on the glittering stainless steel of the knife.

"Well, it. . . ," Laidlaw temporized.

"Look," said Kelly, "that's your quota of stupid questions for the day. You know about me or I wouldn't be here. I don't know a goddamned thing about what you want of me. You want to talk about that, I'll listen. Otherwise, I'll go back to Basel where at least I get paid to talk to turkeys."

"I think I'll take over after all, Mark," said General Pedler with surprising calm. He met Kelly's eyes. "How current are your Russian and Vietnamese languages?"

The civilian blinked and snapped the awl closed. "Not real current," he said carefully, "but I can still communicate well enough, I suppose." Wistfully he added, "I used to be Native Speaker level, 4-4, in both, you know . . . when we were monitoring the message traffic in. . . ." His voice trailed off.

"And your French?" Pedler continued.

"My French customers tell me I have a Corsican accent," Kelly said with a chuckle, "and I once had an Italian wonder if I didn't come from Eritrea the way he did. But nobody takes me for an American, if that's what you mean."

"You won't need Italian for this mission," the general said decisively. "Now, even though you were with a, ah, Radio Research Detachment in Viet Nam rather than a combat unit—"

Kelly nodded calmly. "Right," he interrupted, "I was with the National Security Agency then, just like I was up to five years ago."

"But I gather you did have some combat experience," General Pedler said. "I believe there was even a Silver Star with V. I know what that means, especially for an enlisted man as you were."

Captain Laidlaw started to hand one of the folders to his superior. It was red-bordered and stamped Top Secret, unlike a standard 201 Personnel File. The Defense Attache waved it off without taking his eyes away from Kelly.

"I'd admire to know what's in that file," the civilian said, but it wasn't a real request. He looked at the wall, at a framed photograph of General Pedler as a younger man, grinning beside the nose of an F-100. "That was at Fort Defiance," he said. "They named it that because they dug the Squadron in with a pair of 8-inch howitzers, right in the middle of War Zone C. They dared the dinks to come get us. They did, too; the Lord knows, they did that." He caught the general's eyes. "I didn't get that medal for fighting. I got it because somebody had to guide in the medevac birds with a pair of light wands, and it turned out to be me. I guess I'm about as proud of that as I am of anything I ever did in my life, if you want to know the truth . . . but I'm not looking for a chance to do anything like it again."

"We need," the general said, "someone to manage the defection of a Soviet Bloc citizen in a third country. That will require a certain facility with languages, which you have; but that could be supplied by a number of other persons with active security clearances—yes, yours still is, Mr. Kelly. The—mission, Project Skyripper—the mission, however, must be developed with speed rather than finesse. As I understand it, your name was suggested by General Redstone, who had served with you at one time."

Kelly broke into a smile. "That bastard made general? I'll be damned! I'd heard the Special Operations Group was pretty much a dead end for your career in the brass. Seemed like the folks who'd been running missions into Laos scared the crap out of the War College types back in the World when they got a few drinks in them and started telling stories." The smile broadened. "And Red has some stories to tell, *that's* God's truth."

"You accept the mission, then?" broke in the

Naval Attache, still smiling to hide his discomfort.

Kelly shrugged restively, looking at the picture again. "Five years ago, the NSA decided it didn't need a cowboy," he said. His hands, unnoticed, were still playing with the red and silver knife. "Right now, this cowboy doesn't need the NSA—or any other part—" he glared at Pedler— "of the fucking US Government. Oh, sure, you'll pay me—but last year I cleared, what, $37,000 it'd come to, cleared it honest without anybody trying to grease me or throw me under the jail." Kelly leaned forward in the chair, the words cracking out like shots. "If I want excitement—and I don't—I can get that walking the Genoa docks. Anything in the fucking world I want, I *want*, and I can get it or I know a guy who can get it for me. What do I need the USG for now, except another chance to get the shaft? Why do I need *you?*"

"You don't," General Pedler said, his voice a calm contrast to the civilian's spewing words and the anger growing on Laidlaw's face. "You didn't need a medevac bird in the jungle, either. *You* weren't wounded. You don't need your country at all; but she needs you. And that's enough, or you wouldn't have flown in from Basel when we contacted you. Would you?"

Kelly slapped the arm of his chair. "Don't *give* me that crap!" he said. "The country *needs* a few wogs blown away, so let's get Tom Kelly, he's good at it? No thanks. I had my share of that sort of diplomacy before, remember? Get somebody younger, General. This trooper's learned that the US doesn't need that shit—and the world sure as *Hell* doesn't need it!"

The civilian thrust himself back in his chair, glaring angrily at both officers. To Kelly's surprise, the Naval Attache was nodding morose agreement.

"As a matter of fact, Mr. Kelly," General Pedler said, "I had a very similar reaction when the project was first broached to me. Like you, I've spent a great deal of my working life outside the US proper. . . and I learned very early that you don't work very well with foreigners if you think they're all wogs. What changed my mind about the mission is the information I'm about to give you."

"Ah, Wally," said the captain, "do you think it's a good idea to. . . ."

Pedler looked at the other officer. "Why yes, Mark," he said with a trace of mockery, "I *do* think it's a good idea to carry out this mission. That's why I'm going to give Mr. Kelly enough background to convince him of the same thing."

The Defense Attache stood up and strolled to his window. "The counterintelligence boys check out everybody who rents a room over there that faces the embassy," Pedler said, waving an index finger toward the Boissy d'Anglais. "They still want me to put up opaque drapes. I say screw'em. Didn't join the Air Force to spend my life in a coffin. But a lot of things I say with my back to the glass." He turned toward the civilian.

"Very simply," Pedler continued, "a Russian scientist had found a way to destroy all US strategic weapons within seconds of launch. He had a particle beam device, you've probably heard mention of it before. The concept is simple, but a way to turn the concept into a weapon is something else again. It appears that the Russians have it. Fortunately, the hardware—the electronic nuts and bolts of the device—isn't simple either . . . and that the Russians haven't got." He paused.

Kelly stroked his jaw. "Okay," he said. "They don't have the gadget and we don't have the gadget. I haven't heard any reason to panic yet."

"The reason," said the general, and the intensity of his voice underscored his words more vividly than a mere increase in volume could have done, "is that the Russians will have the necessary manufacturing technology very shortly. If they

can't develop it themselves, they'll get it from the
West. Some nation, some private company or
group of companies, will find it expedient to
provide that technology. We live in a world, Mr.
Kelly, in which nations as diverse as Libya and
Israel find it expedient to send arms to the
Iranians in their war with Iraq. The Russians will
get their hardware. Within five years. There will
be a nuclear exchange; and Mr. Kelly, only the
Russian weapons will reach their targets."

Pedler took a deep breath. "That is what will
happen," he concluded, "unless the Russian physicist who developed the weapon defects to the
West, as he wants to do. As we want you to make
possible."

Kelly eyed the two officers as if they were in a
police line-up. "You could be lying through your
teeth, General," he said flatly.

"No, Mr. Kelly," General Pedler replied, "I don't
think I could—not to your face, not and expect to
be believed. But if you want to think that somebody sold *me* a bill of goods . . . well, I can't stop
you from thinking that. All I can say is that I *am*
convinced, or I wouldn't be talking to you now."

"Jesus," Kelly said, rubbing his temples with
his eyes closed. "Jesus." Then looking at Pedler
with none of the hostility of a moment before,
"Look then, do I have . . . have full control of handling the thing if I take it on?"

"Well, if you want *carte blanche*," said Captain
Laidlaw, consciously trying to smooth the frown
from his forehead, "that might depend on your de-
finition of the term."

"You've got my fucking file, don't you?" Kelly
snapped. "You *know* what I mean by *carte
blanche!*" He looked back at the Defense Attache
and said, almost pleading, "Look, General, my
skills—I'm not a diplomat. You say you need it
quick and dirty, but . . . sir, it can get *real* dirty.
And that's the only way *I* can be sure to get it done.

There's people who wouldn't make waves, not like . . . not like me."

The Defense Attache nodded. "That was considered," he agreed. "But—you see, there were two plans for getting the hostages out of the Teheran Embassy," he continued. "One of them was the CIA's. Everybody knows that one; it's the one they tried. Real slick. Minimum fuss and bother, minimum men and equipment committed so no-body'd make a big fuss in the UN afterward. That was one way."

The general sat down again. Captain Laidlaw licked his lips nervously. "Ah, sir, I don't know—" he began.

"If you don't know, then keep quiet!" Pedler retorted. His heavy voice continued, "The other plan came from the JCS, and as it chances, I worked on it. I'd been Air Attache in Teheran a few years before, you see." The general's thumb riffled a stack of papers on his desk-top. "What we wanted to do was use a ring of daisy-cutters to isolate the compound—" Laidlaw frowned in puzzlement rather than disapproval. "Not a piece of Navy ordnance, Mark?" Pedler asked with a smile. "Fourteen-thousand pound high-capacity bombs, then. They take two pallets in the belly of a C-130 to carry them, and when they go off, they can clear a quarter mile circle of jungle for a landing zone. They'd have done the same thing to the buildings in the center of Teheran. We were going to use Rangers, parachuting in on MC-1 chutes and coming back on a Fulton Recovery System with the hostages."

The general's grin was as cold as a woman's mercy. "That would have taken time, reeling in people who'd never used a snatch lift before. But it would have worked, which choppers couldn't, not flying that far. And there would've been plenty of time. It'd have taken the rag-heads three days to bulldoze through rubble and bodies the daisy-cutters would have left."

Kelly chuckled appreciatively, a sound that could have come from the throat of an attack dog. The hot glare of old emotions was making his palms sweat. "And when they got there," he said, "they'd have found every mothering 'student' with his balls in his mouth, wouldn't they?"

The general cocked his head. "That wasn't part of the written plan," he said.

"Sure it was," the civilian said. "You made that decision when you decided to send in Rangers. Sure you did. . . ."

Captain Laidlaw was beginning to look ill. Both his spit-shined low quarters were flat on the floor. Pedler continued, "This operation is being handled through Paris instead of Rome because my opposite number in Rome refused to have anything to do with it. Well, maybe he was right. But I've been told that *I've* got a free hand, so long as the job gets done. And that means you've got a free hand, too, Kelly. So long as you come back with the goods."

The civilian began rewinding his antenna wire to give his hands something to do while his brain worked. "You've got a full briefing set up, I suppose?" he said.

Pedler nodded. "Are you go or no-go?" he asked.

Kelly looked away and cleared his throat. "Oh, I'm go," he said toward a corner of the ceiling. "In a month or two I'll ask you if you still think you knew what you were doing. If I'm around to ask. But I'm go, provided you take care of one thing."

Pedler's face went as blank as a poker player's. "Let's hear it," he said.

"Somebody may try to run an Article 15 through on the guy who drove me in today," the civilian said. "Specialist 5 Phillips. I want the papers torn up—if there are any papers."

The Attache's expression did not change. "What happened?" he asked. Captain Laidlaw was shifting uneasily in his chair.

"Nothing happened," Kelly said. "That's why I
don't want to see the guy shafted." His smile
flashed, as chill as a polar dawn.

"All right, Mr. Kelly," the general said as he
stood, "I'll take care of it. And now that that's
settled, I'm giving you the only order you'll hear
for the duration: stay off the sauce. Period."

Kelly snapped his eyes back to the Attache's. "I
can handle it," he said.

Pedler leaned forward with his knuckles lost in
the books and papers littering his desk. "Don't
bullshit *me*, Sergeant," he said. "I've worked with
juicers all my service life. Some of them aren't
oiled all the time, and some of them work better
than a lot of the rest of us even when they *are*
oiled. But you're not selling typewriters now. If
you drink the way you've been doing since the
NSA fired your ass, you're going to get a lot of
people killed and you're going to screw up the
mission. Do I make myself understood?"

Kelly stood up, thrusting the radio cord back in
his pocket. "I hear you talking, General," he said.
"Now—I want a shower and a shave. Then we'll
get down to details."

Pedler nodded toward the door. "Have Oanh
look up Morley for you," he said. "He was
supposed to take care of arrangements. Report
back to Room 302 here at—" he checked a massive
wrist chronometer—"1500 hours."

Kelly's hands were full of his own gear, helping
him suppress an instinct to salute. Sergeant. Well,
he'd been one, a platoon sergeant when they booted
him out. He'd refused all offers of warrant rank.
Just didn't want to be an officer, even a half-assed
warrant officer. And now, by God, they needed
him like they needed none of those brass-bound
monkeys in the Pentagon. They needed Tom Kelly.

When the door closed behind the civilian, the

Naval Attache coughed quietly for attention.
General Pedler looked at him. "There's something
in this man's restricted file that I think you ought
to . . . note carefully, Wallie," Laidlaw said.

"Well?"

"He, ah . . . it appears that when Kelly was in
Viet Nam he used to accompany troops on
field operations as a matter of course," the
captain said. He flipped pages up over the binder
clasp until he found the correct one, though the
report was too clear in his own mind for any real
need for reference. "Kelly's duties, his assigned
tasks at the time—this was 1968—did not require
him to leave the base camps, of course."

"So he did things he didn't have to do," the
general said with a snort. "Probably did a lot of
things he wasn't supposed to do, too. That's water
over the dam—and besides, it's just that sort of
thing that gave him the background he needs for
Skyripper."

"No doubt, sir," said Laidlaw acidly. "I'm sure
there must have been *some* reason to decide that
Mr. Kelly was qualified. In this case, however,
Staff Sergeant Kelly—as he then was, accompan-
ied a ten man ambush patrol under a Lieutenant
Schaydin. They dug shallow trenches and set up
Claymores—directional mines—"

"I know a Claymore just as well as you do,
Captain. We used them for perimeter defense ourselves."

Laidlaw looked up. "Yes. They set up Claymore
mines about 25 yards in front of their position.
During the night, a sound was heard to the front.
Lieutenant Schaydin raised his head just over the
lip of his trench and detonated a Claymore. The
mine had been turned to face the friendly po-
sitions. It sprayed its charge of steel pellets straight
back in Schaydin's face, killing him instantly."

Pedler shrugged. "All right," he said, "the dinks
had the ambush spotted and reversed the mines.

Not the only time it happened."

"No doubt," the naval officer repeated. "But one of the men reported to a chaplain that before the patrol set out, Sergeant Kelly had warned each man individually to stay flat if there was any report of movement to the front. It had been on the man's conscience ever since."

"Give me that file," said General Pedler, reaching across the desk with a scowl. He scanned the report, a Xerox copy of a fussy carbon. "Hell, this report wasn't filed till three years later," he said brusquely. "I wouldn't hang a dog on evidence like that."

"Nobody *did* hang Mr. Kelly," Laidlaw pointed out. "I just think you ought to know about it. Since there may still be time to . . . bring the matter to the attention of the Pentagon."

"Well, for God's sake, it's the Pentagon who sent us the file, isn't it?" the general snapped. He was continuing to read, however. His anger was the more real for being directed against a subordinate who was, after all, right. "For God's sake!" Pedler slapped the file closed. "It says Schaydin had gotten three men killed by a friendly mine when he took his platoon through an area before checking whether it'd been cleared." He thrust the folder back at Laidlaw. "Well?"

The captain stood up. "I'll return this material to the vault if you have no further need for it, then, General," he said. He walked toward the door.

"He wouldn't be much use on an operation like this if he weren't willing to kill! Would he, Laidlaw?" Pedler demanded.

The Naval Attache turned. "Personally," he said, "I don't believe *anything* would be much use to an operation which depends on a known drunk and probable murderer," he said. "But I'll continue to carry out the orders of my superiors to the best of my ability. If you'll excuse me, sir."

He slammed the door behind him.

III

"Our contact agent is a Vietnamese national named Hoang Tanh," said the major with the toothbrush moustache. The patch on his right sleeve was the sword-and-lightnings insignia of the Special Forces. The silver and blue Combat Infantry badge glittered over the left breast pocket of his uniform. Kelly had disliked Major Nassif on sight. "He's a physicist, was involved with the Dalat Nuclear Facility before the Communist takeover. The Defense Attache's Office recruited Tanh as a stay-behind agent."

"Hoang," the civilian said.

"What?" asked the major.

"His family name would be Hoang, the first name in the series, not the last," Kelly explained. "Same with most Oriental languages."

"To return to something significant," the soldier snapped, "this slopehead became of some importance during the past year when the Vietnamese government began to explore reactivation of the Dalat facility—it was disabled in 1975, of course—as a counterweight to Chinese pressure. Even if they couldn't build bombs, the option of sowing the border between the two countries with radioactive material might deter another incursion by the Chinks." The major fixed Kelly with what they probably said at West Point was a look of command. Maybe at West Point it *was* a look of command. "The Russians are always looking for chances to stab their former comrades in the back, of course. It's not surprising that they provided fuel and technical support to the gooks. And that's where our man made contact with—" he looked down at the briefing file—"this Professor Evgeny Vlasov. The target." Nassif paused. "Code named Mackerel."

"Christ on a crutch," said Kelly as he stood up. "What's my code name? Turkey?" He paced sullenly toward one of the spotless desks. Not everybody followed the Defense Attache's own sloppy security practices. Though—having met General Pedler, Kelly was willing to believe that he dumped the clutter from his desk by armloads into his Mosler safe every day before he left for home. "What's the hold we've got on Hoang?" Kelly asked abruptly.

"Sergeant, if you'll sit your ass down where it belongs," said Major Nassif, "we'll get through this a lot quicker." He rapped the desk in front of Kelly's empty chair with his index finger.

Head-height, sound-deadening panels divided Room 302 into three alcoves. Everyone had been moved out for the briefing, but the walls and the hallway door were something short of code-vault secure. With that in mind, and the fact that he genuinely did not like to lose his temper openly, Kelly said in a normal voice, "Look, Major, if I'm going to trust my life to this bird, I've got to have *some* reason to hope I'm not being set up. There wasn't a whole lot in the way we left Nam in '75 to make somebody who stayed put want to risk his neck for us, was there? We lied to the Reds and we lied to Congress ... but mostly we lied to the South Vietnamese themselves. And weren't they cute to keep right on believing we wouldn't *really* let'em go down the tubes? Dr. Hoang sounds like the closest thing the new regime has to a home-grown nuclear physicist. That makes him valuable enough to coddle, even if he is from the South. Why should he work for us?"

The major glanced back at his folder, then up at

the civilian again. "Sit down, Sergeant," he said. "You'll be told as much about the sources and methods involved in setting up this operation as you have a personal need to know. As for Mackerel's bonafides, they've been checked by the people whose job it is to check such things. That'll have to be sufficient, I'm afraid."

Kelly sat down, massaging his forehead with his fingertips. He was watching through his fingers, though. When Nassif opened his mouth to continue, the civilian said, "Shut up for a minute, Major. I've got a story to tell you, and then a suggestion."

"Serg—"

"And if you call me 'sergeant' once more, I'll feed you your teeth!" Kelly shouted. His voice was as raw as a shotgun blast, and for the moment as disconcerting. Major Nassif started up, but he locked angry eyes with the squat man and subsided again.

"This is a Special Forces story, so you'll be able to appreciate it," Kelly continued quietly, hoarsely. He nodded toward the losing-unit patch on the major's right shoulder. "I was young, then, and I took orders better. . . ." Kelly coughed, trying to smooth the roughness from his voice. "I was with the Five-Oh-First Radio Research Detachment. We'd go out in the field with ground combat units and set up one hell of a beautiful communications intercept system. We'd pick up everything Charlie was saying on the air, whether it was out at the treeline with a handie-talkie or a divisional command near Hanoi. Everything was taped and flown back to NSA headquarters at Fort Meade . . . but we were language-trained, too, you see. That way we knew to tag anything really hot for cable from Saigon."

Kelly sucked his lower lip under his teeth. He was hunched over as if the rain were driving at his back. "One afternoon we picked up calls from an

NVA forward artillery observer. He was handing out targets to a mortar company getting ready to do a number on a Special Forces camp about thirty clicks away. The way we knew exactly what he was doing is he was using an Army Map Service sheet to give grid coordinates. A US map!

"So we sent a query to Theater HQ in Long Binh requesting permission to release the intercept to the camp. I mean, *they* didn't even know they were going to be hit. *We* knew exactly what targets, what order, how many rounds—and the exact time. We knew everything the dink battery commander did—" the civilian raised his voice and his angry eyes— "and our receivers were enough better than his that we got every coordinate the first time while the dink had to ask for repeats on a couple of them."

Kelly stood up and paced, his hands locked behind his back. The thick, blunt fingers wound together. "Long Binh wouldn't clear it. They shot it on to Maryland, though, in case somebody there would authorize release. We got word back three hours later, about an hour after the bombardment had ended. Fort Meade wouldn't clear it either." Kelly swallowed. "Compromise of NSA sources and methods was more important than the purposes to be served by such a compromise. Permission refused." The civilian slammed his right fist into the table. "I never did learn how many people got killed by that bullshit. They weren't any of them in NSA headquarters, though, and that was all that mattered to the top brass. But it wasn't all that mattered to me."

"Umm, well," said Major Nassif, as if he had understood the point of the story. They hadn't warned him that he would be briefing a psycho. . . ."Well, to continue," the major said.

"Sorry, Major, just one more thing," Kelly said tiredly. "I said I had a suggestion. I'm going back over to my room in the ETAP—" he thumbed toward the blank north wall of the office. "I suggest you check with whoever it takes, General Pedler, I suppose, and then drop the file off with me there."

Nassif started to rise in protest. "I said check, didn't I?" Kelly overrode him. "And the whole file, too—the file and every other scrap of data there is in this embassy, anything that *might* have something to do with it." The civilian opened the door and stepped out into the hall. Turning, he added, "If the ETAP isn't secure, you're *really* up a creek."

Major Nassif plucked at his moustache. Suddenly he glanced from the open door to the open file in his hand. He slapped the file shut, but it was another minute before he actually stood up.

IV

Tom Kelly heard the knock the second time and padded to the door. The fisheye lens in the panel distorted the figures of two men in shirt sleeves. Each wore his hair shorter than civilian standard. "A moment," Kelly called. He set down the short, double-edged knife and pulled on his slacks. When he opened the door, his right hand again held the knife out of sight along his thigh. Hadn't even started, Kelly thought, might *not* start, and already he was getting paranoid again. Bad as he'd been five years before in Venice, when he went to work wearing a uniform. . . .

"Mr. Kelly," said the visitor carrying the briefcase, "General Pedler directed us to bring some material to you. I'm Sergeant Wooley; this is Sergeant Coleman." His black companion, apparently bemused by Kelly's state of undress, blinked and nodded.

"Sure, come on in," the civilian said, stepping back out of the way. Already embarrassed, he slipped the knife hilt down into his side pocket as unobtrusively as possible. "Expected Major Nassif, you know," he said. He looked carefully at the two sergeants. "You fellows wouldn't have Crypto clearances, would you?" he asked.

Sergeant Wooley closed the hall door. Coleman had moved over to the writing desk on which the radio sat, crackling with the odd inflections of an Albanian news-reader. The younger men looked at each other. "Yes sir," the first said slowly, "we're Communicators, if that's what you mean."

"I'm sorry, sit down," Kelly said, waving toward the upholstered chairs as he seated himself on the bed again. He flicked a hand across his own bare chest. "Just sitting here thinking," he said in what was meant for explanation. "When it wasn't that jackass Nassif, I figured they'd sent couriers. But I guess somebody over there—" he waved toward the embassy, beyond the heavy drapes and the other buildings— "got the notion that I might be prejudiced against officers." He smiled. "Might just be right, too. Want a drink? The refrigerator's stocked with one of everything, and I brought a bottle of my—"

"I think we'd better just turn these over, sir," Wooley said. He opened the case. It contained the briefing file which Kelly had already seen in Nassif's hands, plus two other, slimmer, folders and a clip-board with a receipt. The sergeant held out the clip-board and a pen to Kelly. "If you'll sign here, sir," he said.

"43 Documents Classified Top Secret," the civilian read aloud. "Well, that's enough to the point." He signed his name with a flourish and handed the receipt back to Wooley. "If the count's short, I know where to find you."

"What is this?" asked Sergeant Coleman, pointing to the short-wave receiver. "I mean—the station. Is it Voice of America?"

All three men paused to listen to the strident news-reader. He was attacking the Italian Communist Party with a passion that, combined with his accent, made the fact that he was speaking in English hard to ascertain. "Radio Albania," Kelly explained as Wooley's pen scratched his confirming signature. "The Sixth Fleet's about to hold exercises in the West Med, and the running-dog poltroons—don't think I'd ever heard the word spoken before—of the CPI did nothing to prevent this example of bour- geois imperialism. You'd think they'd be scream-

ing about us—" he smiled again—"but with
the Albanians, it doesn't seem to work that
way."

"Thank you, sir," said Wooley, folding the
receipt into his pocket. He left the rest of the
material on the desk. "When you're ready to
return this, or if you have to leave this room for
any reason, will you please check with the Marine
guards in the hallway. They'll escort you or call an
authorized person from the embassy to watch the
documents during your absence."

"I'll be damned," Kelly said. He strode to the
door and opened it. A Marine E-5 in dress blues
stood six feet to either side of the door. They
carried holstered .38s. The one on the left nodded
to Kelly, but his companion kept his eyes trained
toward the end of the hall. "I'll be damned," the
civilian muttered again. "Well, if Pedler's willing
to play by my rules, I can't complain if he plays by
his at the same time."

The two Communicators shook hands with
Kelly as they left the room. Coleman paused a
further moment in the doorway. "Why do you
listen to that?" he asked, gesturing toward the
radio with his chin.

The civilian shrugged. "I spent—a lot of time
listening to signals that didn't mean a whole lot,
piecing things together . . . listening. I think better
now if there's somebody talking in the background, if there's a receiver or two live." He
chuckled to hide his embarrassment. "Besides, I
wind up knowing things that sort of seep in. . . . It
helps, some times."

When the door closed, Kelly was alone again,
just himself and Albania and a case of classified
documents. Sighing, he took the knife carefully
from his pocket. He had replaced the round, thin
handle of the short-wave receiver with a sand-
finished stainless steel strap over an inch wide. A
hand-tooled leather wrapper cushioned the

handle. Kelly unsnapped the two fasteners on the leather and set his knife into the cut-out machined into the steel strap. He had no idea of how many airport security checks he had passed through with this radio or one of its similarly-modified predecessors. He was simply not going to be at the mercy of whatever set of crazies happened to hijack a plane he was on.

Off to work. Kelly stripped to his shorts again and opened one of the supplementary folders. It contained only a four-page Current Policy Statement, issued by the US Department of State. It was the text of a speech delivered by the Under Secretary for Security Assistance, Science and Technology, to a—for Christ' sake!—to a national conference of editorial writers. The title, 'Nuclear Power and the Third World,' was about as clear as the discussion got. The speech was the typical Foggy Bottom bumf sent around to all missions. It was intended to give the official line on how to dodge awkward questions.

The question this time was why the US was opposing the International Conference on Nuclear Power Development. The Conference—though the US did not doubt the good faith of the Algerians who were hosting it—had been politicized in a manner not conducive to world peace and harmony. Israel and South Africa had been banned by a unanimous decision of the Conference Trustees—whoever the Hell they were—though in fact neither republic had expressed an interest in attending. Further, if anything but political rhetoric *should* eventuate from the Conference, it would likely be a heightened interest in nuclear weapons among the nations of the Third World. The effect of this could not help but be unfortunate at a time when all nations must band together in the service of peace, with population control and greater agricultural productivity as primary goals.

Kelly snorted and went on to the file with the Top Secret cover sheet. The Department of State building had more floor-space under one roof than the Pentagon; and there were probably more damned fools per square foot there, too. At least the Department of Defense would have managed to say *something* in four pages, though it would doubtless have been a lie.

The first classified document noted that arrangements could be made for the defection of a Professor Evgeny Vlasov during the—okay—International Conference on Nuclear Power Development in Algiers. The operation would, however, resemble an armed kidnapping or a paramilitary operation rather than an ordinary defection. A scientist of Professor Vlasov's stature would certainly be housed in the Soviet Embassy in El-Biar rather than in the Hotel Aurassi with most of the national delegations. Whenever Vlasov was outside the embassy, he would be escorted by armed KGB officers—intended to protect him, but certain to completely circumscribe his movements. Further, the KGB Residency in Algiers, already substantial, would be beefed up to take advantage of the concentration of Third World diplomats attending the conference. Even beyond that, there were an estimated 3,000 USSR military personnel operating in Algeria as advisors to the People's National Army and to the Polisario Front. These troops normally operated in uniform, though without rank insignia. At need, they would certainly be available to provide additional manpower.

In sum, the faceless DIA analyst concluded, Professor Vlasov's defection would require the neutralization of a minimum of four KGB/GRU officers. In addition, an indefinite number of local security personnel from the National Police and the Presidential Security Office would almost certainly become involved. The Conference would include ranking scientists and in some cases heads of state from countries which were mutually hostile: Brazil and Argentina, Iraq and Libya, Viet-Nam and China, among others. The Algerians would be expecting trouble and would be taking steps to minimize it through a show of overwhelming force.

The analyst had obviously determined to his own satisfaction that the proposed Operation Sky-ripper was impossible for both political and practical reasons. Kelly sighed. He was inclined to agree with the analyst, but it wasn't his job to care. If the USG were bound and determined that he was going to run the operation . . . well, there were plenty of slick types in the CIA, recruited from major universities and used to working through cut-outs, go-betweens. . . . Hiring local agents to hire more local agents, so that if the operation went sour—as it usually did —the President could blandly deny that the United States had been involved. Even the Bay of Pigs, an *invasion*, had been handled that way. . . and no wonder it came out a rat-fuck. But if they wanted deniability, they went Ivy League and Big Ten. If they really wanted results, maybe they went to a cowboy for a change. Maybe they went to Tom Kelly.

Kelly got up and ran the pitcher full of water. There were the usual pair of six-ounce water glasses beside it. He ignored the glasses, sipping from the pitcher itself as he walked back to the desk. He stared for a long time at the AWOL bag from which he had already unpacked his clothes. In the end he sat down without reaching into the bag again. He flipped the Kenwood receiver to 15 megahertz and then dialed up to the German Wave, thundering out of Wertachtal. With the selector set for wide band and the modulator damping the German pop music by 60 db, Kelly began looking at what he had in the way of assets for the job.

Besides himself.

The next document had a separate cover sheet, in some ways the most striking thing about it. It was marked 'Top Secret—Dissemination ONLY by order of Director, Defense Intelligence Agency.' On a separate line, typed in red caps, was the additional warning, 'NO ACCESS BY CIA PERSONNEL!'. Kelly grinned. Well, it was important to know your enemies. And it certainly answered the question of whether he could expect support from the CIA station in Algiers.

The Defense Attache's Office in Algeria consisted of the Attache, Commander William Posner, US Navy; and his staff, Sergeant E-6 Douglas Rowe, US Army. Rowe had an armor specialty. The two men and their predecessors had been trying to get a clerk-typist for their office, but they had been unable to justify one to the boys in budget. The only typist in the mission with a Top Secret clearance was the Ambassador's secretary—who was actually Third Secretary for Administration, in order to get her on the Diplomatic List with all the privileges that entailed. The Defense Attache was rather low on his Excellency's list of priorities, so reports from Algiers were consistently late. That did not seem to bother anybody at headquarters enough to spring for a typist slot, though, probably because the reports were pretty dull reading even by the undemanding standards of the DIA. Posner spoke some French. Neither of the men on the ground had any Arabic, much less Kabyle.

And the Kabyles were the key to Skyripper, if there was a key at all.

At first Kelly thought that he had never heard of the Kabyles, but a quick reading of other background documents showed him his error: he had known them as 'Berbers,' that was all. Berber meant just what it sounded like, barbarian. As with 'Welsh,' 'German,' and 'Eskimo,' it was a name affixed by foreigners and never used by the ethnics themselves when their ethnicity became important. The Kabyles were both the Barbary Pirates and the Moors who overran Spain in the name of Allah.

And they were not Arabs, any more than the Cherokees were English. The West had a tendency to equate Moslems and Arabs. That mistake was made by Arabs only when they were dreaming of Third World hegemony the same way the Russian Pan-Slavs of 1900 had dreamed of an ideal state dominated from Moscow. Every Moslem state had its Arabizers, just as British India had had its babus. The Arabizers tended to be intellectuals with their values shaped at universities in Cairo and Beirut rather than in their native lands. In Algeria, they held virtually all the top posts in the government and army. They had done so since the French were driven out, though the bombed-out farms in the Kabyle Highlands still bore testimony to who had really done the fighting which led to that victory. There were already signs that the fighting was about to resume, and that this time the outside overlords would be Arabs and not Frenchmen.

Operational planning had started even before a courier from the DAO in Berne had caught Kelly making a sales presentation to a Volkswagen dealership in Basel. Another courier had been sent to Algiers, ordering Commander Posner to give full support to the agent or contract officer, as yet undetermined, who would be arriving soon. Further, the Attache was ordered to alert his contacts within the Kabyle underground to a coming need for manpower and other support. The USG would pay for such support with up to one million dollars in gold or any desired currency and—Kelly whistled, clashing with the radio's rendition of

'Danke'—full US support for establishment of a Kabyle Government in Exile in Rabat, Morocco.

Kelly got up and walked to the sink, partly to refill the pitcher. Mostly he needed to move as he thought. He wondered how the button-down types in the Fudge Factory at State had taken that news. Not real well, he suspected. It meant the probable end to diplomatic relations between Algeria and the USG, whatever came of the defection attempt itself. This thing was big, it was so big it scared him. Why in *God's* name they'd picked him to run the show. . . .

Kelly took the 750 milliliter bottle of Johnny Walker Red out of the bag. Scotch to Americans, malt to an Englishman; whiskey to the rest of the world. Kelly preferred Tennessee sour-mash whiskey, but you didn't find that outside the States except maybe as a dusty bottle on a high shelf in big liquor stores. Scotch you could find from Iceland to Japan . . . and besides, it didn't matter that much, Kelly had drunk peppermint schnapps when that was handiest; and if he preferred the taste of hog piss to peppermint schnapps, it had done the job just the same. He needed a drink now, needed it bad. But Kelly gulped water instead and sat down with the file. The dapper man in hunting pinks winked knowingly from the bottle's label at the American.

Outsiders could not be expected to reach Professor Vlasov, but Dr. Hoang would certainly be able to renew his acquaintance. No eyebrows would be raised by a private conference between physicists representing two communist states allied against the Chinese between them. That left the problem of contacting Hoang; but that, given modern electronics, shouldn't be insuperably difficult. As he continued to read through the assortment of documents, Kelly began arraying mentally the support and equipment he would request from General Pedler—and the back-up he

would arrange for himself. There were some
things he did not intend to tell anyone in the Paris
embassy. A passport, for instance. Nobody in the
USG was going to know what documents Kelly
was travelling under. In his years of knocking
around Europe, Kelly had met people who could
do the necessary job as well or better than
anybody in a CIA smokeshop. Why use a false
passport if you knew a Consul who would issue a
real one for the right incentive?

And what if somebody talked to a girlfriend or a
drinking buddy? A salesman who might be
planning to run a load of hash under a squeaky-
clean passport wouldn't interest anybody around
the Russian Embassy. Government ID for Tom
Kelly, a French-speaker who'd been on both ends
of automatic rifles in his day—that was something
else. And people do talk, no matter who they are,
when their pricks are hard or they're half-seas
over.

There was no way to be sure how well Commander Posner would be holding up his end, with his
Level 2 French and a naval officer's rigid disapproval of something this unconventional. Time
would tell, too goddamned little time, ten days.
But at least a sailor could be expected to take
orders, however much he might dislike them.
Kelly sighed and ran his index finger over the
embossed label of the whiskey bottle.

And then he went back to the file.

V

Lieutenant Colonel Nguyen Van Minh dropped
the report back on his desk. He shook his head
toward the mountains out the window. If he read
between the lines correctly, it was not simply a
knifing he had to deal with. The fight between two
of his staff, guards at the Dalat Nuclear Facility,
had occurred during an argument over the
prowess of their respective regiments during the
War of Liberation.

Both men, might they rot in Kampuchea where
he was transferring them, had been on the
losing—Southern—side.

Colonel Nguyen sighed and loosened the collar
of his uniform tunic. Bao, his predecessor as Chief
of Facility Security, had been incompetent, no
doubt about that. But how he had failed to do even
basic background checks on these two ... and
how many other ex-Airborne and Marine
personnel were *still* on the staff of this crucial
part of the defense establishment? The situation
no longer reflected on Bao's honor, it reflected on
Nguyen's own.

The phone rang. Nguyen snatched it as if it were
a rope out of his administrative morass.
"Security," he snapped. The colonel was his own
secretary. He spoke to anyone who called ... and
they had better have *very* good reasons to call him.

This caller did. Even before he spoke, the background wail identified a trunk line from the
North. "Minh, good morning," squeaked the voice
of the head of the Army Intelligence Bureau.

"How would you like to take a little trip?"

Nguyen tensed. "General," he said, "I will be pleased to serve the State in whatever capacity she needs me, of course." For fifteen years, during the War of Liberation, Nguyen had spent more nights in the open than he had under a roof. After the victory, the Northerners had continued to load him with the dog work—including six months of shepherding gas rockets around Kampuchea. "Whatever capacity," the colonel repeated, "but matters here in Dalat are at a—critical stage. Surely there is someone besides my own unworthy self who can deal with whatever problem you are having in Kampuchea?"

"No, no," interrupted General Ve. "You don't understand. This is a sort of vacation, a reward for you, Minh."

"That's what you said about this job," the colonel retorted more bitterly than was politic. " 'Beautiful scenery, no danger—just a few administrative problems. . . .' Do you *know* who that idiot Bao hired for plant security?"

"If you'll listen for a moment, Colonel," the distant voice said harshly, "you'll be better able to judge your orders, won't you?"

"Right, sorry, General," Nguyen said. He forced himself to relax. His service during the War of Liberation had been second to no one's; but Nguyen was a Southerner by birth, a member of the Viet Cong and the National Liberation Front—not the Hanoi establishment. Hanoi was in firm control since its armies had pushed home their invasion and achieved what twenty years of guerrilla warfare had failed to do. It behooved Nguyen to remember his place—or find himself commanding a garrison battalion in Kampuchea, an even worse job than that of the chemical warfare detachment to which he had already been assigned.

"You know this conference in Algiers that your Doctor Hoang will be attending?" said the general.

The momentary asperity seemed forgotten.

"Yes, of course," Nguyen said. "I understand that he'll be escorted by a team from the central office." Of *course* a plum assignment like that would go to toadies from the Hanoi office. During the War, Nguyen had suffered in order to end injustice. Now—but if he thought too long about such things, the result would be a blast of homicidal fury which would serve no one, least of all the State.

"That was the original intention, yes," General Ve agreed. "It appears, however—despite my personal intervention—that the Treasury will not release enough hard currency to permit more than one person from this office to accompany the Doctor."

"Yes?" prompted Nguyen. He held his breath in a hope that he would not admit even to himself.

"And I have determined that you are the best suited member of the Bureau for the assignment as it has developed, Minh," the general went on. "To act as sole escort, that is."

The colonel was afraid to ask the obvious question, but it had to be asked if he were to know what he was getting into. "Ah, General," he said, "I'm flattered, very flattered . . . but why me?"

General Ve coughed, a bark of sound over the bad connection. "Well, you see, Colonel," he said, "I took another look at the list of attendees and . . . the size of the Chinese delegation concerns me. They have, I'm sure, a notion of our purpose in reactivating the Dalat Reactor. And they surely know of Doctor Hoang's importance to the program. Frankly, I tried to quash the whole trip, but Hoang seems to have convinced—certain officials—that his presence at the Conference will be valuable to his work. And also, the head of the Russian delegation has expressed a desire to see Hoang again. . . . Their Professor Vlasov, the one who visited last month. So Hoang is going, and well. . . ."

"General, I'm very flattered," Nguyen repeated. He was waving his free hand in the air in silent joy.

"Well, Colonel," Ve said. "I wouldn't want you to think that we in Hanoi were unaware of your . . . . ability. Not that I really *think* the Chinese would try something at an international conference, but—"He paused.

"As well to be sure," Nguyen completed.

"Exactly," agreed the general, "exactly. We're working in liaison with our Russian friends. I'm sure you'll be able to share the duties with their contingent. You've worked with them before, I believe?"

"The technicians with the poison gas equipment," Nguyen agreed. "Yes, their manpower should be very helpful."

"Well, the written orders will be along in due course," General Ve said. "I just wanted to make sure you had time to take care of any arrangements in Dalat before you left. Good day, Colonel."

"Good day," Nguyen said to a dead line. He cradled the phone.

Arrangements. Well, somebody had to vette the entire guard staff, it appeared. Truong could handle that. Truong damned well *better* be able to handle that. As for trip preparations. . . .

Nguyen opened the top drawer of his desk. He took out the pistol, removing the magazine before he locked back the slide. The round in the chamber spun out onto the pile of paperwork. It was an old weapon, a Tokarev TT-33, thirty years obsolete in Soviet service.

Nguyen had killed sixty-two men with it when he headed an assassination team during the War.

The Colonel worked the slide several times, studying its action with a critical eye. He had better get in some range time before he went to Algiers. Just in case.

VI

"Can't say I'm in much of a hurry this time, Specialist Phillips," Tom Kelly remarked as he got in through the door the driver insisted on holding open for him.

Phillips was grinning as he walked back around the hood and settled himself behind the steering wheel. "I'm glad to hear that, sir," he said, putting the Concord in gear, "because I scared the crap out of myself the last time." He chuckled. "Not as bad as I scared the lieutenant, though."

The gate guard saluted as the sedan passed him sedately. Anybody picked up at the front of the embassy was worth a salute. It was a lot cheaper than explaining to the Gunny why you'd ignored the CinC Med, who happened to have been in civvies that afternoon. . . .

"Ah, look, sir," the driver went on, watching traffic and not his passenger, "I, ah, heard about what you did for me. And well, if there's ever something you need and I've got—well, look me up, huh?"

Kelly grinned back. "Hell," he said, "you just did what you were told to do. I only made sure that if anything happened because you followed a damned fool's orders, that the USG knew it could whistle for any help it was going to need from me." Kelly paused, watching the buildings past Phillips' face. Traffic in the left lane was sweeping around them, but the sedan's tires were riding the rough pavement with only a modicum of discomfort. "Where did you happen to hear about that, anyway?" Kelly added, as if the answer did not matter to him.

"Oh, a buddy of mine drives most nights for the Adjutant," Phillips said. "You know, when he's going off to a reception and doesn't want the flics to stop him driving home plotzed. He was talking to the Assistant Air Attache. . . ." The driver shot a look over at his passenger. "We're machines, you know. Typewriters and telephones and drivers . . . but you know."

"Sure," said the civilian. "I know how it is." His skin was flashing hot and dry in pulses that came and went as his heart beat. "What do they say about my chances of getting the job done?" he asked, wondering if his voice sounded as odd to the driver as it seemed to his own ears.

"Look, sir," Phillips said in sudden concern. "I didn't mean they were talking about—whatever you and the general have on." The driver was frowning, dividing his attention between his passenger and the traffic. "General Pedler's been playing that one real close, I think. That is—I've heard a lot about you in the past couple days, Mr. Kelly, but it's all been about what a mean SOB you are. Not whatever you're doing."

Kelly laughed in a combination of relief and irony. "Yeah, I've been acting ill as a denned bear," he agreed. "Could just be that's the way I am, too." Phillips had turned down the narrow Faubourg St. Jacques, between the massive and ancient hospital complexes of Port Royal and Cochin. Either the pedestrians had a somber look or Kelly's mind gave them one. He wouldn't have been alive himself without a damn good surgeon and all the help that science and centuries of other surgeons trying to improve on past practice could give. Even so, hospitals always reminded Kelly more of death than salvation. These, with their 17th Century stonework blackened and corroded by soot, gave him the creeps even worse than most such places did.

"But it could also be. . .," Kelly continued. He was looking out his window at the domes and colonnades of the Paris Observatory, not toward the man to whom he was speaking. "It could also be that I'm scared, and if I'm a big enough bastard, then nobody else may notice how scared I am. Could just be."

"Everybody gets scared," the driver said, relaxing a little over the wheel. "You aren't the sort to lock up when you get scared, are you? So what's it matter?"

"Sure," Kelly agreed, "sure. The matter is that they want me to do something I've never done before. I'm not sure *anybody* could handle the job, and I swear to God I don't see how I can. I'm over my head and I don't mean a little bit."

They were waiting to turn on the Boulevard St. Jacques, their view of the Place blocked by the closed deuce and a half van ahead of them. The driver turned and looked steadily at Kelly. "If you really thought that," he said, "you'd have told them to stuff the job, wouldn't you? You'll be all right, Mr. Kelly."

Traffic and the sedan began moving again. Kelly laughed, as pleased to be flattered as the next man. After a moment, though, he said with whimsey in only the overtones, "But you know why I didn't? Because they fired me five years ago, booted my ass out of the—well, it's no secret, the NSA. They couldn't give me a damned thing that mattered after that, not a damned thing . . . except a chance to ram that termination back down their throats. And that's what they offered me, that chance. Can't lose, after all. If I pull it off, they were dopes to fire me. And if I screw up, well, I don't have to worry about that or any other goddam thing ever again."

Phillips did not speak as he took the sedan around the fountain of the traffic circle and south at increasing speed down the Avenue d'Italia. He genuinely was not in a hurry. None the less, the mass of traffic jostling for position demanded the driver's skills and awoke the aggressiveness that honed those skills. "Were you," he said at last as he tucked behind the bumper of a Jaguar, "hitting the sauce a little heavier than they liked?"

Kelly glanced up at him sharply. "They do talk, don't they?" he said with something like a smile. Then, "No, then I—I wasn't very much of a drinker, to tell the truth. It was.... Well, I met a girl in Venice when I was back in port, pretty and she, she seemed to like me. I liked her, I—well." Kelly cleared his throat, his eyes on the Jag's British license plate again. "Smart as a whip, that's God's truth. Very sharp, she was."

They were in the congestion of the Boulevard Peripherique, slowing with the car ahead, then slipping sideways as a motorcyclist accelerated up a ramp and opened a gap. The Boulevard was a gapped concrete roof overhead, tire noise echoing from its pillars in a deep-throated rumble. Phillips was taut at the wheel, his hands at ten o'clock and two, making the tiny motions necessary to keep the sedan tracking down what had become the Avenue de Fountainbleu. He seemed oblivious to his passenger as Kelly continued, "She was an American, Polish background but born in Chicago, I checked her passport. You get antsy, you know, when they keep telling you the Russkies are out to learn everything you've got to tell. So I checked her purse when she was asleep, but it wasn't like I was worried, not really. And the passport was fine. Only. . . ."

Kelly wished he could forget they were on the Avenue de Stalingrad now. He didn't need to think of Russians, and he assuredly didn't need to say what he was about to say. But the words were finding their own way out, directed not at the stolid driver but perhaps at the self-righteous man who had been Tom Kelly one day five years ago when. . . . "Languages are my business, though. They were then. And there was something about her English. . . .So I put in a query through channels, insisted they get me a picture from the file at State, no big deal . . . and I still didn't *think* there was anything wrong, just a feeling. Funny. She knew something was up, but I didn't, almost till—" He cleared his throat again.

To the left was the Thinis Cemetery, green shade and an occasional flash of stone past the vehicles in the northbound lanes. Hospitals and cemeteries, take them away and there would be a lot less of Paris. A lot less of the world, but you could have death and corpses without either, and all the canals of Venice flow to the sea. . . .

"The picture was wrong," Kelly said to no one present. "She was a girl, a college student who'd gone to visit grandparents in Poland, her parents had died in a car crash. And one of her friends got a post card from Greece, but that was all, she never was seen again. And now somebody with her passport and a new picture was living with an NSA field man. Oh, the CI boys loved it, they'd play her like a fish and see who she reported to. Only—" Kelly's lips were very dry and the tendons on his neck were standing out— "some girl was gone, gone from the world so that they could play their games, all of their games. You kill enemies, sure, but some kid who just wanted to find her roots and didn't dream a government would have her greased to get a US passport. . . . I—it bothered me. And I let something drop.

"It hadn't been Janna's doing . . . the kid, I mean," the agent continued. "But she was wired, she'd been living with me long enough to—worry what might happen if I learned she'd set me up. So she made a bad move, went for a gun as if she could point it and I'd freeze. Me! And . . . well, some of the old reflexes were there. Reflexes don't care, Phillips. Reflexes don't love anybody."

They were within the airport precincts now. The airliner taking off on a parallel course was an Aeroflot I1-62, carrying civilized diplomats and vacationers to Warsaw and beyond. "When she disappeared," Kelly said softly, "my Janna who wasn't Janna, they figured at first she'd been tipped off. Only they learned that people in the Russian Embassy—she was being handled from Rome, not the consulate in Venice—they were panicked too, thought she'd defected. And then they decided that they'd talk to me about it under pentathol . . . and I told them to go screw themselves . . . and they told me I'd just resigned for the good of the service." Kelly managed a smile. "There were four of them in the room with me at the last, and I swear to God they were wearing bulletproof vests. Four of them and they were afraid of me." He paused. "Well, I'm back," he said. "Tom Kelly is back."

Phillips pulled the sedan into the kiss and go lane in front of the south terminal. "Good luck, sir," he said. "It's nothing you can't handle."

"Hope to Hell you're right," said Kelly. With his radio and his AWOL bag, the dour civilian began to walk toward his future.

VII

The pair of young customs officials peered into the packing crate with more bemusement than concern. The one with the pencil-line moustache turned to Kelly and said in French, "You understand, Mr. Ceriani, that this machine—" he tapped the case with his pen, over the stencilled 'Rank Xerox—London'—"is cleared for demonstration purposes only? It must not be sold."

Kelly nodded in agreement. His lightweight suit had borne up well on the short flight from Frankfurt, but he was already wondering whether April in Algiers would not demand a warmer selection of clothing than what he had brought. The other customs man was poking desultorily through Kelly's suitcases, open on the inspection table beside the crated copying machine. "Yes," Kelly said in his Italian-accented French, "we understand fully. I may invite clients to my suite to inspect the product, but by law there may be no store-front display, and all orders must be shipped from out of country rather than a local warehouse. Ours—Rank Xerox—" Kelly fumbled from a leather case a card identical in format to the ones he really used as an Olivetti representative— "we will ship from our warehouse in Marseilles. We understand that Algeria is choosing the route it deems proper to national self-sufficiency. We will comply fully with all national regulations."

The moustached official riffled the spiral notebook prominently labeled SPESE. It was quite

real, though from Kelly's past and not his present
persona. Its slap-dash listing of business expenses
was the final proof that he was the salesman he
claimed to be. The official said something to the
other in Arabic, apparently a joke because they
both laughed. He gave Kelly a friendly wave of his
hand. "Good day, Mr. Ceriani," he said. "Have a
pleasant stay in Algeria."

Kelly smiled back and quickly loaded his gear
onto a hand truck. The line he had given the
customs men would have been no more than the
simple truth had he been in Algiers as a real
business rep. The big corporations did not cut
legal corners to do day-to-day business in foreign
countries. Only in the aerospace field did the
bottom-line potential of a sale make it justifiable
to bribe—a Dutch prince or a German defense
minister, say. . . . Otherwise, the economic risk of
being banned permanently outweighed the momentary advantage of selling your demonstrator
to a customer who was hot to trot.

And Tom Kelly had learned as well that if you
had a solid product to sell, you could work within
any system. The Algerians restricted foreign
corporations as a proof of their socialism and
their rise from a colonial past. The restrictions
hurt no one as much as the Algerians themselves.
It would be generations, at least, before there
would be any indigenous copier manufacture,
judging from the dismal result when the Algerians
tried to make their own televisions. But it was
their own country, and they had a right to go to
Hell in their own way.

It was only as a representative of a sovereign
government that Kelly could imagine himself
flouting laws in order to do his job.

The first cab in the rank was a white Peugeot
201 with an enthusiastic driver named Hamid. He
helped Kelly manhandle the crate and suitcases
into the trunk, muttering instructions to himself

under his breath. Hamid was obviously impressed both by his passenger's air of importance and the fact that Kelly gave the Hotel Aurassi as his destination. The Aurassi was flagship of the state-owned system and a world-class hotel by any standards. "Ah," said Hamid as he drove out of the cyclone-fenced parking area, "are you then a scientist come for the Conference?"

Gravel brushed from the lot spewed from beneath the tires as the taxi cut onto the highway. The rear wheels twitched, then bit against the two-lane blacktop. The roadway was unexceptional, practically identical to any state secondary road in Kelly's one-time home of North Carolina. In the French fashion the trunks of the palm trees along the shoulders of the road had been whitewashed six feet up to provide cheap warning reflectors. "Ah, no," the American agent said, "I'm only a salesman trying to turn a dinar in copy machines. Have you carried many Conference attendees already, then?"

Traffic was steady and heavy enough in both directions to make passing a suicidal impossibility. Hamid was relaxed, giving more attention to his passenger in the rear view mirror than to the road ahead. "Not as yet, no," he said, "and no doubt they will travel in official cars with no thought of how a poor man like me should feed five children. But perhaps you are not aware, sir, that in three days the Aurassi will be cleared to accommodate guests of the Conference? Zut, out—" Hamid flicked his right hand in a gesture of full dismissal, turning directly to look at Kelly as he did so. The Peugeot quivered no more than the road surface would have demanded anyway—"460 rooms, all turned over to the Conference. There is still time, though—I can carry you to the St. George, very nice also and downtown?"

"Goodness, I didn't know that," Kelly lied with a realistic frown. "Still, the firm will have given the address to customers already. I'll have to check in at the Aurassi, if only for a few days."

Hamid kept up a flow of cheerful information throughout the long ride from Dar al-Beida to the hotel on the western heights of Algiers. There was nothing that could be called a circumferential road per se, but a long stretch of well-laid divided highway sped them more than they were slowed by its increased traffic. Cars were of typical European makes, but they appeared to Kelly to be unusually standardized. When he asked about that, the driver laughed.

"You see the license?" Hamid explained, pointing toward the sedan in front of them. It was a Renault 5 throughout the French-speaking world and 'Le Car' in the United States alone. "One-six means Algiers. One means a car, not a bus, whatever. And the next two numbers—79—are the year Sonacome imported it. *All* cars are imported by Sonacome expect those for foreigners and the very wealthy for their own use. And except for a few limousines for the Presidency and heads of departments, all the cars each year are the same model, whoever offered Sonacome the best price. Still, there are colors—and a car is a car, no doubt."

"Somebody goes first class," the American said, pointing toward the pair of leather-suited motorcyclists talking on a grassed median. Their parked bikes were BMWs, blue-painted and obviously official even without the fact that the riders wore holstered pistols.

"Oh, yes," agreed Hamid, "the National Police. They *are* first class, you must know, but yes, they do not buy their equipment on low bid. When Sonacome buys Volkswagens for you and me to ride in, the cars are built under license in Brazil. When the police buy Volkswagens, they come from Germany, yes."

The terrain on the outskirts of Algiers reminded

Kelly of the two trips he had made between Oakland and Travis Air Force Base, on his way still farther west. The hills looked dry, hinting at the harshness of rock; but this was not desert. Considerable construction was going on, multiple complexes of high rises. The workmanship appeared good and the buildings were attractive in detail. Colored tiles picked out the stuccoed concrete, and each unit had a balcony shaded by a concrete screen in one of a number of patterns. The size of the buildings, however, hit Kelly as his background reading had not done. Each block contained a good 1600 apartment units, and during a twenty mile ride they had passed at least a half-dozen being built. The population of Algeria was exploding. Gas revenues might keep the lid on for a time, but there would be a reckoning in the foreseeable future unless diversification provided something for the new citizenry to do beyond sitting in a government room.

The taxi swept up the long, curving drive to the Aurassi, confirming in Kelly's mind the presumption he had already drawn from the briefing file: the operation would have to take place elsewhere. The Hotel Aurassi was as effectively separated from its immediate surroundings as if it had been on an island. Chopped into an expanse of rock which had been unbuildable until enough money became available—even the Moon is developable if enough money becomes available—the Aurassi could be reached by its drive, a ramped causeway. Even the most limited security precautions would make it impossible for a car to reach the highway if anyone thought it should be stopped before then; and security precautions were not the sort of thing the Algerians skimped.

The building itself, though obviously constructed according to expensive architectural advice, was less attractive than the massive apartment blocks which were being built for the citizenry. The architects were the problem, as a matter of fact. The mass units were built with an eye to efficiency. Because they were to be occupied by people, however, their lines were picked out with local touches, the tiles and moldings and vari-colored stucco Kelly had noticed on the way. By contrast, the Aurassi was classic Bauhaus: a box on a slab, with no more of taste or of beauty than an automobile's radiator has—and far less real functionality than the radiator. Judging from their own attractive blends of practical necessity and human desire, the Algerians had probably wondered at the ugly, expensive block which foreign architects had designed for foreign travellers; but there are men who choose to sleep on nails, and there is no accounting for taste. . . .

Hamid pulled up under the concrete beams of the skeletonized porte-cochere. "Sir," he said, sweeping Kelly's door open. His left hand gestured expansively toward the lobby. "There is a bank at the desk if you. . . .?"

"Thank you indeed," the American said, handing the driver a wad of sixty dinars he had bought from the Bank of Rome. There were ten Swiss francs folded into the midst of the local currency. A pair of liveried porters were approaching. One of them whistled for the boy with the hand truck when he saw the packing case. "If I am served as well during the remainder of my stay in Algeria, the business I do will delight my employers."

Though that was probably a lie, Kelly thought as he followed the porters across the red carpeting of the lobby. This one wasn't likely to delight anybody until, at best, years in the future. By then, most people would have forgotten the cost.

VIII

On the third ring from the embassy switch-board, somebody picked up the extension and said, "Attache, Sergeant Rowe speaking."

Kelly's eyes were on the Bay of Algiers; he had never been enough of a TV viewer that he felt compelled to stare into a dial as he talked on the phone. "Hello," he said without trying to counterfeit an accent, "this is Angelo Ceriani with Rank Xerox. We are informed that you have been requesting a look at our desk-top copying system." The cue was 'desk-top,' the only information about his arrival which Kelly had permitted to be given through the DIA system.

"Huh?"

Jesus Christ. Many of the ships standing far enough off-shore to be tiny white slivers in the sun were in fact supertankers. With a good pair of binoculars—"Yes," Kelly said aloud, with a calm that he could not have managed without a moment to cool off, "my firm received the request through, I believe, a Mr. Pedler of your Paris branch. Perhaps if you would check with your superiors. . . ?"

"From a Mr.—oh. *Oh*!" Sergeant Rowe swallowed audibly. "Sure, that's right, Mr.—well, we didn't have the name is all. Are you at the airport? I'll bring a car right out."

"Oh, that won't be necessary," the agent said through a grimace. "The equipment isn't set up yet, of course. But I'd like to drop by with a brochure shortly, and then later you and your superior may

come here to my room at the Aurassi for a demonstration."

"Right, of course," the sergeant agreed. "Ah,
well, I'll inform Commander Posner. He's been
very interested in the new equipment. It, ah, it
should really speed up office routine."

Yes, friend, it surely will do that, Kelly thought.
Aloud he said, "I'll get a taxi, then. Good day."

Of course, if he really wanted to look at ships,
the Company doubtless had a Celestron telescope
with a coupled 35 mm SLR taking pictures of
everything in the roadstead. More and more it
seemed to Kelly that he would be smarter to spend
his time looking at boats rather than trying to
make bricks out of locally available materials, not
—it appeared—including straw.

What the Hell. He showered and changed, removing the sheath for his knife from the suitcase
lining. He clipped the weapon to his waistband at
the small of his back. What the Hell.

IX

One advantage enjoyed by embassies located in the Mediterranean Basin is that they need not raise eyebrows and insult the host government in order to make themselves secure. The cab pulled to the side in the middle of a curve and stopped abruptly. Kelly was staring at a whitewashed wall ten feet high. It was too close to permit his door to open. The driver reached back and unlatched the back door on his side, ignoring the scream of brakes as a passing Fiat missed them by inches.

"American Embassy, you wanted," the driver said. His passenger paid, then slipped out and around the taxi in a quick motion, hoping the next vehicle would not sheer him off at the knees. The taxi spurted away, leaving Kelly on a street filled with traffic and traffic noise which rebounded between the high walls on either side.

A patrolman in a blue uniform, not the black leather of the National Police, eyed Kelly from a hundred feet away. Presumably the man was an official recognition of the embassy. Kelly walked to the nearest gate. It was steel plating on a grillwork of the same metal, probably the only change in external appearance since the place had been built a century or more ago. When he knocked on the steel, a man-sized door opened in the larger panel and an Algerian in some sort of khaki uniform waved Kelly in.

"American Embassy?" the agent asked doubtfully in French.

"Ah, yes," asserted the guard. Kelly stepped through into the beautifully landscaped grounds. The building itself, set back a hundred feet from the wall, was white with the varied profusion of design which 'Moorish' shares with other popular architectures. There were up to three stories —four, perhaps, because a domed turret or two were visible. Windows, even on the upper floors, were closed by gratings no less functional for being of attractively wrought iron. Glazed tiles set off the border of each flat roof. Against the wall to the right of the gate was a guest house. An archway over the curving drive was covered with wisteria. The vines were as thick at the base as a man's thigh. A red Mustang was parked beyond the arch, and past it along the drive approached a white Chrysler sedan. There was a passenger in the back of the Chrysler, dimly visible through the tinted glass.

The guard was already swinging the squealing gate open. Kelly moved aside, but the car stopped abreast of him anyway. The back window whined down. The passenger was a slender man of fifty or so with perfect features and a look of distaste as he viewed Kelly. He was tall enough to hunch a little in his seat to look comfortably at the agent. "Yes?" he asked without warmth.

"Ah, Angelo Ceriani, sir," Kelly responded. He held a sheaf of Xerox brochures in his right hand. "About the copy machine."

The passenger sneered with the disdain of a man who felt insulted at the suggestion a copy machine might interest him. He turned to the guard and snapped in excellent French, "Badis, you've been told to send tradesmen to the Chancery at once instead of admitting them here. Do so now!" The power window was already rising, clipping the last syllable as the limousine slid out into traffic.

The guard looked apologetic. "The next building," he said, pointing down the street toward the relaxed policeman.

"Guess I've met the Ambassador, hey?" said Kelly. He stepped onto the street again. "This is the Residence?"

The guard's head was nodding, perhaps in agreement, when the gate clanged shut behind Kelly.

X

The Chancery grounds had something less of a manicured look than those of the Residence, but the two main buildings themselves were equally impressive. Further, there was more of a feeling of life to the place. Half a dozen Algerians were lounging on the inner side of the wall, talking and laughing. One, a slim, neat fellow, was in khakis like those of the Residence guard. The other men wore dull-colored sport coats over ordinary work clothing. Only the guard seemed interested when Kelly stepped through the open doorway.

"I have an appointment with Sergeant Rowe," the agent said in French. "My name is Ceriani."

"Sure," the guard agreed, waving his hand toward the building which sprawled on the right of the drive. "Front door, ask the man at the desk."

Kelly blinked doubtfully, then walked on. A magnetic detector arch was set up a few feet within the compound, far enough from the gate that the steel plating would not affect it. Obviously, that was a relic of more troubled times. To the left of the drive and set closer to the front wall than the main buildings was a low outbuilding. He glanced through the open doorway; it was a restaurant of some sort, with what must surely have been one of the best-looking cashiers in Algeria. She was tall and her black hair, held up with combs, flashed highlights. Several men, apparently locals, walked out talking in a non-European language.

The agent felt increasingly uncomfortable about

what he had gotten himself into. Algiers was one
of only a handful of US Embassies which had no
Marine guard contingent. The absence was not
wholly a disadvantage. A dozen young men who do
not speak any of the local languages and whose
idea of a good time may be limited to booze and
broads can provide problems for the diplomats
running the mission. That was especially true in a
Moslem country with strict notions of proper
conduct and a government which was not on the
take from Washington.

But the problems occurred when things were
going smoothly. When the mob was coming over
the walls, somebody had to carry the eighty-pound
sacks of telegrams to the shredder and somebody
had to stand out front laying down tear gas until
the job inside was finished. Especially if Tom
Kelly's name happened to be on some of those telegrams.

And even while things were quiet—tune in again
next week—it would have been nice if somebody
had at least checked the identification of the total
stranger heading for the Defense Attache's Office.

Security improved inside the building. The front
door opened onto a small anteroom with a high,
groined ceiling. The inner door would require
blasting to open it if the magnetic latch were not
thrown. Above, a TV camera flanked by a four-
inch outlet eyed the visitor. Kelly suspected that
the outlet was ready to dump CS on intruders, the
way a similar rig had done in Tripoli a few years
before when Qadafi had sent his thugs to sack
the US Embassy there.

Of course, like the magnetic detector, the tear
gas system might have been disconnected by now.

"I am Angelo Ceriani, to see Sergeant Rowe,"
Kelly said, carefully facing the camera.

"One moment, please," crackled a voice in
accented English. About thirty seconds later, the
latch buzzed and Kelly stepped into the Chancery

proper. He was in a roofed court. To the immediate right was a middle-aged Algerian seated at a desk holding a TV monitor, a telephone, and a separate intercom. A young American in sport clothes but with very short hair leaned over the stone balustrade from the floor above. "Sir?" he called. "Glad you could get here so promptly. I'm Doug Rowe and—oh, come on up the stairs, the commander's waiting."

The steps were of the same polished granite as the balustrade and the railing around the second floor. Kelly trotted up them, then followed Sergeant Rowe down a hall. Someone stuck his head around the corner behind them and called, "Say Doug—"

Rowe and the agent turned. The speaker was a balding man wearing a white shirt and a vest, a little older and a little heavier than Kelly himself. He folded over the cable copy he held when he realized the sergeant was not alone. He said, "Sorry, I'll catch you later," before disappearing back around the same corner.

"Sure, Harry," Rowe said, waving to the man's back. "Harry Warner," the sergeant remarked to Kelly in an undertone as he knocked on the last office door. "He's the Station Chief. Cover's in Econ Section."

"How big's the CIA station here?" Kelly asked.

There was a mumble from within the office. Rowe opened the door, continuing, "Four slots with the one in Oran. Plus the Communicators, of course, though the whole embassy uses them for the cable traffic. Gee, I wish we had the money to throw around that those boys do."

"You must be Kelly," said the Defense Attache, remaining seated. He held a cigarette and the ashtray on his desk was overflowing.

Kelly had never learned a good way of dealing with naval officers. Commander Posner extended a hand over his desk without rising. Kelly took it.

"Yes, sir," he said, "I'm Tom Kelly."

Posner gestured abruptly toward one of the basswood and naugahyde chairs with which his office was furnished. "I think the Ambassador would like to have the money Warner can throw around, Sergeant," he said. "But I gather that's just the sort of budget this office has suddenly been blessed with. *Is* that the case, Mr. Kelly?"

"Well, I understand this operation has a pretty high priority, that's right," the agent said. Posner's trick of staring at him through a stream of cigarette smoke made him uncomfortable. "I suppose if it all works out, there'll be promotions all round," Kelly added in an attempt to brighten the conversation.

Posner leaned forward. "From the little I have been told, Mr. Kelly," he said, enunciating precisely, "I would presume that if your scheme works out, the least undesirable result will be the immediate closing of this mission and the expulsion of all its personnel."

Kelly leaned back in his chair, crossing an ankle over a knee. Fine, if that was the way it was to be played. "Well," he said, "from what I've seen, all Third World countries'd be smarter to close all great-power embassies. It's the only way to keep their elections from being rigged and their politicians bought by outsiders. But since none of that has anything to do with our job—yours and mine and the sergeant's, here—" Kelly waved to Rowe, already seated in another of the American-made chairs— "I propose we move on. Have you got the contact we need in the Aurassi?"

Commander Posner held an icy silence for some seconds while the sergeant twitched on his seat. At last the Attache said, "We have, yes, one of the desk clerks . . . the one who gave us the room numbers you requested. As we expected, none of the Russians attending the Conference will be billeted in the hotel."

"Sure," Kelly agreed, "but the number you sent me is the room that the contact agent, Hoang Tanh, will be using during the Conference, isn't it? That's the one I booked from London as Angelo Ceriani."

Sergeant Rowe fidgeted again. The commander said, "I'm afraid that wouldn't have been possible, Mr. Kelly. We gave you the number of the room across the hall from Tanh's instead. The one in question is kept on a long-term rental for business purposes by the manager of a German cement firm. He'll be put out for the Conference itself, of course, but the clerk refused to take the chance of disturbing that arrangement for us. I made him a very sizeable offer." Posner's face worked, leaving no doubt of how he felt about raw bribery. "Fifty thousand dinars."

"Christ Jesus!" the agent snapped. "This German clown can screw his girlfriends next door for a couple days, can't he? He'll have to make other arrangements during the Conference, so he can make them a couple days early! How did you put it to this clerk, anyway?"

"Perhaps you'd like to try yourself, Mr. Kelly," Posner retorted. "The Pentagon seems to have the impression that you can walk on water, after all!" He stubbed out his cigarette and fumbled for the pack.

"Sir," said Sergeant Rowe. "There was his nephew, you know."

Commander Posner flicked his hand enough to drop the plastic lighter he held. "I checked that," he said. "I told you, it isn't possible."

"This whole damn thing may not be possible," Kelly said mildly. He rotated the chair seat so that he faced the sergeant's profile rather than the desk. "Tell me about this nephew, Sergeant."

"I said—" Posner began.

"If you will!" shouted the agent, snapping his head toward the Attache like a gun turret. His right arm, cocked on the chair back, was tense. The tendons drew the skin of the thick wrist into pleats. In a quieter voice but one which would have been suitable for reading death sentences, Kelly continued, "Commander, I would not presume to tell you your business. This is my business, and I need to know absolutely everything about it." He turned back to the sergeant. "Ah—Doug?" he prompted.

The sergeant looked at Kelly rather than his own superior. Posner's hands were shaking too much to successfully light a fresh cigarette. "Well," Rowe said, "the clerk has a nephew, his sister's son, who wants to go to engineering school in the States. Got accepted at Utah, I think it is. Only—" he waved, caught Posner's eyes, and quickly focused back on Kelly— "the kid had goofed. A couple years ago he'd applied for a US visa while he was in Paris."

Kelly shrugged to move the story along. He had never heard that applying for a visa was a crime.

The soldier bobbed his head and said, "It's a game the State Department plays with the Ministry of Foreign Affairs here, you see. The MFA only grants visas to US citizens who've applied at the Algerian consulate in DC. So we only grant visas to Algerians who apply here in Algiers. It's like asking why they dye pistachio nuts—doesn't make a damned bit of sense, it just happens."

"Rowe," said the commander, who had managed to light another cigarette at last, "keep to the facts and leave the insulting comments for our visitor, if you please."

"The nephew got turned down in Paris," the sergeant continued more quietly, "because of that. That wouldn't have mattered except that when he filled out the new application here, he said he'd never been turned down. Maybe he forgot, maybe he thought it'd hurt his chances the second time to have blown it before. Anyhow, they've got computers in Foggy Bottom, and they turned up the previous application right away. That's lying on a visa application, and that's the kiss of death for *ever* getting a US visa issued. They tell me."

Frowning, Kelly turned to the Defense Attache. "OK," he said, "so we've got a kid who's eligible for a US student visa except for a technical screw-up. And we've got a clerk who'll give me the room I need if the kid gets that visa. Is that right?"

"We *don't* need Room 327, we can operate from 324," the commander said in a clipped voice. "And in any case, the rule can't be waived. I took the matter up with Ambassador Gordon himself."

Tom Kelly gave Posner a smile that no one in the room thought was friendly. "What's the word on commo here?" he asked, a cat testing the surface before leaping. "I know what I've been told in Paris, but that's not always how it looks on the ground."

Sour but uncertain, Posner said, "We received notice of this—operation—by courier. He also brought a set of program disks. We have been instructed to encode all operational materials ourselves on the embassy mini-computer, using the disks we received from the courier. We are then to pass the encrypted message to the Communicators. In other words—" the Commander's voice rose and he had to tent his fingers to keep them steady— "to completely divorce this office from the mission as a whole. I can tell you that the Station Chief regards all this as a serious breach of security—and that the Ambassador is considering filing a strong protest at the insult."

"Yeah, well," Kelly said. "Well, we don't want to add to his Excellency's severe problems, do we? He might get peeved and slobber all over the finish of his limo. . . . So we'll hand in this cable in clear, Immediate—Night Action, addressed—" Com-

mander Posner's mouth opened, but the agent did
not let him speak— "DAO Paris. Arrange student
visa issued—fill in the name and whatever else
you need, Rowe—most urgent, reply copy
Ambassador Algeria, signed Cuttlefish." Kelly's
grin was real this time and a trifle rueful as he
added, "That's me, Cuttlefish. We also serve who
pacify budgies, I suppose."

Rowe was already out of his chair and swinging
toward the door. "Sergeant, come back here!"
gurgled the Defense Attache. With his voice under
a little better control, Posner turned to Kelly and
added, "You can't send that. Are you insane?"

"It's got to be sent," the agent said. "Commander, it doesn't go out over your name, it's in
mine. And if nothing comes back, I'm the idiot for
getting mixed up with the USG again and trusting
them to back me. Sergeant Rowe, I don't want to
put you in the middle. If you'll guide me to the
code room, I'll hand in the message myself."

Rowe looked at the Attache. "Commander," he
said, "the orders were specific. I'll take care of the
cable." As he passed through the door, he added
over his shoulder, "I still go by Doug, Mr. Kelly."

The door closed. Behind Commander Posner,
the great harbor glittered. It was closer than it had
been from the Aurassi, but the film of cigarette
smoke in the Attache's office dulled the view. Coils
stirred in the draft of the sergeant's departure.
"Commander" said the agent, wishing there were
a radio on in the room, "we're got to work
together. I don't have the time to get you replaced,
and you don't have the clout to get rid of me. It's
just that simple." He hunched forward a little and
added, "Would you like me better if I'd been to
Annapolis and wore a yard of gold braid?"

"I wouldn't have liked this operation if the Joint
Chiefs sat down in my office and briefed me on it,
Mr. Kelly," the Attache said. He hammered the
palm of his right hand on the desk. Raising his

eyes he added, "It stinks. It stinks like a *sewer*, and I don't appreciate being dragged into it."

Kelly nodded, holding the officer's eyes. "I understand that," he said as earnestly as any salesman ever spoke, "believe me, I do. But you and I have our orders. And behind those orders stands the nation we serve. There are decisions that are yours and mine to execute but not to make, just as good soldiers have been doing since the world began. If you can't accept that, Commander Posner, your argument isn't with me—it's with your uniform and the oath you swore when you put it on."

Christ, what bullshit, Kelly thought as he leaned back again. But not all of him thought it was bullshit, and he knew that too. . . .

A brick in the face could not have hit Posner any harder. The Defense Attache swallowed. He started to draw on his cigarette, looked at it, and crushed it out in transferred anger. "Mr. Kelly," he said, "I—" he glared at his brass ashtray—"I apologize if I've seemed unhelpful. As you point out, we didn't choose this world, but we have our duties to carry out in it." He swallowed again before meeting the agent's eyes. "As for the Kabyles, I've arranged a meeting with what we believe is their leadership in the city tomorrow afternoon. At least, there is a group of some sort calling itself the Association of Kabyles. They have a rough idea of what you desire—" Posner managed a bleak smile—"which is all that I have, of course. I assume you'll conduct these negotiations yourself."

Kelly nodded. "Right, right," he said. "And we don't need an army, twenty people'll be plenty if they know what they're doing. God help us all if they don't . . ." He looked out at the Mediterranean, the dazzle from blue waves. He shook his head back into the present. He was a black-headed lion who knew the spearmen were close,

knew the odds were with them . . . but also
knew that there was nothing on the plain that he
could not rend if he chose to. "No," the agent
continued in a voice that barely reached the
Attache and was not really meant for him, "it
doesn't matter if they speak for their people,
whatever . . . so long as they can raise the muscle
for one quick and dirty job."

Kelly blinked, fully present again, and added,
"Where'd you get a contact, anyway? Not that it
matters so long as you do have one."

Posner coughed and lit the last cigarette from
his pack. He crumpled the foil and cellophane and
skidded them off the end of his desk into a waste
basket. "I suppose you could call him a walk-in,"
the Attache admitted. It was nothing to be
ashamed of. The Algerians, while not positively
hostile, kept the agents of imperialist powers on a
pretty short leash. "One of the Chancery guards,
actually, Mustapha bou Djema. He'd been working
for a few weeks when he stopped me when I was
going out one evening. I almost brushed him off,
told him he could talk to the GSO if he had a
problem. But it wasn't work, he wanted to talk
about 'politics,' that's the normal formula—"
Kelly nodded in understanding— "and he'd picked
me instead of Warner because I was a military
officer. He'd been in French service, it turned out,
as well as fighting against them later during the
Revolution. I really think that Mustapha's group
may be. . . .," the Attache paused, "quite
significant, but I suppose you'll be able to judge
better. Mustapha's English isn't any better than
my French, I'm afraid."

There was a knock at the door. Both men tensed
instinctively. "Yes?" the commander called.

Sergeant Rowe opened the door. "Just me, sir,"
he said. "DeVoe says the cable's gone out."

"Then," remarked Kelly, rising from his chair
with the awkwardness of a man just awakened, "I

think we've covered all we need to for the moment. Is there someplace around here to get lunch? I don't eat much on planes, and—" he smiled at himself—"I left my packet of Lufthansa peanuts in my other jacket when I changed."

"Ah, why don't I run you down to the snack bar?" the sergeant suggested. "It's a damned good place to eat lunch—and besides, it's about the only place except for the hotels. Lunch isn't an Algerian meal. You want to come, sir?" he added to Commander Posner.

The Defense Attache shook his head, managing a smile of his own. "If DeVoe's seen the message," he said, "then I can expect a visit from Harry Warner as soon as you leave the room. I may as well stay and take my medicine."

Kelly gestured toward the door. "Lead on, Doug," he said. "My stomach follows."

XI

Sergeant Rowe waited until they were outside the building to ask, "How do you like Commander Posner, then?" A haze was banked at high altitude along the line of the shore. The breeze across the grounds smelled of flowers, but it was brisk enough to make the agent's suit more comfortable than the sergeant's short sleeves.

"Well," Kelly said, "things'll work out. Only, people might remember when they're setting up a deal like this that you can't make much of a sow's ear from a bolt of silk, either."

It was almost two o'clock, local time, and the snack bar had generally cleared out. The stunning black-haired woman who had been at the cash register when Kelly first walked by had been replaced by a young Algerian male. The agent realized that he had not seen any local women—except the previous cashier—at work on the mission grounds. Welcome to Islam, where women have their place—and where they'd damned well better keep to it.

Rowe led the way to the counter at the back. A menu was chalked on a dusty blackboard. The room was packed with plastic chairs around small formica-topped tables. It looked much like a big-city lunchroom anywhere in the US. "Do you like veal parmigiana?" Rowe asked.

"Huh?" responded Kelly. He had been expecting a hamburger—with luck. "Oh. Sure. It's good here?"

"Two parmigianas and coffee, Achmed," Rowe

called through the window. He began running
coffee from the big pot into a pair of mugs.
"Everything's good here, Anna sees to that," the
sergeant explained. "Cream."

Kelly shook his head. "Hot and black," he said
with a grin, taking one of the coffees and the chair
to which Rowe gestured him. There were half a
dozen men sitting in pairs at tables. Only two of
them were North Americans, judging from their
appearance. Beyond the partition in back came
the hiss and clatter of kitchen equipment. "What
is this, anyway?" the agent asked. "A private
restaurant?"

"Well, it's operated as a service to embassy
officers and employees," the sergeant explained
as he sipped his coffee. "The prices are good, and
anyway, there really isn't much place to get lunch
in Algiers, like I said upstairs. For a while there,
they were feeding all sorts of people off the street
—which was great for the American School here, it
gets the profits, but it was lousy security, of
course. And even later, there was a problem with
the maintenance people. The mission maintains
all the off-post housing here, you see. The
maintenance crews all decided they'd forgotten
some part or tool and drove back to the compound
here right around noon each day." Rowe glanced
around at the local nationals talking over the
remains of their own meals. "Still some of that,
the GSO tells me. But except for here, you either
carry your lunch or you buy a rotisseried chicken
and eat it on the sidewalk. Somebody really ought
to start a lunch counter, but the government isn't
crazy about private enterprise even in traditional
businesses. They'd probably have a cat-fit if even a
local started something new."

Someone called from the service window and
thrust a pair of heavy china plates out onto the
counter. Rowe heard, even over the clashing of a
boy hauling a tub of dirty dishes into the back.

Before Kelly could get up to help, the sergeant
had fetched the plates and pocketed the check. "I
always eat Italian here," Rowe said as he raised a
forkful of veal, "but believe me, if Anna decides to
fix Eskimo, that's going to be good too."

It was excellent, especially when Kelly had
figured the price chalked on the board in dinars
and found that it was less than three dollars.
Naive travellers were often stunned to learn that a
hotel room or a meal in Third World countries
was generally more expensive than an equivalent
would have been in New York City. Tom Kelly had
not been called naive for a long time.

As Kelly and the sergeant finished their meals,
the two North Americans carried their plates to
the counter. "Say Doug," said one of them, "did
you check about the car?"

"Ah," said Rowe, "Syd Westram, Don Mayer,
this is Tom . . . that is, Angelo Ceriani. Syd and
Don are in Econ Section."

"Actually, I'm in Consular," said Westram as he
shook Kelly's hand.

Kelly grinned. "Right," he said. "I'm in business
equipment." He continued eating without haste as
the other three wrangled quietly over the car the
two Company men wanted to borrow from the
Attache's Office for some trip or other. Rowe lost
interest clearly enough to resume eating himself
in the middle of the discussion. The others
continued to push long after it was obvious that
the sergeant had no authority to clear the loan.
Still muttering to one another, the CIA officers
finally walked off to pay. The kitchen door opened
and out walked the woman Kelly had first seen at
the cash register.

She wore white slacks and a red cotton blouse
that was loose enough to be comfortable but left
no doubt of her sex. She was as tall as Kelly but
her weight was a good forty pounds beneath the
agent's one-sixty. Kelly had never in his life

dreamed of looking that good.

"Anna," called Sergeant Rowe, "we were just saying how good the veal is. Oh, Angelo Ceriani, meet Annamaria Gordon."

Kelly stood up carefully so as not to overset the center-balanced table. He made a half bow.

The woman laughed happily and extended her hand. "My, so gallant," she murmured in Italian.

"Lady," replied the agent in the same language, "so lovely a one as yourself deserves the gallantry of true gentlemen, not such as myself."

"Mother of God, he speaks like a Florentine!" Annamaria cried in delight. She clasped Kelly by both shoulders. "Oh, you don't know what it's like to—the Italian Ambassador is an old stick and deaf besides. And his *wife*—Dougie—"switching to English—"Where have you been hiding this one?"

"Well," said Sergeant Rowe, trapped in his chair by the table behind him and the woman reaching over his head, "he's—"

"Oh, of course!" Annamaria broke in, "he has to be the, the Thomas Kelly who has my husband so angry, that is so?"

Kelly's skin prickled again with fear and anger. This time the fear was not misplaced, though the last of the customers had left the room and it was unlikely that the fellow at the cash register could hear even if he did speak English. Anna was an embassy wife, that was clear, and her husband had done too goddamned much talking out of—

"I'm sorry if his Excellency is concerned," Sergeant Rowe was saying.

Jesus Christ, she was the Ambassador's wife.

Annamaria—Mrs. Ambassador Gordon—tugged Kelly out into the central aisle of the lunchroom. Releasing him and stepping back a pace, she eyed the agent up and down with the dispassion of a horse-buyer. Embarrassed but as much at a loss as was Rowe—who had finally struggled to his feet—Kelly found himself staring back at the lady.

Her chain necklace was of gold and heavy. It was the one thing besides her beauty that seemed to suit her status.

Reverting to Italian, the black-haired woman asked, "Have you seen the city yet? You won't have, will you, since you've just arrived."

"Well, I'm not here solely on pleasure. . .," Kelly temporized, distrusting the conversation though he could not believe it was headed where it seemed to be.

Belief be damned. "Come then, this afternoon. I'll be your guide instead of Doug here," said Annamaria. "It's been *so* long since I've heard Italian spoken by anyone in the least interesting. And if my husband is so angry without even having met you, you must be interesting."

"Ah, Mrs. Gordon," said the agent, switching back to English but trying not to show his horror, "I'd be delighted to see Algiers with you some other time. But we're going to be busy for the next couple days and—"

Annamaria smiled with a cheerful wickedness. Her eyes were set wide, their pupils very dark. She raised one finger and said, still in Italian, "You don't intend to see the city? Poof! And what are you going to do this afternoon, tell me?"

The sergeant blinked, aghast now that Kelly's words had shown him how things were tending. The agent himself met Annamaria's eyes. The humor of the whole business struck him and he started to laugh. The dish boy looked around in surprise, then ducked back within the kitchen. "All right," said Kelly, "to tell the truth, I was going to get a tour of the Casbah. Want to come along?" As a dip's wife, the woman had an automatic 'Secret' clearance, barring the kind of negative evidence that would in all likelihood have prevented her husband from getting an ambassadorship. And by God, if there was a better way of giving the establishment a kick in the ass than this, Kelly couldn't imagine what it was.

"All right, give me fifteen minutes to shower and change," Annamaria said, her smile broader. "And remember, you have to talk to me."

"Sir," said Rowe.

"Tom, for Chrissake," Kelly remarked, his eyes still on the woman. "No, Mrs. Gordon, you two can pick me up in front of the Aurassi in an hour and a half. And one thing—" this in Italian, and the tone brought her around with her tweezer-shaped eyebrows rising—"what you do when you're alone is your own business . . . and slacks are fine with me, make a lot of sense. But if you're going to be with me in the Old City and I'm working, which you know I am—wear a skirt, please? With a skirt, we're tourists and nobody cares. In trousers, we're stupid tourists—and it's not our country to be stupid in."

Annamaria's expression was momentarily as black as her hair. "Do you take particular pleasure in ordering women around, Mr. Kelly?" she asked in a new tone.

"Sometimes I think I get the most pleasure from killing a bottle of Jack Black alone in my room," the agent said quietly. "But that won't get the job down this time. Mrs. Gordon, if you don't like something I say or do, just tell me to go piss up a rope." The phrase had a ring of unexpected obscenity in translation. "But if I'm working, don't assume that I do anything for fun."

After a moment, the beautiful wide smile flashed back across the lady's face. "In person, Rufus is going to like you even better than he does now, Mr. Kelly," she said. "Well—the Aurassi at four, then."

Annamaria strode off without self-consciousness. Her walk had the grace natural to a slim-hipped woman with perfect health and assurance.

"Let's go call me a cab from your office," said Kelly, pulling a wad of dinars from his pocket as he led the way to the cashier. "Just in case some-body's watching, I'd as soon not enter and leave the compound in official cars." Rowe had taken the check, but the prices were in plain sight on the menu board. Kelly didn't intend to bum even a cheap meal from somebody trying to make ends meet on a sergeant's pay. "You know," he added, "Mrs. Gordon isn't what you, ah, expect in an am-bassador's wife."

"A human being, you mean?" Rowe replied with a smile as they stepped back onto the grounds. He sobered. "Yeah, well. I mean, Ambassador Gor-don's a good choice in a lot of ways. He speaks French and he's travelled a lot, that's how he met Anna, I suppose. But he's old money, you see, his family's got a big ad agency in Houston . . . and a lot of the time, he seems to think the whole mission ought to be outfitted with servants' uniforms. There's a swimming pool on the Residence grounds. It's supposed to be for use of the whole mission and their families, but word got out as soon as the Gordons arrived in country that the hoi polloi had better keep to their own side of the wall, thank you."

Rowe opened the front door and paused in the Chancery anteroom. "Henri," he said into the voice plate, "would you call a cab to take Mr. Ceriani back to his hotel, please."

"I'll need to rent a car, I suppose," Kelly said as they walked back toward the gate. "Right now, I need a guide, though."

The sergeant nodded. "Sure, they'll deliver one to the Aurassi, just check with the clerk." He said nothing for a moment, then resumed. "It's the usual thing, big frog in a small puddle. You see it in army posts, God knows. But maybe it's worse in an embassy because there's nobody this side of DC that ranks the Ambassador, even though he's got only twenty people under him."

"Few enough higher in DC, too," Kelly agreed.

"And I don't suppose it was political contributions to the Secretary of State that got him appointed."

"Sure, being able to call the President by his first name may—affect how you feel about a sergeant E-6," Rowe said. "Or a commander O-5, for that matter. But the thing is, I think a lot of the way the Ambassador acts toward everybody else is the way that Anna doesn't give a hoot in Hell for all the crap and ceremony herself. She goes to receptions when she wants to—and she knocks 'em dead in a black dress, let me tell you—not that *I* get invited to many. But that's when she wants to. And instead of running the mission wives like happens at most posts, charities and garden parties and such, she runs the snack bar. And that's great for my wife, she'd be at the bottom of the pecking order same as I am with the mission . . . only I think life with his Excellency might be a little easier for the rest of us if Anna didn't rub it in quite so much."

Kelly chuckled. "When they come up with a perfect society," he said, "let me know about it. Not that they'd want my sort anywhere around."

The group loitering at the gate had changed slightly in composition but not in character. Someone had tuned a French transistor radio to a station that was playing Arabic music. Kelly had never learned the conventions of Eastern music, but tuned low—as this was—he found it soothing. It reminded him of CW traffic received through severe heterodyne, part and parcel of much of his life. "In Nam," he said aloud to the sergeant, "when I was in base camp on stand-down, the hooch maids used to listen to horse operas while they worked."

"Westerns?" Rowe said in surprise.

"That too," Kelly explained with a grin. "There'd be the sound of hoofs as the hero rode up to the ranch. He'd sing to the heroine, she'd sing back, and then the chorus of cow-hands sang to everybody. Eventually the hero would clop off, sing threats at the villain and vice-versa, and then they'd have a gunfight. 'Bang!' 'You scoundrel, you have wounded me, but my love gives me strength to overcome you yet.' 'Bang-bang-bang!' 'Haughty fool, I have slain your betters a thousand times—see the notches here on my gunbutts.' This'd go on through what I swear must've been a mini-can of ammo before the hero triumphed and married the girl."

"Jeez, that sounds awful," said Rowe.

Kelly grinned. "Well, maybe I'm not a good source for opera. I heard *Rigoletto* at La Scala and I didn't think a whole lot of that, either."

Voices loud enough to carry filtered in from the street. The North Americans looked at one another. Both stepped through the open doorway.

A Fiat sedan had pulled up near the Residence gate. The driver, a tall black man in a dashiki and slacks, had gotten out and was arguing with the guard. Both men were gesturing and shouting—the guard in French, the black apparently in English disguised by distance and an accent. "That's part of the Ambassador's management style, what you see there," said the sergeant.

The black strode haughtily past the guard and into the Residence grounds. Still shrieking, the man in khaki followed with his fists clenched. "Jesus," muttered Kelly in amazement, "It's a damn good thing the guards aren't issued guns." Then, "What do you mean about the Ambassador being responsible?"

Rowe stepped out along the wall and motioned the agent to follow him, not that the Algerians within were showing any signs of interest in the conversation. Cars, braking and changing down as they rounded the curve, provided background noise. "The Ambassador's secretary," the sergeant said, "Buffy Tuttle. She lives in the guest house right by the Residence gate."

"I've seen it," Kelly agreed.

"Well," Rowe went on, "that's a good place because she has to be on call pretty much all the time. And she dates a lot—she's single and damned good looking. But his Excellency doesn't like it that the guys courting her park right in front of his door. He won't tell *her* that himself, maybe because she's black and he's afraid of being called a racist . . . so he tells the guards to make all Buffy's visitors park across the street in the Annex lot. And they pay about as much attention to the guard as you'd expect." Rowe nodded toward the Fiat.

Kelly shook his head. "His Excellency's going to have blood all over his gravel if he doesn't watch out," he remarked.

"Sure," agreed Rowe. "And what's even worse is, well . . . there aren't a whole lot of blacks in Algiers, you know. Most of them calling on Buffy are from the Chaka Front office downtown."

"What!" the agent blurted. A great Magirus Deutz truck passed, its diesel blasting as it climbed the hill. During the interval, while both men squeezed their backs still closer to the wall, Kelly decided he must have misunderstood.

"Yeah, that's right," the sergeant said gloomily as the truck disappeared. "Goons from the South African liberation organization. They've got an information office here, may as well be an embassy. Which is fine, but. . . ."

"But this is the secretary who's typing and filing most of the Top Secret material in the mission?" the agent said, not really asking it as a question. "Jesus."

"Neither Harry Warner nor the commander's real pleased about it," Rowe agreed. "In the country team meetings, the Ambassador says it may prove a useful channel of information from the Chaka Front. I don't know. Maybe he'd say the same thing if she was dating Mossad agents, maybe he wouldn't. . . . Anyway, he's the boss in this puddle, isn't he?"

A yellow Renault cab pulled up with a shriek of brakes. "Jesus," Kelly repeated. Then, as he got in, he called back, "We'll meet again soon, then, Sergeant, and get down to business!"

XII

It wasn't particularly a surprise to Kelly that Annamaria Gordon drove up in front of the Aurassi alone. It did surprise him that the Ambassador's wife was at the wheel of a Volkswagen, not the red Mustang which Kelly had seen parked in the Residence drive that morning.

Annamaria started to lean from her window to speak to the uniformed doorman. Kelly, striding from a bench near the lobby doors, caught that functionary's eye in time to avoid being paged. He got in on the passenger side, meeting the woman's bright smile as she thrust the car into gear. "I thought," she said, "that you might want to be driven around in something less conspicuous than an American car with diplomatic plates, so I rented this. If you want to drive it yourself, though, you have to be approved by the rental agency."

"Glad to know you're so scrupulous about legalities," the agent said with a smile. He adjusted the hang of his camera. "I'd figured we'd park at a distance and walk—"

Annamaria nodded. She was wearing a dress of gray silk, simple enough and rather high in the neck. While it showed little flesh, however, it did nothing to disguise the way her muscles worked beneath its opacity. Her hair was held up by combs of black wood instead of the plastic that had sufficed earlier. Annamaria might be unconventional, but she was not wholly unconcerned with the impression she gave, either. "We'll have to walk if you really want to see the Casbah," she said at Kelly's pause.

"Oh, fine," the agent said. "Anyway, it wasn't the end of the world if the car was conspicuous, but that was damned good thinking anyway. I appreciate it."

They were speaking in Italian. It provided a sort of time slip for both of them. For Kelly, the language returned him to his five most recent years as a civilian, where tension was the success or failure of a sales pitch. For the woman, Italian was a return to her early twenties, before the ten years of marriage that relegated the tongue of her birth to diplomatic gatherings—and that rarely.

Thinking about nothing that he should have been, the agent added, "Not that I don't think we'll attract more attention than Doug and I would have . . . but I doubt anybody's going to be looking at me long."

"A tourist couple," Annamaria said. She looked at her passenger and gestured. The habit made Kelly wince internally as they sped south. "And you with your camera for what? Protective coloration? Very clever."

"I told you I was working," the agent said, looking out his window at the two and three-story buildings stepping down the gradient of the street. "I might have needed to talk to Doug, you know."

"Not in front of me," the woman said. "Not business." She flooded Kelly with her smile again. "Besides, a couple blends in. Would you scandalize folk with the appearance of a menage?"

Kelly cleared his throat and turned his attention to the car itself on the assumption that he would be driving it soon. It was a standard VW Passat, basically what would have been a Dasher in the US. A decal on the back window announced in large, blue letters, "Made in Brazil"—surely as striking a monument to the omnipresence of English as one could have found. The engine seemed as peppy as the automatic transmission permitted it to be. None of the inevitable squeals and rattles seemed to signal any major mechanical difficulties.

"Unless you have a preference," Annamaria announced, "we'll park at the bottom. It's all a hillside, you know. The natives got the part of the city that the French didn't want to take over for themselves, and then just enough of them were permitted to stay to be servants for their betters. Not," she added with a rueful smile, "that we Italians can claim much better." Swinging right at a traffic light that had already gone red, she explained, "This is the Rue Bab el Oued, you know?"

"The Watergate," Kelly said, dredging up some fragments of Arabic gleaned during his years in the Med.

Annamaria turned to gesture behind her though there appeared to be nothing but office buildings and apartment blocks. She continued, "Back there in the Bab el Oued was the poor section of the city—but for whites, you see. That's where the Pieds Noirs lived, that's where the Secret Army terrorists hid and built bombs to kill Arabs with, to keep France from ever freeing Algeria. . . . But they weren't French, the Pieds Noirs, except in citizenship the most of them. They were Italians, like me—or truly, they were Algerians or could have been, were they not so quick to slaughter innocents to prevent that result."

Annamaria pulled into a parking space. In the near distance sunlight glittered on a fountain which the agent supposed was in the Plaza of the Martyrs. "I guess it's natural that the people who're worst off fight the hardest to keep the little they think they have," Kelly said as he got out of the car. "And I guess it's natural that they do it in the most self-destructive ways possible, too, because the people with all the experts to advise them generally manage to do the same goddam thing themselves."

He laughed and added abruptly, "They go out and hire people like me, for instance."

There were no vehicular streets in the Casbah save the Rue Amar Ali which bisected it on a diagonal opposite to the one Kelly and Mrs. Gordon were taking. Access was by pedestrian ways, sometimes covered and always lowered upon by jutting upper stories. Sometimes the passages were broad enough that a traveller could spread both arms and touch neither wall. More often, they were so narrow that two persons passed each other with difficulty.

As the couple worked north and steeply upward from the Ali Bitchin Mosque, Kelly took surreptitious photographs. His old Nikon F was fitted with a 24 mm semi-fisheye lens. The pictures would be severely distorted by the short lens, but nothing longer would have been of the least use in such close quarters. Further, the wide angle lens could be used without normal aiming. Kelly had brazed a stud to the camera's back. The other end was hooked in one of his belt holes. That kept the slung camera pointed forward and slightly upward as he walked. Whenever the agent was ready to take a photograph, he would turn his head and say something to Annamaria behind him. His right index finger stroked the release unnoticed. The heavy Nikon shutter made more noise than Kelly would have liked, but there was generally background sound chattering through the narrow passages. At any rate, the agent did not now have time to get used to new equipment.

The ground levels of the three and four-story buildings were mostly shops, less frequently a hammam—a Turkish bath—or even the gorgeously-tiled anteroom of a neighborhood mosque. Store-front churches were not unique to American inner cities. In one open room, a man shaped chair seats with a draw-knife while two

friends argued and smoked hand-rolled cigarettes.
A shop sold horsemeat, dark and without the
marbling of fat typical of even lean beef. That shop
was flanked on one side by a display of wicker
bird-cages, each unique; and on the other by
kitchen equipment of plastic and aluminum, sold
by a heavy-set woman in the white gown of a
widow.

The passages twisted and forked. Rarely could
Kelly see more than ten feet ahead or behind him.
At intervals, a step or a flight of steps would
mount the grade, making the tracks as impassible
by donkeys as they were to motor vehicles. The
thought of carrying out a military operation here,
where the walls were stone and the twists and
turnings left every attacker alone, was chilling.
The Germans had found Stalingrad an icy Hell. For
the French, the Battle of Algiers was a matter of
entering a sarcophagous some moments before
death. Kelly smiled and clicked his camera and
occasionally consulted the French map he held
folded in his left hand.

One could see shops only when on top of them.
Some, however, announced their presence at a
distance with odors as distinctive as display signs.
A bread shop flooded one passage with the smell
of baguettes, freshly baked on the premises; and
the rich, chocolaty aroma of coffee pursued Kelly
a hundred feet from where the beans were
weighed and ground and blended from burlap
bags. There was no stench of dung, of sewage.
Once they passed a man urinating against a wall,
but defecation was as private a matter as in any
American suburb. Further, unlike many Western
cities, the Casbah had no population of domestic
animals spreading their daily burden of waste.

Near the top of the Old City, Kelly paused at a
stone railing to rest and change film. Below them
loomed the Safir Mosque. The ground rose so
abruptly to them that the Mediterranean could be

glimpsed over the roofs and clothing spread to dry. The agent found he was breathing hard. That irritated him. He made a reasonable effort to stay in shape, but age was creeping up on him with its claws out.

"How old are you?" he asked his companion. It was the first real conversation they had had since they left the car.

The woman laughed and tossed her head. "To think I called you gallant," she said. "But I'm 34, since you ask."

"It looks a lot younger on you than 38 feels on me," Kelly said, his eyes on the film leader he was cranking through the sprockets. Carefully, he set the camera back in place, then clicked the shutter twice to bring unexposed film from the cassette. "Well, no rest for the wicked," he said as he rose from where he knelt. "According to the map, the Fort de la Casbah should be just south."

"There's also a section of what Susette—Groener, the Political Officer's wife—says is a Turkish aqueduct," Annamaria remarked. She straightened from the rail against which she lounged. "But I'd swear myself that it's really Roman wall. None of the guidebooks help, even the Guide Bleu."

"That's fine," said the agent with a smile, "but I'll bet it hasn't been converted into a nuclear research facility—the way the fort has." A pace or two later he added, "Might be best if you didn't pay much attention to the place. I don't suppose the government thinks of it as a tourist attraction the way the Casbah itself is."

"Oui, oui," said the woman, and the French made Kelly glance at her face in time to catch an impish smile.

The Fort de la Casbah—more recently the Caserne Ali Khodja and now the Institute for Nuclear Research—squatted on the Boulevard de la Victoire. It looked more like a brick-built 19th

Century prison than it did a military, much less
scientific, installation. The walls were about ten
feet high and topped with triple strands of barbed
wire. The wire was electrified from the look of the
insulators between it and the supporting
posts. There were low corner towers, the one
nearest to Kelly manned by a soldier with an
automatic rifle. Staring at the map with his head
turned up the street, the agent began snapping
pictures.

Annamaria leaned against Kelly's right arm as
he was cocking the shutter. In loud French she
said, "Darling, I'm *certain* the National Theater
must be toward the harbor. Here, let me see the
map."

The sun was low. She should have needed a coat
to stay warm, Kelly thought. But the Lord knew
her breast was as warm as it was soft where it
pressed against his arm. The agent's breath
caught—like a goddam little kid—before he said,
"Well, if we follow this up to the corner and then
left on the Ourida. . . ."

They walked south past the riveted steel gate of
the Institute. The metal was painted a dusty gray,
which made it look as solid as a vault. Not that
Kelly was planning an assault. But it was obvious
that they would have to play a lot of this one by
ear, and the more the agent knew about the
surroundings, the better. Annamaria continued to
cling to his arm. Every few yards, she would tug
him to a halt, facing the Institute and arguing
volubly over the map. The map shaded the Nikon
and Kelly's hand working the shutter. Annamaria's perfume was floral and attractive in its
suggestions.

"And now?" the woman murmured in Italian as
they reached the Boulevard Ourida-Meddad and
the south face of the Institute. She was very warm
against his arm.

"Now, back though the Casbah a different way,"

replied the agent. "I think there's enough light left
if we push-process the film. And anyway, there's
plenty of light to see by."

"You think that you can memorize all the
turnings of the Old City in one afternoon?" the
woman asked with a smile.

Kelly raised an eyebrow. "You doubt it? Tsk. I
can do anything. Just ask the folks in the
Pentagon."

Going downhill, the alleys of the Casbah resem-
bled a bobsled run, steep and narrow. The footing
was mostly asphalt, punctuated by low stone
steps. In earlier times the Casbah had presumably
been paved with cobblestones which would have
been even slicker than ice during rain. Annamaria
followed as before, but the memory of her was soft
on Kelly's arm.

A soccer ball jury-rigged from a plastic bag with
rag stuffing bounced toward the couple at an
intersection. Kelly stopped. Three boys with
bright eyes and hair cut as short as American boys
of the '50s bounded after the ball. They caromed
from the blank sidewalls of the passage, each
blurting an apology to the couple as they darted
past. Kelly waited. Annamaria rested a hand on
his shoulder, but she did not speak.

A moment later, the boys were back, one of them
holding the ball. The agent grinned and called
after them in French. "Please, a photograph?"
Giggling, the three children skidded to a halt. They
arrayed themselves with linked arms across the
passage in which they had been playing. As the
boys mugged, Kelly raised the camera and
checked the viewfinder for the first time that
afternoon. He shot, turned the camera for a
vertical, and shot again. Finally, he adjusted the
shutter speed and f-stop before taking another
photo. "Some day you may be famous," he called
to the grinning boys as he lowered the camera
again. "Many thanks."

"Don't tell me you aren't utterly devoted to work after all," said the black-haired woman as they resumed their descent. "An affection for young children, yet!"

"I'm not utterly devoted to work, no," Kelly said with a smile which the woman could hear in his voice, "but as for those pictures.... Did you notice the two back doorways facing each other across the alley?"

After a moment, Annamaria decided to laugh. She squeezed the agent's shoulder again. "Do you like cous-cous?" she asked unexpectedly.

"Damned if I know," the agent said. He photographed the Rue Amar Ali northward, then turned and pointed toward the Theatre National while he shot the southward length as well. "Do I eat it or—" He stopped himself.

"You eat it," Annamaria said, holding Kelly's arm again as they darted across the narrow street, "and you feed it to me. I think my guiding you has earned me dinner tonight, don't you? Not to mention the fact that I'm freezing myself for your duty."

"Tsk, did anybody make you come?" said Kelly, turning enough to let the tall woman see him grin. "And besides, you—" The agent stopped himself again.

"Doug Rowe couldn't have looked like anything but a soldier, even if you'd put him in a dress," Annamaria said. "And do you think *he* was going to make the guards ignore your camera by cuddling you?" She giggled. "Well, he might have at that.... Still. And as for my husband—" answering the question Kelly had not spoken— "he'll be right down there at El Mouggar where the Lovelace Jazz Quartet is playing on their ICA tour tonight." She waved in the general direction of the National Theatre. "I told Rufus that I'd do my duty at the buffet with the quartet at the Residence Wednesday, but not then and tonight besides."

"That's not quite. . .," the agent began. His voice trailed off when he realized he did not care to say what he *had* exactly meant. Nor, he supposed, did he need to. "All right," he said, "I guess I'm old enough to learn about cous-cous."

Or whatever, he added to himself as he let a pair of veiled, heavy-set women step past. Or learn about whatever.

XIII

Kelly walked along the south side of the street where there was something of a sidewalk, albeit not a curb. He had followed Annamaria's Mustang back from the rental agency in El Biar where the Passat had been transferred to his name. The car was now parked in the GSO Annex, across from where the Mustang had pulled into the Residence gate.

The agent noticed that the Fiat was no longer in front of the Residence. That whole business could lead to bad trouble, international trouble, at the mission—which was about the last thing Sky-ripper needed. Kelly hoped that if somebody, a Zulu from the Chaka Front or an Algerian guard, were going to be knifed at the embassy, that it would happen after Professor Vlasov had de-fected—or the operation had failed of itself . . . in which case Kelly would be well and truly at peace with the universe, he assumed.

The agent darted across the street and rapped on the Chancery gate. A different guard opened the door. This one was a heavy-set man in his fifties, with a thick, black moustache and almost no hair above the eyebrows. The loungers seemed to have gone home. Perhaps they had been friends or family to the man on the day shift. "Is Commander Posner or Sergeant Rowe still here?" Kelly asked in French.

"Mr. Ceriani?" asked the local employee. "Com-mander Posner, no, but the sergeant is waiting for you." He waved toward the Chancery. As the agent strode down the walk he noticed the guard picking up the phone in his shack and dialing. He waved when he saw Kelly looking back at him.

Doug Rowe was coming out the front door of the building before the agent had reached it. The steel door within was open. The receptionist and another man were examining it.

"Anything wrong with the door?" Kelly asked with a nod toward the building.

"Oh, Henri says three men came asking for visas," the younger man explained. "He sent them over to the Consulate in the Villa Inshallah, but one of them leaned against the door or something—and it opened. The bolt must have stuck, I suppose. Seems OK now. Henri hit the siren, and I guess the poor guys are lucky they ran off before he dumped CS over them."

Rowe looked around. "Let's walk on the grounds," he said, waving a white cable copy to Kelly. In a lower voice he added, "All this stuff is making me a little nuts. I keep thinking maybe my office is bugged."

"Planted by a predecessor who was a KGB mole, no doubt," Kelly joked. The sun had set behind the mountains, but there was enough light to see by.

"KGB, Hell," Rowe said. "I'm worried about Harry Warner. He went through the roof when this came in—" he handed Kelly the cable— "and so, I'll bet, did the Ambassador. You got a bull's-eye, Tom, a perfect bull."

Kelly read the brief flimsy. "They want the job done, they give me the tools to do it," he said quietly. Flowers, their colors turned to shadow, filled the air with their freshness as the men walked past. Kelly handed back the cable. "Run it through the shredder, then," he said. "Stapling it to the visa request would be adding insult to injury. Nobody's going to play silly games when there's an order from the Secretary of State in the mission files already."

"You'll handle it tonight, then?" the sergeant asked, darting a sidewise glance at his companion.

"Can you raise the commander if you have to?" Kelly replied obliquely, looking off toward the wall about the grounds.

"Well, he'll be at home. . . . Sure."

"Sorry," the agent said, noting the expected lack of enthusiasm in Rowe's voice, "but I want him to do it. And yeah, I want it done tonight. Posner's had the initial contact. He can follow it up without getting me involved. Let the clerk think I'm being set up, too. At least let him wonder."

Kelly paused. "And as for you, Doug," he said, lifting three film cassettes from his coat pocket, "you handle the darkroom work for the office?"

The sergeant nodded, his rueful smile hardly visible.

"Yeah, that's right," Kelly agreed, "a goddam all-nighter, and I'm sorry, but. . . . It's Tri-X and the cans are marked. Develop One standard, push Two and Three to ASA 1200. Then I need prints from every frame, numbered. Eight by tens. It's a bitch, I know, but we'll need the prints when we talk to the Kabyles tomorrow afternoon."

"I'll phone my wife after I get the commander," Rowe said. "After all—" his teeth glinted— "I wanted the job because of the excitement, didn't I?"

A car pulled in the gate behind them and made a U-turn. Before the headlights were shut off, their reflection from the wall brought out the car's red finish. The engine continued to purr at a fast idle.

Kelly gripped Rowe by the shoulder and squeezed. "Here, you best keep my camera for me too, if you would," he said. He unstrapped the Nikon. Then he added, "At least you know what the Hell you're doing. I swear I don't. Though I suppose I had to eat somewhere tonight, didn't I?"

The two men began to walk back the way they had come—Rowe to a night in the darkroom . . . and Kelly to the Mustang that awaited him.

XIV

Kelly walked around the back of the car to get to Annamaria's door. She had started to unlatch it as soon as she had parked, but she waited when she realized what her passenger was doing. "Madame," the agent said, bowing low in self mockery after he had handed her out.

"You know," said the black-haired woman, "I rather thought you might be the sort of man who insists on doing all the driving himself." She arched an eyebrow. Annamaria wore the dress she had on when they toured the Casbah, but the effect was strikingly different now. Her shoes were straps with spike heels, comfortable for no more than the thirty yards they had yet to walk to the restaurant. Her hair was down in a black flood to her shoulders where it merged with the fur of her wrap—just as black, just as rich, just as clearly expensive. The perfume was the same, but it now was a part of the night.

"Is that what you wanted?" the agent asked, offering his right arm with the stiffness of unfamiliarity. When her hand rested lightly on the crook of his elbow, Kelly began to pick a way for them toward the orange neon sign of Le Carthage. There was a street light at the foot of the Chemin de la Glycines, but parked cars bled shadows that could hide a pothole in the street beside them.

At first, Kelly thought that the woman had not heard his question; but when they had almost reached the doorway of the restaurant she said, "I would have cancelled the table I reserved for to-

night if you had been that way. Men with their
balls on display every day, every minute—" Kelly
opened the door. Annamaria's grimace segued
into a greeter's smile as she stepped down into the
entryway. Within, the lights were low and the
music just loud enough to meld the scores of
separate conversations into an unintelligible
murmur. The tune was Western, a blurred version
of 'The Tennessee Waltz.'

"Gordon, please," the black-haired woman said
to the maitre d'. The Algerian bowed without
checking his book. He led them to a table in a front
corner. Neon through the square-paned window
brightened the table more than did the squat
candle in the middle of it. The two diners
themselves were in darkness.

"Did you know," Annamaria asked as a waiter
took away the third place setting, "that young
Foreign Service employees often have to grow
beards if they're stationed in Arab countries?"

Kelly raised his eyebrow. He flipped his palm up
in question on the tablecloth when he realized that
his hands were the only parts of him that were
visible until Annamaria's eyes adapted.

"Yes," she said, reaching for the wine list, "if
they don't have any children. And especially if
they aren't married. Arabs are likely to misunder-
stand about beardless men, you see, unless they
have some other proof of their virility. Italy, I'm
afraid, isn't a great deal better. I didn't need to see
more of that."

Hanged if I know why you needed to see more of
me, either, the agent thought. Aloud he said, "It
was your car, not mine. You knew where we were
going. For that matter, you're a good driver. It
scares the crap out of me to ride with anybody
else, just about, but that's not to say that you're
bad."

"Since this is an experiment for you," Annamaria said, staring toward the agent's face, "I

think we'll have the Cous-Cous Royal and a plate of charcuterie between us." She could see well enough now to tell that Kelly was grinning. She slapped the wine list shut between the fingers of one hand and said in a harder voice, "And for the wine, a bottle of Cuvee du Président. The Algerian reds are very good, strong but not raw."

"Water for me, thank you," Kelly said. "The meal sounds fine, though."

"You don't trust me to choose wine?" Annamaria demanded. "*That's* a man's job, then?"

"I remember killing a bottle of Juarez Straight American Bourbon one night," Kelly said in a reminiscent tone, his eyes directed out the window. "Haven't the faintest notion of how I got it. For flavor, I guess it was a toss-up between that and diesel fuel. But the stuff had enough kick to do what *I* was after." He looked at the woman across the table. "I'm easy to order wine for, you see, I'm a juicer. Only for the next couple days I'm going to try to dry out, that's all."

Annamaria looked away. "I'm sorry," she said.

"Your husband get on you that bad about climbing back onto your pedestal?" the agent asked.

The waiter appeared at Kelly's elbow. Kelly smiled and gestured to Annamaria. "Two Cous-Cous Royal and a plate of charcuterie," she said in a crisp French. "And a large bottle of Saida, please." The waiter nodded and sidled off. "The local mineral water comes from Saida," Annamaria explained.

"There used to be a training depot there for—" Kelly began. He paused with his mouth open. The restaurant's clientele seemed to be almost wholly foreign, and it was doubtful that even the nearest table could hear anything he said anyway. Still, it had been a long war. Kelly would not have discussed the SS in Tel Aviv, and he would not discuss the French Foreign Legion here. "For the troops headquartered at Sidi bel Abbes," Kelly concluded. "Never occurred to me anything else happened there. Shows where my head is, I guess."

"Rufus doesn't smother me by trying to do everything for me," said Annamaria, speaking toward her folded hands. The bead in her left earlobe, gold or silver, was washed orange by the neon. It winked as she moved her head. "Rufus likes to have other people do for him, you see. And that's not a problem, generally, because he has plenty of people around. . . . But there are some things that only the Ambassador's wife can do—not me, but my position. And then there's friction sometimes, yes." She raised her eyes to Kelly. He could now see the liquid gleam of her pupils catching the candle flame. "It makes me snappish when I think someone is reacting to what I am, not who I am. And so I'm sorry."

"Christ, I've been snapped at by experts," Kelly said with a laugh. "When everything gets straightened out, we'll go off on a toot together. And I promise to drink anything you order."

As they ate cauliflower and French bread, the couple talked about the Bay of Naples. It was a liberty port to Kelly and the site of a beach house owned by Annamaria's family. The locations about which they talked were both as near and as far from one another as Eden and the Wilderness. Annamaria had a quick, bubbling laugh. Kelly brayed like a donkey and knew it, so he kept a straight face throughout most of the things he thought really funny. His control broke several times, however, during Annamaria's description of the thirty-seven days she had spent as an infant-school aide at the American School in Algiers. Other diners glanced at them. Hell, when you were out with somebody as beautiful as Annamaria, you were going to get stares even if you sat on your hands all night.

The dark-haired woman combined the processes

of eating and talking with more grace than the
agent could remember complementing anyone of
her verve. When Kelly blinked at his first forkful
of cous-cous, asking if it were rice, he was treated
to an expert cook's description of how the dish
was prepared. As Annamaria chewed, her hands
demonstrated how the millet flour was rolled into
beads even smaller than rice grains, each one
coated with cooking oil wiped from the cook's
hands. Then the beads spent hours in a perforated
steamer as the sauce simmered beneath it,
cooking and imbibing the very essence of what
other methods of preparation would have left as
merely something to be poured over a completed
dish. Finally the completed meal would be
brought out to grace the low table of the husband
and his honored guests—perhaps garnished, as
here in the restaurant, with lamb chops; but first
and foremost, the cous-cous itself.

"It's no accident," Annamaria concluded, "that
the most stunning examples of Kabyle metalwork
are the cous-cous sets. The great steamer, the
serving bowls . . . the tray to carry it all in with, all
chased and studded and sometimes inlaid. But
that's only the male reflection of the art the wives
perform daily in the kitchen."

"Craftsmanship's never a bad thing," Kelly said
through a mouthful. The individual beads were
crisp, not soggy as rice steamed without the
coating of oil would have been. "Even for a bad
reason, even in a bad cause." After a moment he
added, "I've always told myself that, anyway."

They were getting up to leave when Kelly
paused. His hand froze in the side pocket where he
kept his paper money. His face wore a distant
look. "Something's wrong?" the woman asked in
concern.

Kelly brought out his hand with the fat sheaf of
dinars folded around a bill clip. "No, no," he said
with an odd smile. "Believe me, there are easier

ways to make a living that than to pick my pocket.
Even when I'm bombed. . . . No, it's the tune on the
muzak." He thumbed toward the ceiling, though
the speakers there were not actually visible. "It
just surprised me, that's all. It's an old ballad from
the English side of the border. 'The Three
Ravens.' "

"I don't think I know the words," said Annamaria. She was studying her companion more
carefully than she seemed to be as he helped her
on with her furs.

"Oh, three ravens are complaining," the agent
said, leading the way to the door. "You learn the
damnedest things from the BBC World Service. . . ." The maitre d' and the cashier greeted
them cheerfully. Kelly smiled back as he paid,
adding his compliments on the meal.

The cool air outside the restaurant was a shock.
Annamaria held Kelly's arm more closely than she
had when they walked toward Le Carthage.
"There's a knight lying dead, you see," Kelly went
on. "The ravens can't get at him, though, because
his hawks and his hounds are guarding the body.
And then his girlfriend, his leman, comes along
and buries him before she dies of a broken heart."

In a strong and surprisingly melodious baritone,
Kelly sang:

"God send every gentleman
"Such hawks, such hounds, and such a leman."

They paused beside the Mustang as Annamaria
fished the keys from her tiny lamé reticule.
"There's a Scots version, too," Kelly said, looking
back toward the restaurant. " 'The Twa Corbies.'
Things don't come out so well for the poor bastard
in the ditch in that version. But he was dead, so I
don't guess it really mattered to him."

"Think you can find the way back if you drive?" Annamaria asked. She held the keychain out on the tip of her index finger. The chrome and her short, polished fingernail caught the street light.

"With a little help," said the agent, taking the keys carefully. "I guess I can do most things with a little help."

As Kelly pulled from the parking place into a tight, smooth U-turn, Annamaria said to him, "I suppose it's the Scotch version that you believe in?"

"Don't know that I do," said the agent, shifting without haste as they climbed the hill, then shifting again. "Sometimes seems that way, I guess. But there were a lot of guys I knew back in Nam who made pretty good hawks . . . not the sort of thing you can really tell till it happens. I made a pretty good hawk myself, when it had to be done."

Two Fiats were parked at the Residence entrance, close enough to narrow the gateway still further. Kelly blipped his horn for the guard. Nothing happened except that a car barrelling down the hill locked all four wheels before coming to a stop behind them. Kelly laid on the button and the gate swung back at last. When he slid the Mustang into the grounds, the agent understood the problem. The guest house to the right of the entrance was lighted up. The windows were open and through the curtains bellowed reggae music. It was no wonder that the first beep had been lost in the background.

"I was going to have a discussion about keeping awake on the job with your guard," Kelly said as he pulled up beside the main building where he had first seen the Mustang parked, "but I guess he's got enough problems right now." There was no sign of the Chrysler. It was still a few minutes till ten, however.

"It's easier to be an individual with somebody who's—an individual himself," Annamaria said as she let the agent hand her out of the car. "It's been a delightful evening—" her teeth winked in a wide grin, lighted by the lamp at the side door— "Angelo. I hope there'll be—wait a minute! Do you like jazz?"

"Well enough, I guess," Kelly said, eyes narrowing a fraction at the woman's change of subject.

"Wait here," she called, already darting to the unlocked door. "It'll just be a moment." The latch clicked behind her.

Kelly grimaced, but he realized that he was still holding the car keys. There was no practical way he could leave even if he wanted to . . . and a good deal of him did not want to, anyway. In the event, Annamaria was back in little more than the moment she had promised, holding what seemed at a glance to be a note card. "Here," she said, handing the card to Kelly.

Christ, it was an invitation with a US Seal embossed at the top.

The Ambassador of the United States of America *and Mrs. Rufus J. Gordon*
Request the pleasure of the company of
Mr. Angelo Ceriani
at a *buffet with American Jazz*
on *April 19*
from *8 pm to 10 pm*
R.S.V.P.

'Mr. Angelo Ceriani' was hand written; the other blanks in the printed form had been filled in on a typewriter.

"Anna," Kelly said. He touched his lips with his tongue. "I've got—I don't know what I'll be doing day after tomorrow. It, it's apt to be pretty fluid." He felt that he was stuttering, though he knew he was not.

"Come if you can," the woman said simply. "And—wait." She stepped back and reopened the door. Kelly strode forward with the car keys.

Instead of entering the house, Annamaria only reached inside. The light clicked off. She took the keys in the sudden darkness. Kelly heard them clink in her purse. Then she was in his arms, her waist softer than her furs, her lips softer yet on his.

"Jesus God," Kelly whispered as Annamaria stepped back from him.

"Come if you can," she repeated. "It's more pleasure than I can tell you to—speak Italian again."

Kelly still stood with a bewildered look on his face when the door closed behind her. "Jesus *God*, Mrs. Gordon," he whispered to the panel.

He began to be conscious of the reggae music again. Time to check in with Doug at the Chancery, set up things for the next day. A lot to do the next couple days.

He slipped the invitation carefully into the breast pocket of his coat. A lot of things to do the next couple days.

XV

The voice that responded, "Yes?" to the Chancery bell was American.

"Angelo Ceriani," Kelly said, "to see Sergeant Rowe." The guard had said Doug was still in the compound—where indeed, the photo processing was sure to keep him considerably longer.

The lock buzzed open and Kelly pushed the door back. At the reception desk with the phones and monitor was a blondish man in his late twenties. His suit coat lay folded on the edge of the desk, but he still wore a tie and a white shirt. "Ah, hello," he said, rising to take the agent's hand. He was looking at Kelly as he might have looked at a Doberman Pinscher that had wandered through the door. "I'm Steve Tancredi—I've got the duty tonight."

Kelly laughed and shook hands. "Join the club, I guess," he said. "I need to talk some things over with Doug. Any notion where I'd find him?"

"Down in the darkroom, Mr. K—ah—"

"I figure it'll confuse the other side as bad as it does everybody around here," the agent said, forcing a smile. "The KGB can run around gossiping and trying to straighten out its files, instead of worrying about anything that matters a damn. But can you tell me where the darkroom is?"

"I'd better call Sergeant Rowe up here," the duty officer said apologetically. "I shouldn't leave the lobby, and you'd get lost, the place was built in 1620. Say! Charlie!"

A big, soft-looking man of about fifty was shuffling up the stairs to the right of the lobby. He wore jeans, a gray sweatshirt, and a thoroughly disgusted expression. At Tancredi's hail, he looked up without brightening in the least.

"Charlie," the duty man continued, "I know you're p-oed, but look—could you take Mr. Ceriani here to the darkroom? Or, say, if you'll just watch things up here for a minute, I'll run him down. It's just that I'm sort of expecting a, ah, follow-up on that earlier cable. You know?"

"Say, that's a joke!" said the older man. There was nothing in his face to suggest he saw anything funny about that or any other facet of his recent life. He studied Kelly. The agent met his eyes steadily. "Sure, why not," Charlie said. "He's screwed up the evening so far, why not another ten minutes? Come on, buddy." He turned back down the stairs, beckoning disinterestedly.

Kelly followed. "Sorry about your evening," he said to the man's back.

"Not your fault," the other grunted. "Besides, this gives me a chance to have another slug before I drive home. As a matter of fact—" he halted on the stairs and turned, extending his hand to Kelly— "as a matter of fact, Mr. Kelly, I'm going to give *you* a slug too. I'm Charlie DeVoe, I'm a Communicator as you probably guessed. And you know why I'm giving you a drink?" Kelly's facial shrug was unnecessary, but he offered it anyway. "Because whatever you did, you pissed off the Ambassador royally. And anybody who's in that bastard's bad book is a man I want to drink with. Come on, I'll find you the darkroom and then I'll find us all some Scotch. Doug deserves a shot too—Posner's as big a shit as Gordon, if he just had the rank."

Kelly could have located the darkroom with proper instructions, but the basement corridors of the old building were as complex as the duty officer had suggested. "Code Room's the other way," said DeVoe at a T intersection. "So's the bottle." He laughed. "I keep one in the code safe," he explained. "Nobody but me and the other guys are authorized in it. Not that it matters, I've got my papers in already. Should've stayed in the fucking Navy."

At the end of the plastered corridor was a door with a hand-lettered sign reading "KNOCK DAMMIT!" Kelly knocked, shave-and-a-haircut.

"Who the Hell is it?" demanded the sergeant in a muffled voice.

"Simon Legree," the agent called back. "Here to lend a hand."

"Oh—oh, just a second, Tom. Let me get these in the hypo." There were sounds of movement within. The Communicator gave Kelly a thumbs-up signal and began striding back down the hall.

An inner door opened, then the hall door itself. Sergeant Rowe, looking tired but smiling, stood in the room which was being used as a light trap. "Come take a look," he invited. "Some of them aren't bad, but the angles. . . ."

"Look," the agent said in a low voice shutting the corridor panel behind him, "DeVoe, the Communicator, he'll be back in a minute. He just sent out a cable about me. If you're in a good place to take a break, maybe it wouldn't be a bad time to shoot the breeze and see what we could learn."

Rowe shrugged and gestured toward the dark-room proper. Kelly could hear water circulating in the print washer and the buzz of the dryer's heating element. "Be ten minutes before I can put anything else in the dryer," the sergeant said. "And it turns out there was a pouch for you. . . . It's up in the commander's office now. I don't mind getting out of this hole for a while." He grinned. "Oh—the commander took care of your room. Went out to the Aurassi tonight and just called in a few minutes ago. He's about as happy as you'd figure, but he soldiers on like the rest of us."

Kelly opened the door almost before DeVoe's knuckles could strike it the second time. The Communicator held up what was left of a liter of Glenfiddich in its odd, triangular-cross section, bottle. "Come on upstairs, Charlie," the agent said, "and we'll take a look at what the pouch bringeth."

That was a calculated risk. All Communicators were CIA employees. While they were officially forbidden to discuss cables with anyone, their promotion and merit raises depended on the Efficiency Reports they received from the CIA Station Chiefs at the post where they served. Smart Communicators learned early to run everything of interest past the Company rep—and from what had been said, Harry Warner would have given his left arm to learn what was being pouched to the DIA man.

On the other hand, DeVoe was obviously disaffected; and if he had really put in his retirement papers, he had little to gain from spying on embassy operations in the usual manner. Letting him in on a bit of Kelly's operation was a hell of a good way to get details of the equally-secret cable the Communicator had just sent.

The ploy worked like a charm. "It better be something you can take care of somewhere else than Algiers," DeVoe said as their steps echoed up a back staircase. "Because you're not going to be here any longer than the next flight out if his asshole Excellency has anything to say about it. Took him nearly a thousand groups to say it, but that's what it boiled down to, pure and simple."

"I'll be damned," said Kelly in genuine surprise. "Hell, it doesn't matter to him about one visa request or another, not really. Does he think his prestige is on the line because I've got a channel to State myself?"

"Wasn't that," said the Communicator. He looked back down the corridor. There was no one, of course, but he still waited for Doug Rowe to unlock the Attache's office and usher them in. "No, he got that one before he left the Chancery this evening," DeVoe continued behind the closed door. "Before *I* left, too. I get home and bam! there's a rush call to come back and shoot off an Immediate. Don't eat, don't help your wife move the Bird of Paradise plant in the back yard—she's screaming she's had it, she's going home, and goddam if I don't wish she would sometimes. . . ." Gloomily, the Communicator unscrewed the cap of the Scotch. "Rustle up some glasses, Dougie," he said. "Or Hell. . . ." He raised the bottle and drank deeply from it.

"Let's see what we got," Kelly said, squatting on the floor beside the steel-banded packing crate, the 'pouch." The exterior was stencilled CORRESPONDENCE DIPLOMATIQUE several times, and in all likelihood the Arabic markings said the same thing. Rowe handed a pair of pliers to the agent. Kelly cut the bands with them one after the other. The twang of the tensioned steel was the only sound in the office for some moments.

Under the wood was a layer of lead foil to block X-rays. Kelly drew his pocket knife, the Swiss Army folder and not the double-edged sheath knife clipped to his waistband. The small blade sheared the lead neatly against the top of the case within. This one was stencilled POUDRERIES REUNIES DE BELGIQUE, SA. "Right," the agent murmured as if his mind were not almost wholly occupied with what DeVoe had said about the cable. He lifted the inner lid. The top layer of the twenty-four cylindrical grenades, fused and ready, squatted in the styrofoam packing. "Right. . .," Kelly repeated. "Here's the smoke. I hope the tear gas shows up tomorrow, but we still got a little time."

"Jeez," said the Communicator in sudden awe of the grenades.

"The Ambassador say anything about his wife?" asked Kelly without looking up from the crate.

Rowe started. DeVoe smirked in surmise and clapped Kelly on the shoulder. "Well, you bastard!" the Communicator said with delight, "no *wonder* he was so pissed. Say, that's a goddam fast job, boy. You should've been a sailor." He pummelled the agent again and quoted, " 'Personal activities benefitting neither accomplishment of the task in hand nor the reputation of the American community in Algiers.' Pretty *goddam* quick!"

"He's exaggerating," Kelly said with a false, knowing smile, "but my tour's not up yet either—whatever his Excellency may think." DeVoe handed over the bottle. Very deliberately, Kelly drank. "Well," he said after he had taken a breath, "have we got a place to store these, or do we just leave them here with the radio equipment?"

"We'll put them in the armory, I guess," Sergeant Rowe said after a moment. "The commander'd have kittens if he found them in his office in the morning. Come on, it's right down the hall." He lifted one end of the heavy crate. Kelly took the other after handing the Scotch back to DeVoe. "Oh," the sergeant added diffidently, "why are these French? Are they better?"

"Belgian," the agent corrected as DeVoe opened the door for them. The crate would surprise anybody checking the mission stocks, but presumably that didn't happen very often at a quiet post. "And I think the word is 'Deniability.' Wouldn't be terribly surprised if the fellow who bought these let out that he was from the PLO . . . or Mossad, for that matter. It may not really fool anybody, but the folks in the Fudge Factory like to be able to lie gracefully. Anyhow, the chemistry's pretty much the same in anybody's product."

"You know, I used to get around some when I was younger," said the Communicator, taking another pull from his bottle as he followed the others down the corridor. "Jesus, I'll never forget the day I DEROSed—or maybe I ought to say I'll never remember most of it. But what I *do* remember—" He chortled.

The armory was a walk-in closet in the Deputy Chief of Mission's office. Rowe had keys to both the office and the recent steel door of the armory itself. Within, under the light of the bare bulb in the ceiling, were racked a dozen 12-gauge pump shotguns and a single M16 rifle. Revolver holsters were suspended from pegs across from the long-arms; the handguns themselves were presumably in the metal filing cabinet beneath them. Against the walls were stacked cases of gas masks, ammunition, and a crate of spherical gray grenades. Rowe and the agent set their own load down on the other grenades. "Hope to God those are gas and not the old Willie Pete," the agent remarked, "White phosphorus scares the crap out of me."

"Scaredest I've ever been in my life," said DeVoe, "was getting up the morning after, like I said. See, I'd told my wife I was getting out the next day, so I could stop off in DC. Picked up a black whore on Dupont Circle—" he drank and offered the bottle to Rowe.

"Thanks, but I've still got pictures to print," the sergeant said. "Can't know myself on my ass like I'd like to."

"Anyhow, next morning I felt like all kinds of shit," DeVoe continued, passing the bottle to Kelly. The rest of the story was obscene even for a sailor. DeVoe told it with a knowing smirk, man to man. At the end, his laughter boomed in the narrow room.

Doug Rowe managed an uneasy smile, but Kelly

laughed too, laughed and wiped his sweaty palms
on his trousers and slid open a drawer of the filing
cabinet. From its box within the agent took a revolver, a snub-nosed S&W Military and Police.
"Used to be pretty good with one of these," he remarked as he unlatched the cylinder, showed the
others the six empty chambers, and closed the
gate again with the pressure of his thumb. "Quick
draw, even."

"Go ahead, show us," said the sergeant,
relaxing a little now that the talk was of weap-
onry.

Kelly shrugged and took off his coat. If the
others noticed the sheath knife, neither remarked
on it. The agent belted on one of the holsters,
standard police pattern with a strap to secure the
weapon for carrying. Kelly holstered the revolver
and rotated the strap out of the way. "Now we
need some room," he said, stepping out in the
office proper, "and a quarter."

"A dinar piece do?" asked DeVoe, fishing one
out of his pocket.

"Perfect," said Kelly. "Oh—and some lubri-
cant."

"I've got a can of WD 40 in my office," said the
sergeant. "Shall I get it?"

"Naw, not for the gun," said the agent, grinning,
"for *me!*" He took the Scotch from the Communicator again and drank, his throat bobbling. After
three swallows he handed back the bottle, nearly
empty, and burped.

"Now. . .," Kelly said, facing the hall door. He
held his right hand above the holster with its
fingers extended. The dinar piece lay on top of the
webbing between thumb and forefinger. His arm
moved, the wrist pivoting, down and up. The
revolver was pointed at the center of the doorway
and the office echoed with the dry *clack*! of the
hammer falling on an empty chamber.

"Say, that *was* quick," said Rowe uncertainly.

With his left hand, Kelly gripped the bottom of the holster and lifted it, leaning his body forward to help. The coin, on his hand before he drew the weapon, rolled out of the holster into which it had dropped. The aluminum disk pinged and spun on the tile floor.

"Yeah," said the agent, unbuckling the rig, "quick enough." He handed the revolver and holster to Rowe, keeping the muzzle of the weapon pointed safely toward the ceiling. "Haven't forgotten everything I used to do. . . ."

Grinning like a death's-head, Kelly took the bottle from DeVoe again.

XVI

The car whose lights had been behind Kelly most of the way back to the Aurassi continued up the driveway when the agent turned right into the hotel parking lot. The other vehicle was of no immediately recognizable make, dark and gleaming and rather large by Algerian standards. It was not a tail, at least not a professional tail. Only tension and the whiskey had made Kelly notice it at all.

The lobby of the Aurassi was spacious, but its furnishings showed the same extreme of Western tastelessness as the building's design did. Swivel chairs of molded purple plastic shared the orange carpet with bright yellow sofas and glass-topped coffee tables. Three swarthy men in dark suits sat together at the far left, where the lobby formed an L with the hotel bar. Apart from those three and a desk clerk, the big room was deserted.

"Room 324," Kelly said to the clerk. "Any messages?"

"Let me see, sir," said the Algerian, turning to the mail slots and taking a yellow form from that of 324. He frowned and murmured to himself before raising his eyes to the agent's. "Sir," he continued, in French again, "I'm very sorry but your room had been changed. You're directly across the hall in 327 now."

"Tonight?" said Kelly. He had just enough of a buzz to resent the move he had rung bells in Washington to achieve. "Christ on a crutch!"

The clerk shrugged helplessly and handed over

the key to 327. "Very sorry," he repeated.

Kelly had not bothered to unpack the copy machine or his suitcases, so the move was quick and simple. The packing case skidded acceptably over the carpet when he lifted the front end; the suitcases and radio made only one further load. Kelly plugged the receiver in and draped its wire antenna from the top of the closet door to stretch it out. A commentator on the BBC Italian service was considering and discounting the possibility of a clash as the US Sixth Fleet and the Soviet Mediterranean Squadron prepared to hold simultaneous exercises in the Western Mediterranean. Kelly wondered if he could buy a bottle in the hotel. He didn't like drinking in bars, it made him feel too much like a zoo specimen.

Someone knocked in the hallway.

Kelly had been taking off his shirt. He froze and the knock was repeated, not on his door but on one nearby. He stole across the carpet and put his eye to the wide-angle lens set in the door panel.

Three men stood with their backs to him in a semicircle around the door of 324. From behind and through the fisheye lens he could not be sure, but the trio was certainly dressed like the men who had been waiting in the lobby when he came in. There had been a number of people in the sedan that followed him, too, but—

The man in the center held a wallet open in his hand, obviously official identification. After the second knock went unanswered, another of the waiting trio opened the door. All three slipped into 324 without waste motion. The door closed behind them.

Kelly blinked at his distorted view of the empty hall. 324 had a spring lock as well as a dead bolt to be engaged with the key. Kelly had not bothered to throw the dead bolt when he left the room; but the visitors had not seemed to fumble with a pass key to open the spring lock either.

A moment later, the door opened again. The three men left as quickly as they had entered. One was replacing something in a breast pocket—or a shoulder holster. The strangers were down the hall and out of view in a moment. They moved with quick, short steps, all three sets of legs in unison. None of them glanced at 327 as they passed.

The agent relaxed slowly. Using both hands to keep from jabbing himself, he put his double-edged knife back in its sheath. Police of some sort, clearly. Presidential Security Office?

But what had he done so far to concern the Algerians? Kelly himself had had no contact with the underground as yet . . . and why had they gone to the wrong room—if it *had* been a mistake.

After a moment's further consideration, Kelly slid one of the chairs over to his door and tilted it under the knob. The chain bolt was a joke, scarcely even a delay for a pro who knew how to use his boot. Not that it really mattered. If the authorities wanted in, they were going to get in. But why?

The Italian Service had closed out its broadcasting for the day. The Kenwood hissed with static. Kelly started to play with the tuning, then changed his mind. He stripped and lay down on the bed with the lights out. The radio dials shone as cats' eyes, but he had dimmed them also.

Kelly wanted a drink very badly, but he had no intention of opening his door again that night. After a time, he slept.

XVII

"Seven-zero," Kelly whispered to the mirror front of the bathroom medicine chest.

After a moment, the speaker of his short-wave receiver rasped, "Go ahead," in French.

"Up five," the agent said in the same language. He was still speaking toward the shaving mirror. He reached down and adjusted the receiver so that its digital read-out said 10.430 in megahertz instead of 10.425. He cut the power. From the mirror came the faint, tinny sound of someone counting to ten in French.

At 'dix' Kelly whispered back, "Got it. Four-one out." He turned. Sergeant Rowe was standing in the bathroom doorway. "There it is, Doug," the agent said. "Now, if the rig'll just keep working for the next couple days, we've got our link to Doctor Hoang." He frowned. "Not that that puts us out of the woods either, but it's a start."

The Sergeant stepped past Kelly and slid open the left door of the medicine cabinet. "Pretty slick, even if I do say so myself," he remarked.

A transmitter and a separate receiver, neither of them much larger than a standard hearing aid, had been glued to the inner surface of the mirror. Hair-fine wires spliced them into the circuit serving the shaving lamp built into the cabinet. Spray enamel had melded the wires into the metal surface; it reeked at the moment, but the odor would have dissipated by the time Kelly surrendered the room the next day.

The transmitter had, as a matter of fact, been an

off-the-shelf bugging device, powered by and broadcasting on the building's own electrical circuitry. It was sound-activated with an interlock to keep it from re-broadcasting noises from the receiver. Ideally the transmitter would have been monitored within the Aurassi, but Conference security measures would make that impossible. Instead, Kelly and the sergeant had been forced to position a separate and far more powerful transponder in the outside wall of the bedroom. It broadcast on an integral antenna, easily capable of driving a signal to the American Embassy.

The transponder installation was behind a sculptured divan. All the fragments of drywall had been swept into a bag which Sergeant Rowe would carry away with him. The hole had been covered with an aluminum plate 150 mm square, anodized to a close match for the beige wall paint. With luck, even someone who took the time to cut loose the plate—it was sealed to the wall with quick-setting epoxy—would still assume that the featureless gray box of the transponder had something to do with the power line to which it was connected.

The receiver had been more of a problem.

"Damn thing was a good 25 kilocycles off," Kelly grumbled to the sergeant. "I don't see how a sealed unit like that could slip off frequency, even being flown to Algiers in the guts of a Xerox machine. Either it works or it doesn't work—it doesn't just decide to work on a different frequency."

Rowe slid the cabinet door closed again. In order to see the paired devices, one had to actually stick one's head into the cabinet. That would require more than a mild suspicion that there was a bug in the room. Anyone who searched the medicine chest would already have dismantled all the light fixtures and wall receptacles in the living quarters. "They'd have tested it, wouldn't they?"

Rowe asked. "Whoever made it, I mean?"

The agent cracked a smile. "I wonder who Pedler and the boys did get this one from?" he mused aloud. "It's not quite the NSA's cup of tea, is it? And if it came from the Company's Tech Services Division—" he laughed aloud— "I wouldn't be surprised to learn it had a tracer built into it someplace."

More soberly, Kelly shook his head as if lulling his fantasies to rest. "No," he said, "they probably tested it, but not under field conditions."

"Like the commander wanted to do?" the sergeant suggested.

"Right, right," agreed the older man, nodding vigorously. "If we'd tried this next to the transmitter the way Posner suggested, it'd have worked fine because the signal was so strong. Hell, you can make a light bulb talk if you drive a signal at it hard enough. But a few miles away with some walls in between, well . . . that little matter of 25 kcs—" Kelly had been in radio before 'hertz' replaced 'cycles per second'— "isn't so little any more."

"Lucky thing we had your short wave so that we could be sure it wasn't the base unit that was messed up," the sergeant said, kneeling for a closer look at the Kenwood.

The agent raised an eyebrow. "Luck?" he said. "Luck isn't planning Skyripper, Doug my boy, Tom Kelly is." He paused, then went on, "God knows we're going to need more luck than I expect us to have. . . . But that doesn't mean I haven't crossed as many Ts as I could."

The two men looked at one another for a moment. "Well," Rowe said, rising, "it's time to get ready for the meeting. It took longer than I expected, setting up this commo."

"Yeah," Kelly agreed. He unplugged the Kenwood and lifted it carefully. "It'd have been quicker if I'd run it up first, instead of going down

fifty kcs before working up from what it was
supposed to be."

"If you'd done that," said Sergeant Rowe,
following the agent out of the bathroom, "they'd
have been off on the low end instead."

The communications set-up, including the transponder, was live only when the bathroom light
was on. There were ways to control units from a
distance, switching them on and off as the person
monitoring desired; but that added a level of complexity and potential failure. If a switch failed in a
satellite, tens of millions of dollars might be
pissed down the drain. If one failed *here* it would
very likely mean Kelly's ass . . . and that was not
something the stocky agent trusted to high-tech
solutions when there was any other way.

There was a fair likelihood that Hoang—or
rather, the security people sure to accompany the
physicist—would sweep the hotel room for bugs
as a matter of course. The usual technique
involved a sensitive receiver that lighted in the
presence of a signal. The searcher walked around
the subject area, talking in a normal voice and
seeing if the indicator lighted up as a bug
broadcast his speech. Unless the bathroom fixture
were on, the bug would not be live; and it was very
unlikely that the searcher would turn on the light
and risk masking the weak glow of his own
indicator.

Kelly took from his closet a brown corduroy
blazer and stuffed a blue knit cap in the side
pocket. He folded the jacket over his forearm,
lining outward. "Let's go, then," he said. He
glanced sidelong at Rowe as they walked to the
door. "Ah, Doug," he added, "you'll be at the
meeting too?"

The sergeant shook his head sharply. He did not
look up from the carpet as they strode down the
hall. In a low voice he said, "No, I . . . the
commander won't let me get into something like

. . . illegal. I've got a red passport, you see. The commander'll drive you. Any anyway, he's had all the contact with the group himself."

Kelly had said nothing about the three visitors across the hall. Rowe was too subdued by his own circumstances to notice that his companion kept darting glances to the rear as they walked toward the elevators. Someone could run up behind them, his or their footfalls swallowed by the soft green carpeting. "What about your passport?" Kelly responded in vague irritation, wholly alert but only partially listening to what was being said.

"Oh—red," Rowe explained. "Official, not black like a dip's. The Attache has a black passport—and diplomatic immunity. Staff travels on red and takes its own chances when something blows up." He pressed the elevator button, staring morosely at the bag of wall fragments in his hand. "He's doing it for me, really; but it's the way the book says, and that's the way the commander was going to do it anyway. Well, it's a direct order."

The elevator signal pinged. "Look," said Kelly in sudden decision, "meet me at your car. I'm going to walk."

Before the elevator doors slid open, the agent had rounded the corner to the stairs. Rowe heard his shoes echo briefly within the smoke tower before the door swung shut behind him. Frowning at last in perplexity, the sergeant waited for the passengers within the car to exit before he could ride it down.

XVIII

Kelly got into Posner's rented Peugeot 204 before the vehicle had come to a full stop. Cigarette smoke twirled into phantom hands at the suction of the door.

The commander pulled away from the curb with only a glance of irritation at his passenger. Wearing the brown jacket and knit cap, the dark-complexioned Kelly was scarcely distinguishable from the local men lounging back at the Chancery gate.

"I don't know what you're playing at," said Commander Posner in a tight voice. "There's nothing suspicious about two foreigners visiting an antique shop. Perhaps it's as wise not to use a car with diplomatic plates, I'll agree. But that doesn't mean you have to dress up like a thug. . . . And it *certainly* doesn't mean I have to pick you up on a street corner, instead of at the Chancery as we'd arranged previously."

The agent rubbed his temples tiredly. "Tell me, Commander," he said, "how many salesmen do you take on shopping trips?"

Posner cleared hs throat. He glanced sideways in more of an apology than Kelly had expected to receive.

It didn't make the agent feel more comfortable, however. The excuse was fine for silencing the Defense Attache, but Kelly himself knew that he had begun acting irrationally. There *could* be reasons for his sudden paranoia; but if there were, he was not consciously aware of them.

He wasn't sure which was worse—having premonitions or going nuts. Kelly had wondered the same thing toward the end, there, with the girl in Venice whose name was not Janna. He had not reached a solid conclusion that time either.

"No problems with the radio gear at your end, then?" Kelly asked to break his own train of thought.

Posner stubbed his cigarette out into the ashtray and tried to get another one-handed from the pack in his pocket. "No, no, it appears to be quite in order, once we found that fuse this morning," he said. He looked at the agent more fully. "Once you found the fuse, I should say."

"Sometimes they're blown right out of the box," Kelly agreed mildly. "There's people pretty much that way too, so I guess we ought to figure it for fuses." The Attache was trying to pull a disposable lighter from between the cellophane and the liner of his cigarette pack. The Peugeot did not have a resistance lighter. "Here," said Kelly, taking the pack. "I'll do it."

Commander Posner was not a natural driver; he constantly overcorrected with jerky movements of the wheel, brakes, and gas. Still, he relaxed a trifle with the fresh cigarette between his lips and said, "I'm surprised there's no scrambler in the system. Of course, it's possible that no one will be monitoring the frequencies—but quite frankly, I can't conceive of Washington authorizing you to give operational directives this sensitive in clear."

"Yeah, there's people who'd have conniptions if they knew," agreed the agent with a wry smile. He cranked his window down an inch but found as he expected that it simply drew more smoke past him instead of clearing the air. "Thing is, there's no way to fit a scrambler/unscrambler to hardware as small as what we've got to use in the Aurassi. Our contact'll almost certainly be sharing the room with a security man. We can't just stick a

PRC-77 in the closet for him to use . . . or phone
him."

"I should have thought that a risk of the sort you
intend to . . . put us all through would have had to
be cleared at very high level," Posner said dis-
tantly. The car wheels thumped on the right curb
and rubbed for several yards. The commander
continued on, apparently unaware of the scraping.

Kelly wiped his chin with the back of his hand.
His whiskers bit at the skin. "Look," he said, "we
do what we can. Nobody'll be talking on the
system but me and the contact—and we'll be using
Vietnamese. Sure, it can be recorded; but unless
we're completely SOL, it'll be days before anybody
here'll have time to figure out what the language
was, much less translate it. There are risks; but
that's a fact of life."

The Defense Attache snorted in what turned out
to be an unexpected outburst of humor. He looked
at Kelly despite the fact that a boxy, green bus was
stopping in their lane. "There *was* a Vietnamese
community in Algiers during the last years of the
French, you know," he said. He looked up just in
time to jam on the brakes. Algerian passengers,
loaded like cattle in a truck, peered down from the
back window.

"Yes, secret police—refugees after Dien Bien
Phu," Posner continued. "The French brought
them here to deal with the FLN. Torturers, of
course. . . . The FLN blew up a barracks full of
them, killed over fifty. And after Independence,
well,—I don't think we need worry about local
Vietnamese speakers, you're correct."

The two-stroke Fiat diesel of the bus whined.
After a moment, the commander realized that the
lane was no longer blocked and drove off himself.
"I think it's—Yes, we turn here."

They were far to the south of the Casbah, in one
of the small connecting streets near the Boulevard
Victor Hugo. The buildings lining the street were

two-story. They had flat roofs with iron railings
around the upper-floor balconies. At street level,
most of the buildings were shops. Plaster,
originally painted white or light gray, flaked in
patches from the masonry beneath. Save for the
ironwork, the block could have passed for an
aging downtown anywhere in the United States.

Posner pulled up behind a panel truck. The shop
directly beside them had no sign, but the metalwork displayed on faded velvet in the windows
was an adequate description. Kelly got out
quickly, scanning the street in both directions as
unobtrusively as haste permitted. There was
nothing untoward. The parked cars were the usual
mixture of small European makes, with light
colors predominating. The Defense Attache was
slow locking his door. Kelly waited for him, needs
must, but he felt a helpless fury at the delay that
kept them in the open. It was like the moment your
chopper hovers, just before dropping to insert you
in somebody else's jungle.

Brusquely, concerned only about political and
not physical danger, Commander Posner strode
past Kelly and into the shop. A string of bells rang.
Within, the unassisted light through the display
windows was barely adequate. It would have given
the advantage—should the need arise—to the teen-
ager seated in the corner to the left of the door.
"Ah—good afternoon," the Attache said in his
stilted French. "My American friend here is
looking for brass of exceptional quality."

Instead of answering, the boy gestured toward
the back with his left thumb. His right hand was in
his lap, under a copy of *El Moudjahid*, the French-
language official newspaper. Not lazy or disinterested, Kelly realized. The kid was so hyper
that he was afraid to attempt anything as complex
as speaking.

The center of the shop was a large, cloth-
covered table which supplemented the broad

shelves around all four sides of the room. The wares were a medley of work, ranging from obvious antiques to the glisteningly recent. A copper cous-cous steamer, decorated with curves of hand-applied stippling, lay beneath a 20-inch bayonet. The weapon itself was French, of the narrow-bladed Gras pattern of the 1870s. The scabbard, however, was of brass lacework, almost a filigree—weeks or months of work for some craftsman in a Kabyle village. Elsewhere, the eye met lamps and trays and an incredible variety of bowls; brass and copper predominantly, but with an admixture of silver, gold, and even aluminum. Even at this juncture, their craftsmanship impressed Kelly. If Kabyles could execute Skyripper with the same meticulous ability, things were going to be fine.

The two Americans walked past the guard, feeling his eyes on their backs and hearing the paper in his lap rustle. In the shop's rear wall were a curtained stairwell and a door. Posner hesitated at the door. Kelly wondered whether or not the Attache had ever been through it before. With only the brief delay, however, the commander pulled the panel open. The agent followed him in to join the five men and two women already there.

This time the gun—one of them, at least—was quite openly displayed. A Mauser 98 was aimed squarely at the center of Kelly's breastbone. The agent smiled, wondering what that implied about his status relative to that of Posner. "God be with you," he said in French as he pushed the door closed.

The waiting group was varied. One man wore a suit as good as any of those Kelly owned, while another was the man the agent remembered as the late-shift guard at the Chancery. He was still in his khakis. Most of the Kabyles, including the women, were smoking. The odor of their tobacco was harsh and thick in the small office. The middle-aged man with the rifle bore a strong facial resemblance to the youth in the shop proper. He sat on the only chair in the room and supported the Mauser along the slanted top of an old writing desk. Even if he were the shop owner, however, his eyes glanced deference to the patriarch wearing a flowing white jellaba.

The old man nodded severely to Kelly. His moustache was huge and as white as his outer garment. Looking at the agent, he spoke briefly in a non-European language. His eyes were fierce.

Kelly glared back. He could make an educated guess as to what the Kabyle demanded. There was nothing to lose by trying—and perhaps a great deal to gain. Standing at a rigid parade rest, the agent retorted in French, "No sir, I cannot speak your own language—nor can I speak the Arabic of those who would demean you. I come to you as a man needing help—but as a strong man ready as well to help you and help your nation. If we can speak together as men in a tongue foreign to all of us—" he nodded around the circle— "so be it. If not, we each will fight our enemies alone."

"I am Ali ben Boulaid," said the old man in French. His face broke into an enveloping smile. The Mauser clicked on the desk as the hand of the man holding it relaxed minusculy. "Ramdan, coffee for your guests!"

The shop owner stuck his head back into the shop and shouted instructions. His Mauser disappeared behind a section of wall panelling and he brought out a rug for the office floor. There was no room for more chairs, even if they might have been available. Kelly joined the Kabyles, sitting with crossed ankles and no particular discomfort. Posner attempted to squat with his back against the shop door. He had to move when a woman bustled in with a beaten silver coffee set carried from the living quarters above the shop. The Attache slid his balancing act into the corner by the desk. The unfamiliar posture cut off his circulation. At intervals during the discussion he had to hop up embarrassingly and massage his calves.

A few years before, the Kabyle movement had been little more than demonstrations—often spontaneous—against the tendencies of the government. Every such attempt at public protest had been put down with riot sticks backed with machine guns. Arrests were ineffective against a movement without leaders. Mass beatings by the police were seen as more likely to get results.

The results they got were the creation of Kabyle leaders all over the country.

The old networks still existed among the survivors of the War of Independence. After the victory, leadership of the Front of National Liberation and of the new state had been taken by those who had spent the war in French prisons, planning their memoirs. Those who had done the fighting, though, were still in the rural areas and the Casbah. If a new need to fight arose, well . . . it mattered little, after all, if the enemies of freedom spoke French or Arabic.

As generally happens, the government itself had been the dissidents'—now rebels—strongest recruiting agent. Now there were nodes around which could coalesce those dissatisfied with any aspect of autocracy, any aspect of rule: tribal chauvinists, goat-herds disgruntled by reforestation projects intended to block the advance of the Sahara; squatters evicted from public housing so that the proper applicants could move in. . . . The sufficiency of the reasons for which people will fight is determined by the individual fighters alone.

The coffee was thick and sweet, cloying on Kelly's empty stomach. He continued to drink it anyway as he argued quietly and listened to the others wrangling among themselves. The agent had expected to meet a single leader. What he got instead was democracy with a vengeance. It was

possible that Ali ben Boulaid could have made and
enforced the decision himself, but the old man
showed no sign of wishing to do so. There had
been no decision on whether the group—they did
not use any formal name in Kelly's hearing—
would go through with the operation.

Finally the agent opened his attache case of 8x10
glossies of the Casbah. That killed theoretical discussions about whether an office in Rabat outweighed the risks of a gunfight in the center of
Algiers. The arguments slid at once into the
practical questions of who and where, how many
and by which route. Kelly sipped his coffee. He
made small comments when he had something
useful to add . . . and he kept his smile inside,
knowing that he had just begged a question that
was likely to get a number of people killed.

After the initial discussion had burned out,
Kelly took charge. He used both the map and the
corresponding photographs. "Here," he said,
pointing with a blunt forefinger, then stirring the
glossies to find the same location, "a truck blocks
the complex of streets from the south by sliding
across the intersections just west of the Institute.
On the other end, the motorcade will be coming
and we won't be able to insert a blocking vehicle
into it. We need to cut the intersection of the
Boulevard de la Victoire and the, whatever,
Boulevard Abderrazak. Can you handle that?" He
looked challengingly around the circle of Kabyles.

A young man with sideburns and a black turtle-
neck sweater glanced at his companions. When no
one else spoke, he shrugged and said, "There must
be a drain there from the Institute . . . the main
sewer's on the east side of the boulevard. Twenty
pounds of *plastique* in that and—" he gestured
with his hands and lips. "Sure, we can cut the
street."

Kelly felt Posner beside him shiver. "Right," the
agent said, "and that'll make the perfect signal for

our boy to run. He'll have plenty of company when
pieces of the pavement start raining down—it
won't get him shot by his own people." Kelly
cleared his throat, hoarse and dizzy from the
layering smoke. "Next," he said, "we need to cut
off visibility on the ground. We can fill the truck
with oily rags and set them afire, that may help,
but the wind's going to be straight uphill from the
sea unless we're lucky. I've got a case of smoke
grenades. If you've got a few people to volley them
from upper floors at that end of the street, they'll
do the job for as long as we need it done."

"The roof will be best," said the man in the
three-piece. He had a nervous trick of inserting a
finger under his collar-facing, but to Kelly's surprise he had been one of the hawks of the earlier
discussion.

Now the agent shook his head in violent dis-
agreement. "There'll be troops on the wall and
towers of the Institute," he said. "Will be or
should be. And look, this is dangerous, maybe the
most dangerous part of the whole deal. Those
smoke grenades'll leave a track back to where they
come from as broad as a highway. The guards
across the street won't shoot down maybe because
they won't know what's going on down there with
so many of their own people. But they'll damn well
open up on the windows things're being thrown
from. We'll tie the grenades in bundles of six.
There'll be plenty of range from a third floor
window."

"They won't shoot if we've shot them first," said
the younger of the two women. "They made their
choice when they put on the uniforms of the
oppressors." She mimed a throat-cutting with her
index finger.

"Look," said Kelly, "the less shooting, the better
off we all are. Bullets'll ricochet like a bitch
between those walls and the pavement. Even if
you know what you're doing with a gun you don't

have any notion where the slug's going to wind up. I've got some gas grenades which we can use as soon as the, ah, the target's clear—"

"Tear gas?" interrupted the older woman. Her hair was black save for a thin white zig-zag that marked old scarring as surely as an X-ray could have.

Kelly met her fierce eyes. "CS," he said with a nod of agreement. "The kind of 'tear gas' that makes people puke their guts up if they get a good whiff of it. Toss that into the smoke and you don't have to worry about anybody on the ground chasing you."

"Toss satchel charges into the cars," said the woman, "and nobody chases you either."

Posner was swearing or praying under his breath. Kelly shrugged and turned his palms up. "Look, what you do *after* my man clears the area is your business. But you might keep in mind that it's not just troops and cops and security people going to be down there. There'll be scientists from maybe fifty countries. I don't know and you won't know just who it is in the line of fire. Start throwing bombs and you'll be able to read the body count in just about every paper in the world, right on the front pages. That won't bother me a bit . . . but I'm not about to start a government in exile."

"We will consider that among ourselves," said ben Boulaid, his cracked voice sweeping through the others' miscellaneous chatter like a horseman through wheat. "There is still the matter of price. Qadafi paid *ten* million dollars to have the Jewish athletes killed in Munich."

"Did Qadafi stand with his gunmen or did he send them off alone to die?" the American agent snapped back. "*I* offer a million dollars and recognition that you would not be able to buy at any price, not even from the enemies of the government you oppose. *And* I stand with you, a warrior among warriors."

"Good God, man!" blurted Commander Posner in English. "You *know* that's against your orders. It *must* be!"

"If I must stand alone," Kelly continued, ignoring the Attache, "so be it. I do not need the help of those who can be bought for cash alone." He was light-headed, had been for what seemed like hours. He almost burst out laughing at the image of himself charging the motorcade alone, hurling CS grenades with both hands. Might be better than going home and trying to explain to folks how he'd blown the deal before it even got off the ground, though. . . .

"I did not say that *we* were merely terrorists seeking dollars," the old man said stiffly. "We will consider the offer among ourselves."

"How are we to know the person you want?" asked the man who knew about the street drains. "You say 'when he's clear'—but who?"

Kelly took a thick 9x12 envelope from the lid of his case. Commander Posner was already saying, "Obviously, that has to wait until you have decided if you are going to—"

The agent opened the envelope and began handing fuzzy enlargements around the circle of Kabyles. "We are warriors," he repeated. "Will we betray each other, even if we cannot agree? This one is Vlasov, a professor, a scientist. He wishes to escape to freedom. We wish to help him because that is our way."

Ben Boulaid stared at the photograph and nodded solemnly. "We will reach you soon—through bou Djema, as usual." The Chancery guard bobbed his head enthusiastically. The old man rose, his compatriots to either side braced to help him. They were unneeded.

Kelly quickly swept the photographs of the Casbah back into his case. The locals could study the site on their own, he could not. "Peace be on you," he said, bowing first to Ben Boulaid and then to each of the other Kabyles in turn.

"The peace of God be on you," replied the patriarch, bowing back to Kelly. "If it pleases God, we will speak again soon." The agent tugged the weak-kneed Attache erect and opened the door. The still, cool air of the shop washed his face like a shower.

The Americans had barely closed the door when they heard the voices behind them resume. The words were indistinguishable, but the tones were not those of peace and moderation. "Hooked them," whispered Kelly in English as they passed the guard again. "Hooked them, by God, as sure as I got hooked myself!"

Posner turned the car in the street, heading back toward the embassy complex. As they cornered onto the Boulevard Victor Hugo again, Kelly caught a glimpse of something in the rear-view mirror. He spun to look over the back of his seat, but the Attache had already pulled through the intersection. If there had been a black sedan turning toward the shop from the direction of the Rue Boukhalfa, it did not follow them to the embassy. Kelly was quite certain of that, because he kept looking back the whole way.

XIX

Commander Posner had not spoken on the trip back, even to ask what his passenger expected to see out the window. Any hopes the Defense Attache may have had that the operation would be bloodless—or better, would not even be attempted—had evaporated during the meeting with the Kabyles. There would be blood in the streets, and the leader on the ground would be an American working for the DIA, just as Posner himself did. . . .

The car stopped in the lane between the Chancery and the Villa Inshallah, the building in which Admiral Darlan had been assassinated in 1942. Posner set the emergency brake. He looked at Kelly and said with a deliberate absence of inflection, "I—am told that his Excellency received a cable regarding you this morning."

The agent regarded the naval officer levelly. "I presume," he said, "I would have been notified if I'd been booted out. So I presume further it wasn't that. Shall we play 'Twenty Questions,' or are you going to tell me what it really was?"

Posner scowled. "I could only speculate about the contents, and I have no doubt that you can do that with at least equivalent accuracy yourself, Mr. Kelly. The—the DCM is a friend of mine. He was, I think, warning me. . . . Ambassador Gordon is very angry about what he sees as the situation. And while you will no doubt be going home, the rest of us may have an unpleasant aftermath to deal with."

The commander paused. Kelly put his hand on the Peugeot's door handle, but before he opened it the Attache went on, "Mr. Kelly, I have no reason to doubt your abilities, since obviously they are held in high regard by my superiors . . . and of course, what you said earlier about a soldier following orders is quite correct. But I think there may come a time soon when I will take the second option you suggested and resign my commission. I only hope that if I do make that choice, I will make it soon enough."

Posner got out and began walking rather quickly toward the Chancery. Quickly enough that the agent would have had to run to keep up with him. Kelly did not do that. The sea was already dark with the shadow of the mountains. After waiting long enough to permit the commander to get inside, Kelly strolled toward the Chancery himself. He needed to run a cable out to Paris. It was better to hold one of the Communicators over than to call one back as the Ambassador had done the night before.

Kelly still needed to clear out of the Aurassi and pick up his VW from the hotel lot. The place would be tight as a tick from midnight on; and Kelly had seen and heard enough about Algerian thoroughness to know that they would damn well clear things out themselves if he did not do it in time. When the Pan-African Games had been held in Algiers, the government had decided as an aesthetic measure to clear the balconies of the high-rise apartments fronting the parade route. Clearance had been effected by squads of troops who marched from room to room. Everything found on a balcony was pitched over the rail. Not infrequently that meant the sheep which recently-rural families stabled on the balconies in anticipation of the Feast of Muharram. The pictures of sheep flung twelve stories onto concrete looked like nothing Kelly had seen since the days VC prisoners were transported by helicopter.

The Algerian employee at the reception desk admitted the agent before he had time to ask through the speaker. Kelly gave the local a V-sign and trotted up the stairs to Rowe's windowless office next to the Attache's. There was no light on in the latter—Posner must have been with one of his friends elsewhere in the building. Sergeant Rowe was just setting down the intercom, however. His door was open and he gestured to Kelly happily when he saw him. "Say, that was for you," he said. "Anna. Do you want me to buzz her back?"

"Business first," the agent said, trying to manage a smile. He had not thought about drinking since he got up and started to install the communications rig in his room. Mention of Anna reminded him that he had meant to pick up a bottle in the Aurassi that morning. "I need a desk to draft a cable on," he said. "Then you or I are going to have to encrypt it on the computer." He smiled ruefully. "And we're going to have to hold somebody to shoot it off, it won't wait till morning. See if you can get DeVoe—I've got some other stuff to talk to him about. . . . Oh—and I want to sweeten the pot a little on that one, too. How do I get a bottle of booze around here?"

"Well, from the top," Rowe said, smiling back, "you can have my desk while I go see that the computer'll be free." He frowned. "You know, the Code Room's down in the basement with a lead lining on all sides and cushioned floors. There's no way anybody could eaves-drop while they're encrypting. The computer, that's in one corner of a hallway with movable partitions around it—that was the only place there was room. It's not exactly the most secure spot in the mission, you know."

Kelly waved a hand. "Sure, the Company boys may record the click of the keys and fire them off to Langley—or Meade, for all I know—and they can read them out in clear. But by the time they get that back—" his grin was a wolf's grin— "I'll be long gone and they'll have a better notion of what we were up to than the cable could give them anyway. That's the name of the game on this one, you see—the main enemy's the guy in the next office."

The sergeant shrugged. "Ours not to reason why," he said. He picked up the intercom and punched 121 on its pad. "Say Pete," he said after a moment, "we've got a TDY officer—" he winked at Kelly— "here who needs a bottle of. . . ." He paused.

"Johnny Walker Red, I guess," the agent supplied. "Say—there wouldn't be some Jack Daniels around, would there?"

"Walker Red and Jack Daniels," Rowe relayed. "Yeah, the Black, I suppose." Kelly nodded vigorously. "And 750s—" Another nod. "Sure, Pete, I'll be over in a minute or two—I know you want to close up and get home. . . . Yeah, don't feel like the Lone Ranger."

The sergeant hung up. "I'm going to get over to the Annex and pick that up right now," he said. "The GSO's a friend of mine, but you don't stay friends if you keep people around this place after hours." He smiled broadly. "Meaning nothing personal, you know. . . . Oh—I'll get Charlie on the way. Better see him than ringing down to the Code Room, I suppose."

Kelly sat at the sergeant's vacated desk and began composing, using a single sheet of typing paper and a soft pencil. He had deliberately left the office door open, so that he could hear any movement in the corridor. The footsteps a moment later were not precisely surreptitious, but neither did they call unnecessary attention to themselves.

Kelly folded the draft with three quick motions and thrust it in the breast pocket of his coat. Then he stepped to the door. Harry Warner, the CIA

Chief, was coming down the hall very slowly. The agent grinned at him. "Good evening," he said.

Warner nodded abruptly. "Wanted to see Bill," he said.

Kelly stepped sideways and rapped on the door of the Attache's dark office. "Sorry," he said to Warner. "I'll tell him you're looking if he comes by."

"Funny as Hell, isn't it?" the Station Chief snapped. He turned on his heel, repeating, "Just funny as Hell!"

"Want to buy a copy machine?" Kelly called to the man's back.

He had scarcely begun writing again when another set of heels began slapping down the hall—wooden-soled sandals and a long leggy stride. Kelly sighed and refolded the draft. Perhaps he should have done the work at his hotel, where the door locked and CW traffic on the Kenwood would blur even the sound of knocking. But that would also mean driving back to the Chancery with the draft cable in his pocket. Most security precautions were silly on a realistic level, but carrying that cable in clear would have been a violation of common sense as well as tradecraft.

"Anna," the agent said as he stepped to the door. "Look, I'm sorry but I'm busy like you wouldn't believe right now. If you really need something, I'll give you a ring when I'm clear—whenever that is."

Annamaria smiled. She was back to Western Informal, blue slacks and a red and blue pull-over which read 'Sun Walley'—local manufacture, obviously. "You still have to move and pick up your car, don't you?" she asked.

That was no secret, but it made Kelly uneasy all the same—for reasons that had nothing to do with business. "Yeah," he said nodding, "that's part of it. Look, Mrs. Gord—"

"Doug and I can take care of that, then—I

caught him as he was going past the snack bar,"
the woman said. "You don't have to do that in
person, and the car will take two to get it anyway.
Give me the keys and we'll leave you to your
work."

Kelly brought out the Passat's keys. He was
unable to argue with the logic and unwilling to
argue with the rest. As he held out the chain, however, he hesitated and instinctively closed his
fingers back over the keys again. "Oh, look, Anna,"
he said, his eyes frowning at the chain and his
mind somewhere else. "Have Doug give my car a
quick once-over before he drives it back, will you?
I mean, just so there's no extra wires from the dis-
tributor, that sort of thing. I'm getting screwier as
I get older, that's all. But—" he raised his eyes—
"carry him over in your car, OK? And he drives
back in mine."

The woman's fingers touched Kelly's as she took
the keys. "We'll see you soon," she said, "so work
hard."

The basic preparations for the extraction had
been made before Kelly left France. The MARS
both had preceded him by diplomatic pouch in the
same shipment that brought the base unit transmitter and receiver to be used for Skyripper. The
timing had to be adjusted to circumstances as
Kelly found them on the ground, however; and the
method put enough other people at risk that the
agent had directed that it not be executed until he
had given a specific go-ahead himself.

The cable he was drafting was the go-ahead. He
combined it with a Situation Report with enough
detail to see whether anybody had gotten faint-
hearted in Paris or DC. It was no worse than they
must have expected, though. Presumably the
Powers That Be had decided they wanted the
omelet before they contacted Kelly in the first
place.

The agent left Sergeant Rowe's door unlocked

behind him because he did not have a key to re-admit himself if he needed to. His trouser cuffs swished and echoed at every step. They sounded much like a blade on a whetstone.

Ideally, the mini-computer would have been located with the General Services Officer in the Annex across the road. The system's main day-to-day use was for inventory control. Other officers, with more clout if less need, had lists of their own which they wanted on disk too, however. There was also some reasonable concern, Doug had said, that the local employees who swarmed about the Annex would find the new Western toy irresist-ible—and fragile—if it were where they could get their hands on it. That meant that Kelly had only to walk up to the third floor of the Chancery instead of hiking up the Chemin Cheikh Bachir Brahimi and back.

The computer sat on its cabinet, partially ob-structing the entrance to the tower from which the harbor was monitored. The agent cut on the power, then checked the tower room more or less for the Hell of it . . . though it wouldn't have been wholly beyond possibility for one of the Company men to have been inside, 'checking the cameras.' When the CRT screen announced the machine was PRET—Christ, it was a Thomson-CSF unit with all its commands and controls in French—Kelly took a program disk from his inside coat pocket and inserted it.

There was a set of similar—though not, of course, identical—code programs locked in the safe in the Defense Attache's office for emer-gencies. For the purpose of Skyripper, how-ever, Kelly was assuming that the disks issued to Commander Posner had already been compro-mised; that is, that CIA officers had made a sur-reptitious entry to the office, burgled the safe, and copied the programs therein.

In all likelihood, that had in fact occurred.

Kelly began typing from his draft. He turned off the CRT since the letters that would be appearing on it were garbage anyway. The program simply coupled the keystrokes into a series of random numbers generated, Kelly had once been told, by cosmic ray impacts. It was the electronic equivalent of a one-pad code, totally indecipherable without an identical program. Because the patterns were random, even possession of the clear text of one message would not have permitted the deciphering of the next.

With the report complete and stored in the working memory of the computer, Kelly checked to see that the paper was straight in the sprocket feed of the printer. It was. Sighing, he punched COM and watched with his usual fascination as the daisy wheel raced back and forth across the paper. Even after five years of selling and servicing the damned things, Kelly still got a wrenching feeling every time he saw a machine working happily away without the necessary attention of any human being. It made the agent think of missile siloes in North Dakota and Siberia, controlled by computers just as conscienceless as this one.

Of course, somebody still had to punch START.

The printer was a fast one. It had completed its task before Kelly's mind had proceeded from the air bursts at 10,000 feet to the firestorms sucking houses and men into the heart of Hell. Somebody else's worry, that. Kelly pulled the sheet from the printer and checked it. Satisfied, he removed the program disk, put it back in its envelope, and cut the computer's power—dumping the internal memory. With the encrypted sheet folded in his hand, he walked down the empty stairs to the basement and the Code Room.

There was no response when Kelly knocked on the heavy steel door. The agent's frown began to smooth into the blankness his face took on when

he was really angry. Then Charlie DeVoe called,
"Hey, Cap'n," from behind in the corridor. "Let
me take that." The Communicator was grinning.
"Sorry I wasn't here, but it hasn't come to the
point we can't take a leak while we're on duty, you
know."

"Just got here myself," the agent said, handing
over the encrypted report. At the top he had
printed in block capitals the cable address and
priority. No one had thought to tell Kelly where
the normal word-processing program was kept.
The address, if typed on the code program, would
have been just as indecipherable as the text.
"Sorry as Hell to keep you on again," Kelly said,
"but maybe Doug told you—I hope a fifth of
Scotch'll make things a little smoother for you."

The Communicator raised his eyebrows at the
statement, then glanced down at the coded document. "Oh, didn't have to worry about that. . . ," he
said, meaning one fact or the other. Then, "Yeah,
that sure as Hell does smooth things. You kow
what a fifth of Johnny Walker runs me?"

Kelly was taken aback by the question. The
liquor was, after all, a gesture rather than
payment *per se* for work within the Communicator's normal duties. "Well, about three bucks, I
suppose," he said mildly, "but I've always found
it's a good way to spend three bucks."

"Three bucks to somebody on the dip list,"
DeVoe corrected. "Somebody who can order duty-
free from Justesen, sure. To Foreign Service *Staff*,
like yours truly—" he thumped himself on the
chest— "It's the full duty. That's about eighty
bucks in Algiers, that's what it is."

"Christ," said Kelly in amazement, "I knew it
was that way on paper . . . but I thought missions
generally pooled their duty-free allowances and
everybody got some. I mean, they keep telling us
America's a democracy, don't they?"

DeVoe sneered. "Not the Algiers mission," he

said. "And that's not a policy that'll be changed by his Excellency Rufus Jackass Gordon, either." The Communicator's face brightened. "Say, you know that bastard's looking for you, don't you?"

"Heard there was a cable on the subject," admitted the agent. The situation reminded him of the business deals he had made in men's rooms across Western Europe. DeVoe could not take him into the Code Room, and a suggestion that they move anywhere else would have broken the rapport.

"Sure was, short and sweet," the Communicator said. The problem with making people violate their oaths in order to keep their jobs was that once the initial sanctity was gone, the oath itself meant very little. DeVoe had lost his cherry a long time back. " 'Request denied,' it said, and I'd have given a month's pay to see Gordon's face when Buffy carried it over to him. God *damn* I would!" He sobered, even as his hand raised to slap his thigh. "Say, though, that's not what I meant. The duty officer's been calling all around the building looking for you. He had Gordon on the line, wanted you ASAP." DeVoe waved the sheet of gate-fold paper and grinned. "Guess he didn't try the computer, did he?"

"Hell, I was busy," said the agent. "I wouldn't have answered if somebody did ring. Though come to think, I didn't see an intercom up there anyway." He sighed. "Well," he went on, "I guess I better go put in an appearance or you'll be here to morning with the Ambassador's cable traffic. . . ."

XX

Kelly could hear the angry voices as he mounted the stairs to the lobby. Even so, he was surprised when he stepped through the doorway and saw that one of the three men wrangling in the reception area was Ambassador Rufus Gordon himself.

"Ah—" said the youngest of the three men, presumably the duty officer. He pointed toward the stairs and Kelly.

Ambassador Gordon and the plump, suited man of about forty turned at the gesture. "What in *God's* name do you think you're doing?" Gordon demanded in a voice on the high edge of control.

"Ah, Mr. Ambassador—" the plump man beside him said anxiously.

"Reeves," quavered the Ambassador, "when I need the warnings of my DCM as to what I should say in my own embassy, then I'll ask for them!"

The Deputy Chief of Mission bit down on his lower lip. Kelly said very carefully, "Sir, I'm doing my job, just like anybody else. I'll be leaving—"

"Who told you you could waltz around the Chancery unescorted?" Gordon shouted. He wheeled on the duty officer like the cutting head of a turret lathe. "You—Byrne! *You* let him loose this way?" In his silver-gray suit and agitation, the Ambassador looked like a man who had witnessed a murder on the way to a dinner party.

Kelly did not know the junior officer, but he knew his own duty as a human being. Raising his voice in a verbal lightning rod to draw the anger back on himself, the agent said, "My permission to use embassy facilities freely came to me through Major General Wallace Pedler, the DA in Paris. If you feel the confirmation of those orders which you've already received is not enough, then I suggest that's a matter for General Pedler's superiors and yours. *Sir*."

Ambassador Gordon's face was pale enough under ordinary circumstances. Now its pallor was less that of a corpse than of the bone beneath the flesh. He took a step toward the agent. Kelly, with the chill certainty of the knife he would not need to draw, spread his feet a half step and waited.

"Good *God*!" cried the DCM, leaping between the two men. Kelly had not advanced, and the Ambassador had paused when he met the agent's eyes. Reeves bobbed between them, suddenly ridiculous—separating two motionless men already ten feet apart.

"Kelly, I swear one thing," the Ambassador said, breathing hard. "*I'm* the President's representative here, and *I* decide the use of embassy premises. And if you don't leave my wife alone, you'll rue the day you were *born*!"

It wasn't the parting shot Kelly had expected. Gordon turned and strode out of the Chancery. The entryway door was too heavy to fling open as the Ambassador would have liked, but it made a satisfying slam behind him.

The three men in the lobby looked at one another for a moment of silence. Then the agent said quietly, "Look, I don't suppose either of you like me worth a damn . . . and I don't blame you. But I'm sorry, for what's gone down and what's coming."

Reeves rubbed his fleshy cheeks with his hands. Instinctively, he glanced at the TV monitor as if to be sure that the Ambassador was not in the anteroom with his ear glued to the door. "This is officially a hardship post, Mr. Ceriani," he said. "A

15% differential over base salary is paid to personnel stationed here. The weather is splendid, the government is stable—the people are quite friendly, really, if you go out and meet them, none of this 'US go home' stuff or jacking up the price for an American. . . . But there are times, you know, that I don't think 15% is nearly enough."

He drew himself up. "Well," he concluded, "I will go back to my wife and cold dinner and *not* explain to her why his Excellency saw fit to call me away." Shaking his head, he left the Chancery.

Kelly waited for the door to close. Without looking at the duty officer, he said, "Look, it doesn't matter to me . . . but I'd suggest you not tell anybody about this either. If it gets beyond the, well, four people who were here, somebody's going to get real embarrassed. That wouldn't be good for anybody who needs a fitness report to get promoted . . . however much fun the embassy wives might find the story." He looked up at Byrne at last. The duty officer nodded agreement.

"Well, I'm gone then," said the agent, striding to the door. He closed it gently behind him, then waved to the TV camera before stepping out of the antechamber. He had forgotten to check on Sergeant Rowe, who should have returned by now. And on the liquor.

The first question resolved itself, while the need for a drink became more acute: Annamaria sat on one of the benches beneath the cantilevered roof covering the entryway.

The tall woman was dressed as Kelly had seen her earlier that evening, but with the addition of a dark jacket, suede or wool so far as the agent could judge in the entrance light. She was smoking a cigarette as well, something Kelly had not seen her do previously. She ground it out against the side of the stone bench before she rose. "Your things are in the St. George, the room your 'firm' had booked," said the woman. "Your car is parked at the Annex, all very proper—Doug insisted. Now, if *I'd* been driving, you'd be right down there where I am." She pointed toward the lane between the Chancery and the Villa Inshallah.

"That's fine, sure," Kelly said. "Look, Doug—"

"Doug has gone home, I told him to," Annamaria said. She raised a finger to forestall any comment by the agent. "Of course, you can call him there if you really need to destroy his little girl's birthday supper, which was supposed to have been last night."

"Oh, Hell, he didn't say a thing about that," Kelly mumbled. "Not that there would've been a choice—we needed those enlargements."

"Well, tonight there was a choice," Annamaria said primly. "I can't imagine any errands Doug could run that I can't . . . or any keys that he has and I don't, either, though I suppose I shouldn't admit that. Oh—" she reached down behind the bench and straightened with a topless Haig and Haig box— "Doug says these are for you."

Kelly took the box. The metal foil seals of the two bottles winked above the cardboard cells. "Yeah," he said, wetting his lips and pretending he had not heard the question in the woman's voice. "Look," he went on, facing the ground, "I need to get these inside. . . ."

"I'll wait out here." Annamaria spoke brightly, but as Kelly buzzed the Chancery door he noticed the flame of a cigarette lighter behind him.

Byrne turned out to be one of the vice consuls. If he was surprised at the agent's request that he give the Scotch to DeVoe when he left, it did not show. Kelly had no intention of disturbing the Communicator while he was in the middle of sending Kelly's own urgent cable. As for the sour mash waiting for the agent's return—it was more than a temptation to open it and take a quick slug before walking back into the night. Kelly did not do so; but he was not sure he would not until he had closed the outer door behind him.

"Look, Anna," he said as the woman stood again and the second cigarette joined the first, "maybe we need to talk, but I don't think—this—is the place. . . ."

"I brought my car," she said smiling. She held out her arm, insisting on linking it with Kelly's despite his hesitation.

"Your husband—" the agent began as they walked to the Mustang.

"Hush, you said you didn't want to talk here," Annamaria retorted, patting the inner angle of Kelly's elbow. "We'll find a place that's quiet. Here, I'll drive."

They pulled past the Residence gate, accelerating. Two Fiats were parked there again. For an instant a reggae beat puffed over the wall before Kelly rolled the side window firmly closed. Annamaria showed no sign of wanting to talk as she whipped the little car north. Kelly said nothing either. The woman was driving over her head at the moment, and the agent did not want to distract her. Besides, he didn't really know what he was going to say. He very much wished he had brought the whiskey along.

They climbed west toward Village Celeste, around switchbacks so sharp that the tires squealed at little more than a walking pace. The gradient was well over 12%. Unexpectedly, Annamaria pulled hard right and braked. The headlights glared back from the pressed steel guard rail; then the black-haired woman cut the lights and the engine together.

Both of them sighed. Annamaria took out a cigarette but did not move to light it. "That's Notre Dame de Afrique," she said, gesturing through the windshield. Below, the dome of the 19th Century cathedral shone in the moonlight, barred by the shadows of its own towers. Beyond the black slither of National Highway 11, the main

coastal road, the Mediterranean was itself a
metallic shimmer. Mercury vapor lights were
blue-white pinholes in the fabric of the dark city.

"You must have been there when your husband
came out of the Chancery," Kelly said finally as he
studied the ghost of his own reflection in the windshield. "What did he say?"

"Nothing," Annamaria said quietly from her
side of the car. "Which is what I expected." Her
lips quirked. "Chuck Reeves said, 'Goodnight,
Anna.' But Rufus didn't say anything at all. When
he gets very angry, he's like that—he pretends I
don't exist." She was looking at her fingernails,
flared on the steering wheel in the moonlight.

She flicked the cigarette, still unlighted, up onto
the dashboard as she continued, "The last time he
did this was when I told him I was taking over the
snack bar. Chuck had been complaining about the
problems—they'd fired the local manager, he was
robbing the place blind and couldn't do even *that*
well. I said I'd take over—I'd heard that an ambassador's wife had run the place a few tours
before, and I figured it was something I could do
as well as anybody else. I told Rufus, and he said I
wouldn't, and . . . it was two weeks or so before he
spoke to me again. I think he'd ruin Chuck's career
completely if he even suspected the notion had
anything to do with him."

Annamaria reached over and took Kelly's hand
with her own. "It bothered me, it bothered me a
lot when we were first married. But not now, not
for years. It's only when I really *do* exist, when I'm
doing something that isn't being his shadow, that
Rufus pretends I'm not there."

Kelly leaned toward her. They kissed. His arm
bumped the steering wheel as he reached around
her shoulders, his fingers caressing the black
suede and feeling the coat slide over the light shirt
beneath.

Annamaria fumbled with the steering wheel

latch. She swung the column as nearly vertical as
it would go. She reached back for Kelly, her knee
now pressing against the gearshift.

"Anna, wait," the agent said. He caught her
hands in his, bending to kiss the backs of them.
Their bones and tendons were tense beneath his
lips. "Listen," he said, speaking to her hands as
she had done moments before, "I want this a lot,
more than—" he paused, swallowed and dropped
her right hand into his lap. Her fingers gripped his
erect penis through the trousers, stroking
greedily, but he lifted her away again.

"A lot," he continued huskily. "And I don't give a
God damn about what your husband can do to me,
because he can't do a thing. Wouldn't matter anyway. And you—" he looked up, met her eyes—
"you're an adult, you know what kind of trouble
you're going to get in or not, that . . . that's your
business, not mine. My business is to finish a job,
though . . . a job I've been sent to do."

Annamaria squirmed, her left hand slipping
under Kelly's jacket and trying to tug him closer.
His rib cage was as hard as an oak tree—and as
immobile.

"Anna, listen," the agent repeated desperately,
"I can't handle this, not without blowing the
other—I just *can't*. And I don't want to screw it up
because my mind's on you. *Please*, Anna, for God's
sake understand."

"God?" Annamaria said. She straightened. "Oh,
God, yes, God *indeed*," she repeated and slammed
the heels of her hands against the steering wheel.
She bent forward, her face against the hub, her
arms straining on the woodgrained plastic. At last
she took a deep breath and faced Kelly again. In
the lights of a passing car, her face looked calm
except for the strand of hair twisting across it like
an unnoticed serpent. "Yes, you're really going to
leave me this way," the woman continued in a
savage voice. "I really have a talent for bringing

out the cold fish in men, don't I? Rufus freezes up
when he's angry enough to chew nails, and now
you—with a sense of duty that makes you
impotent!"

The agent said nothing. He bent his head down
but did not turn away. He had in fact lost his
erection, but it was not a subject he would have
debated in any case. "Anna," he said into the
waiting silence, "until Professor Vlasov's in somebody else's hands, you're right. I'm no kind of man
at all. Afterwards, if you really care, I'll come to
wherever you are, but . . . I'm sorry. My God but
I'm sorry."

Annamaria sighed. "Oh, lover," she said under
her breath, "you're sorry and I'm sorry and we're
all a lot of sorry fools, aren't we?"

She started the car, glanced over her shoulder
and backed onto the road again. Before Kelly
could speak, she had cursed and pulled the headlights on. "I'll drop you by your car, then," she
said as they lurched forward and down the hill.

"Oh, Chancery gate if you would," the agent
said. "I've got. . . ." his voice trailed off. "I'm
sorry."

"It's not your fault I'm a fool," the woman responded coolly. After a moment she added the last
words that were spoken between them until she
let Kelly out of the car: "Or mine if you are, I
suppose."

XXI

The liquor in Kelly's gut was sending little tendrils through his whole body like mold spreading across a bread loaf. He had not drunk much, well aware of how long it had been since he ate. Still, his step was jaunty and the bottle now had enough air in it to slosh. Byrne had found him a paper bag to carry it. Kelly shouldn't have broken the seal—Lord knew what Algerian liquor laws were like. All he needed was to be jailed after a fender-bender because he had an open bottle in the car . . . and no trunk to lock it in, either.

As Kelly slanted across the street to the Annex, he saw in the corner of his eye the glow of a car's courtesy light winking on as the door opened. A tall man was getting out of one of the parked Fiats. The distant street lamp turned the black of his aristocratic face to something near purple.

The agent stepped up on the far curb. He wondered if the Chaka Front could possibly do a more brutal job of governing South Africa than the present government did. Possibly, yes; it was barely possible. Look at Idi Amin, Macias Nguema . . . Bokassa the First—and, thank God, Only—who gave diamonds to a European President and tortured young girls to death by the hundreds. Look, for that matter, at King Chaka himself . . . though in comparison to some of *his* European contemporaries, the great Zulu leader did not seem so bad. God knew that he hadn't done as much bloody evil as Napoleon.

But that was State Department business at the

national level. And here in Algiers, it was the
business of his Excellency the Ambassador. No
business of Tom Kelly, who had more than enough
on his plate right—

Two men stepped from the shadowed trees
between the street and the sidewalk. They were
blocking the dirt pathway some twenty feet from
the Annex gate. The men wore dark slacks and
dashikis decorated with incongruous floral prints.
They were smiling as they faced Kelly; at least, the
agent caught the flash of their teeth. There was
nothing at all cheerful in that.

"Hello, hello," Kelly murmured and jumped
back for the street. The third Zulu, the man Kelly
had seen getting out of the Fiat, caught him about
the arms and waist. He held the American with the
ease of a father with a six-year old throwing a
tantrum. The Zulu was not wearing shoes. The
whisper of his long strides across the pavement
had been lost in the buzz in Kelly's skull.

A hundred yards up the street, the headlights of
a parked car went on and froze the struggle in
their glare. The car began to move with only the
hiss of its tires on the pavement.

"Help!" Kelly shouted.

The car passed, still accelerating. It was large
and black. The faces of the three men in the front
seat were dim, silent blurs.

The absence of the headlights deepened the
earlier darkness.

The man holding the agent wrestled him back
onto the pathway, away from even the dim blue
security of the distant street light. One of the two
waiting Zulus joined him, seizing the American by
the left wrist and elbow. Kelly kicked at the man's
groin, missed, and tried to stamp on the bare in-
step of the one holding him from behind. His crepe
heel connected, but it did not affect the Zulu's
diaphragm-level bear hug. Kelly had no illusions
about his ability to match three bigger, younger

men in hand to hand combat.

The third attacker stepped forward; light danced over his right hand for the first time. He chuckled.

The weapon strapped to the Zulu's hand and wrist was known the world over, but it was most common in societies existing in proximity to big cats. Four tines had been opened from a section of ductile iron waterpipe. The metal had been twisted and sharpened with a file into ragged edges that winked like diamonds where they caught the light. They could kill, of course, as even a rolled newspaper can kill; but the real purpose of the claws was more dramatic than mere death. . . .

The man with the claws laughed and feinted with his weapon. Kelly screamed and kicked harmlessly. There was no one on the street. The courtyard walls were as blank as those of a Roman amphitheatre. The three Zulus snickered together. The one to Kelly's left grabbed a handful of the agent's trouser front. He pulled. The belt held, but the fly and the cotton briefs beneath ripped away. The sagging fabric hobbled Kelly's knees. The man behind the agent shifted his grip, now holding Kelly by both elbows. The claw-wielder said something abrupt and strode forward.

Kelly screamed again and slammed the liquor bottle down with all the strength of his freed right hand. The thick glass held, but bones smashed in the knee of the man behind him. The Zulu's grunt of pain mingled with Kelly's own outcry. The claws missed because the injured Zulu could not prevent the agent's backward lunge.

One man still gripped Kelly by the left wrist. The American, supported in a half-squat by that grip, brought his paper-clad bottle around like a flyswatter. The Zulu threw up his free hand to protect his face. The side of the bottle caught the point of the man's raised elbow. This time glass and bag burst together in a spray of sour-mash whiskey. The Zulu cried out and loosed Kelly to hold his own damaged limb. Kelly jabbed him twice in the face with the ragged neck of the bottle.

Like a sap glove, the iron claws were heavy enough to impede the user's coordination. By the time the third Zulu had recovered from his vertical swipe at Kelly's groin, his two companions were down. The Zulu's face was in full shadow. Light washed between two tree boles and lapped about the American. Behind Kelly on the pavement, the man with the crushed knee was retching. The agent reached out with his left hand and peeled the remnants of the bag from the neck of the bottle. He held it advanced. The glass winked in a tight circlet. There were no long blades like those of resin dummies used in films. The stubby edges were smeared with blood and humours from the eyes they had just destroyed.

The Zulu raised his claws. Kelly lunged forward with a guttural cry. He stumbled on his torn trousers. The Zulu dodged around a tree and into the street. As he ran, he was calling to his companions and fumbling with the strap that bound his weapon to him. He had learned a lesson that his ancestors had taught the British at Isandhlwana: if your opponent is willing to die to get to you, you had best be willing to die yourself.

Kelly picked himself up from the dirt. He shuffled a step forward, then regained enough composure to tug his pants up with his left hand. He staggered to the Annex gate, walking with an adrenalin tremor. He banged on the steel with the heel of his right hand. Nothing happened. "This is Ambassador Gordon, you wog bastard!" Kelly shouted in English. "Open up or you're out of a job!"

The gate swung open abruptly. Kelly stumbled within and closed the portal behind him with his shoulders. Then he doubled up in front of the nervous guard to vomit bile and whiskey onto the drive.

At last the agent managed to raise himself into a kneeling position. He mumbled in French, "Do you have something to eat?"

The guard gave him a terrified smile but did not speak. "Food!" Kelly shouted. He got control of himself again. He found the pocket of his torn trousers with some difficulty and drew out the money clip. "Food," he repeated more calmly, peeling off a pair of hundred-dinar notes, enough to buy a meal in the best restaurant in Algiers. "I'm drunk, maybe you heard me shouting in the street. . .? I just need to get something in my belly before I drive home."

This time the guard nodded. He slipped back into his shelter. In the street a small car roared to life and squealed into a turn. The shouting was muffled by the wall and gate. But the time the guard returned with two navel oranges and a baguette of bread, the car had started again and was screaming north at too high a speed for the gear.

Kelly wolfed a bite of the crisp bread, choked, and swallowed it anyway. His fingers shook too badly to permit him to peel the oranges. After a moment's hesitation, he took out his jackknife and cut each orange across the axis. He squeezed the halves into his mouth. The tartness of the juice masked and almost smothered the bite of stomach acids high in his throat. Then, methodically, the agent finished the bread.

The guard stared as Kelly stood. The American looked down at himself, torn and bloodied and reeking of his own vomit and urine. "Tsk," he said, "I'll certainly have to change before I go to his Excellency's musicale tonight, won't I?"

Kelly watched cross streets and his mirrors as he drove downtown to his new hotel. He was not followed so far as he could tell.

XXII

The window in the Defense Attache's office looked north, toward the sea and directly away from the Aurassi. Kelly, no less than Posner and Rowe, found himself staring anxiously through the glass anyway as they all waited for the radio to speak.

"I don't know why I'm worried about this," said the Attache, turning sharply in his chair and standing up. He paced toward the closed door. "Best thing that could happen would be this whole house of cards coming down before anyone gets hurt. Either the equipment doesn't work or your contact wasn't told how to use it after all. I had *nothing* to do with that."

And nobody said you goddam did, the agent thought. Aloud he said, "Well, if they didn't make contact en route like they were supposed to, then we'll have to arrange something here. Phone from the desk, ring off if the security man answers instead of Hoang. . . . I dunno, whatever. Right now, all that I'm afraid of is that our boy isn't in 327 after all. Then we *have* got a problem."

"For Christ's sake, man!" the commander snapped, "you heard Tarek on the phone yourself. They've checked in, they're in 327—and Hoang isn't contacting us, for whatever reason!"

"Or Tarek," Kelly said, standing to stretch his legs more than to look at the scintillating water again, "was afraid to tell us something went wrong for fear we'd jerk the kid's visa again. Which we by God *will* if this falls through. I don't care why!"

The intercom buzzed. The three men froze; then Sergeant Rowe, who would normally have screened incoming calls from his own office, reached over his superior's glass-topped desk and took the instrument. "Rowe," he said. He listened intently for a moment. Cupping the receiver with his palms, he whispered to the others, "There's a crate like yesterday's in the pouch for you, Tom."

"Can they—" Kelly began. He pursed his lips. "No, I want to check it before we dump it in the armory after all. Doug, can you have somebody haul it up to your office until things are straight here?"

Rowe gave him the high sign. "Henri," he said, "I'll be down for that in a—"

The radio blatted, "Hello, are you there?" in loud, distorted Vietnamese.

Kelly motioned a fast, unnecessary 'Cut' to the sergeant as he twisted back the gain with his other hand. He keyed the mike. "We're here, Doctor," he said in the same language. "Can you hear me all right?"

"Not so loud, please!" the other voice hissed desperately through the receiver. "I have the bath running, but my guard is very close."

The agent dialed back on the transmitter's output. "Can you hear now, Doctor?" he asked.

"Yes, yes. . .," said the receiver, tinny but no longer a painful roar. "But go quickly, I am very nervous with this."

Kelly paused a moment to make sure the Vietnamese had finished speaking. "All right, Doctor," the agent said, "listen and don't speak until I say so. You must deliver this message to—" he paused. Did Hoang know Vlasov by the code name Kelly had been given? Hell, better discovery than misunderstanding.

"You must deliver this message to Professor Vlasov tonight at the banquet. Tomorrow morning you are scheduled for a tour of the Institute for

Nuclear Research near the Casbah. The signal will be either an explosion or a nearby traffic accident. This will be as soon as the Professor gets out of his car. A bomb or a crash, either one." The timing on the truck shouldn't be that close, but Kelly was afraid that the driver might get overanxious.

He cleared his throat and continued, "At the signal, Vlasov is to run across the road, the Boulevard de la Victoire. People will probably be running or ducking under cover. There will be one man standing up across the street with a white coat over his arm. Vlasov is to make for that man as fast as possible. If he can look like he's in a panic, so much the better.

"Is that clear? You can speak now."

Briefly the only sound from the radio was the popping and hiss of the electrical sea which surrounds the planet, the archetype of the theoretical ether. Sergeant Rowe had slipped away, his leaving unnoticed in Kelly's total concentration on the microphone in his hand. Then the speaker said, "I understand that, I will tell him. But what about me?"

The agent blinked. "You'll, ah—" he began. Kelly had not been interested in the arrangements already made with the Vietnamese physicist. Setting up a one-time net in Algiers had been plenty to occupy his imagination. Hoang Tanh was like the US Navy: necessary to the ultimate success of the mission, but out of Kelly's own hands and therefore not to be worried over. Otherwise, you worked yourself into a complete and completely useless dither.

Maybe, however, Kelly should have learned more about Hoang.

"You'll be handled by your regular control," the agent said, adding with what he hoped was assurance, "The arrangements will be carried out to the letter. In fact, there'll be a bonus for you."

That much Kelly could guarantee, even if it had

to come out of his own pocket. Why the *Hell* didn't somebody warned him that Hoang would need his hand held?

Because any control officer knows that, just like you don't have to tell a radioman to key the mike before speaking, the back of Kelly's brain told him. He hadn't known it, because he didn't have any goddam business—

"No," the radio was saying in southern-dialect Vietnamese. "I must come too this time. This is very big, yes? You must now give me a position in one of your universities—that is fair payment, is it not?"

Christ on a crutch.

Well, it probably *was* a fair deal; and yes, assuming Doctor Hoang had half-way reasonable credentials, the USG probably could find him a slot somewhere. . . . The Pentagon laid out a lot of grant money in the course of a year, enough to convince more credentials committees than not. But why in *God's* name was Hoang springing it now?

Or was it the first time the matter had been raised? "Ah, Doctor," Kelly asked carefully, "what have you been told so far about provisions for you to defect?"

"Told? Told nothing!" the voice spluttered through the atmospherics. "In good time, yes, they tell me, but stay a little longer. I have stayed long enough, I say! I have earned my reward!"

"Yes, of course, and we've anticipated your request," Kelly lied. "You will be taken out in Frankfurt, while you change planes. The German Federal Police will separate you from your, ah, bodyguard at Passport Control. You'll be rushed straight to the American Consulate. You need do nothing—by telling me you want to come over, you've done everything necessary. Do you understand?"

The agent's grip on the microphone was tight

with anger rather than tension. He forced his fingers to relax. You don't get mad at guns that jam or cars that won't start. It doesn't change things, they're just the way they are. And you don't get mad at people who act like fools either, not unless it's going to change things. What the Hell, the plan as described might work—if Pedler and the boys back in Europe got on the stick. At least, it ought to keep Hoang happy until the snatch had been executed. Or at least attempted.

The Vietnamese did not sound particularly happy, though, when he said, "I hear you. All right, I understand. And I will carry out *my* part. "Now I must go."

White noise from the speaker replaced the contact agent's voice. Kelly shook his head wearily and cut the transmitter power. "We need to keep the tape recorder hooked to the receiver until all this is over," he said, speaking indiscriminately toward Posner and Rowe—who must have returned. Presumably one or the other of the men could handle it. If they didn't, the Hell with it. . . .

"No," the agent said, aloud but to himself. Then, "Doug, got the recorder? I'll hook it up myself."

The heavy reel to reel recorder fit comfortably beside the receiver on top of Posner's desk. A length of coaxial cable bound them into a neat unit. Whenever a signal was received, the recorder would tape it and shut down again. Generally, since the pick-up was automatic, that meant that they would get a tape of the toilet flushing and perhaps the security man singing in the shower. There was an off-chance that the rig would function as a true bug and hear an important conversation; and a rather less improbable chance that Hoang would try to contact them again. The recorder made sense.

Kelly had a splitting headache, compounded of the dry air and the smoke-filled meeting with the Kabyles the day before. Well, if it weren't his sinuses, it might have been his prostrate. . . . He turned from the recorder to the Defense Attache. Posner's smoking wasn't helping a whole lot either, but it *was* the man's own office. "Commander," the agent said, "there's a glitch with our contact—he wants to defect too."

Both the other men grunted in surprise. Kelly nodded. "Yeah, I about danced for joy myself when he dropped that one. I told him sure, it was already set up. The Germans'd take him away from his guard in Frankfurt, then *zip* off to the States and Ivy League tenure. Or whatever the Hell. Thing is—and it's not that I'll shoot myself if it doesn't work out . . . but I did tell him that."

The agent looked from one of the military men to the other. He was embarrassed that it mattered to him that he had made what amounted to a promise. "Anyway, we need to get a cable out to Pedler to see if he can pull the deal off on pretty goddamned short notice. I'm not going to be able to handle it and check out the drop site during daylight. Can you, Commander?"

Posner jetted smoke from both nostrils. "Yes," he said, "yes, that's reasonable enough." He managed a smile at Kelly. "It's even the sort of thing I imagined I might be doing when I transferred to the DIA. Which, God knows, very little else that's going on is."

Kelly handed Posner the program disk. "Fine, sir. Here's the code. And—ah, if you'd keep this on your person at all times, I'd appreciate it. Orders, of course."

As they closed the Attache's door behind them, the agent said, "Let's take a look at that pouch before I forget it, Doug. Then we can haul it to the armory too."

The grenades in the second case were similar in size and shape to the previous load of smoke bombs. The tops of these were painted white, however, in line with US practice for marking CS.

Kelly drew out one of the heavy bombs and looked at it for a moment. "Got some Kleenex or a roll of toilet paper handy, Doug?" he asked.

The sergeant shrugged and tossed over a box of tissues from his lower desk drawer.

Carefully, the agent matted three tissues together. Then he unscrewed the fuse assembly from the grenade canister itself. The assembly was a slender tube that fit the length of the grenade's axis. It contained the striker, fuse, and the black powder booster charge that actually ignited the filler and caused it to spew tear gas. Kelly stuffed the tissues down into the well to keep the filler where it belonged. Then, with another wad of tissue, he wiped the tube clean before dropping it into his side pocket.

"We'll bury this under a rose bush after dark," he said with a grin, thumbing toward the defused canister. "Till then, let's hope nobody knocks the thing over, or else you don't use your office for a while. A *long* while. And now—" he bent over to take one end of the packing case— "let's get this to the armory and ourselves to lovely Tipasa, resort of the best defecting physicists."

XXIII

"I want you to take a look from up here," said Sergeant Rowe, panting a little with the climb from the parking area. "Otherwise when you see the harbor itself, you'll bitch. This isn't much of a coast for fooling around with rubber boats, Tom."

"Hell, you can say that again," Kelly muttered. "You mean this is a *good* area?"

"Typical," corrected the sergeant. "The harbor's good, but you can't really tell from this angle."

The cliff on which the Americans stood dropped eighty jagged feet to the Mediterranean. Tipasa's Roman wall, four feet of rough stone in a concrete matrix, had ended just short of the edge from which they watched. Only the foundations remained, their massive construction belied by their state of total ruin. Over a kilometer to the west, another promontory completed the bay into which harbors had been cut ever since the Carthaginians settled here. Knowing that, and seeing the chop of the Mediterranean, Kelly appreciated how rare decent harbors were in North Africa.

There was nothing like a beach at any point the agent could see, although the ground fell away along the southern edge of the bay and gave him a good view. Low cliffs, the corniche, alternated with jumbles of rock which stretched far out into the water. There the waves bubbled away from the ruddy stones like foam from blood-smeared teeth.

"Now, I think this is going to work," Rowe said. He was pleased at the impression the view had

made on his companion. "But you've got to
recognize that if you're being extracted by boat,
you're pretty limited. Closer in there's the beach
at Chenona, but the buildings all around it are
housing for government employees. And on the
other side of the mountain, at Cherchell—" He
pointed. A cone at least three thousand feet high
stabbed abruptly from the coast just west of
Tipasa. Clouds blurred its peak— "there's an even
better beach. But there's also an armor school,
and *no* foreigner wants to get too close to that. So
Tipasa's pretty much the choice."

Kelly shook his head. "Damn," he said, "you
look at charts; and sure, there's enough water to
get a sub in close enough for a pick-up. Looking at
those rocks down there, I—well, I sure hope they
don't scrape the bottom at any speed, because I'll
bet it doesn't look any softer half a mile out than it
does here."

"Well," Rowe suggested cautiously, "the first
thing is to get the rubber boat out half a mile, isn't
it? Let's take a look at the harbor."

The modern city of Tipasa stretched somewhat
farther south than had the ancient one, but its
total occupied area appeared to be much smaller.
Much of the area enclosed by the fallen walls was
now meadow. Sergeant Rowe drove carefully back
to the highway from the parking area east of the
city.

They were paralleling the foundations of the
Roman wall. Kelly noticed that the grassy slope
was littered with hollowed stone blocks. Each was
more than five feet long and a foot in width and
height. A few of the blocks still had their stone lids
in place. "What the Hell are they?" the agent
asked. "They look like coffins."

"Right, sarcophagi," the sergeant agreed as he
turned onto the highway. "Nothing fancy, just the
local stone squared and hollowed. Once in a while
you'll find a Chi-Rho cut on one end, but usually

not even that. And they weren't buried, just placed
on the hillside outside the walls."

Kelly licked his lips. He did not reply. It would
have made no difference to his plans if he *had*
known the extraction point would be in the center
of an arc of ancient graves.

It did not make him like the situation any better,
however.

Just inside the ancient walls, the marked
highway branched left and away from the bay.
Rowe continued straight, toward the row of
buildings that looked like a business district. The
hundred yards of ground between the street and
the sea was broken and overgrown. "Shall I drive
all the way to the harbor?" the sergeant asked.
"Or do you want me to park on the street for now?
It's not far to walk."

"No point in calling attention to ourselves,"
Kelly decided. "Let's walk."

Two blocks away, near the entrance to the
excavated portion of ancient Tipasa, was a group
of boys. One of them broke away and began
running toward the two men. Rowe locked up the
car and the men walked seaward. The breeze was
mild.

There was no chop to speak of here to mark the
brilliant, ultramarine water. None the less,
frequent tongues of foam reminded Kelly that
there were rocks near enough to surface to gnaw
the bottom out of his boat. He leaned forward.
"Christ," he said. There was a beach of sorts after
all. It was narrow and of pebbles rather than sand,
but it would do . . . except that it was a good ten
feet below the sharp lip of the corniche.

The boy came running up to the Americans.
"Watch your car," he panted in English. American
cars were identifiable and virtually unique to the
national community here, it seemed.

"No," said the sergeant harshly.

"A dinar," said Kelly. He flipped the aluminum

coin high in the air, then repocketed it with a smile.

"*Two* dinars," said the boy in pleased surprise.

Kelly pointed to the car. "Watch it well," he said. After only a moment's hesitation, the boy began to saunter back to the Volare.

Looking out over the crystalline sea, the agent said, "First, we can't afford even the *tiny* chance that he'd let the air out of our tires. Second, it gets him away from us quicker than trying to ignore him. And third—" he looked at Rowe and grinned— "I sort of like kids. But don't let word of that get out or I'll lose my all-star bastard rating."

Rowe cleared his throat. "Well," he said, "well. Where we want to go is back to the east. We'll drive it when we put the boat in the water, but for now. . . ."

The ground just beyond the corniche was driveable, though it was not in any sense a proper road. Absinthe bushes—wormwood—must have been planted ornamentally at some time, perhaps millenia in the past. The bushes grew profusely, their white-dusted leaves shading the rust-red native stone. Ahead, foam and rocks shared a deep cavity which the sea washed but did not hold. Closer yet, there was a trench cut in the—

"Well, I'll be damned," Kelly said. "It's a staircase cut down to the beach!"

"As requested," the sergeant agreed. "One beach, with access. And as open as all this is—" he waved his arm in a southerly arc, taking in the blocks of stone and scrub to the nearest buildings— "nobody can see you launch the boat. The cliff hides you to anyone on the road until you're out beyond the breakwater. Okay?"

Kelly clapped the younger man on the shoulder. "You're the best damn travel agent *I've* ever met," he said. "You know, I was worried that the local support I'd get would . . . leave a lot to be desired. But I was wrong, at least about you. . . . I'll tell the world!"

The sergeant blushed and looked away. "Well," he said, "glad it's okay. We'd better take a quick look at the safe house now and stash the gear. Hope it does as well as the sea did for you."

Their car was visible around the edge of the nearest building. It would have been half a block shorter to cut straight to the vehicle, but the waste area was a tangle of uncertain footing. They retraced their steps along the sea front instead.

Kelly noticed a simple shaft monument. He had ignored it before when his mind was on other things. "Just a second," he said. There was a small bronze plaque set in the concrete face of the shaft. Translating its French inscription aloud for the sergeant's benefit, the agent read, "Sacred to the memory of six sailors, their names and nationalities unknown, who washed ashore here on March 6, 1942. Rest in peace.' "

There was a small cross incised beneath the inscription. Someone had made repeated efforts to gouge away the relic of Christianity. The message had been scarred as well.

They walked on. "Interesting," Kelly said in a neutral voice. "There's a political statement made with a chisel. Made by somebody who was probably illiterate, at least in French; but he knew that defacing crosses was a patriotic thing to do. . . . It doesn't give me a lot of hope for world peace and understanding."

After a moment he added, "A guy in Paris convinced me I wasn't going to be doing the same goddam thing myself. He'd better have been right."

The house Commander Posner had managed to rent on short notice was several blocks south of the harbor, near the present edge of town. It had a courtyard wall and a wooden gate which Kelly unlocked to pass the station wagon.

The building was not prepossessing. The plaster had cracked from much of the facade and lay scattered in the courtyard. Patches of discoloration beneath the windows, and the areas of bare concrete elsewhere, combined to give the house the look of something in wartime camouflage. It would serve though.

"The phone's connected and the electricity," Rowe said as the two men wrestled the boat out of the back of the wagon. "Other than that, it's pretty much what you see. Concrete and dirt." He kicked at the baked ground. It was as bare and as refractory as the walls of the building.

Kelly shrugged. "That's fine," he said, staggering a little with the weight of the collapsed MARS boat. "Just so long as we can stash the boat and radio here, and we can lay up until dark tomorrow ourselves." He laughed. "I have simple tastes," he added. "I want to get this whole thing over so bad I can simply taste it."

The men grunted simultaneously as they set the package down in the hall. "We should have brought the other five men this damned thing's built to hold," Kelly grumbled. "Though I swear, it'll look small enough tomorrow when I get to take it out to sea. Well, one more load."

"Ah," the sergeant said. "We thought—my wife and me, Tom. Maybe you'd like to have dinner tonight with us?"

The agent stopped in the doorway. "Doug, that's—well, I really appreciate it. I—I've got something else that I—" and his tongue stumbled, but he got the next word out anyway— "need to do tonight. But I really appreciate it."

"Well, let's shift the other stuff," Rowe said. He smiled cheerfully. "And good luck tonight."

XXIV

The upper lot by the DCM's house was already crowded when Kelly arrived. Mercedes predominated, but there were a fair number of top-quality Citröens and Renaults as well as more exotic makes. At least one of the Citröens bore cream-colored Presidency license plates with a damned low prefix: either the Minister of Foreign Affairs himself or someone high-ranking from his shop. The agent smiled and shook his head as he eased past. His VW was going to feel lonely.

Loneliness was the wrong subject for a joke, even to himself . . . especially to himself. Kelly's stomach knotted around the liquor he had drunk in his hotel room to nerve him for the evening. Scowling, the agent pulled into a space between the GSO Annex and the line of brown-painted Conexes. The building was a metal temporary, and the Conexes were shed-sized shipping containers that doubled here—as in Nam—as lockable storage for the General Services Officer. In sum, the scene was as romantic and Eastern as downtown Milwaukee.

Kelly got out of his car, locked it, and checked his pockets. The invitation was in the breast pocket; and the grenade fuse made an unsightly bulge on the right side. Kelly removed the fuse to check it. He had put thirty wraps of plastic electrician's tape around the charge tube and the arming spoon. Henri, the Chancery receptionist, had found him the tape without asking questions. Doug could have gotten it, but Kelly did not want to involve the sergeant.

Working by the light outside the GSO building, the stocky American pulled the cotter pin that locked the spoon in place. The tape wrappings still kept the spoon from flying up to hit the striker and ignite the fuse. The plastic tape was amply strong to hold for the foreseeable future.

With the doctored fuse concealed in his hand, the agent began to stroll up the long drive toward the gate to the Annex grounds. Under his breath he was mouthing a phrase from the folk song 'Sam Hall':

". . . you're a bunch a' bastards all,

Goddamn your eyes."

There were cars parked solidly for a block either way from the Residence on both sides of the street. Most of the vehicles had green Diplomatic plates. Those which did not were of a luxury which conferred equal immunity. Pairs of Civil Police stood at the limits of sight in either direction, directing traffic with yellow light-wands on the ends of flashlights. Another pair of blue-suited patrolmen lounged against the wall outside the open Residence gate. They were laughing and talking to one another unconcernedly, but their pistols were real and they each carried a walkie-talkie—unusual for the regular police. It was not a gate that anyone smart would try to crash.

The Fiat was right where Kelly had spotted it when he drove in, fifty yards from the DCM's entrance and on the same side of the street. A little farther than the Zulus normally had to park from their lady friend's front door, but not much. Kelly had not expected the car to be there, not tonight, maybe never again . . . but he had been prepared just in case. The agent's lips were dry, his right palm sweating on the fuse assembly. He sauntered toward the car, his mind tumbling over the last stanza of the song though his mouth was too stiff to pass even the shadow of the words:

"Now up the rope I go, now up I go. . . ."

Kelly's suit was of a wool-silk blend, well-cut as befitted a man who sold big-ticket items to conservative businessmen. It was also charcoal gray. Even if any of the policemen had made the effort, they would have seen only one more shadow gliding between the parked cars and the courtyard walls. The Fiat's gas cap was not of the locking type, though Kelly would scarcely have been delayed if it had been. He twisted it open, using only the tips of his left fingers on the knurled rim. He dropped in the taped fuse, then replaced the cap when the splash assured him that the fuse had slid into the tank proper. He gave an extra twist after the gas cap had seated, smearing his prints illegibly instead of wiping the metal with a rag. Whistling under his breath, Kelly walked back to the Annex gate before stepping into the street and the view of the policemen at the entrance.

The blue-suited men straightened slightly as they saw Kelly approach through a gap in the traffic. Cars were being fed in alternate directions by the police with wands. There was not room for them to pass both ways at once with the parking as it was. The agent tipped his invitation toward the men in a mock salute, smiling. They smiled back and relaxed again, young men in long, boring duty. They were not westernized enough to appreciate the jazz from beyond the wall as music, and they were not affected enough to succumb to its snob appeal.

At the Residence entrance proper, a tuxedoed servant checked Kelly's invitation with no more than the usual care. He gestured ceremoniously within, saying, "Refreshments are being served to the right, by the pool, sir."

The Residence grounds were lighted by yellow paper lanterns spiked to the lawn on iron bases. Couples and small groups—mostly men—strolled on the grass among the cedars, in separate, low-voiced conversations. A sidewalk curved to the entrance and across the front of the house. At the right end of the rambling building was a blaze of electric light. The guest house was lighted also. Kelly noted with amusement that there was no reggae tonight from behind the closed, curtained windows. He walked along the sidewalk without haste, his eyes open for anyone he knew—and for anything he needed to learn.

The social area proper was a flood-lit patio to the right rear of the building. It was a full story lower than the front entrance. The swimming pool was near the courtyard wall, a lighted jewel dazzlingly brighter than the moonlit Mediterranean visible over the wall coping. A temporary stage had been constructed against one wing of the Residence, but it held only instruments and a pair of large speakers at the moment. Either Kelly had arrived between sets, or the entertainment was over for the evening.

Commander Posner was resplendent in dress whites for the occasion, talking with animation to the Station Chief near a tiled wall fountain. Kelly started toward them, hesitated, and walked to the bar instead. Three tuxedoed Algerians were decanting wine, mineral water, and a variety of fruit juices. There was no hard liquor in evidence, perhaps in deference to the fact that more than half the guests were locals. Kelly snagged one of the glasses of red wine and sipped. After a quick glance around, he slugged down the rest of the glass. Reaching around a portly, bearded man in a fez, the agent traded his empty glass for a full one. Annamaria had been right: the local vintages did have a bite.

Harry Warner saw Kelly approaching. He waved to silence the Attache. Commander Posner turned, his face registering multiple levels of surprise.

Kelly smiled easily, the portion of his mind that

was tuned to business slipping to the fore. Everything was stable, was crystalline, when he concentrated on the job. Though that was only by contrast, of course. "I won't intrude now, sir," the agent said, "but if you have a moment later, I'd like to check on our business."

Warner waved dismissal. "Sure," he said, "I was going to get another drink anyway." The CIA officer smiled coldly at Kelly as he walked to the bar.

"For God's sake!" Posner whispered, "what are you doing here? This is a Section Heads Only affair!" He looked around hastily. "You know I can't pass you your code disk here."

"No problem," the agent said, swallowing more wine without really tasting it, "you can hold it. I just wanted to make sure the cable got off okay."

"Well, I said it would, didn't I?" snapped the commander. "You're an *idiot* to come here tonight, you know. How did you ever get past the gate?"

The fountain was dry, but the alcove itself was tiled in a running-water pattern. Blue and yellow slip glazes rippled over a white background. More than a hundred individually different tiles had been arranged in a unitary design which had been planned at a factory . . . perhaps four centuries before. Kelly let his eyes rest on the soothing, hand-painted curves as he said, "Oh, I had something to attend to . . . and I felt like coming, I guess that's the reason I do most things. Thank you, Commander."

Both men were shaking their heads when they parted.

Annamaria was nowhere to be seen; neither was her husband. For all his bravado in attending the affair, Kelly rather hoped that he would not meet the Ambassador again. He was not sure what either of them would say.

The general language of the gathering was

English, though there were varieties of it that had
more to be translated than understood by a native
speaker. At the hors d'oeuvres table was an
obvious member of the jazz group, a gangling
blond man in slacks, a long-sleeved shirt, and a red
vest. He towered like a derrick over an Algerian
girl who was perhaps older than the fifteen she
looked. The American was offering the girl stuffed
olives and very earnest conversation. To the
musician's other side was another, shorter,
American in a light sport coat. He was equally
earnest and far less relaxed.

The musician finally turned to the shorter man
and said, "Say, Cal, can you speak to her? Don't
think she knows any American at all."

"Gerry, when is the *set* going to start?" the other
man demanded.

"When Dee gets out of the shitter, I suppose,
Cal," the musician said. He turned back to the girl.
"Go tour-direct somebody else, man," he added
over his shoulder.

The girl was very nice indeed. She was wearing
clothes from Paris with a style that belied her
youth. Kelly grinned and started to join the couple
as an interpreter. The girl was obviously flattered
at the attention—and obviously, as even Gerry had
surmised, completely innocent of English. Before
the agent could speak, however, the musician
made one last thrust at international understanding. He bent down so that his face was on a
level with the girl's. Then he asked with the exag-
geratedly slow delivery of a Voice of America
language lesson, "Would . . . you . . . like . . . to. . .
fuck?"

Kelly turned, choking to keep from spraying out
the mouthful of wine he had just taken.
Annamaria stood three steps behind him, wearing
a black silk dress and a look of delighted amazement.

"Angelo!" she cried, "you *did* come! What a

surprise." She touched Kelly's hand in friendly greeting.

The agent checked his watch. "Well, I. . .," he said. "Things happen and things, ah . . . things change." He wished to God his glass was not empty. "Look, Anna, I need—" he looked at his watch again, this time to take his eyes off the woman— "I'd like to borrow a phone for just a moment. But I—" he faced her but lowered his voice— "I don't want to fall over your—his Excellency. I'll go next door if I need to."

"Not at all," Annamaria said, using her fingertips on the back of Kelly's hand to draw him after her. "We'll use the extension in the front hall, if that's all right. Rufus has been upstairs with—" her own voice fell— "someone from the MFA since the reception line closed. If he *does* come down, he'll go out by the back door anyway."

The wisteria overhanging the entrance was a rich purple fragrance that penetrated the flagged court within. It even touched the hall beyond. The ceiling light was small, but it glanced in more than adequately from the blank, white walls. A phone sat on a circular table, beside a coat rack of age-darkened wood. "I'll wait around the corner," Annamaria said, gesturing toward the instrument and walking on. "Call when you're through."

The agent opened his mouth to say that was not necessary; but then again, the less known. . . . God she was lovely. Kelly's mouth was dry again as he dialed the six-digit number he had memorized from the register on Sergeant Rowe's desk. Dryness was good. It would change the timbre of his voice, and a trace of nervous anticipation was just what the doctor ordered on this one.

"Yes?" said a woman on the other end of the line. Kelly had never met the Ambassador's secretary, but it was her home phone he had dialed.

"Buffy," the agent whispered urgently, "this is

Chuck Reeves. You've got to get him out *fast*. The
Ambassador's going to cover up for last night by
getting them all thrown in Lambése Prison on
open charges. The Minister's just agreed and the
arrest team's on the way. If he's still there in five
minutes, he'll only leave the prison when they put
him on the roads!"

Kelly slammed down the phone on the yelp of
alarm from the other end. He was smiling, and it
was not a nice smile to see. Then he looked down
the hall and saw Annamaria looking back at him,
alerted by the clash of plastic. Christ, he was
trembling again. "Let's get out of here," he said in
an attempt at a normal voice, "and—but, Hell, I'm
sorry, you'll have things to do."

Annamaria's heels clicked even through the
thick carpeting as she strode back to the agent. "If
his Excellency the Ambassador can disappear,"
she said, linking arms as she had before, "surely
her Excellency the Ambassador's wife can do the
same. My car?"

"No, I. . .," Kelly said. "I don't really need to go
anywhere. Let's walk over to the Annex grounds,
that's—" The stocky man met her eyes, finally. He
smiled without the murderous delight of a
moment before. "Just want to talk, that's all."

They were another indistinguishable couple on
the lawn as soon as they stepped beyond the
lighted sidewalk. It was warmer than it had been
for the past few evenings. Annamaria had not
bothered to wear a wrap. Her dress was slashed
off the right shoulder, leaving her skin to glow in
the ambient light. Worth a glance, even in the
darkness, but the attention of all those nearby
seemed to be focused on the scene taking place at
the guest house.

The front door was open, a harsh rectangle in
contrast to the light diffusing through the window
curtains. A slim woman with a splendid Afro stood
in silhouette in the doorway, shrieking back into

the house.

Annamaria missed a half step in wonder. Kelly continued walking, his gentle momentum drawing the woman on. "What on earth is Buffy doing?" Annamaria marveled in an undertone. "Goodness, if word gets back to Rufus that she's had a public scene with her boyfriend tonight, with everyone here, she'll be shipped back to America by the next plane. Of course," she added thoughtfully, "he'll have someone else sign the orders."

A tall black man stamped angrily out of the house, snarling something to the woman. His shoes were in his hand. "God damn you!" she screamed in reply. "Go on! I won't have them taking me too!" Her gesture was imperious. She looked like a back-lighted statue of Queen Ti.

The man bent to don his shoes, then changed his mind and loped for the gate. The house door slammed. He looked back over his shoulder and light from a window fell on his face. As Kelly had assumed, he was the man who had held the claws the night before. The American agent kept his right hand unobtrusively under his coat tails, thumb and forefinger resting on the steel hilt of his utility knife. There was no cause for concern. The Zulu was not looking at him, was not really looking at anything at all tangible. His sculptured face bore an expression melded of fear, anger . . . and the indescribable tension of something that knows it is hunted.

"Lovely sky," Kelly remarked conversationally as they walked through the gate a moment later. He nodded past Annamaria toward the two policemen on duty there. One nodded back, but they were more interested in the Fiat. Its headlights dimmed with the starter whirr, then flared as the engine caught. Police the world over suspect the unusual, and a Zulu running from a diplomatic function with his shoes in his hand was nothing if not unusual. "Electric lights every few yards may make the streets safer," the agent continued, "but it's a shame the way they hide the stars over most cities."

Annamaria looked at the American strangely. Her mouth quivered with the questions that she did not express. The Fiat pulled away hard enough to make its tires and engine howl. Kelly paused on the curb. The black-haired woman clung to him with a shade of nervousness. The policemen tracked the car with narrowed eyes as it accelerated past them. One man fingered his walkie-talkie.

Gasoline had been dissolving the plastic tape ever since Kelly had dropped it in the tank. Thirty wraps, thirty minutes, as a rule of thumb. The tape must have finally parted under the spoon's tension a moment after the Zulu had started his engine. The timing could not have been closer if Kelly had been waiting to put a rocket-propelled grenade into the Fiat as it slid past.

The first result was a mild thump, as if the car—twenty feet down the street—had rolled over an empty box. The booster had gone off in the sealed gas tank. The explosion itself was almost lost in the engine noise. It was quite sufficient, however, to rupture every seam in the tank and spray gasoline over the road and the car's undercarriage.

A fraction of a second later, five or so gallons of gasoline ignited. Because the fuel-air mixture was unconfined, the result could not technically be termed an explosion. The *whump*! and the fireball from the finely-divided mist made a damned close equivalent.

Kelly swung Annamaria to his right side as the tank burst, interposing his own squat body between her and what was about to follow. The blast flicked across his neck between collar and hairline, heat in momentarily palpable form. The Fiat twisted, out of control but running on the gas still trapped in its fuel lines. It side-swiped a parked Mercedes and swopped ends in a spin. The street behind and beneath it was a gush of flames. A moment later the back tires exploded from the heat, one and then the other. They sounded like the double barrels of a shotgun, louder by far than the fuse detonation that had started the process.

The side-swipe had torqued the car body enough to wedge the doors shut. The driver was trying to get out. One of the Algerian policemen who had been directing traffic threw down his flashlight. He took two steps toward the car before the flames beat him back. The screams from inside could not be heard over the roaring fire, not really.

The patrolmen at the upper side of the embassy complex were gaping, forgetting the traffic they were there to control. The huge flaming barricade brought cars to a halt in front of the Chancery gate and back up the street in screeching sequence.

"Let's cross quick," the agent said. He still gripped Annamaria by both shoulders. People were jumping out of their stopped cars, babbling in polyglot amazement. Kelly and the woman darted between the bumpers of a Peugeot and a Dacia pick-up as quickly as Annamaria's spike heels would permit her to follow the guiding hand. The flames, fed now by the asphalt roadway itself, threw their capering shadows down the street in demonic majesty.

XXV

The gate of the GSO Annex had been left open during the affair at the Residence. The guard was the man who fed Kelly the night before. He stood open-mouthed beside one of the gateposts, his eyes filled with the nearby inferno. He gave no sign of noticing Kelly and Annamaria.

The agent started down the drive, primarily from inertia. Annamaria halted him with a gentle tug on his arm. "People will be getting cars," she said. "They won't be able to leave, but they'll be coming over here anyway. There's a place we can talk, though. . . ."

Kelly let the woman direct him to the right, along the inner face of the compound wall. They passed the playground and buildings of the American School. Kelly had not realized the Annex area was so extensive. The path narrowed between the wall on one side and the steep hill down to the Conexes on the other. The shrubbery was rough, obviously untended. Suddenly there was a small, square building in the midst of the trees and brush. It was barely touched by the streetlight reaching over the wall and through the foliage.

The white exterior plaster had flaked somewhat at the corners and around the jamb of the round-topped door. It gave the squat building the look of a soldier who has gone through a battle in his parade uniform. A double band of ceramic tiles encircled it just below the roof line. The flat roof humped in the center into a dome.

Annamaria reached up and fingered one of the

smooth tiles, the care of its decoration obvious though the dim light washed its varied colors into shades of gray. "The tiles are mostly Dutch, you know . . . here, the Residence, most of the really old buildings in Algiers. 16th Century Delft tiles here. . . . It was a saint's tomb, a sidi was buried here. The body is long gone, of course."

The door was a thin plywood panel, clearly original to the building. It was held shut with a twist of wire, perhaps part of a coat hanger. "Why the mania for Dutch tiles?" the agent asked as he unwound the wire. "Not that they aren't very pretty. . . ."

"The price was right," Annamaria said. She was so close to Kelly that her breast touched his left arm. "Charitable societies in Holland used them for centuries to ransom Christian seamen from the pirates. The Barbary Pirates, the Berbers. . . . Do you suppose he slept better, the saint, knowing that his tomb was covered with the ransom of infidels?"

Kelly swung the door open. It scratched on the stone flooring. There was nothing within but hollow echoes and a few leaves. He turned deliberately to Annamaria and kissed her as her arms slipped under his jacket. When the pressure of her fingers on his back relaxed, Kelly also relaxed slightly to allow their mouths to part. He murmured something that even he did not understand, his eyes screwed shut in hope and pain.

"Darling," said Annamaria quietly, her fingertips ten moth-wing touches above the line of his belt, "what happened to you last night after you left me? Or was it this morning?"

The agent's eyes were open, now, and as still as pools of quicksilver. "Oh," he said with a smooth, false nonchalance, "did your husband say something was going to happen?"

"It was Rufus who did something, then," the woman said. She stood with the perfect calm of a

gymnast the moment before she executes a particularly difficult series. "No, darling, Rufus said
nothing. . . . I told you, Rufus doesn't talk when
he's angry, not to me. But you—" She raised one
hand and traced the index finger from Kelly's earlobe down his jaw line, then back and down his
chest. He shivered. "You made a decision, and you
stood by it last night when I think it might have
been easy not to." Her finger tapped Kelly's belt
buckle and skipped lower, briefly, enticingly. She
giggled.

Kelly mumbled and tried to draw the dark-
haired woman close again. Annamaria leaned
back, away from the fulcrum of his hands. "No,
darling," she said seriously. "I have to know."

"I—" Kelly began. Then, his eyes on hers, he
went on. "Last night I got reminded that people
don't live forever. I won't live forever. You know,
the plane you were supposed to be on crashes, or a
roof tile nips your ear before it busts to Hell on
the sidewalk. I'd decided, maybe I couldn't handle
two things at once. But I decided, yeah: and maybe
I can't handle either one alone. But even if I live in
a cave and have people slip food through a slot,
something can still go wrong. That's not a reason to
be afraid to try. . . ." He swallowed. "Afraid to do
things that are important to do."

Annamaria's left hand still held Kelly gently
where his rib cage tucked under. She spread her
right hand on his shirt, over the nipple, and looked
at her own fingers rather than the agent's eyes.
She said, "Darling, if you were very angry
with—my husband, with Rufus—" she looked up.
"How would you get back at him? You *would* get
back at him."

Kelly took his hands away so abruptly that the
woman stumbled back a step. He did not notice because he had turned and smashed the heel of his
palm against the tomb as hard as he could. He
slowly raised his left hand to the arch of the door,

feeling his way along the plaster. His face was bent toward the empty floor within.

After almost a minute poised against the tomb, the stocky man faced about. In a hoarse, tired voice he said, "I've done things, Anna, you're right. . . . Not, not just to get even, but why should you believe that? And anyway, it doesn't matter." He wet his lips and paused. Annamaria stood with her arms crossed, her long fingers touching her own shoulders. Kelly said, "Anna, I'm not subtle. I—I might kill, sure, because there're some things, some people that—I'm not going to have go on. But—not your husband, because he *is* your husband. And I. . . . Nothing I—" he looked away— "nothing I wanted from you had anything to do with your husband."

Annamaria's face warmed by stages in a broad, slow smile. "Wanted?" she said, extending her right arm with the delicacy of a plant sprouting. "Want-ted? Darling, don't try to tell *me* that you don't want it still." She continued to caress his groin until she moved her hand to permit their bodies to press closer together while they kissed.

Kelly slid his hand up and cupped a breast through the silk dress and nothing more, Jesus, nothing more. The nipple hardened beneath his palm. Annamaria leaned away, raising her hand to Kelly's. Their lips parted. An apology rose in his throat but caught there as the black-haired woman slid the silk off her left shoulder and let the dress fall free of her torso. It was caught momentarily by Kelly's hand on her breast, then held at her waist as they embraced again. The aureolae were small and very dark against Annamaria's white skin, black in the diffused light of the street lamp.

Kelly bent. She touched her own left breast, lifting the erect nipple to meet his lips. When his tongue began to quiver over the surface of the nipple, Annamaria moaned and sagged a little against the hand with which Kelly supported the curve of her right hip.

Annamaria reached down and touched her groin, through the dress at first, sliding a finger up and down over the slick fabric as she arched herself to meet her hand. Then she gave a tiny gasp, a catch of her breath, and hiked her skirt up with a convulsive movement that threatened the material. Kelly knelt in front of her, feeling but ignoring the bite of pebbles on his knees. When his mouth left her breast, Annamaria touched the wall of the building with her left hand and leaned sideways until her shoulder braced her. Her face was slightly lifted, her eyes closed. From her throat came a purr that may have been intended for words.

Annamaria's panties were simple and very brief. They were white and more noticeable against her skin for their reflectance than for any difference of shade. Kelly hooked his thumbs under both sides of the garment, then gently tugged it down. The fabric clung at mid-thigh, then dropped around her ankles.

She tossed her head sideways, looking down past the dress she held bunched at her waist. She lifted her left foot carefully clear of the panties, then kicked out sharply with her right leg. The slight garment flew off into the darkness from the tip of her open-toed shoe. Annamaria giggled and ran the fingers of one hand through Kelly's hair.

Bending forward, Kelly divided the lips of the woman's vulva with an index finger. They were already moist. Her pubic hair was a small black wedge with a stem up her midline toward the navel. He touched, then kissed, her exposed clitoris, slipping his finger back and deeper as she thrust her pelvis toward him.

Annamaria began breathing with short, rasping intakes. The fingers of both her hands danced over Kelly's scalp, guiding his rhythm with their pressure but never attempting to force what they already controlled. After a moment, she began to caress his earlobes between her thumbs and index fingers. The skirt had tumbled across Kelly's face in a spidery flood. He lifted it away with his right hand while his left hand and tongue continued to probe gently and rhythmically.

Annamaria's gasps stilled, her hands froze in brushing contact with the man. Only her hips continued to move, once, twice, and as she thrust the third time she screamed in a perfect counterfeit of pain. Kelly continued to hold her, continued to stroke, until her body relaxed and she bent over him. Annamaria murmured endearments as she drew him upright, kissing him and clinging with a supple muscularity.

After a moment, the woman stepped back. "*This*," she said with an angry intensity, looking down at her dress. "*This!*" She found the concealed zipper in the side, then pulled the garment off over her head insted of stepping out of it.

Kelly, grinning, took the delicate dress from Annamaria's hand as she turned to fling it into the dark after her panties. "Now, always treat your equipment kindly," the agent said. "Never know when you'll need it again." He leaned into the tomb and hung the dress carefully from the upper edge of the door. He tossed his own suit coat over the panel as well.

Annamaria giggled again and bent to test the ground. "I think," she said as she straightened, "that cracked stone has it over cedar twigs." Wearing only high-heeled shoes and the dappling shadows, her beauty was startling. Kelly had tossed his shirt over his coat. He was leaning against the door jamb, struggling with a shoelace and wondering if there were not somehow a more sensual way to undress. The dark-haired woman stepped close and kissed him. "Well," she said, eyeing the tomb floor speculatively, "not the most romantic setting I could have found, is it? But I doubt somehow that I'll notice that the stones are cold."

"Romance is something you bring with you," Kelly said, "not something that's there." He lifted his right foot out of his shorts and trousers together. Without being fully conscious of the fact, he was using his torso to keep the small sheath knife out of the woman's sight. Her eyes were not on his clothing. Her hand reached out again to stroke his genitals. "And as for the floor," he added in a huskier voice, shifting his weight to clear his left leg in turn, "I know a trick worth two of that. . . ."

Kelly spread a hand under each of Annamaria's buttocks. Their groins pressed together. He was a strong man, proud of his strength, and never more of his mettle than now. Their lips met, damping to a murmur the question in Annamaria's throat. Kelly lifted her easily, her calves wrapping instinctively around his thighs and taking much of the weight off his arms. The lips of her vulva, spread naturally by the motion, slipped easily as he entered her for the first time. Her cry was a muted echo of her previous climax. They rocked together, Kelly's knees flexing and straightening. Annamaria's head was turned to the side, her fingers splayed on her lover's shoulders. She gasped and gasped, and at last cried out in pleasure that wracked a spasm from her vagina and brought Kelly to climax as well.

For him, the experience was a unique combination of delight and a bludgeoning. His blood pressure went momentarily off scale, a vise over his skull and the veins of his throat. Then his whole body relaxed, the muscles of his legs trembling. His arms felt as if they were no longer parts of the body he controlled.

Annamaria felt his sudden weakness. She uncoiled her legs, setting her feet on the ground again. The two of them leaned against the plastered wall, still joined, their arms tightly around one another. The woman's high heels had been pressing against the muscles of Kelly's thighs without either of them being consciously aware of it. Both of them were flushed, able to ignore the increasing cool of the night, but the noises of the outside world began to reenter their awareness. The sirens had stopped. Cars were moving in the street and the lot by the DCM's house. Headlights swept within the compound wall. Horns and curses, mostly in French, marked the labored departures.

"I suppose I've got a handkerchief in my pants pocket," Kelly said after a time.

Annamaria ran a hand over his left hip, feeling the play of muscle beneath the skin. "What do you do tomorrow?" she asked, her head turned aside and her eyes half closed.

"Work," the agent replied. He was interested to note that he had not tensed at the question. "All day. I'll—I'll see you again, if you . . . if you want that. Not tomorrow, and maybe not in Algeria. But again, I hope."

Annamaria turned and nibbled at his left earlobe. "Well, we shouldn't waste what we have, then, should we?" she whispered. She felt him stir within her. "Now, if we're careful, I think we can lie down without—oops!" She giggled again as Kelly slipped out of her. "Well. . . ." She sat back, first on her heels and then on the stone floor of the tomb. She stretched her hands toward Kelly from the darkness. "Come here, darling. I told you the stone wouldn't feel too cold."

Later, the walls were an echo chamber for her happy cries.

XXVI

"Oh, by the way, Kelly," said Commander Posner, "we got a reply from Paris on your cable. The general will look into it."

Kelly straightened from the recorder more abruptly than he should have. The shock of motion was as severe as if he had brought his head up under a cabinet door. It drew a wince and a muffled groan from the agent. "Which cable was that?" he asked, fashioning his pain into a frown of question. Drinks in the bar of the Hotel St. George were just as expensive as Charlie DeVoe had suggested, but Kelly had pretty well decided that he had enough money to last the rest of his life.

Sergeant Rowe rapped on the office door. He unlatched it before either of the others had time to grunt him an invitation. Rowe was keyed up in a cheerful, anticipatory way quite at variance with the other men. The Defense Attache's face was a map charting the alternate disasters of success and failure. As for Kelly—Kelly would have been grim and tense had he not been hung over. To the extent his pain distracted him, he became less grim—and more dangerous. "Say," said the sergeant happily, "what's the Company doing here so early on a weekend? I saw all three of their cars when I parked. Harry got something on too, do you suppose?"

"Maybe they've got a tap into the MFA sewer and they're raking shit," Kelly snapped, more sharply than he had intended to speak to Doug.

"Christ," he added more plaintively, "we've got enough here to hold us, don't we?"

"The cable is the one you requested me to send, you might remember," Commander Posner said with a hint of his own frustration. "The duty officer brought the reply over to me at the Residence last night. I looked around for you, but you seemed already to have disappeared—" Kelly was tense but he did not jerk his eyes toward the Attache— "and I eventually decrypted it myself. There was a traffic accident on the street that took hours to clear up. I decided I might as well use the time by reading the cable, since I couldn't get home and you had left me with the program." Perhaps misinterpreting the agent's stiffness, Posner added, "If that was a mistake, no doubt you can put enough in my next Fitness Report to quite destroy my career, if you so desire."

Kelly shook his head, then winced again. "Oh, Hell, that's fine," he said. "Like you say, you had the program disk. I. . . . Pedler's going to get Hoang out through Frankfurt, then?"

"Apparently there's some problem with that," the Attache said, speaking somewhat more mildly himself. "The Vietnamese—Hoang and his escort —are flying in and out through Paris . . . and of course our relations with the French aren't quite what they are with the Germans, especially on a matter that could be seen as impinging on the Arab world. The Conference being in Algiers, that is. But the General will make an attempt."

Kelly managed to grin, then forgot it and let it fade. "Well, I said I wasn't going to worry about what I couldn't change." He glanced at his watch. It was a good half hour before he wanted to leave. They would be using one of the mission's Plymouth Volare station wagons. It was as conspicuous as an ox in a sheepfold, but it was so obviously the property of a foreign diplomatic mission that the Algerian police were unlikely to try to stop it. If worst came to worst. . . . "Doug, you still have your key to the armory?" Kelly asked in sudden decision. "I need to get in for a moment."

"I—" the sergeant began.

"Sergeant Rowe has already delivered the grenades," said the Defense Attache sharply.

"Yeah, I put them in the trunk of Mustapha's car," Rowe said with a glance between the other two men. "He parks on the grounds when he's on duty. That way there wasn't anything happening except on—" his smile was wry— "diplomatic premises. Just like I can't come and help today."

"Tell the truth," the agent said, facing toward the window but not seeing any of the things toward which his eyes were trained, "I thought I'd borrow one of those Smiths for the morning. Just to have in my trouser pocket." He slapped his pants, shapeless corduroys of a blue as drab as the brown of his jacket. "Not one chance in a thousand it'd make any difference, but . . . but then, it doesn't do any harm sitting there if it's not needed, does it?"

"No," said Commander Posner. "You can't have a pistol."

Kelly turned to the taller man. The first touch of conflict was clearing pathways in his brain that the night before had clogged. "I can be trusted with a revolver, Commander," he said in a voice with a rasp in it. "I've never shot anybody who didn't need shooting."

"You can't be trusted with an *embassy* gun," the Defense Attache said on a rising inflection. He shook his right index and middle fingers in Kelly's direction. The cigarette he held jerked its trail of smoke in nervous angles. "*I* can't tell you you can't go armed," the officer continued. "It's an act of *war*, you know, an act of war—but I can't help that. What I can stop is the notion that you'll be found with a weapon straight out of embassy stores. And if you think you can ruin me for that, then you go ahead and do it. I swear, I'll make the whole business public!"

"For Christ sake!" the agent shouted, "How the hell many Smith and Wessons do you think've been made, anyway? A couple million? Unless the damned USG *gives* the Algerians a list of serial numbers, how do you think it's going to be traced anywhere?"

"I said no and I meant no," the officer repeated flatly. "You're responsible for planning the operation, I'm well aware of that. If your plans require that you be armed from the embassy arsenal, then you should have said so in time to have it cleared by the competent authorities. What you're suggesting is contrary to all the regulations under which those weapons are stored. 'Defensive Purposes Only' does *not* include using them for kidnapping and murder on the streets of a friendly power."

The veins in Kelly's head were pounding him hard enough to make him nauseous. Sergeant Rowe put a hand on the agent's arm and said, "Ah, Tom. . .? I've still got the packing cases from those grenades in my personal car. You've got a minute—come down and give me a hand getting them up the incinerator, will you?"

Kelly blinked. The sergeant's thumb squeezed his biceps. "Yeah, I guess I can handle that," the agent said, surprised at the apparent calm of his own words.

Rowe gestured toward the dingy trench coat Kelly would be carrying to mark him for Professor Vlasov to home on. "Might bring that too, sir; it's still cool."

The commander's face registered only relief when the other men left.

In an undertone as the door latched shut behind them, Kelly asked, "You want to tell me what this is all about now?"

"When we get to the car, sir," the sergeant whispered back.

"Look, you weren't just afraid I was going to deck the sanctimonious son of a bitch, were you?" the agent pressed. "I wouldn't dirty my hands."

"At the car," Rowe repeated.

The sergeant owned a Plymouth sedan. At an appropriate charge, embassy mechanics and stores could be used to repair the personal vehicles of mission members; but that was a benefit only if the personal vehicle were similar to those of the mission fleet. Rowe unlocked his passenger door and the glove compartment while the agent waited with a frown. The white walls of the Chancery and the Villa Inshallah were glowing with the coming dawn. Details were still indistinguishable.

"Here," said the sergeant. He handed Kelly a box about two inches square and an inch deep.

"Jesus," whispered the agent, his hand accepting the unexpected density of what it had received. Across the top of the green paper tape sealing the box was the legend:

25 CARTOUCHES DE 11,43 MM
POUR PISTOLETS

"Didn't want to carry it loaded in the car," Rowe explained as he walked around to the trunk. "And that's all the ammo I've got, I'm afraid."

"Not that I'll really need a gun. . .," the agent said in a low voice, his eyes scanning the barred, black windows of the flanking buildings. "I don't know, I've been antsy, real antsy the past couple days. It's not—"

The trunk lid swung up. The sergeant tugged aside a folded blanket— "Jesus," Kelly repeated. "Doug, I don't want to get you in trouble. Does Posner know you've got this?" The agent ran the fingers of his right hand over the square, gray receiver of the silenced sub-machine gun the soldier had just displayed.

"Oh, no," Rowe said, "but in my last post—Qatar, when they were having the trouble, you know—I told my CO that I was worried about my wife having to be alone in the house. . . ." He smiled reminiscently. "The Colonel was a Marine. It was a different world from working with Commander Posner . . . but I told him what I wanted and he signed the paperwork, 'Required by serviceman on active duty,' you know the drill."

Kelly turned the weapon over with one hand. He was careful not to raise it above level of the trunk well or into a position that could be seen from any of the windows of the flanking buildings. It was as square and functional as a traffic sign; and like the sign, it was stamped in the main out of sheet steel. The bolt enclosed most of the barrel, so that the whole gun was only 10½ inches long when its wire stock was telescoped back against the receiver.

The silencer almost doubled the length.

"Who made the can?" Kelly asked, touching the inch and five-eighths tube that had been Parkerized the same shade of grays as the weapon itself. "It isn't a Sionics."

"Better," said the sergeant, grinning with pride.

The agent turned to look at Rowe directly. "If it's better than Sionics," he said, "it's pretty damn good. Whose product?"

"LARAND," explained the sergeant through his smile. "Instead of baffles, it's filled with thick washers woven from stainless steel wire. Mitch WerBell did a fantastic job with the Sionics, but I don't think there'll ever be a machine that's perfect." His face sobered. "You know, the gun's one of the lot the government tried to confiscate when WerBell left MAC. I couldn't believe the way they've been persecuting somebody who's served this country as long as he has."

The agent tossed his coat into the trunk, then

removed it with the weapon hidden securely in its folds. "It's like Kennedy's ghost-writer said, Doug," Kelly remarked. " 'Ask not what your country can do for you.' Absolutely right. The *real* question is what your country can do *to* you if somebody sitting on his ass in DC decides it's a good idea. Somebody figured WerBell had spent long enough in clandestine ops that they wanted to be real sure he was under control . . . and framing him into a three-year fall in Atlanta seemed about as good a way as the next to take him out of circulation." Kelly patted the sergeant's shoulder with his free hand. "See why I've spent the past five years in Europe? Maybe I'm crazy, but—it still seems like it was a pretty good idea."

Sergeant Rowe thumped the trunk lid down. "Well," he said toward the car, "I just don't like to think the USG treats its people that way, I suppose."

"And your boss doesn't like to think the USG treats friendly countries the way I'm about to treat this one," Kelly agreed. "The world might be a better place if either one of you were right, I suppose." He turned back toward the Chancery door, his arm guiding the sergeant; but before the agent actually stepped forward, he paused and said, "Seriously, Doug—this could be trouble like you wouldn't believe. Maybe—"

"Tom, listen," the sergeant said. He looked older and more certain of himself than Kelly had seen him look before. "The commander says I don't have a black passport so I can't get involved in anything illegal on Algerian soil. Like you say, he's my boss, it's an order. OK. But this is something you think you need and I happen to have. Don't *you* come all chickenshit over me and talk about regs and trouble. It's my decision, I'm an adult, and by God I'm a soldier in the US Army!" The corners of Rowe's eyes crinkled again with humor. "Beside, if anybody but you and me learn about this gun today, you're in a lot worse trouble than I am."

Kelly clapped the younger man on the shoulder again. His headache was almost gone. "That's nothing to the trouble the folks on the muzzle end are in," he said as they walked toward the door. "Now look, you tell the commander my tummy's acting up and I'm going to be in the john for a while. And that's God's truth, because there isn't any fast way to load twenty-five rounds without stripper clips that I don't have."

XXVII

With the stall door bolted and his trousers around his ankles for verisimilitude, Kelly began to load the borrowed weapon. The French ammunition had an abnormal appearance. The bullets and cartridge cases were of the same, unusually pale shade of brass. The agent wondered briefly whether the bullets might not be solid gilding metal as some French rifle loadings had been, instead of having a jacket of the harder metal over a lead core.

Better his mind should wander that way than that it should fill with images of the Ambassador's wife, her nipples shrunken to black spikes, beckoning toward him. . . .

Like the Uzi's, the Ingram's magazine slipped into the hand-grip as if it were an ordinary auto-loading pistol. That put the weight of the ammo in the best location and permitted the off-hand to find the shooting hand easily in the dark to reload. That wouldn't matter now, the Lord knew, since Kelly had less than the full 30-round capacity of *one* magazine. . . . And anyway, this was just a security blanket. An eight-pound, .45 caliber, security blanket. . . .

By the time Kelly had finished loading the magazine, the ball of his thumb hurt from pressing each round down against the follower spring. The magazine lips had rubbed into the skin in parallel grooves. Part of the cost of doing business, like crazy fears and a tendency to duck when a car backfired. . . .

Kelly slipped the magazine into the butt well and rapped it home with the heel of his hand. Only then did he unlock the bolt by twisting the knurled knob on top of the receiver. He did not draw the knob back to cock the weapon. No safety in the world could keep a sub-machine gun's bolt from jouncing forward if the weapon dropped the wrong way. The Ingram had no firing pin, only a raised tit on the bolt face that fired the weapon as soon as the breech slammed closed.

Besides, Kelly was not going to *need* the gun, not really . . . any more than he needed Annamaria Gordon, so supple that her heels could stroke his buttocks in time with his thrusts within her. . . .

His headache was back. Kelly methodically cut the ammunition box into quarter-inch strips, then flushed the cardboard down the toilet. Don't make mistakes just because you feel like death warmed over, no. . . . Adjusting the coat over his right arm to conceal the weapon, Kelly stepped out of the stall just in time to catch the rest room door as someone opened it from the outside.

Sergeant Rowe looked in. His worried expression smoothed as soon as he saw the agent had the gun covered. "Ah, the commander—" he began.

Posner himself looked around the door jamb. "It's getting later, Mr. Kelly," he said, "and I thought I'd see if you were about ready to go." He seemed inclined to be pleasant rather than gloating as a result of what he had been told was the human weakness of Kelly's bowels.

"Ready as I'll ever be, Commander," the agent said hoarsely. "And I hope to God that's ready enough."

XXVIII

"Beep," went the receiver as its loop antenna rotated slowly. "Beep beep beepbeep-beep-bee-beebee—"

Harry Warner turned the volume down. "Well," he said to his two subordinates, "it works when it's attached, too. I'd breathe a lot easier if we could be sure they'd be using the wagon and not one of their personal cars, though."

Syd Westram had a scholarly forehead which he knew was as prelude to his father's baldness by age 40. His expression was always gloomy, and it fit the present circumstances perfectly. "They should have sent us more tracers," he said. He glared at the receiver's directional antenna. "We could have put one on each of their cars."

"*You* could have put one on each of their cars," retorted Don Mayer. "Look, I can understand why we had to wait to the last minute to save the battery life. That *doesn't* mean I wanted to get caught by that Kelly, planting a tracer under the bumper of his car."

"All right, it's an embarrassment," Westram said, "but the worst thing that could come of it is we lost our tracer. After all, what can Kelly do? Complain to the Ambassador?"

The Station Chief glanced down at the red-bordered file on his desk. He had not shown its full contents to either of his subordinates. "Well," he said, "maybe Don's right. This Kelly. . . ."

As Warner's voice trailed off, the muted tone of the tracer slowed also. Westram strode quickly to

the window and peered through the gap in the
blinds. "It's the station wagon," he reported
tensely. "Kelly's in it with Posner driving. I don't
see Rowe, but they're the main ones."

"All right, boys, you'd better get moving yourselves," said Harry Warner. "I'll give you
directions, and the second channel of these ought
to buzz when you get within fifty feet or so of the
tracer." He slid the two walkie-talkies an inch
closer to the edge of his desk to call attention to
them. "Remember, keep these plugged into the
chargers except when you're using them—and for
God's sake, don't walk off and leave them in your
cars. They're fifteen hundred bucks apiece. It'll
come out of your next check if you lose one, I
swear."

The two operatives picked up the hand units
with the care which the threat demanded. "Right,"
Mayer said slowly. "Well, I hope you can vector us
onto them with the direction finder. I never
trained to follow people in a car."

The Station Chief nodded. "This will work," he
said, "Your own receivers are just for searching
an area if they park. Call me when you've got their
car in sight."

As the others started to walk out to their vehicles,
Warner added, "Oh, boys?" Mayer and Westram
turned. "This one *is* going to work," their superior
said. "The first word to Langley about what those
uniformed twits are up to *is* going to come from
this station. Understood?"

Both men nodded. As they walked through the
door, Mayer began to whistle under his breath.
The tune was the first few bars of the 'Dead
March' from 'Saul.'

XXIX

"It is very good of you to permit us," the little Vietnamese colonel was saying in his accented English.

"We are always ready to join our socialist brothers," said Colonel Korchenko with only a perfunctory smile. "Professor Vlasov wished to spend some more time with your Doctor Tanh." And besides, Korchenko had come with instructions from Moscow to help with security arrangements for the Vietnamese physicist. It was desirable to keep up the fiction that the nuclear devices to be emplaced on the Chinese-Vietnamese border were of indigenous Vietnamese manufacture. A Vietnam without a single known nuclear physicist would embarrass the plan.

The tall KGB colonel glanced toward the door of the Ambassador's residence. The physicists should already have come out by now. The circular drive was crowded with waiting men and cars. One sedan would be filled with KGB personnel. Two more would transport a mix of lower-ranking scientists and more security men. The fourth car was the Ambassador's own armored limousine. In it would ride Professor Vlasov, under the care of Korchenko and the colonel's personal aide and driver.

And with them, at Vlasov's insistence and Moscow's prodding, would be Hoang Tanh and this absurd little colonel who stank of fish sauce.

Even Nguyen had to bend to see into the low-slung Citröen. Schwartz and Babroi were seated in the front bucket seats. They stared back without interest. "A very beautiful car," Nguyen said appreciatively. "Our Ambassador tells me he is trying to get a new car for the mission here, but Hanoi will not approve it."

Korchenko smiled patronizingly. "Yes, well," he said. "Foreign missions always pretend they need more glitter to impress their opposite numbers." Which, of course, explained the limousine, even though Ambassador Miuseck was not the head of the Russian mission to Algeria. In normal fashion, the chief of the KGB Residency—in this case Kalugin, the Consul—had such real authority as Moscow chose to delegate. The Ambassador was still permitted to glitter, however; and the car was useful for functions like this one, squiring around dignitaries from home.

And what the *fuck* were the scientists still doing inside? Having a circle jerk?

"You have two radios?" asked Nguyen, still bent to study the interior of the Citröen. The big pistol made the tail of the Vietnamese officer's coat jut out absurdly.

Colonel Korchenko glanced down. "Oh, the large one's for communication with the other cars and the base unit here," he said. "That other thing's a toy of Babroi's own—he picked it up in Tokyo last year. It's a—" Korchenko paused to get the technical term correct— "a programmable synthesized scanner. Babroi likes to listen in on local radio traffic wherever we go. He says it keeps him alert, so that he never goes on the air himself unless the signal will be scrambled."

Nguyen nodded in what the KGB man thought was a counterfeit of understanding. The Vietnamese did not say what he was thinking. His eyes compared the flat, off-the-shelf Japanese scanner with the bulky tube-driven transceiver which was presumably the height of indigenous Russian manufacture. "Yes, very interesting," Nguyen said as he straightened up.

The door of the building opened. First voices, then the clot of scientists themselves spilled out. Vlasov and Hoang walked in the middle of the group. They were talking in French. All the security personnel, even Colonel Korchenko, struck a brace.

Damned well about time, the KGB officer thought. The sooner this was over, the sooner he could get back and explore just what the First Secretary's wife had meant by her invitation. With any kind of luck, this was going to be an interesting day.

XXX

The sun over the Church of the Holy Cross was in Kelly's eyes every time he glanced across the boulevard. It bothered him that he did look around, toward the Institute and the ambush site. It was a sign to himself of his own nervousness.

It was not, at least, out of his assumed character. Kelly was portraying a friend of the owner of a small epicerie. He lounged against the glass case of crackers and Camembert, sunglasses and the rack of fly-specked post cards. The real owner was at a wedding in Oran. He was sympathetic to the cause, but his shop would still be there after the security forces had time to catch their breath and examine what had happened. The human participants in the operation, with luck, would all be gone. The owner's cover story would simply be that he and all his household had closed the shop to attend a family wedding 400 kilometers away. The owner would have no idea of who might have broken in during his absence.

Taking the owner's place behind the counter was Ramdan, the heavy-set proprietor of the brassware shop. Though middle-aged, the Algerian was as wired as Kelly had ever seen an 18-year old rifleman on his first insertion. And, speaking of rifles, the agent had cringed to see Ramdan stuffing his Mauser into the cabinet below the display case. Although—if the police were going to search the place, that was not the only gun there were likely to find in the Casbah.

Kelly glanced at his own trench coat, lying

folded atop the case. No, not the only gun.

A woman in a veil and black wrapper stepped in to buy a handful of hard candies for the three children she had in tow. The agent tried to talk to the eldest child, a boy of eight or so. His French pleasantries got first a blank stare, then a quick and meaningless rattle of Arabic or Kabyle. The mother herself watched for a moment as Ramdan tried to find, then weigh out, 'his' wares. Suddenly the mother snapped an order and hustled out of the shop gripping the two younger children by their hands. The eldest continued for a moment to stare at Kelly. The woman turned and shouted at him with a touch of hysteria in her voice. All four of them disappeared down the mouth of a nearby alley into the heart of the Casbah.

Christ on a crutch. . . . But it was already very close to time.

Two BMW motorcycles led the motorcade up the Boulevard Abderrazak. They had their sirens wound out and their blue turn signals flashing alternately. The black Citröen DS 23 that followed mounted a blue light on the dashboard. Its headlights pulsed nervously, like the heart rhythm of a man on the point of death.

Below the counter, Ramdan's handie-talkie babbled in excited Kabyle.

"For *Christ's* sake!" Kelly snarled at the older man. "Turn that thing off till I tell you to transmit!" He should have disabled the sending keys of the other units before he turned them over to the Kabyles, the agent thought angrily. Their only proper purpose on this operation was to permit Kelly to order the other personnel into action. No one but Ramdan should have been talking, and Ramdan only at Kelly's direct order.

The two bikes swung expertly at the guidance of their leather-clad National Police drivers. They halted on either side of the Institute's main entrance, facing back toward the street with their

engines throttled to a fast idle. The pair of military
guards at the door braced to attention. They wore
dress uniforms finished off by pistols in white-
leather holsters. The soldiers in the tower above
wore their dress uniforms also. Kelly had little
doubt, however, that their AKM rifles would
function just as well as if they were used by men in
battle dress. The Algerians held their rifles slung
from their right shoulders with the muzzles forward and their right hands resting on the hand-
grips.

"Get down behind the counter where nobody
can see you with the radio," the agent ordered
Ramdan. Without waiting to see if he had been
obeyed, Kelly draped his white coat carefully over
his right arm and strolled back to the edge of
the sidewalk in front of the shop. He resisted the
impulse to grip the Ingram so tightly that his hand
would cramp.

The entrance of the Institute was at one point of
an extremely complex intersection. Five vehicular
streets from the south met there, while the whole
warren of the Casbah lay to the north. With the
truck jamming the intersection proper, though,
and the fork of the Victoire and the Avenue Taleb
Mohammed blasted where they met the Boulevard
Abderrazak—almost on top of National Police
Headquarters—nothing would be driving through
any time soon. For now, though. . . .

The leading Citröen swung halfway across the
boulevard, just beyond the entrance. Its ready
position would aid the Kabyles immeasurably
when the burning truck careened down the hill
and into the intersection. Three men, then a
fourth, got out of the sedan, leaving the driver
behind the wheel. The three doors were open. The
security men were not carrying long-arms, but
Kelly did not need X-ray vision to guess what was
racked within the car.

The Algerians wore dark suits which tweaked an

uncomfortable memory . . . but the car that had been—following him?—had not been a Citröen, whatever it was. None of these men looked anything like the three who had entered the room at the Aurassi.

The second car was a Mercedes limo. It had green diplomatic plates, though Kelly had not been in country long enough to recognize the particular mission. Three men in London-tailored suits and Arab burnooses got out of the back. As they walked toward the door of the Institute, the steel leaves opened inward. A pair of suited Algerians stepped out to bow in greeting. The Mercedes pulled carefully around the security car and turned up the Ramp des Zoaves, past the south front of the building.

The next car was not an old Fiat but rather a Volga, Russian-made and almost certainly Russian-occupied at the moment. The American tensed. He spread a meaningless smile across his whisker-stubbled face. His peripheral vision showed him that there were a number of other bystanders watching events. The escort had cut its sirens, but the procession of expensive cars was still more interesting than most of Algier's drab scenery. Despite the company, however, Kelly felt as obtrusive as a prisoner facing the sentencing judge.

Three men got out of the Volga. All of them were obviously low-ranking security men from their bulk and East-Bloc clothing. Rank hath the privilege of a decent tailor. . . . But that meant the next car, another Citröen limo, this one with AMB—Ambassador—on the plate was—

"Roll the truck!" Kelly shouted back over his shoulder. "*Just* the truck!"

The Volga sedan showed an inclination to hold its position at the intersection. One of the Algerian security men walked over to it and began talking and gesturing to the driver. The Russian car moved off slowly in the wake of the Mercedes.

The Citröen behind it pulled up under the watchful eyes of the Algerians and the three Russians who had dismounted from the Volga. The long back doors opened. From the right-side jump seat a—for God's sake, a *Vietnamese* got out. Another tall European got out a moment later, also from the right side, toward the Institute. He wore an excellent suit but he was too young to be Vlasov. And from the left door, staring at Kelly even before he was out of the car, climbed another Vietnamese. Their eyes met at twenty yards distance. Kelly remembered in a series of flashes strobing between visions of Anna displaying her body that he had told Hoang that his defection would take place in Frankfurt. Since the physicist knew that his flight was through Paris, he had known that he was being lied to.

The last man out of the car was Professor Vlasov. The cuff of his right sleeve was pinned against his shoulder. He followed Hoang through the left door, putting the car between himself and his escort.

"Hit it!" Kelly snapped, and the truck, howling down the Rue Debbih Cherif, unexpectedly exploded just as it came in view.

The cab of the big flat-bed dissolved in a white flash so bright that the sunlight a millisecond later seemed dim. The explosion was oddly muffled. It sounded more as if a safe had fallen onto concrete than the crackling propagation wave of high explosive in open air. Perhaps because the light was so intense, the relative silence did not seem out of place. Sensory cross-over was telling the brain that the ears as well as the eyes had been numbed. Somebody had put an anti-tank rocket into the truck, Kelly's instincts told him. The hood and even the engine block were gone, blasted away, and the shredded front tires were letting the vehicle slow to a halt well short of where it was supposed to stop.

Because the noise was that of metal shrieking and sparking over concrete, the security personnel reacted a hair less quickly than they might have done for a true explosion. Hoang darted toward Kelly and the épicerie behind him. His escort's smile was only beginning to slip as the Vietnamese glanced across the car to the physicist. Then both Vietnamese, like Kelly and everyone else within a block, were dumped to the ground by the explosion beneath the intersection to the north.

Part of what went flying skyward was a car, but it was omelette time and too bad about the other poor bastards who found themselves eggs. Kelly got to his feet. His left palm was bleeding from its scrape along the sidewalk as he fell. He racked back the bolt of the Ingram without noticing the pain.

Instead of a twenty-pound charge, the Kabyles must have filled the sewer pipe with explosives. Hoang Tanh was on his feet and running again. Vlasov himself still lay groggy on the pavement. A pair of the Russians from the Volga were up and staggering toward their charge. The Vietnamese security man vaulted the hood of the Citröen. He was shouting something inaudible in the aftermath of the huge explosion. A ragged disk of asphaltic concrete, six inches thick and the size of a man-hole cover, spun out of the sky. It hopped once on the roadway and took the Viet's legs from under him as neatly as ever a bowler made a spare.

Kabyles were hurling smoke grenades as directed, the streamers gushing into parti-colored floods as the compound burned. It was a scene not of Carnival but of Hell. Against specific orders, somebody opened up from the Casbah with an automatic rifle. The muzzle blasts could scarcely be heard through the ringing of the agent's ears, but plaster and powdered stone spurted from the upper facade of the tower. The guards there went down, one of them spinning under the impact of a bullet.

Kelly was standing as upright as a reviewing officer. Both of his hands were now hidden by the folded coat he held as a beacon. Vlasov stood up. The two Russians grabbed him and threw him back for safety. They knelt above the physicist, each with one hand on their charge's back to keep him down. Their other hands held pistols muzzle-high as they looked for targets through the wisps of smoke already swirling. Kelly cursed and killed both security men with short bursts from the Ingram.

Compactness is fine for something you have to carry, but for use it would have been nice to have a proper stock . . . or at least to have had time to extend the latch-and-wire contraption with which the sub-machine gun was fitted. Christ, it would have been nice to have a rifle and an explosives expert who would not have leveled a square block when his task was to cut a street. But you use what you got. Sights at eye level, bloody left hand gripping the suppressor tube, Kelly aimed to the left of one Russian and let recoil walk the second and third rounds into the man's chest.

As his partner collapsed, the remaining security man screamed and fired into the rooftops from which he thought the shots were coming. This one was trickier, because the target lay squarely over the physicist's body. The agent held higher than he should have, but one of the gleaming bullets caught the Russian at the hairline and dropped him dead as Trotsky. The two rounds that missed spalled plate-sized flakes of paint from the doors of the ambassadorial limo. They did not penetrate the armor beneath.

Hoang Tanh snatched at Kelly's left arm, shouting for help. He was tall for a Vietnamese, scarcely less than Kelly's own 5'9''. The physicist was a rotund man whose pleasant face was now distorted by tension and the need to be heard over gunfire.

"Get in the goddam shop!" Kelly shouted, turning the Vietnamese and shoving him toward the épicerie with the full strength of his left arm. Hoang staggered forward and almost collided with Ramdan. The Kabyle was shuffling out onto the sidewalk with his rifle at high port. "Put that away!" the American shrieked at him, but the Kabyle leveled his weapon and slammed a shot at something across the street.

By now the smoke was as thick as pond water, translucent or less beyond arm's-length. The lighter grit and dust drifting down from the explosion site added its own camouflage and the tang of burning tar. Kelly ran forward, waving the coat like a flag in his left hand. Blended red and purple smoke roiled about the sweeping fabric. A bullet whanged off the pavement near his feet. Momentarily it was a spark, incandescent with the energy released on impact. The American had no notion of whether it was a stray round or one deliberately aimed at him.

He tripped over Vlasov. The Russian scientist had crawled free of the pair of bodies that had pinioned him and was closer than Kelly had expected. The agent sprawled. A burst of automatic fire laced across the boulevard close to where Kelly's torso had been a moment before. The shock waves of the bullets spun curls of smoke as they cracked past.

Kelly could be sure the man he now held was Vlasov because of the pinned-up sleeve. "Come on, Professor," he shouted in Russian, "we have to run!" He waved the raincoat, his identity signal, then tossed it onto the street to free his hand.

Vlasov did not get up. He seemed to be staring through the smoke at the suppressed Ingram. Kelly remembered too late that the defector was

nuts—and what he was nuts about. The Lord
knew, the gun and can did look more like something whipped up for a sci-fi film than the piece of
functional, real-world ordnance that they were.
Screw that, there was no time. "Go!" Kelly
shouted. "I'm your contact!" He tried to tug the
Professor upright by a handful of shirt front.

The black snout of a car thrust toward them
through the man-made fog. Kelly dropped the
scientist and hosed a burst through the windshield, just above the hood line. The car accelerated as the driver's muscles spasmed. The
vehicle missed Vlasov by inches, missed Kelly
only because he leaped sideways. It was the
security vehicle that had led the procession. It
must have doubled back into the chaos for reasons
the driver, at least, would never be able to explain.

Even in normal surroundings the suppressed
weapon would have made less noise than a bottle
being kicked along a hallway. Under the present
circumstances, it was effectively silent. The bolt, a
tool-steel clapper ringing back and forth against
the breech, was overwhelmed by the ringing of the
explosion in everyone's ears. But the empty
cartridge cases dancing from the ejection port
were the same as those of a more standard sub-
machine gun. Unexpectedly reassured, the
Russian defector jumped to his feet as the car
rolled past. "Quickly, then," he said, his lips close
to Kelly's ear to be heard. "For they are here, I
have seen them."

There is no good way to cross a flat area raked
from all sides and elevations. Running upright
made as much sense as anything else. While
Vlasov was evidently crazy, Kelly found no reason
to question the Russian's courage. The older man
sprinted beside the agent toward what Kelly
hoped was the doorway of the épicerie. The smoke
swirled. Ramdan faced them over the sights of his
old Mauser. Kelly struck the weapon away and

screamed in useless Italian, "Back, for God's sake, play your war out later!"

Flames were beginning to envelope the security car wrecked to the north. The draft caused a freak of the breeze to tug clear a lane in the smoke boiling across the boulevard. "There!" cried the Kabyle. He made a quarter-turn and fired without seating the rifle against his shoulder. He spun again as return fire gouged his thigh.

Two uniformed soldiers stood twenty feet away with pistols and a clear field of fire. Standard service handguns are man-killingly accurate at fifty yards or more, but accuracy in combat is something more than an exercise in paper-punching. Kelly had time to turn and sweep a burst across both Algerians. One of them was still trying to fire with his slide locked back on an empty magazine. They were brave men, but soldiering was a bad business for people who make mistakes . . . and they were not the first to make the mistake of shooting at Tom Kelly and missing.

"Now *go!*" the agent shouted again at his charges. He planted his left hand in Vlasov's back and the Ingram's receiver in Ramdan's—the *idiot!* The Kabyle had dropped his rifle and was clutching his right thigh with both hands, but he staggered forward at Kelly's push. Vlasov followed him into the épicerie.

"Take him out the back," the American shouted as he tossed the sub-machine gun to the countertop and turned. An accordian-pleated metal screen could close the front of the shop when it was unoccupied. Kelly unlatched the screen and slammed it down. He shouted curses in several languages when one side caught momentarily in its track. The only light within was the back door opening on another unlighted room. That was a gray blur to the agent's day-adapted eyes. The Ingram met his groping hand—and so did the CS grenade which he had snuggled into a corner behind the counter.

Kelly pulled the pin with his right thumb and stumbled through the back door. He tossed the grenade into the shop as he closed the door behind him. It was a piss-poor thing to do to a supporter's property, but there were other people out there catching bullets. It had to be done. The Casbah was a maze. Closing the entrance to the track the fugitives were taking would, with luck, delay pursuit until there was no longer a trail to follow.

With luck.

XXXI

The back room was furnished as living quarters. Vlasov waited uncertainly at the door in the far end. Ramdan was doubled up on the rug, moaning and clutching again at his wounded thigh. "Come on, Professor," Kelly said in Russian, opening the second door for the defector.

Beyond was an alley less than a meter wide— Alexandria Street, if you wanted to believe a French map-maker to whom there was no such thing as *terra incognita*, even if the cognition were in the map-maker's office alone. A Kabyle with a Kalashnikov half-hidden in the folds of his robe beckoned them urgently from the top of a pole-supported staircase a few meters away. Kelly gestured Vlasov toward the stairs, then called over his shoulder in French, "If you don't roust, you'll be there when they come looking—that'll hurt worse'n now, believe me."

No one ran toward them down the alley from the killing ground on the Boulevard de la Victoire. Vlasov mounted the steep, unrailed stairs with as much agility as could be expected of a scientist in his mid-60s.

Kelly risked a glance down at the Ingram. His left palm was throbbing and beginning to swell. Long bursts had heated the suppressor tube enough to make the air above it dance. It had seared the abraded flesh of the hand that gripped it. Like the gas-filled épicerie, that came with the turf. Kelly tried to extend the sub-machine gun's stock, but he found that he could not figure how to

233

lock the folding butt-plate into position in the instants he was willing to spare. It was more important to spot the people coming down the alley whom he might have to kill.

Vlasov squeezed by the guard at the narrow landing. The American pounded up the stairs himself. The guard ducked inside behind Kelly and slammed the blue-painted door panel.

An entire family waited inside the room. There was a grandfather, parents, and four wide-eyed children spaced from six to the infant in the woman's arms. The rugs that provided bedding were rolled up against the wall. A table holding a plastic bucket of water completed the furnishings. The family might be related to someone taking an active part in the operation . . . or it might not. No matter. In all likelihood, the father had been a babe in arms when similar scenes were played out in the struggle against the French; and his father had not talked, either.

At the end of the room, where a hanging blanket filled the place of a door, stood Hoang Tanh. "You did not tell us about him," said the rifleman accusingly to Kelly.

The agent nodded curtly. "Let's go," he said. No point in trying to explain. The Kabyle, after all, did not have the real problem of trying to get the stupid son of a bitch out of the country.

It would have been faster to run to the Rue Amar Ali down the Rue Porte Neuve. The latter was one of the few pedestrian ways in the Casbah that deserved the name of street. It would be faster for the security forces too, if they blew their way past the gunmen who were supposed to lie in ambush at its head. To the Kabyles, a room to room, central courtyard to stairs route had the advantage of involving large numbers of people who therefore had excellent reason to fear the police and army. In for a penny, in for a pound. . . . Kelly himself had spent enough time in another

kind of jungle to have learned that you did not
follow established trails if you wanted to go back
to the World under your own power. It did not
occur to him to question the technique as the
Kabyles applied it.

They reached the Amar Ali through a hammam,
a Turkish bath, which they had entered by a trap
door from the cellar where the oven was. In the
cellar, dampness was a thing you could touch.
Kelly had shrugged his jacket off. He carried it
slung over the Ingram as he had the trench coat
when the morning began. With his dark com-
plexion and his cheap, styleless clothing, the
American agent was not worth a second glance
from the bath attendants and their early
customers.

The two defectors were another matter. Hoang
had generalized Oriental features. There must
have been Chinese or even Korean in the
physicist's ancestry. Conceivably, he might have
gone unremarked in the dim light. Professor
Vlasov, on the other hand, stood out like a preg-
nant bride. He was six-foot three, and his fore-
bears had certainly included many a blond 'Rus'
as the natives called the Viking 'rowers' who had
founded Novgorod and the Grand Duchy of Kiev
before the Mongols swept across the Siberian
plains. But no one looked at Vlasov, either, proof
that the would-be rebels had done their home-
work—even if their aggressiveness had put Kelly
and the operation in jeopardy.

At the entrance of the hammam, the plain,
cream tile of the hallway gave way to a mosaic of
intricate knots on a golden background. Kelly
blinked at the sunlight of the open street beyond.
Their original guide had been replaced by an older
man whose right hand never left the side pocket of
his coat. "Quickly, get out," he hissed to Kelly. The
agent still hesitated. "This was all our arrangement."

The Volare wagon waited across the street. Commander Posner was drumming on the steering wheel, his eyes trying to look in all directions. The Attache's nerves were screwed as tight as the breech of a cannon. Ordinary traffic noises had given way to sirens from all directions. In the open air again, the thump of gunfire could be heard.

The car parked three spaces behind the Volare was a Volkswagen Beetle. Presumably the Defense Attache had not noticed it pulling in. The driver was Mayer, one of the CIA personnel Kelly had met in the snack bar.

"I'll go first," Kelly said in French. His right arm crawled with a sweaty desire to put a burst through the Beetle's door. If those bastards thought they were going to get in his way, they'd better be ready to die. . . .

He started across the street with the quick, nervous stride of a man dodging traffic on any busy artery. Kelly's eyes darted around him at street level and above, trying to anticipate the shot that would pay him back for the many mistakes of others on which he had capitalized. There was no shot, though a van missed him by less than the small part of his mind devoted to traffic had calculated. The Company man saw Kelly before Commander Posner did. His eyes widened and he raised a walkie-talkie enough for Kelly to see it.

"Start the goddam engine!" Kelly shouted to Posner through the open window. His anger was flashing out at the closest victim, not the cause. Face black as thunder, the agent waved curtly across to the hammam entrance.

It said something about the sparseness of CIA assets in Algiers that Warner had to use Amcit officers for a surveillance operation. It said something about how badly Langley wanted to know what the DIA was up to that they had gone ahead with the surveillance regardless.

Vlasov, his white hair flashing like a marker

pennant, stepped into the street. He was more cautious than even Kelly had been. The American agent still stood on the traffic side. His thigh was trembling as the door transmitted the vibration of the engine's initial fast idle. Posner was saying something, but the words made no impression on the mirror surface of Kelly's mind. Something was about—

Hoang ran past the tall Russian scientist. His body, ten feet or less from Kelly, disintegrated in a white flash like the one that had vaporized most of the truck cab.

The vehicle from which the rocket propelled grenade must have come was a black sedan a hundred yards away. It was just turning left out of the Boulevard Ourida-Meddad, the shortest way from the Institute by car. That was goddam good shooting, even with the scope sights fitted to the RPG-7, Kelly thought as he blew out the sedan's side windows with the last four rounds in the Ingram.

"Get over!" the agent screamed to Posner. He tossed the empty gun through the window with little concern for where the Attache's head might be at the moment. With his freed right hand, Kelly jerked open the driver's door. A weary Simca screeched to a stop in the traffic lane. Its driver looked as horrified as Mayer. The CIA officer was gaping through his windshield at a scene right out of *The Battle of Algiers*.

The Russian had been thrown sideways by the blast. He lurched upright under the tug of Kelly's left hand. On the pavement beneath Vlasov lay a shoe, sock, and probably a foot from the ankle down. The American had seen its like before, when a dink had been almost on top of a Claymore mine as it went off. Hoang had made his own choice, and it appeared to have been a very goddam bad one for him. The chance of his location, however, had saved Professor Vlasov from taking the grenade himself.

The Defense Attache had not yet grasped that Kelly was taking over the driving. When the operation had been planned, they had decided that Posner, who knew the city, would drive. Too much had hit the fan in the past few minutes for Kelly now to trust the naval man's reflexes to get them out of what might be coming next. The agent threw the Attache aside with as little ceremony as he bundled the Russian in after him. That put the defector between the two Americans with no chance of changing his mind and leaping out of the car again.

The driver of the Simca had gotten out of the car. She was staring at the disembodied foot on the pavement. The knuckles of both her hands were pressed against her mouth. Welcome to the world of international diplomacy, Kelly thought as he jerked the wheel left. He took the Volare into the street with as much verve as its slant-six engine could muster.

"We'll go straight up along the coast road," Kelly said, remembering to speak in French so that both his companions could understand. He cut right at the first intersection, feeling his guts tense as he waited for a trio of white-robed widows to cross in front of him. Things were not quite bad enough that Kelly was going to kill old ladies to save a few seconds. Not quite.

"They have decided to kill me," said Professor Vlasov in a voice that belied the apparent calm of his face. "I thought they would, if I tried to reach the West."

"Why did you turn, then?" Commander Posner demanded in peevish English. He had just stuffed the sub-machine gun gingerly under the seat. "We could have gone straight and turned at the Abdel Kader Lyceum."

The agent heard brakes and felt metal jolt as he pulled left across traffic onto the Rue Bougrina. A

Peugeot's driver had not been alert enough when the relatively huge American car took his place in what was already a solid line of traffic. The Peugeot's bumper dragged off with a clang on the Volare's right rear fender. The Defense Attache stared open-mouthed at Kelly. His cigarette, still unlighted, stuttered like a telegraph key between his fingers.

Kelly ignored the sounds. He said, "Because traffic on the Abderrazak'd be blocked by that procession even without that goddam bomb cratering the road four blocks south. God willing, we can get through by the Lyceé if we're on the north side of the square."

"My hope was," the Russian said in the same taut voice as before, "that they would be taken off guard. Before, they spared me because I was harmless with no one to build my devices. Killing me would prove that I was right."

He raised his head. "Now that I have started," he said, "I must succeed. If they catch us, we have no hope and the world has no hope."

XXXII

The nearby shooting had stopped. Most of the smoke particles had settled to paint the street like the wing of a giant butterfly. The screaming still continued.

Someone was plucking at Korchenko with maddening persistence. The colonel rushed back to awareness with a flush that made his whole skin prickle inside. Babroi had an arm under Korchenko's shoulders and was trying to feed him a swig of vodka. The colonel did not need either the help or the liquor. He needed full consciousness—that was returning—and better luck than seemed probable.

"Get away, dammit," Korchenko muttered to his aide. He rolled to all fours and stood. Babroi hovered beside his chief. He had dropped his flask uncapped into his pocket to free both hands in case the colonel fell. Only Schwartz' own door was still closed on the limousine. The driver was hunched over the wheel, as rigid as a gargoyle. Schwartz was the best driver Korchenko had ever met, skillful and utterly fearless while performing his functions. When he was faced with any other sort of danger, however, he froze—until someone ordered him to drive.

The back compartment of the Citröen was empty. Through its open doors Korchenko could see bodies sprawled on the pavement. The Professor's body was not among them.

The other shoe dropped. "The bastard is defecting!" Korchenko shouted. He slammed his hand down on the limousine's roof.

The Vietnamese security man raised himself by his grip on the car's bumper. His face was as blank as a pelt stretched to dry. The pain within illuminated the skin. "If you please, sir," he said in a calm voice, "where is Doctor Hoang?"

"Shut the Hell up, I'm busy!" Korchenko snapped. He forgot to use English, but the tone translated well enough. The KGB colonel ducked to use the microphone. The motion made him dizzy for a moment. Angrily, Korchenko blipped the mike button three times for attention. The nervous babble on the control channel ceased.

Car One was the Citröen, Car Two the Volga which had dropped off the KGB team in front of them. Three and Four were the Volgas further back in the procession. "This is Korchenko," the colonel snarled into his microphone. "Everybody shut their fucking mouth. Car Two, report your location."

Nothing. "Car Two, come in or I'll—" Korchenko shouted.

Beside him, Babroi clucked in the back of his throat and said, "Colonel, their radio wasn't working in the compound when we tested it."

Korchenko licked the edges of his front teeth. The sole survivor of the team from Car Two was wandering dazedly down the street with his pistol in his hand. The man's eyes appeared fixed on the bodies of the men who had accompanied him moments before. "Right," said the colonel. Then he keyed the mike and went on, "Car Three, report your location."

"We're not up to the National Police barracks yet and everything's stopped," the radio responded. The speaker's calm was surprising until Korchenko remembered the situation. No one more than a block from the explosion and firefight knew more than that *something* had happened. "What's going on?" Car Three continued. "The police are all running out and it sounded like there were shots?"

"Shut up," the colonel said. The Vietnamese officer had groped his way around the hood of the car. He stood, listening intently as if he understood the Russian being spoken. "Can you turn—" Korchenko began to the microphone.

Babroi's scanner blurted unexpectedly in English, "Harry! Good God! He's got a machine gun! They're *killing* people here!"

Korchenko stopped speaking with his mouth open. The two-way set asked, "Say again?" in Russian. "I didn't copy that."

"Shut up," the colonel screamed into his microphone.

The scanner picked up a different voice saying, "Don, cool *down*. Who's shooting? Are you safe?"

"It's Kelly," responded the first voice in a less shrill tone. "He's got somebody with him in the station wagon besides Posner. I'm all right, I'm . . . they're driving off east on the Rue Amar Ali and I'm staying here. He's shooting a machine gun. Harry, there was a bomb and somebody. . . ."

"Tell the other cars to turn around. One of them goes up the Arbadji Abderrahman, the other Rue Bab el Oued," said Nguyen. Because he spoke in English like the voices on the scanner, Korchenko listened instead of shouting him to silence reflexively. "Look for an American car, there can't be any other here."

The scanner was moaning in the first voice, "They blew somebody *apart*, Harry. There's a *foot* here in the street."

Korchenko relayed Nguyen's suggestions— orders, from the tone!—in quick Russian. The KGB officer had not memorized the street layout of Algiers, and for all he knew there was no map of the city in the car—even if he had time to check it out. But if this fish-eating nigger was wrong, the colonel would personally see to it that he never saw home again.

The trunk lid closed solidly. Babroi strode around to the door again. He was holding out to his superior one of the automatic rifles he had gotten from the trunk. At the head of the street, an armored personnel carrier nosed around the truck still burning in the intersection. There had been no shooting for several minutes. Now some unseen marksman down the Rue Porte Neuve spanged a round off the APC's glacis plate. The vehicle halted with its front wheels up on the curb. The heavy machine gun in the turret blasted a response to the rifle fire. The whole steel-clad mass of the APC rocked with the recoil of the automatic weapon.

Korchenko cursed. "We've got to get past them," he said. He waved forward as he slid into the seat beside the driver. His rifle was impossibly awkward in the space cramped by the floor shift and the tube-driven radio. The colonel dropped the weapon over the seat as Babroi got into the back.

The rear doors slammed, one and then the other. Korchenko drew the pistol from his shoulder holster. "Sir, we'll try," Schwartz said. He put the Citröen in gear.

A second APC from the Mobile Guard barracks south on the Avenue Mohamed pulled up beside the first. Both began ripping long bursts down the pedestrian way. White smoke from their guns drifted to mix with black curls from the burning truck.

Instead of trying to force his way through the firefight, Schwartz cramped the wheel hard and took the limousine up the narrow alley between the Institute and the Church of the Holy Cross. A squad of Algerian troops was coming the other way. The KGB driver went through them. He

slowed just enough that the car's glass leading
edge did not shatter as it brushed a pair of soldiers
out of the way.

"Call your base," directed an unexpected voice.
"Have them alert all other available cars."

Colonel Korchenko jerked his head around. His
throat was caught between a curse and inarticu-
late rage. The Vietnamese officer was poised
behind him in the back seat, holding the rifle
Korchenko had tossed there.

But before the colonel's anger could find words,
the speaker of the two-way radio bleated, "We see
them! We've got them for sure!"

XXXIII

Islam's day ends at sundown Friday. The downtown traffic was therefore roughly what was to be expected in an American city on Saturday morning. Many of the cars were filled with shoppers and families headed out of town for the weekend. The paved square surrounding the tawny, Romanesque pile of the Ketchouan Mosque was thick with pedestrians, many of them foreigners. Kelly was momentarily more concerned with the pedestrians than with vehicles, so only the squeal of tires warned him that a Volga sedan on an intercepting course from the Rue Bab el Oued was trying to ram them.

With one hand, Kelly slammed the gear selector into low, cursing the car for having a slush box instead of a standard transmission. His left hand was spinning the wheel to the right. The agent did not brake. His tires had limited traction. At this point, he needed cornering force a lot worse than he did braking. Broadsiding around an acute corner scrubbed off enough speed anyway.

They might not have made it, but the lighter Russian vehicle brushed the rear of the Volare. It hit with enough force to crumple sheet metal and keep the back end of the station wagon from breaking away as it had started to do. Vlasov jolted forward. Posner's head rapped against the side window. The man in the back seat of the Volga was jolted badly enough that only Kelly realized that the Plymouth was being fired at.

The agent kept his foot in it, winding the slug-

gish engine to five grand in low before he let it
shift. They were barrelling up the center of the
Rue Aboulker, past the only Protestant church in
downtown Algiers. Twice Kelly used the Volare's
bulk to muscle a lighter car into the curb. As they
blasted through the Place Touri, between the
National Theatre and the Square Port Said, a city
bus took their right headlight out in a glancing
blow.

Kelly was pretty sure that the Volga just behind
them now was not the car they had bumped. It
would have taken longer than that to get the first
car backed off the sidewalk into which it had spun
with the impact. But that meant that there were at
least two cars in immediate pursuit, the reasons
did not matter now, and Kelly had to shake them
goddam fast or it was a question only of who
tortured him to death. The KGB might hand him
over to the National Police, or they might keep
him and do the job themselves.

"Posner," the agent said, "you've got *some*
weapons here, right?" He did not look away from
the road.

The Defense Attaché's forehead was swelling
under the pressure cut it had taken when he
bounced against the window. "Of course I don't,
you idiot," he said, squinting as he tried to squeeze
the pain away with his palm. "What in *God's* name
is going on?"

"The aliens are going to kill me," Professor
Vlasov muttered. It must have been coincidence,
because he could not have understood the
question in English.

The Volare's mill was no hemi, but they still had
a better power to weight ratio than Volgas loaded
with three or four big men. What was keeping the
Russians in the race, and indeed on their bumper,
was the fact that the American car cleared a path
through obstacles like a Rome Plow in brush.

Something had to change suddenly or it was going to change for the worse.

"Hang on!" Kelly shouted. Instead of speeding through the Place Emir Abdel Kader, he slewed to the right, then counter-steered to bring the Volare out at right angles to its original course. They were squealing down the Rue Morris, using all of the sidewalk on the left side of the street to do it without exceeding a 15° turn—all the soft tires would allow.

The four corners of the square between the central and circumferential vehicle ways were grassed and set off from the pavement by curbs and slack chains. The driver of the leading Volga tried to follow Kelly. He had less time to react and an even lower threshold of control. The Russian exceeded that threshold, trying to hurl his over-loaded car into a corner that it could not have negotiated empty at the speed it was travelling. In panic, the driver touched his brakes. Their limits exceeded, traction and cornering force dropped instantly to zero.

The Volga slid off the pavement. It maintained exactly the angle and attitude it had when the brakes were applied. When the left-side wheels hit the curb around the green space, the tires stripped off and the car overturned sideways. It rolled three times before coming to rest on its side, against a utility pole. Gas, oil, and radiator fluid pooled in the street. There was no fire until one of the Russians tried to kick open his door with a steel-shod boot.

Two more black Volgas skidded across the far end of the Rue Morris, four hundred feet away and no cross streets between.

They had probably come from the Palais du Gouvernement, less than a block away. That mattered, because it meant they would not be stuffed with armed security men. Kelly kicked down the emergency brake with his left foot, locking the rear wheels. He cramped the power steering hard left. The back end broke away and the station wagon swapped ends with a suddeness that cracked Posner against the window a second time. Vlasov's considerable weight slid against the Attache's hips.

The Volare had been at less than 30 mph when the Russian cars appeared in front of them. Now Kelly was braking to a dead stop, using a steady pressure that laid rubber on the street but kept the tires rotating enough to preserve traction. The air in the Volare stank with their own burning tires and brake pads.

The driver of one of the blocking cars reacted with an initiative that would have been commendable had it turned out better. When the Russian saw the Volare had turned in its own traffic lane and was about to speed off in the direction from which it had come, he turned his own wheel to follow. The Volga accelerated out of the crosswise blocking position.

The bootlegger turn had slammed all three men in the American car against their seat back. When the car momentarily stopped, Kelly reached away from the steering wheel with both hands. His right slid the selector back into low range while his left popped the emergency brake release. The agent tweaked the wheel just enough to keep the tires off the streaks of slick, fresh rubber they had laid on the pavement in stopping.

A Volga with a crumpled fender, the car that had made the initial pass at them near the Ketchouan Mosque, turned onto the Rue Morris. The gouting pyre of the leading Russian vehicle marked the intersection for its consort. A man with eyebrows that met in a black bar was leaning out of the passenger side. He fired a pistol at the Volare. Kelly cursed and steered directly toward the Russian car.

There was nothing of the kamikaze in the
agent's action, nothing of patriotic sacrifice and
noble self-immolation. It was berserk bloodlust,
pure and simple, the rage that had sent the Kellys
of a thousand years before across the beach at
Clontarf, as naked as the axes in their hands. As
the armored Vikings broke that day in bloody
ruin, so the KGB driver, neither coward nor incompetent, violated training and orders. He
snapped his car to the right, out of the path of the
great square grill. The Russian tires squealed but
the driver had not lost control, not really, until his
car slammed head-on into the Volga that had
begun to pursue from its blocking position.

At the moment, Kelly did not particularly care
what might be going on behind him. The latest
brush with a Russian car had stripped chrome
from the Volare's left side and replaced it with
smudged black paint. None of the tires were
rubbing and there were no other immediate
mechanical problems.

Ammunition was exploding within the first
wrecked Volga. It was harmless enough without a
gun barrel to channel the energy, just bits of metal
spitting and whining like bees and no more
dangerous.

The smoke rending the clear sky in whorls from
the flame tips was as black as what spewed from
the ovens at Dachau.

"What's the fastest route to Tipasa from here?"
Kelly asked. He turned onto the Rue Larbi again.
He swung as widely around the balefire as the
street's width allowed.

XXXIV

When the Citröen's windows were rolled down, the wail of sirens made it difficult to speak in a normal voice and still be heard. Babroi had locked the scanner onto the channel the Americans were using. Otherwise the car would have been flooded by the sudden torrent of emergency traffic in Arabic which none of the four occupants understood.

A squad of troops in red berets diverted the limousine a block west of the Place Emir Abdel Kader. The pall of smoke beyond was the visual counterpart of the sirens. Before the radio in Car Four went permanently silent, it had transmitted the sound of rending metal.

Schwartz turned left in obedience to the directions waved by the muzzle of an automatic rifle. Korchenko cursed under his breath but said nothing. "Pull up here," suggested Babroi. "I'll run over on foot and see what happened."

The driver glanced uncertainly at his superior. "Yes, that's a good idea," the colonel said abruptly. His face became fractionally less grim. "Who knows—maybe they collided with the American car and *all* of them are dead."

"Syd," said the scanner. "I'm getting a clear direction." The occupants of the limousine held their breath. "They're heading south and pretty fast, from the way I'm having to turn the antenna to keep it on them. What's your location?"

Colonel Korchenko put a hand over the back of his seat needlessly to keep his aide from getting out of the car. All of them, even Schwartz who did not speak English, waited like snipers.

"Look, I'm down by the train station, Harry," said the American with the mobile unit. "But what do you mean by south? There's a whole desert out there."

"Dammit, Syd, you know I can't give you more than a direction from here," said the voice of 'Harry.' "Turn south and we'll trust to luck."

"Harry, this isn't going to work," Syd's voice responded. "Look, I think I'd better go find Don. He may be in real trouble."

"God dammit, Westram, this is a direct order! The car we want is going south and you're as far north as you can get without falling into the harbor! Now, get off your duff and head south!"

"Acknowledged." The voice from the scanner was cold and formal. "Proceeding south to the Malika and then south on it until ordered otherwise. Mobile One, out."

"From here they must be intending to take National One," said a voice. Again it was an instant before Korchenko realized the Vietnamese behind him was speaking. Again also, the colonel's flash of anger was quenched by the reasonableness of Nguyen's plan and the fact that he at least had *some* plan. Like the puzzled CIA operative, Korchenko could only think that the Sahara was a big place.

"We'll follow," Nguyen continued. "Tell your driver to turn right, then right again at the Rue Mellan Ali, that seems as good a way as any. If we do not catch up with them before they reach National 38, we'll turn right anyway. They were trying to go west originally, before we headed them off. Likely they will try to go west again when they are out of the city." He paused. "It is some chance; and if you will just bring in the Algerian authorities, a very good chance."

Korchenko gave his orders in crisp, command-

ing Russian. Schwartz slid the Citröen back into
traffic like a shark joining a school of mackerel.
The colonel picked up the two-way radio again.
He had no intention of bringing in the locals. In
the end, that would require explanations at the
ministerial level. The colonel's superiors were not
going to be pleased with events in Algiers. They
would be even less pleased if the matter were not
somehow kept in the family.

But at Blida, there was a training cadre of three
hundred Soviet troops. They had both ground
vehicles and helicopters available from stores
being supplied to the Polisarios. Those troops
could be fanned across possible escape routes,
looking for an American station wagon. With luck,
they would be able to strike a more direct blow for
the safety of Mother Russia than anyone had expected.

Korchenko began giving instructions to the
operator on the base unit in the embassy. The
troops would find Vlasov again, that was almost
certain. The Americans with the Professor clearly
did not know their own personnel had put a tracer
on them.

But the colonel very much hoped all those involved would be captured without injury. He
wanted to conduct their interrogations himself,
and he wanted them to be in good physical condition.

When he began.

XXXV

On the outskirts of Birkhadem, ten kilometers from the center of Algiers, construction vehicles had blocked one lane of a bridge. Traffic on National Highway 1 stopped abruptly, then resumed in fits and starts. A flagman using a T-shirt on a pole directed clumps of cars in alternating directions like beads on an asphalt wire. Two National Policemen leaned against a house wall close enough to the road that Commander Posner could have touched them as the Volare halted for the third time. Posner was unlikely to do so. He sat so rigidly in his seat that his front-facing eyes seemed not to blink.

Kelly put the transmission in neutral so that the radiator fan would run. The water temperature was already higher than he liked to see it at idle. He leaned past his companions for a glimpse of the Algerian policemen. The roof of the car still hid their faces. The black leather suits must have been warm, but only one of the men had even bothered to unzip his tunic as far as the belt that slashed across it. The cross-belt supported his pistol holster and mounted his star-burst badge. The agent could hear only enough of the Algerians' conversation to be sure that they were not speaking a language he knew. From their gestures and cheerful volubility, though, Kelly was pretty sure that they were laughing at the condition of the American car.

The flagman waved, a circular gesture in time with the beat of the transistor radio in his left hand. Kelly put the car in gear and followed the vehicles ahead of him around the back of a truck loaded with sections of concrete culvert. "You know," he said in French, "I'd really like to know how the KGB had us spotted but the Algerians themselves could care less."

"This is all insane," the Defense Attache muttered with his eyes closed. "To die for my country, well, I swore my oath. But to die only to harm and humiliate the United States—" he faced Kelly to glare at him past the disinterested Russian— "I should never have come, I should have resigned."

"We're not dead yet," the agent remarked mildly.

"Those aren't KGB," Professor Vlasov said. "They're the aliens who want to kill me." He sounded more impersonal than was to be expected from a man contemplating his imminent murder.

"Professor," Kelly snapped, sick to death of the counterpoint of disaster from his passengers, "I can't swear what language the people after us were talking, but the cars they drove were made in Smolensk, not Mars. And I'll need a Hell of a good reason before I believe this—" he fumbled between his seat and the side panel— "was done by a ray gun and not a Makarov." Kelly found what he was after, the left wing mirror which he had wrenched off as they sped south from the Place Emir Abdel Kader. Angrily, he dropped the mirror in Vlasov's lap.

All the bullet had left was the chromed shield, and even that with a puckered hole in it. The glass and the thin metal that backed it lay in shards somewhere on the Rue Morris. From the direction of the impact, the shot had been fired in the instants that Kelly and the Russian sedan were headed straight toward one another.

Less emotionally, his eyes still on his driving, the agent said, "I'm not worried about dents in the sheet metal, not the way traffic is in Algiers. . . . But I sure hope we didn't pick up any more bullet holes besides this one. I'd hate to have had to explain *that* to the police."

The Russian turned the mirror shell in his hand, closing the bullet hole momentarily with the tip of one finger. As Kelly had said, it was about the right size for a jacketed 9 mm bullet to have made in light metal; though there was no real way to deduce a brand of weapon from a bullet hole. "Ah, well," Vlasov said tiredly, "you think I am mad also, do you? Well, I have gotten used to that from my colleagues, from the officials I have tried to talk to. I say, 'My conversations are being listened to, I'm being followed.' And of course they think me mad, because the KGB follows everyone, listens to everyone, doesn't it?" He waved his hand parenthetically, adding, "Everyone like me, who knows things that our enemies would wish to learn."

Commander Posner looked at Vlasov with more interest than approval. "You mean ex-enemies," he said.

Kelly could not see Vlasov's eyes when the Russian turned to stare at the Attache. No one, however, could mistake the chill in Vlasov's voice as he repeated, "Enemies!" More gently, the older man went on, "But human enemies, you see. We have known many of these, we Russians, from East and West. We will deal with you as we dealt with Hitler, with Napoleon, with the Khans . . . time and courage . . . we will deal with you. But these others, who can say?"

Kelly knew he had to defuse the conversation fast. Though he had no desire to hear a nut expound on the subject of his nuttiness, he said, "Ah, why do you think these aliens are after you, Professor Vlasov?"

The Russian turned around. "Oh," he said, "for the same reason everyone else is after me—you, the Kommission, yes. . . ." He juggled the mirror in his palm so that light danced on the chrome. "Unscientific, was I not? To assign causes without inspecting the data . . . but still, I am sure that they must have informed the KGB, they like to work through humans, I believe, it keeps their true role hidden. . . ."

"Go on, what purpose, then?" Posner interrupted needlessly. At least he wasn't trying to rake the scientist over the coals for inadequate US patriotism. They had too many miles yet to go to spend them wrangling.

"Why, the beam device," Vlasov said in genuine surprise. "The focusing lens, really, the principle. They did not tell you, your people?"

"We know a little, but we're not scientists, Professor," Kelly said with a smile that had time now to be sad. There was no time to reflect when your life depended on keeping the muzzle down and killing the other bastard first.

Vlasov studied the agent with more interest and a touch of respect. "Yes," he said after a moment. "I have seen that. I too was not always a scientist, you know, Mr. American."

Kelly looked the defector in the face. "All I know about your present work," he said, "is that I'm told you're respected by the front rank of scientists. Well and good . . . but Professor, I can see your empty sleeve myself, and I need no briefing book to tell me why you are to be respected for that."

The Russian smiled broadly. "Come," he said, "I have already defected. You do not need to stroke me any more." He looked out the windshield again. The landscape was undistinguished. Even plants in the gardens near the road looked dusty. They had driven through the initial ridge of the Atlas Range which pinned Algiers against its gulf. The reverse slopes now rose abruptly to the right as they followed the highway west.

"You want to know why they pursue me, these aliens that you do not believe in, eh?" continued the Professor. "I think because they will be coming to Earth in great numbers soon, they plan. And if Earth is protected by weapons that kill fifty targets with a single shot, then their fleet, their Armada—" he smiled at the Spanish word— "will come no closer to Earth than we, its inhabitants, choose." Vlasov's smile slumped like wax in a fire. "No closer than you, the inhabitants of Earth who are Americans, choose . . . but I had no choice, my own, my fellow children of my Russian soil, can not turn my formulae into weapons. Not quickly enough." The defector swallowed. He looked at neither of the men flanking him. "I pray that we are in enough time now. There is very little grace remaining, I am afraid."

The notion intrigued Kelly enough to cause him to treat it seriously. He asked, "Aren't these, ah, weapons pretty vulnerable themselves, Professor? I mean, as I understand it, you're just hanging a bomb up in orbit with a lot of electronics around it. Or do you plan to armor them or whatever?"

Vlasov seemed to have forgotten that he was on the verge of certain death. "Vulnerable you say?" he responded. "Yes, in the sense that any object in space would be equally vulnerable to another. These beams, these particle beams have no limiting range, you see, not if the focus if tight enough—as it can be. They command the Solar System; and beyond, even, if targets could be found for them. So our satellites could be destroyed by the fleets that are coming, to be sure. But the risk is equal, attacker and satellite. And here, not light years away from our bases, we can replace *our* pawns indefinitely. The aliens must spend the very heart of their invasion at every attempt. If they were not threatened by my research, they would not have bothered about me . . . as they have. And they are concerned as well to keep their dealings on Earth secret, for what I could do, another might equal."

"So we're fine so long as we can keep building rockets, hey?" Kelly joked. He immediately regretted his flippancy. This was not a bull session with everybody half looped, this was a very bright boy who happened also to be nuts in one area—and who had better stay happy until he was delivered to the submarine. Then he became somebody else's problem.

Vlasov chose to respond to the agent's question as if it were real. He raised an eyebrow and said, "Rockets? Why bother? These are small packages, I tell you. *Shoot* them into orbit. Twenty years ago, you and the Canadians were doing this, two battleship cannon end to end. . . . How could the aliens invade when the Earth is ready to fire scores of new defensive satellites into orbit in a few hours?"

The road signs did not help since they were in Arabic alone. Kelly had been watching the odometer, however. A cluster of one-story houses had been a cross-roads village. It would soon be dwarfed by the apartment block under construction on the near outskirts. "Commander," the agent said in English, his foot off the gas, "is this where the Vilayat road goes straight and the National bends more to the south?"

The Attache bent over a Michelin map, unprepared for the question. "Yes, yes; I guess it does," he said after longer than Kelly's temper cared to wait. "It seems to be called Four Roads—the village. But I'm sure Route 1 would be faster."

"That may not be all we have to worry about," the agent said grimly. He pulled through the controlled intersection at speed, avoiding a southbound Mercedes tour bus by less than its driver or his own passengers could believe. Kelly had his foot to the floor again. He had been looking in the rear-view mirror as he spoke to Posner.

"You—" the commander cried, but as his eyes
turned to the agent, they took in the blank rigidity
of Kelly's face. Posner had seen that look before,
when the agent was hauling them through Algiers
with death on their bumper. Posner and Vlasov
both turned to stare out the back window.

"You thought me mad," said the defector with
flat certainty. "They could not get the Kommission to kill me, so they are coming to do it
themselves."

The square back end of the station wagon had
sucked a layer of road dust over the window like
frosting. Vlasov turned around after only a glance,
satisfied that any and all possible threats were his
aliens. Commander Posner continued to lean over
the seat back, squinting. The local road was
narrower and significantly less smooth that the
National route had been. All that the dust and
hammering left certain was that there was a car
approaching.

It was approaching very fast, despite anything
Kelly could coax out of the Plymouth. This was not
an underpowered Volga. . . .

Ten feet from the American car's rear bumper,
the pursing vehicle slowed to match speeds as perfectly as the road surface would allow. "AMB-51,"
Commander Posner was saying. "Why—I believe
that's the Russian Ambassador's car! Surely—"

"Get your head down, Professor," Kelly interrupted, his thick wrists trembling as they fought
to hold the wheel steady. The Volare was rapidly
overtaking a truck which filled more than half the
roadway.

"It doesn't matter," the defector replied
gloomily. He was staring at the approaching car.
"You saw what their weapons did to Hoang at
the—"

"*Get your fucking head outa the mirror!*"

"Kelly!" cried the Attache. His voice was as

sharp and sudden as the bullet that snapped between the passengers and out through the windshield.

Kelly braked, half in hope that the pursing vehicle would overrun them. Its driver, however, was very possibly as good as Kelly himself was. The limousine's four-wheel disk brakes scrubbed off speed in a straight line while the Volare wallowed across the road. A long crack staggered the width of the windshield from the starred, milky area around the bullet hole. There, only the interior layer of gum held the two shattered layers of safety glass together.

Kelly let up on the brake and steered right in the same instant. He threw the Volare into a sweeping turn that took the near corner and the far edge of the dirt track he had seen as the truck rolled on.

Vlasov was hunched over, deferring to Kelly's wishes if not his beliefs. In the rear view mirror, the agent saw the pursuing vehicle spin on the asphalt as it overran the turn-off. It was not, Kelly realized, out of control. Rather, the driver had used a controlled drift as the fastest way of reversing, much as Kelly himself had done on the Rue Morris. The bastard was good, all right.

Kelly recognized the car now that he had caught a broadside glimpse of it. It was the limo that had brought Vlasov and Hoang to the Institute, a Citröen SM Sedan. With four doors, jump seats, and the armor that stray shots had displayed that morning, the sedan version was slower off the line than the 1,500 kilogram coupe with which it shared an engine and drive train. That did not mean that its 260 kph speedometer was for show. Powered by a Maserati V-6 with six Weber carbs and a 6,500 rpm red-line, the Citröen was definitely the class of *this* race.

Kelly had turned into a track meant for 4x4s—or perhaps for camels alone. The Plymouth jounced. Its oil pan rang on something solid. All three occupants bounced in their seats. "That bastard'll just dial up the air suspension and clear these ruts!" Kelly shouted pointlessly. Vlasov was as tense as a martyr at the stake. Commander Posner had the wide-eyed disbelief of a skydiver whose reserve chute had just streamed.

Unlike the others, Kelly had something to do. That fact kept him out of the utter despair which circumstances made reasonable. He could hear the shots being fired as the limousine closed again. The guns were less of a threat now than they had been on the highway, however. The Citroën was being hammered despite its high clearance. The KGB men within could not lean out of the windows for fear of being cut in half by the coaming on a particularly bad bounce. They were thrusting their weapons in the general direction of their quarry, a pistol from the right front and an automatic rifle from behind the driver. None of a dozen shots had been close enough to ring from the Volare's sheet metal. Still, if the Russians fired long enough, they were going to get lucky . . . and if Kelly ever bogged his car in a sand-swept hollow. . . .

The Citroën had moved up within a few meters again. Its driver began to ease it into a line to the right of the one Kelly was taking. Either the Russian planned to pass or he was giving the rifleman a clearer field of fire. The cars were climbing a slight rise, the road straight within reasonable parameters of the term. "Hang on!" Kelly cried. He took his foot off the gas and dropped the gear selector into second, tramping the throttle simultaneously.

The wagon trembled in an incipient fish-tail. The skittering induced by the road surface masked the change. 45 mph was as fast as the agent could hold the car to. The feedback to the wheel even through the power steering mechanism was brutal on his flayed left hand. The Citroën moved up another two feet. Its glazed front slope grinned above its bumper like a

demon's smile. Two of five bullets ripped the
Volare right to left, entering through the side window a few inches from Commander Posner's face.

Kelly stamped on the emergency brake as his
right foot came off the gas.

The Russian driver was good, but the Volare's
mechanical brake was not connected to the stop
light. The first warning any of those in the Citröen
had was sight of the blunt wedge of the Volare's
left rear fender swinging toward them as the tires
broke away. The collision anchored the station
wagon's rear end and kept it from continuing
around in an uncontrollable spin on the loose road
surface. Glass from the Citröen's leading edge
exploded back toward the windshield like a charge
of langridge. Kelly flipped the brake release and
tried to accelerate smoothly away.

The closing impact had been less than 15 miles
per hour. With tons of metal on either side of the
equation, however, the kinetic energy involved
was awesome. The Volare's frame was buckled,
but there was none of the steel-on-rubber howl
which Kelly had dreaded would announce the incipient blow-out of their left rear tire.

The Citröen had gone into a wild skid, but the
Russian driver recovered with the skill which
Kelly had learned to fear and respect. Without
losing the car into the shallow ditches to either
side, the Russian straightened out and came on
again. The Citröen's notched leading edge snarled
like a boxer with his bridgework out. The AK's
muzzle was already beginning to poke out of the
back window again.

The Volare cleared the top of the rise and hung
with all four wheels momentarily airborne. The
shock when the car hit would have tested the suspension of a Baja Unlimited. The station wagon
rang like an ingot dropped on stone.

"P-professor—" Kelly tried to say.

The Citröen topped the hill behind them. It spun

in a huge explosion of dust and gravel as the engine locked up. All fourteen quarts of coolant lay in a black splash at the crash site where the Volare's fender had ripped the core out of the horizontal radiator. The alloy block of the Maserati conducted heat splendidly, but it had nothing like the latent heat capacity of a cast iron unit. When the coolant went under stress, the engine welded itself into a 6-cylinder brake in less than a quarter mile.

"Jesus!" Kelly cried in delight as figures spilled out of their hopelessly wrecked pursuer. "If this road just goes somewhere and we don't have to turn around and go past them a—"

Steel bullets on sheet metal slapped like traps closing on the Volare. Two, three more. Posner grunted and the windshield starred to either side of the hole already there. More impacts, a thump as something hit a back tire and then the *whang*! and explosive decompression of a round through the wheel itself. Unlike punctured tires, the track drilled through the steel would not pucker closed and let the car run on a slow leak.

The Volare spun, trading ends twice. That may have been a blessing, because during the seconds that Kelly was fighting for control nothing else hit them. There was nowhere to go but forward, away from the gunner. When the bullets had started sleeting in on them, Kelly had already assumed they were a safe distance from the fellow bracing an AKM against the roof of the Citröen. Bad guess, real bad guess.

One of the last rounds smashed the rear-view mirror out through the windshield. Kelly struck at the crazed, opaque glass in front of him with the palm of his right hand. He tore loose a hole through which he could again see enough of the road to drive whatever the gunfire had left him. At last the road dipped, cutting the two shattered vehicles off from one another.

XXXVI

Colonel Nguyen raised the muzzle of the AKM as he pushed himself upright again. The rifle's wooden foregrip was already hot with the thirty rounds he had fired.

Babroi had staggered out of the wrecked Citröen just in time to see the distant American car spin as well. "You hit it!" the Russian shouted. The station wagon was under control again, pulling out of sight. "You hit it!"

"While our car was moving, I could not shoot," said the Vietnamese. "When we stopped—well, a target going straight away from you is not difficult, surely? Have you never used a rifle yourself?"

The aide jerked back, but after a moment he decided that the comment had been only naive. Korchenko, glancing up from the microphone, was not so sure. The Vietnamese was the member of an inferior race, the representative of a nation which would not exist at all without aid from the USSR. None the less, the KGB colonel had the impression that Nguyen's bland face and bland words cloaked raw scorn for his Russian counterparts.

The Vietnamese knelt. He massaged his left thigh where the block of pavement had spun him down. As the radio answered Korchenko, Nguyen asked the aide quietly, "Is there more ammunition for the rifles? I emptied my magazine."

Korchenko cursed, but there was an under-current of satisfaction in his voice as he said,

"Well, we know where *your* charge is, Nguyen.
The Algerians have found part of his body in the
Casbah. Witnesses say the Americans—the people
in the big car—blew him up before they drove
off."

The Russian began to speak into his radio again.
Nguyen frowned and pulled himself erect. He
used the edge of the back door as a handhold and
the automatic rifle as a crutch in order to manage
unassisted. Babroi and Schwartz were struggling
to pry open the hood. It was obvious that the
Citröen was beyond any repairs they could make
in the field.

Korchenko flung down the microphone with a
curse. "Junk!" he shouted, "junk! Now they're
saying that they can't hear me!"

The Vietnamese officer did not speak Russian,
but he had enough experience with the language
and with problems in the field to add them up this
time. "With the engine dead," he said in English,
"the battery does not have the power to transmit
from here to Algiers very long. Especially a tube
radio, so much is lost in heat."

The look Korchenko gave him would have killed
if the KGB man could have arranged it. "Very
fine!" the Russian spat. "An explanation for every
failure. No doubt you will explain to your
superiors why there is so little of Doctor Tanh to
ship home?" The colonel's venom was punctuated
by squealing metal. Babroi and Schwartz had
finally wrenched apart the warped hood and
fenders.

"I do not understand that," Nguyen responded,
as if to a question and not a gibe. "Why should
they kidnap Hoang first and then kill him at once?
Perhaps it was an accident. There was too much
shooting, too much smoke. . . ." He smiled, and
Korchenko wondered that he had ever thought the
little man was bland. "It reminded me of Hue in
'68," Nguyen concluded. "Yes."

Colonel Korchenko opened his door and got out. He towered over the Vietnamese officer. That gave back some of his confidence. "There's a group of military vehicles being diverted to us," he said. "We'll go back to Algiers in one of them while the rest track down the—Americans." He had almost blurted, 'defector,' a word that must not be used outside KGB circles if Korchenko were to have even a prayer of a career remaining.

Nguyen stripped the empty magazine from the AKM, wincing as the motion put weight on his right leg again. "Is there more ammunition?" he repeated. "I will accompany the troops. I want to—catch—the men who killed Doctor Hoang."

"Little fool!" Korchenko shouted. "Shall I leave you here, is that what you want? *I* shall be in charge of the operation from my base in the embassy. But the capture shall be the responsibility of the army alone, the *Red* Army! Do you understand?"

"Yes, I understand perfectly," said the Vietnamese officer in a soft voice. His nod could have been mistaken for obsequiousness. "I hope we will be informed of your success," he added. "From government to government, if you think it would be improper to exchange such information between ourselves."

Behind his still face, Nguyen was balancing possibilities. The Algerian government had a stake in the day's events which the Russians seemed willing to overlook. Nguyen had made only a courtesy call on the Algerian responsible for Conference security, a Captain Malek; but that should be sufficient entree under the circumstances. With the manpower and records of the local authorities, and the skills that had sometimes made Nguyen's own superiors look askance at him, it should be possible to get a quick break in the affair. The Vietnamese officer was quite sure that Korchenko was not the man to defeat the one the radio had called 'Kelly.' The man orchestrating things from the American—was it really American?—side was very good.

"It shouldn't be too difficult," the KGB colonel was remarking. "Their vehicle is unmistakable—and very likely damaged as well." He gave Nguyen a patronizing nod. "And most important, the fact they didn't answer our fire . . . well, it's obvious that they don't have guns or shells any more. Didn't want to compromise a diplomatic vehicle, I'll bet—the fools!"

Korchenko chuckled. "No," he repeated, "it really shouldn't be too difficult."

XXXVII

"Professor, are you all right?" Kelly asked. He dared not stop yet. A quick glance to the side showed him only that his two passengers were sprawled across the seat.

Vlasov straightened up slowly. He had been pressing his ear against the Defense Attache's chest. "Yes," he said quietly in Russian, "but your friend, I am afraid, is dead. I am very sorry."

Kelly slammed his hand against the padded dash as he had hit the wall of the tomb the night before. "Shit," he whispered. He had not cared for Posner, an officious turkey who let his illusions get in the way of doing the job . . . but he had lived by those illusions, and now he seemed to have died by them. "The world," muttered the agent, "just might be a better place if everybody was a Posner and there weren't any Tom Kellys to fuck things up."

"Eh?"

"I'm going to pull over and change tires," Kelly said aloud. "This wasn't autostrada even with four tires."

They were three quarters of a mile beyond the Citröen, and there were a number of twists and turns besides. In theory, that was a matter of only some minutes run for a trained man. It was still an adequate safety margin with this surface, this sun, and with the probable burden of fifteen pounds of automatic rifle if somebody really was determined to run after them.

Vlasov had tried to straighten the commander's

body against the seat back. The bullet that ripped through the top of Posner's chest had already been tumbling. Death might have taken a few minutes, but consciousness must have spilled out instantly with the hemorrhage through the fist-sized exit hole.

"Shit," Kelly repeated as he swung open his door.

The smell of raw gasoline warned him. Besides the *ping* of hot metal finding new tolerances, there was a muted gurgle at the back of the car. Kelly swore and flopped on the ground. One hole was round and neat and could have been plugged; but it was already above the level of the gas remaining. The other hole was the work of a ricochet, skipping up from the road metal and doing a job that could not have been bettered with a cold chisel. The bullet had spun through the bottom of the gas tank in a long line.

The left rear tire was dead flat and the right rear was noticeably slumping, but there was no time now to worry about them. By the time Kelly had changed a tire, there would be no fuel left to drive away on. The agent jumped back into the car and put it in gear.

"Where are we going now?" Professor Vlasov asked. In the interval, the Russian had struggled one-handed to lay the Attache's body out in the back seat.

"As far as we can this way," Kelly said dourly, "which won't be very goddam far, I'm afraid." He paused. "Somebody back there is good with a rifle. He managed to hit us ten, maybe fifteen times out of a thirty-round box—if it was even full when he got the gun. I'd like to meet him again some time, when I've got more than a steering wheel to hold myself."

"There is something up on the next hill," Vlasov noted. He pointed forward. The best speed they could manage with the road and tires as they were was under 20 mph. It was slow enough that the lack of windshield was not a handicap.

"Given what the gas tank looks like," Kelly said, "I wouldn't bet the farm that we were going to make it that far. It's a mile and a half, and it's uphill, which is worse." But at least it was a better goal than anything else on the immediate, dingy landscape.

The object was a square, flat-roofed tower on a hilltop overlooking the road and many miles of countryside. At its base, the tower was surrounded by a low wall. "It's a granary," Kelly explained aloud. "Kabyles've been building them like that to store grain for a couple thousand years, my background stuff said."

Vlasov frowned, then looked at the American. He smiled. "You are joking of course. That is a fort."

Kelly flashed a grin back at the defector. "You could make a case for that, couldn't you, Professor? Well, all I know is what I read ... but it just might be that it wasn't only long droughts that families built places to protect their grain from."

The top of the tower was notched with embrasures. Below them, on what was presumably the second floor, there was a single slit window per side. The slits flared outward to give a rifleman within the broadest possible field of fire while only his gun muzzle was exposed to the shots of his opponents. The tower itself was plastered, but the core was almost certainly stone like the fabric of the wall around the tower's base. If the stones were as thick as their length and breadth suggested, more than light artillery would be required to blast them aside.

"Professor," the agent said, "if we've got a chance to stay clear for the next couple hours, it's up there. I ... if I hadn't screwed up, you wouldn't be in this mess. It's not much consolation, I know ⌐.. but I'm as sorry as I can be."

Vlasov smiled at the American sadly. "It is not you," he said. "Perhaps there is nothing that human beings could have done against—these others."

Kelly's face worked in disgust. He did not like being whipped by the KGB. Coming in second to non-existent aliens turned the thought of defeat into insult.

The slant-six engine continued to chug away happily until they crested the hump in the road beneath the granary. The Volare rode like a sled in the summer, but that was as much as could have been hoped under the circumstances. Kelly grinned. Perhaps he should have been thankful that the ricochet had only ripped the tank and had not ignited it. And then again, maybe he ought to wish he was dead in the back seat instead of Posner. Kelly had been in the business long enough to know that there are worse things than death, especially if the other side has questions they need answers to.

When the nose of the Volare pointed down at a noticeable angle, Kelly shut off the engine. None of the remaining gasoline would drain out, at least, though he was sure that the car would not carry them much further. "Professor," he said, "we're going to walk up there and I'll try to talk to the people. Hope to God they speak French. . . . If we're lucky, they'll give us a drink of water before they shoo us out the door. And if we're real lucky—" he fumbled beneath the passenger seat and came out with the empty sub-machine gun— "if we're real lucky, they just might have some .45 ammo. Who knows?"

XXXVIII

There was no path from the road to the granary. The soil was friable, a mixture of baked dirt and soft stone. It was spattered with close-cropped plants that seemed each to defend a barren territory a foot or more in diameter. Vlasov and Kelly proceeded slowly. The ascent was over 30°, and the soil rolled and crumbled from beneath their shoes. Both men dabbed a hand down repeatedly, the touch of the grit taking just enough weight to give them traction again.

At first, Kelly could see only the surrounding wall and the tower when he paused and looked up from the ground before him. As the agent drew nearer, however, the design became more clear. It was as much a dwelling as a place of refuge. The wall around the base of the tower proper was of ashlar-cut stones laid in courses and mortared into place. This wall had been extended forty feet to one side by a wall of much cruder construction in which stones of varied shapes and sizes were fitted to one another dry. Within the courtyard thus created could be seen the roof of either a house or a stable.

There was a wooden gate in the newer wall. Standing ten feet from the gate and in plain view of whoever was moving behind the gun slit in the second floor of the tower, Kelly called, "Friends, we are travellers in need. For your souls' sake, aid us!" He held the Ingram in his right hand, muzzle down and with the stock extended. In his left hand, Kelly waved the empty magazine.

After a long time, the gate creaked back. An old man walked out and dragged the gate panel to behind him. He wore a dun-colored robe and a burnoose. The old man did not hold a weapon, but someone still watched from above.

"Father," the agent said, "we have run far, but our enemies still pursue. Grant us water before we go on."

The old man's face rumpled in disdain. He gestured toward the sub-machine gun and said in cracked French, "Do peaceful travellers come calling with guns in their hands, then? Go on about your business."

Kelly swallowed on a dry throat. "Father, our business was with the Association of Kabyles. In Algiers this day we have struck down some of the tyrants who would forbid the Kabyle language, who would prevent grandfathers from speaking to their children's children who have gone to the city. We do not ask for shelter; that would be your death. But God will reward those who offer water to the thirsty."

"Come in, then," the old man said abruptly. "Mind the hens." Stepping back, he called to someone inside in what must have been Kabyle.

The chickens running loose in the courtyard were white and scrawny and berserk at the sight of strangers. There was the usual farm odor of dung, though no animals larger than the chickens were evident at the moment, such as the sheep and perhaps goats would be penned here during the night. Now they were presumably at pasture, doing whatever further damage they could to the already barren hillsides nearby.

There were four humans besides the old man lined up in front of the low, beige-plastered house. Three were children, none of them more than six years old. The last was a black-robed woman as old as the man. She had not bothered to veil for strangers: these were Kabyles, not Arabs. There

were no men of—military age, that covered it.
They would be off with the flocks.

And there was no woman young enough to be
mother to the children. Kelly did not need the
crawling between his shoulder blades to guess
where the mother was or what she held in her
hands.

Still, what the *old* woman offered was a copper
cup and a ewer of water. She filled the cup first
for Vlasov as the elder of the guests. The Russian
drank and passed the cup to Kelly, for whom the
woman refilled it in turn. The agent nodded and
passed the cup back to Vlasov. He took the empty
magazine from the waist-band of his trousers
where he had thrust it to free his hand. "Father,"
he said to the old man again, "men cannot reward
men for the gift of water which is the gift of life;
but God will reward you and your house. There is
a thing, now, that I would ask without offending
you—though it involves laws that are strict and
would be enforced with rigor."

The Kabyle chewed the inside of his lip. "Ask,"
he said. "This is not the City, that every man must
beg permission to shit."

Kelly nodded in solemn agreement. "While it is
well known that the government of the City—" he
had not been five years in sales without learning
to pick up a cue— "forbids men to own guns today—though it was those same men and guns that
drove out the French—if it could be that you knew
someone with 11,43 mm pistol ammunition. . .? Or
it may be called .45 ACP, as for the Colt pistol and
the tommy gun . . . that would serve a great need
of ours. We are men, we fight our own battles; but
without ammunition for our gun, we are un-
armed."

The old Kabyle took the magazine Kelly handed
him. He studied it at length while the American
drank another cup of water. The others in the
courtyard were spectators as silent as the woman

in the tower. At last the old man fumbled in a pocket somewhere beneath his robe and brought out a loaded pistol cartridge. It winked as he compared it with the magazine lips. It was patently too small, either a .380 or the short 9 mm Makarov round on which the Russians had decided to standardize their sidearms.

The Kabyle shook his head sadly. Kelly nodded glum agreement. "Father," he said in decision, handing the Ingram to the old man, "to us, this would be only a burden. Take it and use it in the cause of freedom as a man should." He tapped the LARAND suppressor. "With this attached, the gun will make less noise than you would believe possible. Out here—" he waved toward the miles of empty sky— "that is a little thing. But the day will come that you and your sons may have to go to the City to make your will known. . . . This will serve you well, there."

The old man took the sub-machine gun and turned it over in his hands. Kelly touched Vlasov on the shoulder. "Come on, Professor," he said wearily, "we'll drive as far as we can and then hoof it. Until they catch up again." He turned.

"Wait," the Kabyle said. Carrying the Ingram, the old man strode through the door at the base of the tower. Voices echoed from the building. They were muffled by the thick walls but still loud enough to be intelligible had they been in French. The old woman gave the strangers another hard look, then darted through the doorway herself.

"Do you suppose he is going to give us the ammunition after all?" asked Professor Vlasov. He spoke in Russian. He might be crazy, but Kelly had no reason to think the defector was stupid.

"What I'm hoping," said the agent, "is that they've got an old pistol in there that they'll part with. Even a .380's better than nothing." He shook his head. "Didn't like giving away Doug's gun that way, but it made a Hell of an impressive gift. If I get back, I can get him another one."

First the old woman, then the man, and finally a woman in her twenties spilled back into the courtyard from the tower. The younger woman carried a Garand rifle at the balance. She held the weapon easily despite its size and her slight frame. There were a lot of Garands knocking about the world, and you could still make a case for it being the finest weapon ever issued to American troops.

What the old man had brought out with him was considerably more interesting, however.

The magazine well was in the top of the receiver, and for a moment Kelly thought he was being handed a Bren gun. The double trigger—front for single shots, rear for full auto—corrected him even before he took the weapon from the Kabyle. It was a Chatellerault, the French copy of the BAR, and an excellent automatic rifle for all its weight and complexity. The bipod had been stripped from this one some time in the past, but even so the rifle had an empty weight of at least 18 pounds.

Weight made a gun difficult to carry, but it also meant that you could control bursts of the powerful cartridge for which it was chambered. At this point, that looked like a good trade-off.

The old man gave Kelly a long, straight magazine. Apologetically, he said, "We do not have much ammunition for it—only seventeen shots. But—if Allah wills, it may help you."

Kelly locked the magazine home. That freed his hand to take the Kabyle's. The old man's palm was dry and rough and as solid as a tree root. "If Allah loves warriors," the agent said sincerely, "we two shall meet again in Paradise. Go with God."

In brusquer Russian he added to Vlasov, "Well, Professor, let's see if we've got any gas left."

Kabyle voices resumed their argument behind the two men as they skidded down the hill to their car.

XXXIX

The Volare started and bumped off along the road. The right rear tire was by now as flat as the left. Kelly was no longer interested in getting somewhere. Rather, he was hoping to put at least a mile between himself and the Kabyles. It was the least he could do for people who had helped strangers at such obvious risk to themselves. Folks with guns in their homes were often willing to make their own decisions. That was a fact that had not escaped many governments.

The car made it about the hoped-for mile before the road began to struggle upward again. The engine sputtered only once before quitting for good.

"Well, Professor. . .," Kelly said. He took a last look at the road map before he stuffed it into his hip pocket. "If we're where we seem to be, Douéra's that way a few miles." He gestured up the road. "Farther than I'd like, and I figure word'll have travelled there faster than we could anyway. But I don't know a better way."

"There is a helicopter," Vlasov said.

In the stillness after the Volare died, the chop and even the turbine whine of the bird should have been obvious to the agent before it was called to his attention. Kelly cursed and stuck his head out the window. Nothing was visible. The aircraft must be flying very low and slow. The sound of its passage was echoing off the rocks ahead of it. "Quick, Professor," the agent said, "out your side and under cover fast. They may strafe the car."

Even as he spoke, the American was rolling out his own door and darting toward a bush twenty yards away up the low hill. Its foliage was sparse, but the shadow itself would go a long way toward hiding the outline of a man and an automatic rifle.

The station wagon was beige. Kelly had planned to shove it to the side of the road. With a little luck and the long shadows that would be on the hills in half an hour, the car might have been hidden from observation from above. No hope of that now. The helicopter was searching the length of the road from a hundred feet in the air. It was no chance overflight but a searcher summoned by either the KGB or the Algerian authorities themselves. Or by the little green men, of course, but this was not the time to mock Professor Vlasov. He had proven as cool as a paramedic in circumstances that would have reduced most civilians to mewling incapacity.

If there was one good thing about the helicopter, it was the fact that it was not a gunship as Kelly had initially feared. The agent squinted at the aircraft through the warped branches of the stunted fig that hid him. As soon as the pilot saw his presumed quarry, the bird lifted. The maneuver would have given Kelly a criminally easy shot had he wished to advertise the fact that he was armed again. He did not dare do that until he was sure of his opposition.

The twin-turbine helicopter was much the same size and shape as a Bell Iroquois, though the two designs could be quickly told apart by the fact that this one had tricycle landing gear in place of skids. This was an Mi-2. Though its fuselage and rudder bore the Algerian star and crescent on a green and white field, Kelly knew the crew was likely to be as Russian as the aircraft's designer. At any rate, all the pursuit to this point had been Russian.

The helicopter rose vertically to a thousand feet. It began circling slowly. The pilot had either been told to take no chances after he located the car, or he had made that decision himself. "Professor," Kelly called, "can you hear me?"

"Yes, of course," Vlasov's voice responded, slightly attentuated by the wind. "What shall we do now?"

Kelly could not see the Professor, though they were probably level with one another on opposite sides of the Volare. "Without transport, we're screwed," the agent said. "That bird's bringing somebody, sure as Hell. Could be that there's more coming than we can handle, but right now I'm looking to hijack a Russian car as the best ticket out of these rocks. Thing is, Professor, it'll work a lot better if you're willing to draw their attention. Can you run up the hill when I say to?"

"Of course," responded Professor Vlasov. "We are all soldiers now against the coming invasion. We all must do our part."

"Well, for Christ's sake, hit the dirt if they start shooting," Kelly called. He would not have minded having Vlasov guard his back in Cambodia, the agent thought. Except that Vlasov would have been on the other side there. . . .

The sound of two vehicles long preceded the machines themselves. The road kinked a hundred yards short of where the Volare lay. Kelly could hear engines roaring beyond it as the vehicles backed and filled in the narrow road. Then the blunt steel prow of an eight-wheeled armored personnel carrier lurched around the corner.

All the APC's hatches were buttoned up. Gun barrels projected from the three rifle slits on the side of the troop compartment which Kelly could see. There was a small turret forward. It seemed to hold an automatic grenade launcher in place of the more usual 14.5 mm machine gun. The vehicle paused while its turret scanned the rocky slopes to either side of the road. The grenade launcher twitched as if it were the whiskery muzzle of a mouse. Neither Vlasov nor Kelly moved. They were practically invisible at this time of evening, especially to men who were handicapped by searching through prisms or armored glass.

The armored vehicle began to roll forward again. Its separately-sprung wheels lifted and fell in individual rhythm as it presented its left side to Kelly. The APC stopped again. The American heard a hatch open on the other side. A moment later, a soldier in mustardy-green fatigues swung around the vehicle. He ran to the Volare in a crouch. The soldier carried a folding-stock AK ready for action, and his eyes flashed around in all directions. He moved too abruptly, too nervously, to notice the waiting fugitives. Though the man wore no rank or unit insignia, his uniform marked him as Russian as surely as if he had been covered with red stars.

The soldier peered into the car, then snatched open the back door. With his rifle advanced in his right, the Russian reached in with his left hand and touched the Attache's body for reassurance. After a quick look around the car's riddled interior, the soldier ran back to the APC and banged on the bow slope.

The turret hatch opened. Another Russian with steel-gray hair and an aura of command raised himself far enough out to see the trooper. The scout and the vehicle commander talked, neither's voice fully audible to Kelly. At last the commander dropped back out of sight. The soldier scurried to the side hatch.

An open-topped Land Rover drove around the corner a moment later. It carried two more men in unmarked Russian uniforms. The plump passenger still held a radio handset. The vehicles had apparently switched position when they neared potential trouble. The officer had proceeded only after the scout had signalled that the Volare was abandoned to the dead. Overhead, the chopper dropped again to about two hundred feet. The officer in the 4x4 glanced upward at it as he continued talking on the radio.

"Now, Professor!" Kelly shouted in French.

The noise of the helicopter and the engines of the two ground vehicles pulsed within the shallow bowl. Professor Vlasov heard the command, however, and he responded like a veteran paratrooper getting the green light. The defector scrambled from the base of an artemisium bush and began bounding uphill with an agility that belied his age. The Land Rover's driver saw Vlasov before anyone else did. He pointed, shouting. Kelly's signal had either been ignored in the ambient noise or forgotten in the new excitement.

The Russian officer shouted into his handset. The Mi-2 dipped and rotated 30° while the APC commander popped out of his turret for a clear view. With everyone's attention on the running defector, Kelly began killing people.

Off-set to the left of the Chatellerault's magazine was a tangent rear sight. It was screwed all the way down for point-blank fire. Using the front trigger, Kelly put single shots through the chests of both the men seated in the Land Rover. Echoes from the sharp reports rang among the rocks like a long burst from a machine gun. The officer flung the handset in the air as he died. The body of his driver flopped over him.

The armored vehicle was within thirty-five yards of Kelly's muzzle. The driver had already started to cramp his wheels right to follow Vlasov up the hill. Kelly put a five-shot burst into the wheel well, which he knew was not armored. The tracks of his bullets crossed the seats of both driver and co-driver. Sparks flew from the shadowed well as the bullets spat back chips of steel ignited by the friction of their passage. The APC's diesel roared, then died, as the drivers fell over their controls.

Vlasov had thrown himself down at the first shot. The vehicle commander had disappeared into his turret as quickly. Now the grenade launcher began to rake the slope around the Professor. Echoes had hidden the source of Kelly's shots. The Russian was aiming for the only target he had. The muzzle blasts of the grenade launcher were hollow *chunks*, but its projectiles burst on the rocks with a cracking as sharp as the white flashes that accompanied them. Pebbles and fragments of casing zinged through the air. Kelly ignored the shrapnel because there was nothing he could do about it for the moment. He cocked his left elbow under him at a sharper angle as he raised his rifle toward the helicopter.

The helicopter crew was insulated from events on the ground by the racket of their turbines and rotor. The bird was still hovering, turned away from Kelly and within a linear hundred yards. Nobody could call himself a marksman and miss a target the size of a bus at that range. The agent used his front trigger again, holding the foresight just above the rear notch to adjust for range.

A helicopter is nothing but a frame of thin aluminum on which are hung engines, fuel tanks, and seats for the occupants. Anyone who had ever been inserted into a hot landing zone knew exactly how vulnerable a chopper is. It was with feelings that went beyond revenge that Kelly turned the tables. He fired, the heavy weight of his weapon muting its recoil against his shoulder.

There was nothing in the helicopter that would keep the powerful 7.5 mm MAS round from drilling a path straight through it the long way—through fuel lines, hydraulic lines, power cables, and the pilot himself if he happened to be in the way. As Kelly's brass clinked on the rocks beside him, he squeezed off a second, then a third shot. The Mil yawed until its rotor was cutting an arc like a table saw. Then the whole aircraft spun down with the suddeness of an EKG going flat. It struck on the rocky hilltop beyond where Vlasov was hiding. The fuel tank went off like a napalm bomb. One of the broken rotor blades whirled into the air. It reflected sunlight and the ruddy gasoline flames from angles like the facets of a jewel.

The soldiers within the APC's troop compartment were firing in aimless abandon to either side. The tracers interspersed in their magazines were green sparks howling off the rocks with the other, invisible ricochets. Many of the bullets bounced back against the vehicle itself. They sang off the sloping steel sides. The raving blasts of the grenade launcher had paused on the far slope, perhaps while the commander fitted another belt of ammunition.

Kelly rolled twice to the side, using an almost non-existent swale as cover. He had expected at least one of the Russians to notice his muzzle flashes and answer them with aimed fire, but apparently none of them had. Panic and the restricted view from within the troop compartment were as much shield as the agent could have hoped for. The wild bursts of rifle fire were all high. Ricochets were the only danger—and Hell, you could get run over crossing the street.

Kelly aimed at the side of the vehicle. At this short range, the Chatellerault had a fair chance of penetrating the armor. This was not a tank, after all, but a truck with a steel shell. Then, even as the agent's finger started to take up the slack in the trigger, a side hatch swung open.

Almost by reflex, Kelly shot the soldier poised in the opening. The hatch was an empty black rectangle two feet square, framed in his sights. A bullet which entered that opening would have no other way out of the angled steel box. It would clang and howl within the troop compartment until it had spent all its momentum on the

occupants and their equipment. Kelly slipped his
fingertip back to the auto trigger. The hatch was
beginning to swing closed. Before it could shut,
the agent poured every remaining round into the
APC.

The first result was silence. All the firing from
the troop compartment stopped as abruptly as if a
switch had been thrown. The shattering muzzle
blasts of moments before had been so loud that
Kelly was too deaf to hear the sounds that
remained to the landscape: the sucking breath of
the blazing helicopter, and the moans from within
the APC.

The gasoline burning on the hilltop lighted the
road which the sun had by now practically
abandoned. The armored vehicle's shadow pulsed
in counterpoint to the fire above. The firing slits
on the side toward Kelly were glowing. Tiny
flames had smoldered into life within the troop
compartment.

Kelly stood up. He left the empty Chaterllerault
on the ground. "Professor," he called as he
stumbled toward the road. He stepped between
the Volare and the armored vehicle, each of them
at present a steel coffin. The APC was not quite
silent. Flames were crackling within the armored
box—paper and fabric and insulation had all been
sewn with flecks of blazing metal as the bullets
passed and repassed inside. "Professor!" Kelly
shouted again more nervously. He began to
scramble up the slope with the pyre of the helicopter's crew in his eyes.

Vlasov rose to a kneeling position, a sharply-de-
fined silhouette against the red background. "I am
sorry," he said in carefully enunciated Russian,
"but I do not seem to be able to hear any more.
Perhaps that will change. The shells. . . ."

Professor Vlasov had been at the white center of
a storm as the vehicle commander poured a
30-round belt of grenades in his direction. His

clothes were ripped in a score of places. Sometimes the torn edges were stained with blood as
well. But Vlasov had known to stay low, the only
real defense during shelling and a better one than
most people realized. The shrapnel that had
grazed him must have been uncomfortable.
Indeed, he probably felt as if he had been rolling
on barbed wire. But from the way the Professor
moved, and from what Kelly could see in the fire-
light, there were no dangerous or even in-
capacitating wounds.

"Professor," the agent said, bending close to the
other and raising his voice, "we'll take the jeep
and get the Hell out of here before somebody
else—"

Vlasov tugged urgently at the American's arm.
He pointed back down-slope. "Quickly," he cried,
"run! I've seen that before!"

Kelly scowled and glanced over his shoulder at
the vehicles. As soon as he saw the armored
personnel carrier, he understood why the Russian
was trying to pull him away from it. Though that
would mean leaving the 4x4 as well. . . . The steel
hull of the APC had been as black as the death
within it only a minute before. Now the armor was
glowing dull red like an overstoked furnace.

The two men stumbled forward, hindered by the
slope on which they stood and the darkness. The
billowing gasoline above them was little help. It
washed the ground with shadows that waved like
momentary trenches in the rocks. Vlasov tripped
in a runnel notched down the hard soil by the last
heavy rain. He risked a look back. The red glow
was now a lambent white. Heat-waves dancing
from the armor made the outline seem to quiver.
"Down here!" the Russian shouted, suiting his
motion to his words. He dragged Kelly with him.

For several seconds, defector and agent tried to
wriggle into a wash-out only inches deep at the
most. Then the shock wave turned the ground it-

self momentarily fluid. Both men bounced into the air.

The interior of the APC had been brewing up in a near absence of oxygen. When the grenades cooked off, the compartment ruptured and the whole superheated mixture within detonated. The closest equivalent would have been a 500-pound bomb.

The roof of the troop compartment was a steel plate weighing half a ton. It spun skyward like a flipped quarter. Diesel fuel, atomized by the first explosion, equalled it with a bubble of orange flame which swelled to a diameter of thirty yards before it collapsed in sudden blackness.

The ground pounded Kelly and Vlasov even as it protected them from shrieking metal. They jounced under full-length blows that bloodied cheeks and left Kelly feeling as if a horse had repeatedly kicked him from groin to shoulder. The airborne shock wave stunned both men for long enough that the knife-edges of pain were blunted by the time they became aware of them.

When Kelly returned to full consciousness, the night had taken on a campground hominess. Scores of tiny fires had been scattered by the explosion. Bits of rubber and cloth, some of it still dressing body parts, had been fountained across the rocks. The fragments glowed where they had fallen. Higher on the hill, the helicopter was more a bed of coals than a bonfire. Its fuel had roared up with a savage intensity that had quickly consumed itself and everything else inflammable. Even the aluminum fuselage was gone.

One gasoline fire still burned. The Land Rover had been hurled twice its own length when the APC exploded beside it. It was ablaze, and with it vaporized Kelly's hopes of driving quickly into Douéra.

Professor Vlasov was already moving. He appeared to be uncoordinated rather than seriously injured. Kelly tried to sit up and felt a rush of nausea. "Your timing was great, Professor," he said. His voice sounded thin even in his own ears. "But I'm damned if I don't think walking into town isn't going to finish what the explosion didn't."

Vlasov patted the agent's shoulder. He pointed north, in the direction they needed to go. At first Kelly thought the Russian was urging him on with more enthusiasm than the agent could have managed at the moment. Then he realized that there was a powerful headlight bouncing and thrusting down the road as a vehicle from Douéra negotiated the ruts.

The light was a halogen unit. On high beam it was so intense that it completely hid the vehicle which mounted it. The nervous pitching and rolling of the lamp indicated an ultra-short wheelbase, however. Even before it had driven slowly past the hidden fugitives, Kelly had identified the newcomer as a BMW motorcycle—ridden by a National Policeman.

The Citröen had been summoned by God knew what, the chopper and the APC by the Citröen. This bike, the first Algerian involvement in the chase, had come from Douéra in response to the fires and explosions.

The BMW pulled up alongside the wreckage of the armored personnel carrier. All four tires on the left side had been deflated, and the wheels themselves had been blown off into the dark on the right. The policeman stood, balancing the motorcycle between his thighs as he surveyed the carnage.

Kelly stared down at the bike. It was an old machine with drum brakes front and rear instead of discs. Its two opposed cylinders pumped away with the ease which made BMWs the standard of motorcycle reliability.

Finally the Algerian kicked down his sidestand

and dismounted. After a pause, he switched off the
engine and headlight. The night was left to the
hellfire illumination of the burning vehicles. The
policeman's leather suit was no more stark than
the shadows. Still wearing his helmet, he approached the overturned Land Rover as closely
as the flames would let him.

"Professor," said Kelly in a whisper he hoped
was audible, "could you make it to that bike if you
had to?"

Vlasov frowned. "To divert the rider, you
mean?" he said. "I suppose so. If the shells did not
kill me, perhaps the pistol will not kill me either."

Kelly shook his head and winced at the pain.
"No," he said, "I'm in no shape to jump a healthy
cop, even if you've got him looking the other way.
But if he'll just move a little farther, I'm going to
try to steal that Beemer."

The Algerian was alone with a catastrophe. His
radio could not raise help through the intervening
rocks, and it was obviously necessary to learn as
much as possible about the occurrence before he
left the scene to phone in a report. After poking at
the crumpled Volare, the policeman began to
scramble up the slope toward the helicopter, a
hundred yards from the road.

"Easy now," the agent murmured as the
Algerian scuffed his way further up-slope. He had
continued to wear his white crash helmet. It
obstructed the policeman's peripheral vision,
though it also kept Kelly from trying to club him
with a rock. When the Algerian was well above
them, Kelly led the defector down toward the
silent bike at something more than a crawl.

The fugitives paused in the pooling shadow of
the APC. The agent motioned Vlasov to stay where
he was. The policeman's helmet was bobbing, half
way up to the smouldering red of the helicopter.
Kelly darted from the shadow to the motorcycle.
He used the massive tank and air box to shield him

in case the policeman should glance back. The agent reached upward, feeling rather than exposing his head to check the ignition lock in the headlight nacelle.

The key was not there.

His face as calm as that of the Sphinx, Kelly reached into a trouser pocket and came out with his Swiss Army knife. He clicked open the awl blade. It was not what the knife was meant for, but beggars can't be choosers. . . . Rising to his feet, the agent rammed the thin wedge of the awl down into the ignition.

Older BMWs did not have true keys. Rather, they had plungers with a transverse groove cut for spring detents to hold them depressed. The edges of the awl cut into the brass keyway, holding the blade down as securely as the detent could have. Three tiny indicators lighted on the speedometer face—neutral, alternator, and oil pressure. Kelly swung his leg over the seat, cracked the throttle, and mashed the starter button with his right thumb. The hot engine wheezed angrily as it spun; then it fired and Kelly kicked the bike into gear.

The agent turned the motorcycle, slipping the clutch and feeling every rut on his bruised groin. "Get aboard and hang the Hell on, Professor," he shouted as he pulled abreast of the APC. Vlasov mounted awkwardly, his legs dangling against the pipes before he locked down the rear foot pegs. Kelly gassed it, ignoring the jolts as best he could. As the bike spat gravel backward, Kelly twisted the knife to turn the headlight on.

Anything the Algerian policeman cried was lost in the whine and clatter of the bike's long pushrods. As they twisted around the first bend on to Douéra, Kelly could hear the pop-pop-pop of pistol fire. Ed McGivern would not have been a threat at that range.

Operation Skyripper was go again.

XL

The Renault Dauphine had not been a particularly well-built vehicle at the time of its introduction. The example Kelly had stolen had been deteriorating for the past twenty-five years besides. Even so, the car had been a better choice than the police motorcycle for reasons beyond the latter's conspicuousness. BMW has an international reputation for building reliable, comfortable motorcycles. On rough roads, however, no motorcycle is comfortable—or, for that matter, particularly reliable. That was especially true in the dark, when pot-holes sprang out like missiles and the forks had not recovered from one jolt when the next compressed them.

This Renault had been parked behind the closed Sonatrach gas station in Douéra. It had half a tank of gasoline and it had started when Kelly shorted its ignition. For the hot wire, the agent had used a piece clipped from the car's own instrument panel; not pretty, but it worked. The Renault wallowed on the wilayet road, and when they reached National 11 it developed an alarming steering hammer at 70 kph. For all that, it was a Mercedes-class ride compared to that of the motorcycle pitching along ruts.

Professor Vlasov was still daubing at his wounds. They had both gotten through surprisingly well, the agent thought. It would be several days before he knew for certain whether his ribs had cracked or not when the ground rose up and slammed them. In a couple days, that would not matter—one way or the other. The other injuries the pair of them had received were extensive enough, Lord knew; but they were also superficial. They were the sorts of scrapes and cuts and bruises you got from high-siding a dirt bike, if you were lucky.

The pair of them. Not Commander Posner. Well, Posner had gone west with an escort. However this one ended, the Russians were not going to feel it had been cheap.

The highway bent sharply to the left, then back, to avoid the buildings of a pair of farms. The Renault's one, dim headlight flashed red from the retinas of a goat which was peering over a stone wall. Then the road dipped toward the lights of the town below.

Kelly began squinting through the dusty windshield, trying to imagine the look of the intersection he had seen only once—and that by daylight.

"This is the Tipasa we are going to?" asked the defector. "What do we do here?"

"Hell," Kelly said, "I never told you how we were going to get you back to the Land of the Big PX, did I? Hell, I'm sorry, I always get hacked off when people keep me in the dark. I didn't mean to pull that on you."

"Pardon?" said Vlasov, patiently hiding his confusion.

The agent was feeling more than a little dizzy. His ribs and his left palm were both afire. Too close now to lose it. . . . Aloud he said, "There's a submarine waiting for us off-shore. We've got an emergency radio beacon; they'll be monitoring that frequency. We blip the beacon, then they blip back at ten point four one, short wave so I can pick it up on my Kenwood and low power so that nobody else pays much attention. We inflate a rubber boat and head on out. When we're a quarter mile or so off-shore, we kick the beacon on again and leave it on till they locate us. Then it's somebody else's problem."

"We must reach international waters in a rubber boat, then?" said the Russian. "Or—oh. That was very foolish, I see."

Kelly smiled and wished he had not. Torn patches in the skin of his face had dried. The smile cracked them open again. "Yeah," he said, "there's been a lot of things worse than a violation of Algerian territorial waters lately, hasn't there? But I tell you—there's the goddam turn!"

Kelly swung the wheel left and his chest felt as though it were being broken on a rack. "*Jesus!*" the agent gasped. Then, in a tight voice that underscored the pain it tried to conceal, he said, "I tell you, Professor, the sub is the dicy part so far as the USG's concerned, though. If they catch me, the President can stand up and swear I'm an Italian national and never got within a thousand miles of the US. Hell, he tells bigger lies than that every day, he's a politician.... But if something goes wrong and the Algerians catch a State-class submarine in their back yard—well, that's a lot bigger than the U-2 was. And it'd be bad even without a Russian defector and twenty thirty bodies scattered all over the Algerian countryside. *Hell*!"

The iron-sheeted gate registered in Kelly's mind as the Renault rolled past it. The car's brakes were in no better shape than its lights—or Kelly's body, for that matter. Cursing, the agent twisted to look over his shoulder. He gasped and froze on the wheel. After a moment, he backed up with his eyes on the rear view mirror. "Professor," he said, almost too quietly to be heard over the car's rasping idle, "do you think you could unlock the gate and open it?" Kelly took the paper-tagged keys from his pants pocket, rising a little in his seat so that his torso could remain straight. "I'd do it, but. . . ."

Professor Vlasov took the keys solemnly and ducked out of the car. He looked like death in the side-scatter of the headlight, Kelly thought, but compared to Kelly, the Russian was in good shape. Posner might yet turn out to be the lucky one of the three.

The agent used his left arm to turn the car into the opened courtyard. Even so, the pain almost made him black out. There was no choice. They were going to have to call for help.

Vlasov had locked the gate behind them before Kelly could hoist himself out of the Dauphine. The Russian hovered solicitously, willing to help but well aware that any outside torsion could make a bad situation worse. "Just unlock the door, Professor," the agent wheezed. He held himself braced between the roof and the door of the car. "I'll be fine. Just get the door open and see if you can hunt up a phone."

The safe house was as cold as it was empty. Kelly stared at the collapsed boat and his radio receiver. Both sat on the bare tiles of the entrance hall. The MARS boat with its motor weighed over two hundred pounds. Hell, Kelly could not have managed half the receiver's weight in his present condition, much less that of the boat. And launching it into surf was going to be interesting at best.

"Here is the telephone," Professor Vlasov called from further inside.

The agent found Vlasov in a living room as empty as the hall had been. No one had told Posner to waste money on furnishings. The phone sat on a window ledge, more than ample for the purpose because the concrete walls were a foot thick. Kelly had been in bunkers less solidly constructed than an ordinary Algerian house. That was part of the reason that this one *rented* for the equivalent of $45,000 a year, of course. Cheap if it got Vlasov to the folks who were footing the bill.

The long-distance operator answered in Arabic, but he handled without comment Kelly's request in French for "60-14-26 in Algiers, please." As the

phone clicked and buzzed in proof that something
was going on, the agent lowered himself gingerly
to the floor. The cold tiles might have felt good on
his ribs. After a moment, Kelly did lay his left
palm on them.

The ringing on the other end of the line shocked
Kelly out of a revery. He was momentarily uncertain of where he was or what he was doing. He
had recovered a moment later, however, when a
voice answered in English, "Embassy of the
United States. Can I help you, please?"

"This is Angelo Ceriani," Kelly said in the same
language. "It is absolutely critical that I speak at
once with Sergeant Rowe. I need his home phone
or the number of whatever other phone you think
he might be near. I know this may be irregular,
but I swear it's as important as you can imagine."

"Ah, one moment," said the duty officer. There
was a click and Rowe's attentuated voice called,
"Tom, is that you? Jesus, we've been sitting by the
phone ever since the reports started coming in.
Are you all right? Is Vlasov?"

"Ah, Doug, do we have a secure line?" the agent
said. Though anybody with a tap on the embassy
phone was about to get an earful, even without
proper nouns. "Things could be worse," Kelly
went on, "though not for your boss. Or the car.
We're where we're supposed to be, but I don't
think we can move the goods without help. Doug, I
need you to get here as quick as you can. I'm sorry.
These are my orders and they take precedence to
any other orders you may have received. There's
nobody else I can trust."

"You can trust me," the sergeant said simply.
"That's why we're waiting here. See you—I hope
before midnight."

"Oh, Doug," Kelly added, "try to get a van or
another wagon. The stuff's pretty bulky, you remember."

"We'll be there," Rowe said. He broke the connection before the agent could.

Kelly cradled the phone and looked up at Vlasov. The Russian was standing beside the curtained window, as erect as a hatrack. "Well, Professor," the agent said wryly, "I suppose I ought to be doing a lot of things . . . but what I'm going to try to do is get some sleep. We ought to have some help here in a couple hours. I suppose that means you can change your mind about defecting. Wouldn't blame you after the way I've bitched things up so far."

"On the contrary," said Vlasov, his face and tones as serious as those of a priest at a memorial service. "Everything I suspected earlier has been proven to be true. I *must* escape the aliens and the humans they use as tools. I must, because they strive so hard to prevent me."

Kelly took off his coat by himself. He rolled it up as a pillow. The chill of the tile on which he carefully stretched himself seeped into his bones. The numbness it brought was a sort of relief.

After Kelly closed his eyes, the thought of Vlasov kept him some minutes awake. Vlasov, brave and brilliant and quite surely as cracked as a coot. But if Tom Kelly were damned to hell for exploiting a madman's obsession, then he was damned for a thousand better reasons besides.

Sleep came not as a relief but as a hiatus.

XLI

"Someone is here," a voice in Russian whispered harshly. Something was gnawing Kelly's earlobe. He flashed awake and caught himself before a sudden lunge reknotted muscles which had relaxed somewhat while he slept. Professor Vlasov knelt beside the agent. He was pinching Kelly's right earlobe between thumb and forefinger instead of shaking the battered body awake.

A large engine was idling nearby. Its exhaust note echoed within the courtyard walls. Doug must have kept a key to the place. "Tom," called a low voice through the bolted door.

Kelly stood, slinging his jacket over his right forearm and the knife which had been bare in his hand all the time he slept. He walked to the door. His smile was as stiff as one painted on the face of a golliwog. Kelly unlocked the door, then drew the panel open. He hoped to see Doug Rowe, but he was perfectly willing to meet the muzzle of an AKM.

Rowe was there, a step behind Annamaria Gordon.

"My God," Kelly whispered.

Annamaria's face when she saw Kelly went whiter than her breasts had been in the starlight by the tomb. Then she stepped forward deliberately and kissed the agent's bruised lips. She guided Kelly, drawing him back into the house and making room for the sergeant to enter.

In the courtyard beside the Renault stood a

Chevrolet Blazer. It loomed as huge as a tank over the stolen car. The Blazer would be perfect for running the boat down to the harbor, better even than the station wagon would have been.

"I was waiting with Doug," Annamaria said. "If you need help, then we're here to help."

Kelly licked his lips. "Professor Evgeny Vlasov," he said nodding. "Annamaria Gordon, Doug Rowe." Kelly's left arm was around the black-haired woman's waist. He clung as if she were a spar and he a shipwrecked sailor. "That's bad tradecraft, I suppose, but if we're any of us caught, we're beyond tradecraft for help."

The tall Russian bowed, offering his hand first to the woman and then to Sergeant Rowe. He looked at Kelly. "I know it makes no difference, sir," he said, "but—what is *your* name?"

The agent blinked. "Christ on a crutch," he said. "I'm Tom Kelly. And Professor, if we get out of this, I want to sit down with you and a case of beer some evening and swap stories. I—you aren't what I expected. And you're a lot of the reason we're still golden."

Sergeant Rowe had not followed the last of the discussion, since it was in French. After fiddling for a moment with the massive 10x70 binoculars on his neck strap, he said, "Ah, Tom—what do you need us to do?"

"Right, right," Kelly agreed. He sheathed his knife with care before he donned his coat again. "First, we load the gear into your car and carry it down to the waterfront. We unload there and you take the car back up to the street—it's too conspicuous right on the water. We get clear with the—" he looked from Rowe to Annamaria, then back; she had not been specifically told about the submarine—"with the sub and go out to meet it. You make sure we've gotten fairly away and you—both of you—you get the Hell outa Dodge. Clear?"

The boat and motor were a job to maneuver over
the high tailgate of the Blazer, even with the new-
comers doing most of the lifting. Kelly found he
was in better shape than he had expected, but that
still left him far from being the dark-haired
woman's equal at the moment. Annamaria should
not have come, but thank God she had.

The agent smiled as he thought of her. When
they all stepped back from the car, breathing hard
with the successful effort, he leaned over and
kissed her lightly on the cheek. Professor Vlasov
looked bemused. Sergeant Rowe stared at his
hands and said nothing, though he cleared his
throat.

"All right," Kelly said, "let's roll. It's going to be
a while before we get out far enough to meet the
sub, and I want to be underwater before daybreak.
It'd be nice to be out of the shallows, too, but we'll
do what we can."

The agent sat on the passenger-side bucket seat
while Rowe drove. The MARS boat was a four and
a half by two foot package. It took up all the floor
in back between the two facing bench seats. Annamaria rode leaning back against Kelly's seat with
her legs stretched out to the rear. Her hand
reached back to clasp the agent's between seat and
door. The four-block ride to the harbor was as
soothing to Kelly as his hour of comatose sleep
had been.

The brief calm ended when the sergeant pulled
up beside the sunken staircase. The ancient
harbor was empty but not still. The wind over the
rocks had a constant static hiss. Its amplitude
went unremarked until one noticed that the
rambling idle of the V-8 engine was completely
masked except when one stood in the lee of the
vehicle itself. The waves could be heard though, a
vicious, unmastered sound like zippers rasping to
open the fabric of the world. Kelly checked the
tuning of his short-wave receiver. He was running

it now from its separate battery pack. The blue digits were correct. He faced seaward and tripped his beacon for a five-second count.

The submarine's crew was as tight as Kelly was. Their response began to beep from the Kenwood within fifteen seconds of the moment the agent shut off his beacon.

Kelly cut the receiver power to save the batteries. "Let's move," he said. "One more stop and we're shut of this deal."

Unloading the Blazer was fast and comparatively easy, but it seemed like a lifetime's task to all four of those involved. Professor Vlasov was becoming increasingly nervous. Kelly could not be sure whether this was a return of the defector's old fear of aliens or if it had a more rational cause. The sand-colored Chevy looked square and huge on the corniche. Anyone strolling about at night was apt to wander over out of curiosity. Any policeman who was out would almost certainly do so.

As soon as the gear was on the ground, Kelly said, "OK, Doug—run the car up the street and park it, then get back as quick as you can to help launch. Up there it won't call attention to us."

"I'll go," said Annamaria. "You'll need Doug to get the boat down the steps without wrecking it." She slipped around to the driver's side of the Blazer without waiting for a response.

The agent glanced at her, a slim figure in a dark windbreaker. The breeze molded the nylon to her breasts like a silken sheath. The car door closed. "Right," he said as the Blazer pulled away.

Annamaria had been correct. The stairs were perfect for concealment, but they were barely wide enough to pass two men abreast. Without Sergeant Rowe's strength up front, the boat would have brushed the stone walls and stone steps repeatedly on its way to the beach below. The nylon was tough, but there was a lot of water out there. The stone as building material was no less able to scrape holes in the rubberized fabric than it was in its natural state in the surf beyond.

The tide had been going out for an hour or so. At the foot of the low cliff was a beach of coarse shingle. Panting and thankful, Kelly grounded his end of the boat on it. Sergeant Rowe began unfastening restraints, preparing to inflate the vessel.

The agent scrambled back up the stairs for his Kenwood. He was feeling a dreamy lightness after his exertion. It did not keep him from being aware of the pain in his torso, but it allowed him to perceive the pain as something happening to another person. Kelly stumbled on the last step as he returned with the radio, but neither of the other men seemed to notice.

The defector was rigid, but his eyes moved with the quick jerks of a mouse looking for a bolthole. He was as patently fearful as he had been when the shooting first started in front of the Institute. At that time, Kelly had taken the panic as a normal enough reaction to a firefight. Now that he had witnessed the Professor's calm under shellfire and worse, Kelly realized that there was something else going on.

Time enough to worry about that later, he decided. Doug Rowe was ready to inflate the MARS boat. "Just a second," the agent said. "Let's make sure I'm still on frequency." He pushed the receiver's power switch.

The noise blasting from the speaker was as unexpected as a bomb. It seemed for an instant to be as loud. Kelly twisted the attentuator dial by reflex. Even damping at 60 dB—each decibel a log-3 diminution in intensity—made no discernible difference in the beeps. The agent punched the power button again. He stared at Rowe in amazement.

"What the Hell are they thinking of?" Kelly

said. "They're putting out enough signal to rattle china. That's *bound* to bring somebody down on them—on us!"

Rowe had been shaken as well by the unexpected blast of noise. He shook his head. "Maybe it's not the sub," he said. Raising his glasses toward the horizon, he added, "Something's up there now, a plane. Maybe it's broadcasting."

Lights were coursing over the waves at low altitude, only a half mile out. Kelly was sure they had not been there when the Blazer was being unloaded. Now, when he listened carefully, he could hear the breeze-pulsed whine of a jet engine. "Doug," he said, "you don't understand." He was squinting toward the intruder, wishing he had the glasses. "That signal's like tuning to Die Deutsche Welle when you're in Wertachtal. It's nothing you could transmit from a plane, a signal like that. Christ, I'm surprised they've got that kind of power in the sub!"

"They have come for me again," said Vlasov in Russian. "They are broadcasting to thwart us."

A white spotlight glittered at sea. It disappeared as the aircraft banked abruptly. The plane's new course brought it shoreward. It was no more than twenty meters over the water. "What is it, a helicopter?" Kelly said, though even he could clearly see that the red and green lights were outboard on wing tips.

"No," said the sergeant in an odd voice, "but it can hover like one. It's a Yak-36. Tom, we're in trouble."

"Great," said Kelly, "those idiots have called the Algerian Air Force down on us now. These Yaks are armed, I suppose? If they're not, maybe we can run for it in the boat after all."

"It's not Algerian," Rowe said. His voice was barely loud enough to be heard. "The Russians have kept all of these for themselves. The Mediterranean Squadron's holding maneuvers off the coast, you know. This one must have flown off the *Novorossik*. It might have some underwing stores of its own, but I'd say she was dragging a MAD package at the moment. I guess there'll be a couple frigates along soon for the heavy work."

There was a scuffing of shoes down the passage behind them. Both Americans turned. Kelly had palmed his knife again. "Is everything all right?" Annamaria asked as she rejoined them.

Rowe lowered the glasses. "The sub can't go deep," he said, "not anywhere near this coast. Maybe they can run for it—it depends on just where the Russian ships are. But if the Algerians give them the go-ahead to use their anti-sub missiles—well, they don't have to be very close to drop an SSN-14 in, not with that Yak overhead to guide them."

"I don't understand." the black-haired woman said. She put a hand on Kelly's forearm, feeling the concern but without knowledge of the cause.

"Okay," said Kelly, "we pack up and run. The boat and motor are US Marine issue and I don't want to leave them if there's a choice. We'll—"

"Tom, there's a hundred and fifty men out there going to surrender or be killed!" shouted the sergeant.

"*I* didn't tell them to signal that strong!" the agent shouted back. "Come on, let's move!" He tried to reconnect the ends of a turnbuckle that would hold the boat in a tight package. The metal slipped in his hands. "Besides," he added in a voice as weak as a child's, "I told them I'd only consider using a sub in these waters if they'd promise to give it air cover. I can't make them—not have lied to me. But when I get back, I'm going to—"

The sky flashed dazzlingly red. The four of them on the beach looked up.

"Well," said Kelly in a changed voice. "I don't

have to kill anybody in Paris after all. But we do need to move.''

Where the Yak had been quartering the sea with its magnetic anomaly detector, there was an expanding cloud that rained fragments of burning metal. Before the explosion itself rocked houses, the crack of a sonic boom reached the shore at the tangent of a line of flattened waves. Spewed jet fuel began to dance and burn on the water.

"But what happened?" Annamaria said. "Did it just blow up? I don't see another airplane."

Sergeant Rowe connected the strap Kelly was struggling with, then a second one. The MARS boat was tacked into a manageable package again. "They credit Phoenix missiles with a 60-mile range," the soldier said as he worked. "I hear it's about twice that. And I think you just watched the first field test of a Phoenix."

"The first was off the coast of Libya in '79," Kelly said. He was smiling with relief. The extraction had been blown, he wasn't sure how; but they were alive and he'd find another way out. "I couldn't have found a better time for an encore, Lord *knows* I couldn't!"

Several lights had gone on in houses along the street, Kelly noted as they staggered back up the stairs. The Yak was a dying glow out at sea. Doug Rowe supported the upper end of the boat again. He set it down beyond the last step. "I'll bring the car around," he called to Kelly and Annamaria across the burden. He began striding across the broken terrain toward the Blazer parked a block away.

"Come on up, Professor," Kelly called over his shoulder. "We'll get out of this one yet." It felt good to have Annamaria's arm around him and her scent in his nostrils. He gave her a peck on the cheek, but when she turned to respond, he patted her away. He sat carefully down on the boat, watching activity in the town.

Doug Rowe was just getting into the Blazer. The courtesy light winked on, then off as the door thumped closed. Spies were not supposed to have cars with dome lights, Kelly thought. Well, maybe none of the batch of them were much in the way of spies. Stick to selling typewriters in the—

The flash that ate the Blazer was as bright as that of the exploding Yak.

The forty-gallon fuel tank spread orange flames the width of the street. The initial flash had been blindingly white. It left imprinted on Kelly's retinas the image of the hood and tailgate of the car collapsing inward because the steel body between them was gone.

"Professor, come on!" Kelly shouted down the black pit of the stairs. Behind him, the fire leapt and roared. "*Come on!*"

"Where's Doug?" Annamaria cried.

Kelly swung his legs over the boat, ignoring the woman's question as he struggled to get to the defector. Annamaria began running toward the flames.

"They are here to kill me," said the Professor, standing at the foot of the passage. His voice rasped.

"Then we'll have to kill them first, won't we?" the agent snarled. "Move! This beach is suicide if they come looking for us!" He clenched his left fist around the fabric of the taller man's lapels, guiding and dragging him up the steps. The knife in Kelly's hand was pure silver in the moonlight, but the blazing gasoline touched it with hellfire as they dodged through the jumbled rocks.

"Where are we going?" panted Vlasov when they had scrambled to the road a block from the fire. The uncertainty that had momentarily frozen him was gone. "Where are the others?"

No one had menaced them as they stumbled away from the corniche. With every step Kelly had expected a shot. He was moving on his nerves now, his nerves and a killing fury. It would drive him until he found an outlet for it or found his death first. "The KGB didn't have us," he said as he led Vlasov across the road at a clumsy trot. First south, then east to the safe house and the stolen car. "They didn't have us, then they did again. Maybe you're doubling, maybe the embassy's tapped or bugged. . . . Nothing I can do about that."

They were walking now, leaning forward as if to speed progress that their weary legs could not maintain. A mercury-vapor lamp on a street corner distorted their shadows into blotches on a pale blue field. "Nobody connected with the embassy's going to hear a goddam word about this from here on out."

"You still think it's humans, don't you?" remarked the Russian wearily. "Well, in the long run I don't suppose it matters."

"You're right," said Kelly harshly. "It doesn't matter at all!" But his waist was cold for lack of the arm that had encircled it.

The safe house was quiet, the gate locked as they had left it an hour before. Kelly pulled the gate open and then unlatched the Renault's engine compartment. "Stand back, Professor," he said.

"What are you doing?" the defector asked as he watched Kelly probe at the shadowed engine block.

"Wasting my time in the dark," the agent responded. He lay down on the gravel, wincing as he tried to see the underside of the engine. "Don't have a light, though, and we don't have time to get one. So. . . ." Kelly stood up again and slammed the engine cover. He wished that he had found something, a bomb, *something.* . . . If he had disarmed a bomb, he could have felt that much more confident that he was going to survive the next few seconds.

He got in on the driver's side. Vlasov started to
open the other door. The agent snapped, "Get
clear, goddammit!" He began fumbling with the
hot wire.

If there had been a key to turn instead of a pair
of bare leads to twist together, Kelly would not
have noticed it. Now his fingers brushed against
something beneath the ignition lock which had not
been there when he stole the car.

The agent bent over. He could see nothing because of the darkness and the sudden rush of
dizzying pain. The object was no bigger than a
button. From the way it slipped as he applied
pressure it was magnetized. Holding his breath
unconsciously, Kelly pried the thing loose from
the lock. A twitch of resistance suggested that a
hair-fine wire had parted after the magnet
released. Even trying to silhouette the object
against the streetlight showed nothing but a thin
disk.

Without speaking, Kelly got out of the car. He
hurled the button over the wall to the street. The
tiny tick of metal on cold asphalt could not be
heard above the breeze. There was no other response.

"Come on, Professor," the agent said as he got
into the car again.

"But what was that?" Vlasov asked.

"A bug, I guess," said Kelly as the motor fired
raggedly. "And I hope it was the only thing somebody decided to leave this car with."

As they turned east toward Algiers again, the
mirror showed that the sky over the center of
Tipasa was aglow. If Kelly lived, that fire would
not be the only monument to Staff Sergeant
Douglas Rowe, 23, husband and father . . . and a
better man, perhaps, then some of those he had
just died for.

XLII

The door had a spring latch and a draw bolt in the center of the panel. There seemed to be a second draw bolt just above the threshold. Kelly kicked the keyplate squarely with the heel of his boot. The blow tore the bolt from its seat in the jamb and left the lock sagging on half-stripped screws. The panel was only ½ inch plywood.

"Brace me," the agent muttered to Professor Vlasov. He kicked again, angling his heel toward the lower bolt. It gave and the spring latch fell off as well.

"I never figured," Kelly said as he pushed the panel out of the way, "how anybody managed to knock a door down with his shoulder. Or why anybody'd want to try."

Moonlight through the doorway let the agent find the cord to the desk lamp. He tugged it on, reaching past Vlasov to push the door closed now that they were inside. The office of the brass shop looked larger than it had with nine people filling it during the meeting. "Ramdan!" Kelly shouted. "Ramdan! Come down, we're friends!"

"This is a friend's house but you smash in the door?" questioned the defector.

"This isn't the time to be standing in the street shouting," Kelly said grimly. "Besides, I don't think he'd have opened up for us."

The alcove behind the panelling where the Mauser had been hidden was now empty. The agent had seen the rifle abandoned during the fire-fight outside the Institute, but it would have been

nice if there were something remaining there now.
A gun might change their negotiating posture
somewhat for the better. Or again—perhaps this
was just as well.

There were muted sounds from the living
quarters above. They changed abruptly to footsteps on the stairs. Heavy steps, shuffling; and a
lighter pair behind them as nervous as a mosquito
readying to land.

Vlasov seated himself on the swivel chair and
fiddled with the dark tie he still wore. As the steps
neared, the Russian stood and took a half step
toward the door. The agent stopped him with a
shake of his head. "No," he said, in French lest the
Kabyles think something was being hidden from
them. "We'll wait here real quiet and not take a
chance that anyone gets startled." Kelly's own
hands were empty and in plain sight in front of
him. They itched to at least palm his sheath knife.

Ramdan jerked open the door from the shop. He
had lost weight, and the flesh of his face seemed to
have been replaced by sagging gray wax. It was
less than eighteen hours since the gunfight, but
fear and his leg wound had aged the Kabyle a
decade in that time. "What are you doing here?"
Ramdan demanded in a voice as haunted as his
eyes.

Behind the shop owner was the boy who had
been in the front of the place during the meeting.
His eyelids flickered but the pupils did not move a
micron. They did not even tremble, as did the hand
holding the Enfield revolver. The muzzle of the old
gun wavered in an arc that covered Kelly and
Ramdan's kidneys about equally. The elder
Kabyle was nuts, thought the agent, to allow the
boy behind him with a gun. The kid was wired like
a carnival wheel.

"We need a little help, Ramdan," Kelly said
aloud. His hands were still, his voice reasonable.

"Everything's fine. Just a little help, and that we'll
pay for."

"*Help*," Ramdan repeated. His tongue hissed on
the French syllables. The shop owner took a
further step into the office itself. He supported his
weight on the right side with a crutch-headed
cane. His slippered feet glided over the floor,
rasping in the grit. "Three of us already have
died—perhaps more! *My* leg, it could have been
my *head*! They say 'Flee!,' but my leg . . . and who
would look after my wares? And you want help!"

The boy behind the shop owner had not moved.
His eyes glittered above the older man's shoulder.

Kelly shrugged. "You wanted to make a battle
out of it," he said. "Me, I'd already seen as much
shooting as I thought I needed to. . . ." He held
Ramdan's eyes, the cold certainty of his gaze
quenching the Kabyle's anger. "You've got
channels across the border, Morocco or Tunisia,
right? I want you to smuggle us out."

"Madman!" Ramdan shouted. "Get out of here!"
The Kabyle raised his stick to gesture or threaten.
Weight shifting onto his right thigh seared him
like a fresh wound. His mouth gaped soundlessly.
The cane wavered, its ferule flicking back to the
floor and skidding. The heavy man started to fall.

Kelly did not move. The boy, startled back into
reality, tried to catch the older man. The angle was
wrong. The Enfield clubbed at Ramdan's back as
the boy grabbed reflexively. The agent stepped
forward then and took the shop owner's weight on
his own shoulder and flexed knees.

Professor Vlasov stood and pulled out the chair.
Kelly guided the older Kabyle into the seat as
gently as if he held an equal weight of electronic
gear. When the agent straightened, he plucked the
revolver from the boy's hand without looking
around to give warning.

"We want you to smuggle us out," Kelly repeat-

ed in a voice from which his control kept the need
to pant with exertion. He thumbed the Enfield's
latch and dumped the six fat cartridges into his
left palm. He laid the empty revolver on the desk
top; the ammunition tumbled into the pocket of
the agent's shirt.

The boy snatched up the weapon again.

"How do you know we could get you out if we
wanted to?" Ramdan asked in a sick, weary voice.
His words were an affirmation of what had been
no more than an assumption in Kelly's mind until
then.

"Hell, are we little children?" the agent sneered.
He deliberately turned his back on the others and
sauntered toward the alley door. His thumbs were
hooked in his belt. "You need to raise money, to
talk to journalists . . . to buy guns and ammo, for
Christ's sake! Don't you?"

Kelly spun more abruptly than he would have
done if the .38 S&W cartridges were not a shifting
weight in his pocket. "And I don't suppose your
couriers get their visas stamped every week at the
border, do they?" he continued, hectoring the
injured man. "We need a quick trip out and we'll
pay for it, like I said. And I don't mean some Swiss
cloud-cuckoo land, either—green dollars, five
thousand of them, cash in hand when you've
earned it."

Both of the Kabyles were watching Kelly with a
different sort of interest. The boy had cradled the
Enfield to his chest as if it were a kitten. Now, the
fingers of his left hand paused in stroking the
empty cylinder.

The agent unbuckled his heavy belt. His face
wore a sneer as professional as a rock star's. He
slid the belt through the pants' loops, stepping
past Ramdan to use the desk front as a support.
The belt was thin leather, folded lengthwise in
three overlapping layers. Kelly raised the top
layer.

The chair squealed as the shop owner swiveled to watch. Kelly reached into the pocket formed by the middle and bottom layers. He plucked out part of the stuffing and dropped it into Ramdan's lap. "Forty-nine more where that came from," the agent said. "Just get me and my friend across one border or the other."

The Kabyle's hands quivered as he opened what had been tossed to him. It is one thing to talk of a million dollars in the abstract. A US hundred dollar bill, folded into sixteenths, is money in human terms.

"Just get us out," Kelly said very softly.

Ramdan smoothed the bill with the edge of his right hand. "It is. . .," he said, staring at Benjamin Franklin's face. "Just perhaps. . . ."

The telephone was in a lower drawer of the desk. The Kabyle took it out and dialed quickly. The instrument was balanced on one knee, the crinkled bill on the other. The phone rang repeatedly. Ramdan looked up in nervous embarrassment. Kelly was buckling his money belt on again.

"I'm afraid—" the shop owner began. All four men could hear the click of someone finally answering on the other end of the line.

Ramdan's eyes immediately flashed down to his lap again, the telephone and the money. He began talking, low-voiced but very quickly. The burr of response was not to his liking. The shop owner began to speak louder and even faster. His voice gained back the timbre and animation it had had the previous day, before a bullet had tempered his spirits in his own blood. He picked up the hundred with his free hand and began to snap it back and forth in the air, as if the person on the other end of the line could see it.

The exchange in Kabyle was long and heated enough that by the end, the other voice was audible also. Ramdan lowered the handpiece but did not cradle it. He was breathing hard. "All right," he said, "Tunis. But only one of you. That is all that will be possible for three weeks, perhaps a month. And the money in advance."

For the moment, Kelly ignored the demand about the money. He slotted home the tongue of his belt and said, "Why only one? What's the deal?"

Ramdan looked at the phone, then the agent. Vlasov was silent in a corner of the room. Only his eyes moved. The older Kabyle said at last, "It is a plane, a very small plane. We must land and take off outside the regular airfields, even in Tunisia. The ground is rough, we must not overload the plane." He paused, then concluded with a note of anger, "It is only because there is room available that Sa'ad would agree. Not the money. And because he said you fought like a tiger yesterday."

Kelly's smile was as stark as a gun muzzle. "Does he say that?" the agent asked with a mildness that deceived no one. Then, "Well, I don't try to fight the laws of physics, though. Okay. It's a deal." Everyone else in the room tensed. "You land near Tunis, I suppose?"

Ramdan nodded. The telephone blipped an interrogative. The shop owner snapped back at it in Kabyle without taking his eyes from Kelly's face.

"Okay," the agent repeated. "You'll take my friend here. We aren't going to use names, you understand, because I don't like some of the things that happen when names are used. . . ." He looked at Vlasov. A tiny smile lifted the corner of the Professor's mouth. "Sure, you hang out with crazy people and you start to get funny yourself," Kelly added. He rubbed his face with the knuckles of his left hand.

"My friend will have the money in his pocket," the agent continued in a stronger, certain voice. "He'll hand it over as soon as somebody delivers him to Carthage-Tunis airport on—" Kelly looked at his watch— "Monday morning. He'll also turn over that revolver—" he pointed to the Enfield— "which he'll be carrying until then."

The boy sprang back. "No!" he gasped. He pointed the weapon in what would have been a threatening gesture had it been loaded.

Ramdan looked up at Kelly and sighed. "In the base of the lamp," he said, gesturing behind him. "I understand."

Kelly nodded and unlocked the porcelain fixture from the wall. As the American slid the fiberboard cover off the bottom, Ramdan went on curiously, "But why at that time? That means we must feed him, hide him two days?"

There was a tiny Beretta .25 pistol in the lamp base. "Because," Kelly said as he checked the magazine—it was full— "it's going to take me that long to get there myself if you won't take me." He handed the autoloader to Vlasov. "Tell you the truth, Professor," he went on in French, "I don't doubt their honesty or I wouldn't be doing this at all. But if I can't be with you myself—" he smiled—"the next best thing is a gun."

No one laughed.

Kelly sobered. "One more thing," he said. "I've got a car of sorts, but I'll need plates for it. 58 through 60 series'll do, or out of country—I don't care which. They just can't be reported stolen until Tuesday, that's all."

Ramdan still held the telephone. He raised the handpiece and began talking into it in muted tones, looking up at the agent repeatedly.

"You are going to drive?" asked the boy. Both Kelly and Vlasov stared at him. That was the first connected sentence either of them had heard him speak. "They will stop you at the border if your license and registration do not match."

"Yeah, I'll have to think about that one, won't I?" the agent said. The kid might have a future after all. Not for field operations, though. He was the sort who threw the igniter and crouched down holding the fused satchel charge until it went off.

Ramdan lowered the phone again. "No more demands, then?" he pressed. "The deal as you leave it now?"

"Well, clothes—a jacket, Hell, that'll do," Kelly said. His smile was back and there was at last some humor in it. "And one more thing—a bed for a couple hours. Or a floor where people won't mind stepping over me." He stretched. His yawn camouflaged the stabs and ripples of pain that avalanched through his body.

Ramdan began speaking into the phone.

Aloud but to no one in particular, Kelly said, "Got a long way yet to go." His mind chorused from 'Sam Hall'—"Now up the rope I go, now up I go. . . ."

XLIII

The Temple of Minerva in Tebessa was almost four hundred years older than the city's Byzantine walls. As one of the best-preserved Roman temples in the world, it was an obvious magnet for tourists passing through the border city. Kelly was pretending to study the Roman funerary monuments in the fenced temple yard when the Renault 18 pulled up across the street beneath the massive wall. The car had Tunisian plates. Even better, they bore a CD prefix—Corps Diplomatique.

The American agent continued to face the stele as he watched the two couples. They locked up the car, laughing. They were all on the young side, the women in particular. One of them had black hair and a bouncing giggle that cramped Kelly's groin despite his nervousness. It was the men he needed to concentrate on, however, and one of them would do well, do very well. . . .

The couples were talking in French as they entered the gate. They passed Kelly with a murmured "Bonjour," all around. The temple had become a museum while Algeria was still a French colony, and the Algerians had kept it up to the extent of having a caretaker present.

The leader of the visiting couples was a half-step ahead of his companions. He was speaking volubly as he waved toward the carven transoms of the pillared but roofless entryway. He was in his mid-thirties with a dark completion; he was Kelly's height and weight besides, though he carried more of the latter in a chair-bottom spread. The French-

man was contrasting the temple with the one they
had seen in Djemila, and that was especially good.
It meant that they were returning home after a
stay of at least several days in Algeria. It would
have been more awkward if they had just crossed
the border, though you could finesse a lot with a
diplomatic passport. . . .

Kelly strolled out of the temple yard. His hands
were in the pockets of the jacket Ramdan had been
cajoled into giving him. In the borrowed clothing,
Kelly was not a prepossessing figure, but at least
he was no longer dressed in blood-stained rags.

"Well, I hit him on the head," the agent sang
under his breath, "and I left him there for
dead. . . ."

The hilt of his knife was blood-warm in his hand.

XLIIII

It was chill and dark in the hour before dawn. Lieutenant Colonel Nguyen Van Minh felt as weary and gray as the sky. They had to wait for the other team to get in position in back of the shop, and they seemed to be a long time doing so.

This was the sixth arrest—or arrest attempt—the Vietnamese officer had participated in during the night. Two of the suspected Kabyle terrorists had been missing. The squad, three civil police under Captain Majlid of the Presidential Security Office, had ransacked the houses and arrested all family members present. That might in time help the local security forces with their Kabyle problem, but it was of small use to Nguyen.

He had not found the three successful pickups to be a great deal more helpful to him. Nguyen was quite certain from their reactions that two of the Kabyles arrested had known nothing about the plot. The third man had owned the shop through which the kidnapped—or defecting, that was obvious—scientists had been spirited away. The Kabyle was anything *but* innocent . . . but his claim to have been attending a wedding in Oran would probably hold up. It meant that he had isolated himself from the operation. Whatever the prisoner might divulge in the interrogation rooms next to the Civil Prison, it would not include detailed information about the American operatives and their plans.

"Allah, four more of these," muttered the Algerian captain. "And then they'll add more to

the list if I know them." He took out a French
cigarette and looked at it before dropping it back
in the packet. The policeman with him at the front
door said something in Arabic. Majlid laughed and
took the cigarette out again.

Faintly through the air came the whistle that
meant the other two men had found the correct
back door. Radios were less common than was
need for them this night in Algiers.

The captain cursed and threw the cigarette
toward the squad's blue and white Mikrobus. He
hammered on the door and shouted in French,
"Open up in there! At once!"

Nguyen stepped instinctively to the hinge side of
the shop door. The front wall was mostly display
window and no protection, though. The police
seemed only tired. The uniformed man clicked off
the safety of his sub-machine gun without any
apparent concern. Out of deference to his hosts,
Nguyen kept his hand away from his own pistol.
He was taut, ready to move in whatever direction
was required.

Majlid cursed again. He nodded to the man with
the sub-machine gun. The uniformed man stabbed
the butt of his weapon through the glazed door
panel. He jerked the tube stock up, then sideways,
spilling more glass on the floor within the shop.
Nguyen thought that he could hear movement
inside.

The Algerian captain reached carefully through
the opening to avoid the rippling edges above the
putty. He worked the paired locks without haste.
When he had turned the knob to actually unlatch
the door, Majlid withdrew his hand. He kicked the
panel open, shouting, "Come out, Ramdan!"

There was a crash within the shop as someone
met the pair at the back door and tried to retreat.
Majlid frowned and took a step into the darkness.
He tugged at the pistol in his shoulder holster.

"*Don't!*" Nguyen shouted. His Tokarev was already in his hand. "The light's behind you!"

A red cordite flash hit the interior of the shop. The captain's head snapped up. He toppled against the policeman behind him.

The Vietnamese officer shot twice, aiming for the muzzle flash. Through the echoing shots cut the howl of a ricochet. That did not mean Nguyen had missed. The high-velocity bullets of his pistol would not have been stopped by anything as slight as a man's chest.

Within, something hard dropped. The uniformed Algerian was trying to clear his own weapon. "Not now!" Nguyen screamed. He dived into the shop just as somebody in back found the switch for the overhead fixture.

A stepped display platform filled the center of the shop. A boy gripped it to hold himself upright. The revolver with which he had shot Majlid lay on the floor at his feet. The boy's face was as white as a flag of surrender—except for his lips. His lips were brightened by bubbles of orange pulmonary blood. There were two holes a finger's breadth apart in the center of the boy's shirt. In his back would be matching holes.

The team from the back door was pushing a third, heavy-set Algerian ahead of them. There was blood on the prisoner's trouser leg. Since there had been no shooting from the rear, it was probably a reopened wound. As the older man was frog-marched in, the boy slumped to the floor of the shop. He covered the revolver with his corpse. The older prisoner wailed and tried to catch him. The policeman holding his arms jerked him back.

"Are you all right?" cried one of the men from the back. "Look what this one had—good thing he didn't pull the pin!" He raised a fragmentation grenade with a block of plastic explosive molded around it. The combination would lift the roof of a bunker or spread pieces of an automobile over a square block.

"Hey, where's the captain?" asked the man holding the prisoner.

"Him? Oh, dead," Nguyen said absently. He threw the safety of his pistol and holstered it without unloading the chamber. Majlid had taken the bullet through the bridge of his nose. His eyes bulged in ultimate surprise.

The Vietnamese took the bomb from the Algerian who was holding it. The prisoner inches away stank of fear and urine.

"Yes," Nguyen said as he examined the explosive, "this is very good. It will save us going back to headquarters to question this one."

"Wait a minute," objected the man with the submachine gun. "You can't—"

The Vietnamese colonel turned and looked at him. Words choked in the policeman's throat.

After a moment's silence, Nguyen began to give his instructions.

XLV

When the French couples came out of the museum, Kelly was standing on the broad firing step of the city wall. He was gazing out through one of the crenelations. The firing step was a good five feet above street level, so that even though the agent was standing beside the Renault, the grade separation kept him from being a part of the scene. The couples ignored him as he seemed to ignore them.

The tourist who looked most like Kelly began to unlock the driver's door. Kelly dropped into the street in front of the Renault. "Excuse me, please," the agent said with a smile. His hands lay atop one another, waist high.

The would-be driver scowled at the American. "We don't need a guide, thank you," he said, holding the door ajar with his hand. Behind him on the street side stood the black-haired woman. She looked more interested than anxious at the moment. There were other cars, other people, nearby, but no one else was within fifty feet.

"Oh, not a guide, no," Kelly said with a chuckle. He stepped around so that the man and woman were to either side of him. Their bodies masked the knife which the agent suddenly displayed. Only they and the other couple, staring across the car's low roof, could see the steel shimmer in the bright daylight.

"I am an agent of the Second Bureau," Kelly continued in soft, persuasive French, "but there is neither the time nor the opportunity for me to

make this request through channels. I am so sorry,
but three of you—" his smile and the splayed
fingers of his left hand indicated the woman
beside him and the other couple— "must accompany me back to Tunis."

"You're mad!" blurted the nearest man. "We
have done nothing!" The woman beside him had
drawn in her breath, but she was staring at Kelly's
battered face and not at his knife. The other
couple was straining, wide-eyed, trying to hear
what the agent was saying in his deceptively mild
voice.

"Of course you have done no wrong," the
American agreed. "You have by chance the
opportunity to serve France at only a slight incon-
venience to yourselves. Here, give me the keys—"
Kelly did not force the key ring from the other
man's hand, nor was the way his knife rotated
actually a threat. Between firm pressure and the
winking edge, however, the Frenchman released
what he at first had intended to hold.

"Madame," Kelly went on with a nod to the
black-haired woman, "if you will enter and admit
your friends?" He swung the door open, keeping
his body in the opening so that he could not be
closed out. Puzzled and hesitant, the three tourists
got in the car. The knife was hidden again, but it
was more real to the others than was the smile
which never slipped from Kelly's face.

"And you as well, sir, for the moment," the
agent said to the last Frenchman. The man obeyed
awkwardly, because he kept his eyes on Kelly
instead of watching what he was doing himself.

With all four of the tourists inside, Kelly knelt.
He braced his left hand on the top of the steering
wheel. A small rubber band was wrapped several
times around the last joint of his little finger.
Blocked circulation darkened and distended the
fingertip.

"Now, it really doesn't matter whether you

believe that what I am doing is necessary to the survival of France," the agent continued reasonably. "You can believe I'm a Mossad assassin, if you like, it's all one with me. But—you must believe that I am serious when I say that none of you will be harmed if you cooperate, yes?"

The others nodded, mesmerized by the gentle words and the mirror-finished steel.

"But you are not, I judge," Kelly continued, "persons used to violence. It is necessary that you believe me utterly when I say that I will kill you all without compassion if there is the least trouble from you."

The blonde woman in back nodded again, but the meaning of Kelly's words had not penetrated the gloss of fear upon her.

Kelly reached up with his knife. He slashed off the last joint of his own left little finger. The fingertip spun into the lap of the man behind the wheel. The Frenchman sagged as if his spinal cord had been cut. There were tiny droplets of blood spattering the inner slope of the window.

Kelly felt as if he were being bathed in hot sand. There was a notch and a streak of blood on the steering wheel where the blade had cut through his finger. In a voice that rushed through fire, the agent said, "I am very serious. Now, madame, please remove your husband's passport and identity papers. He will stay here. You will drive, I will sit beside you . . . and you will all be released unharmed near Tunis as soon as we can get there."

Kelly carefully wiped both flats of his knife on the coat of the man who had fainted. The wet streak soaked away instantly in the dark fabric. There was very little blood. The rubber band tourniquet prevented that. The bandage Kelly would apply when they got moving would handle infection for as long as it would have to.

The blonde woman managed to stick her head

out the window before she vomited.

"Sorry," the agent repeated, "but it can't be helped."

There would be no trouble from this crew on the long drive. Of that, Kelly was sure.

XLVI

Fear had drawn all the blood from Ramdan's skin. The pigment remained to turn the prisoner's naked body into a construct of yellow wax. Only his eyeballs and the occasional tremors that shook his whole plump frame proved the shopkeeper was still alive.

The two policemen still on the lower floor were silent and increasingly uncomfortable. Nguyen himself kept up a constant flow of conversation as he completed his preparations. "Did they ever talk of Doctor Hoang Tanh?" he asked with a glance at Ramdan. "You see, I'm not in the least interested in your friends, only in the foreigners who were involved in all this."

One of the policemen stirred uneasily. He said nothing. Nguyen turned to him sharply. "Here," the Vietnamese said. He held out a shallow silver bowl. "Take this upstairs and fill it with water. When you've brought it back, you can go up again and help your colleague guard the women."

The Algerian hesitated only a moment before he clumped up the stairs on his errand.

"Or perhaps," said Nguyen, again in a mild voice, "they talked of Professor Evgeny Vlasov?"

That brought a tremor from the prisoner, but he still did not speak.

The police had cleared the central display platform. They had bound the shop owner to it in a sitting position after stripping him naked. The swivel chair in the office would have been too easy to tip over. That would have given the subject

325

something to think about other than what Nguyen intended. Ramdan's limbs were tied to the platform supports. A final loop locked his waist to a pillar behind him so that he could not throw himself forward. The edge of the platform's second step caught the prisoner in the small of the back. That provided just the slight measure of discomfort which the Vietnamese officer wanted for the moment.

"I don't suppose you know the real name of the American in charge," Nguyen said, "but perhaps you'll tell me what name he used? Kelly, perhaps? Ah, well."

He found what he wanted for the demonstration in the tangle of objects which they had brushed off the platform. It was a glass plate on a stand of bronze filigree. Nguyen held the plate up to the light fixture and rotated it. The heavy glass threw a lens across the floor. It wavered briefly across the head of the teenage boy who still lay where he had fallen. The blood which had gushed from his mouth was dry now. It was as black as his hair. Ramdan's eyes followed the light across the floor. He began to tremble again.

The policeman who had been sent for the water returned. He carried not only the bowl but a full plastic bucket as well. "In case you need more," he muttered, keeping his eyes turned away from both Nguyen and the interrogation subject.

"Very thoughtful," said the Vietnamese, "but I would not have called you back anyway." Torture requires a particular mind set, the capacity to think of the subject as a thing to be manipulated rather than a human being.

Effective interrogation, which is not necessarily the same thing, requires the same mind set.

Nguyen set his paraphernalia on the ledge of the display window where it was directly in front of Ramdan. Most of the objects were not threatening. There was the bowl of water, the plate . . . a roll of adhesive tape from the office and a pad made by folding a strip of the velvet which had covered the platform. The incongruousness of the objects was itself disconcerting.

"You know," said Nguyen, working a bit of plastic explosive off the block, "I could understand if you were doing this to save your friends. But I'm not interested in your friends, you see, only in the foreigners. Who they are, what their plans are . . . where I might find them, yes. . . . That's all."

The explosive was white, with the consistency of grainy modelling clay. The piece Nguyen's thumbnails had cut from the block was no bigger than the last joint of a man's little finger. The Vietnamese officer rolled it into a ball, set it on the glass plate, and began to repeat the process. "Yes, I'm really sorry that you're doing this to yourself, Ramdan," the Vietnamese went on. "The only people who deserve to be punished are the foreigners who used you and your friends as pawns in their own games. But if you insist. . . ."

Nguyen set down the second bead of explosive—on the ledge rather than the plate. Both Ramdan and the remaining policeman were watching him with a similar mixture of curiosity and repulsion. "Did you know," the Vietnamese said cheerfully, "that *plastique* will burn without exploding? You mustn't step on it then, but otherwise it just burns. Very, very, hot."

Nguyen took a disposable lighter from his pocket. Smiling once more at his subject, he thumbed the flame to life and began to play it over the explosive on the glass dish. The bead of *plastique* quivered. A thread of black smoke wobbled up, and the point at which the lighter touched looked momentarily green. Then the explosive ignited.

The flame was sword-thin and a foot high. It twisted like the blade of a kris. Nguyen dropped his lighter and picked up the bowl of water. He gripped the metal through the velvet pad as he held the bowl over the flame.

"Isn't it an interesting color?" the Vietnamese remarked. "The way it seems to be pure white, but its light makes other things show a green tinge?" He did not raise his voice. The hiss of the fire and the hiss of air being driven out of the water overlay his words.

"How hot, do you wonder?" Nguyen asked. The last of the explosive was burning from the puddle it had made on the dish. The heavy glass exploded at the direct touch of a 1200° flame.

"*How hot?*" the Vietnamese repeated in a shout, and he flung the water boiling in the bowl across Ramdan's chest.

The Kabyle's screams took almost a minute to die away. He strained at the ropes holding him. The heavy platform rocked and thumped on the floor. The skin of the prisoner's chest blushed a bright scarlet and began to puff up.

"Now you see what I mean," Nguyen said reasonably when he could be heard again. He was using a shard of glass from the shattered plate to cut a length of tape from the roll. "*You* don't deserve to be punished. It's the foreigners, Vlasov and the American. . . . They're the ones who are at fault. Where are they now, do you suppose?"

Ramdan was blubbering now, but he still would not speak. Fresh blood was again leaking from the bullet wound in his thigh.

"Well, if we must, we must," murmured the interrogator. He spoke barely loud enough to be heard. He set the second bead of plastic explosive on the edge of the strip of tape. "Perhaps you think," he continued, "that I plan only to scald you with water? No, no . . . that was only a demonstration. I thought it only fair that you learn how hot the *plastique* burns. Learn indirectly, that is, before you learn...." Nguyen stepped forward with a sad smile.

Ramdan began to scream again before the Vietnamese officer had even touched him. His body thrashed to the narrow limits of the ropes. They threw him back against the wood of the platform each time. Nguyen waited for the moment of exhaustion. The policeman was staring in horrified fascination.

Ramdan paused, gasping for breath. Nguyen's hands darted for the Kabyle's groin. He wrapped the ends of the tape around Ramdan's genitals before the subject could even scream. The bead of *plastique* poked out from beneath the tape. It was clearly visible against the dark skin of Ramdan's penis beneath it.

"What a monster that American is to put you through this," said Nguyen sympathetically. He clicked his lighter. The flame was turned high, wavering.

"No," begged Ramdan. "No! *No—*" He tried to jerk back and the jet of butane singed hair from his scrotum. "*No-no-no—*Allah *I'lltellyouI'lltell I'lltellI'lltellI'lltell.* . . ."

Nguyen stepped back. The subject's voice had sunk into bubbling sobs. "Ramdan, my friend?" the Vietnamese said quietly.

The room stank with the feces that the shop owner had evacuated. He tried to raise a hand to wipe his eyes. The bonds stopped him. "I'll talk," he said dully. "Only before Allah, take the tape away. . . ."

"As soon as you have told us what you know," the interrogator promised. "As soon as you've helped us punish the foreigners who did this to you."

The remaining Algerian policeman suddenly bolted for the stairs, retching. Effective interrogation requires a particular mind set.

XLVII

"American Embassy," said the bored voice through the crackling of the Tunisian phone system.

"Don Marshal, please," replied Kelly in English. There was no pay phone in the restaurant, but the proprietor had no objections to Kelly making an important business call with the phone beside the cash register. No objections when he had assured himself that the American hundred dollar bill was real, at any rate.

The agent could have used the phone in the office, as a matter of fact, but this way he could keep an eye on his three companions. The French tourists were at a booth in back of the Western-style restaurant. The waiter had already arrived. Lucie, the black-haired woman, was ordering for Kelly as well as herself. The American smiled. Lucie waved a reply. The other couple, the Clochimonts, looked askance at her.

The Clochimonts had slept all night in the hotel's small bathroom. A string tied from the knob to Kelly's wrist would have awakened him if the door had been opened. Lucie, though, had spent much of the night talking to the agent. Whatever she might believe about Kelly's real mission, she and the agent were no longer on terms of mutual mistrust.

"Two-one-two," said the phone.

" 'Working,' you mean, don't you, snake?" Kelly replied, dropping into the past with the tremble of an anchor through deep waters.

"Who the Hell?" said the voice on the other end of the line. "This is extension two-one—"

"Think way back," the agent continued. "Nineteen and sixty-eight. A buck sergeant with black hair, one-sixty . . . I wore a bandanna for a sweat band back then—"

"*God-almighty!* Carried a Swedish K? Sergeant Tom Kelly! God almighty, man, I thought I'd never see you again!"

Bingo. "Tell the truth, snake," Kelly continued, "I wasn't just sure I'd ever see you again either, the way you looked when they started slapping IVs in your arms."

"Hell, yes," agreed Marshal more soberly. "I was conscious there for a while, you know, before the morphine got to me. I wouldn't have had a snowball's chance in Hell if you hadn't packed me back to the bird, man. And I know it." The speaker paused. "Ah, what brings you to Tunis, Tom? Or are you even here?"

"Well, a friend and me'll be getting in tomorrow morning," Kelly said. The cashier met his eyes occasionally, but there was no harm done even if the Tunisian did understand English. "That's sort of what I needed to talk to you about. You see, I've been selling office machines for a few years, but right now I'm back with the old firm again."

"Oh?" said the other man carefully.

"And I hear you never left the, ah, company you were with back in '68. In Cambodia. I need help, snake, and you're the only one I know who can give it."

Marshal's voice was more distant than the breadth of Tunisia accounted for. "I'm not sure what kind of a mistake—" he began.

"Listen, man," Kelly cut in harshly. "I didn't call to embarrass you, I didn't call to put you in a bind. I'm telling you, I *need* you and our Uncle needs you bad, worse'n you'll ever know. If I go through channels, I'm dead and *every*body's dead, just as dead as you'd have been if there hadn't been somebody to carry you back to the slick under fire. Now, you can turn your back on that and on me—or you can take my word for it that there's no other way that'll work for Uncle. And snake? This doesn't go in my report. I've got other stories I don't tell besides this one."

After a long pause, the other man said, "What do you need, then?"

"Well, my friend and I thought you might meet us for a drink at the airport tomorrow before we fly out. Got a pencil?"

Marshal grunted.

"Six-three, one-eighty, age 61 . . . white hair, blue eyes. And five-nine, one-sixty, age 38, black and brown. Europeans, I think . . . or Hell, US is okay, this is a one-shot anyhow."

There was another brief pause. Then the other man asked, "How good are you expecting these to be, then?"

"Man," Kelly explained, "if they're looking for us, we're shit outa luck anyway. But it'd be a real pisser to have the deal blow up because somebody forgot there should've been an entry stamp for Tunisia, hey?"

"All right," Marshal said. "Noon in the airport lobby. I'll see what I can do. I don't know why I'm doing this."

"Because it's your job," the agent said softly. "Oh—and snake? One more thing."

"What the Hell now?" But Marshal's voice too was soft.

"Could be I need that Swedish K again, but it wouldn't do me much good what with metal detectors and all," Kelly said. His eyes were on the booth and the French tourists. The food had come. Lucie beckoned him with an impish smile. "I hear you boys got involved in some of the off-shoots of the Sky Marshal program. If anything like that was lying around—it'd come in handy. I'm not going to beg you, man . . . but I need it worse than anybody who's ever carried one so far."

"Tomorrow at noon," Marshal said. The phone clicked dead.

In 1968, Don Marshal had been CIA liason to the Special Operations Group. Most of Marshal's peers had left the heavy work to Special Forces and indig—Hmoung—troops. Marshal, however, had gone on an operation into Cambodia. That had earned him a line of bullets across the abdomen and a ride on Kelly's back to the extraction chopper.

At the time, Kelly had thought the Company man had been in the wrong place at the wrong time. But after getting out of the hospital, Marshal had been reassigned to the Middle Eastern section. He had risen there—and he had missed the post-Nam RIF that had caught hundreds of his former colleagues. Kelly had heard in a bar in Rome about Marshal's later history. The information had not been of any importance when he first heard it, but it got filed in Kelly's brain for future need.

The future had arrived when the agent began developing his private contingency plans, to get out in a hurry and without using channels that anyone knew he had open to him.

"Excellent, excellent," Kelly said as he walked back to the booth and the chicken dish which awaited him. "Madame—"

"Lucie." She pouted, patting the seat beside her.

"Lucie, your taste is excellent," Kelly continued. His left hand felt as if a truck had run over it, but he forced himself to use it to unfold his napkin. He smiled at the woman, then the Clochimonts. "You have all been very kind in the hour of your country's need. It will be with regret that I leave you tomorrow. But I will leave you with hope that your vacation has not been too badly disarranged."

Lucie snickered. "Poor Jacques," she said. "Back in Tebessa worrying himself silly. We'll have to phone him at once." She looked at Kelly in concern. "As soon as you say we may, Angelo."

"I am a luckier man than your friend," the agent said after a mouthful, "for having had the pleasure of your company for a day."

And *that* was a goddam lie, thought the agent as he ate: but at least Tom Kelly was a damned sight luckier than he might have been. The morning would tell.

XLVIII

A Boeing 737 was landing with a whine and a
roar as Kelly walked to the terminal building. The
plane bore the blue and yellow livery of Cub
Scouts and Lufthansa . . . and Christ Jesus! he'd
better not start free-associating at passport
control or he'd blow this one yet.

Jacques Blondin's suit fit Kelly rather well,
though the agent doubted that he looked much
like a Second Secretary of the French mission to
Tunisia. He was not going to use Blondin's passport anyway, not unless it became absolutely
necessary.

He wished he could have treated the tourists a
little better at the end. He had dumped them afoot
on the outskirts of Tunis and doubled back to
reach the airport without their knowing his destination. Their car was now abandoned in the
airport lot. With luck it would be days or a week
before it was located there. And of course they had
all been more or less terrorized, while Blondin
himself had been left across the border with no
passport and no way of knowing what was happening to his friends and mistress.

Lucie had not been all that terrorized, come to
think.

They had been civilians, and that was a damned
shame . . . but it did not seem so very long ago that
Kelly had been wrapping a poncho around what
was left of a 14 year old boy. The kid had been
driving his water buffalo down a trail before
dawn. The Claymores of the automatic ambush

335

had put between fifty and a hundred steel pellets
through his body. This was a war, baby; and if you
doubted it, ask the ghost of that Yak-36 pilot.

Carthage-Tunis was a tourist airport; but it was
also the port through which hundreds of
Tunisians came and went to jobs in France. The
locals and their families stood in voluble clots
within the terminal. They were more colorful than
the modern pastel mosaics on the walls of the
lobby. Kelly walked among coherent groups,
watching carefully for Professor Vlasov. A man
nine inches taller than the average of the crowd
should not be able to—

"I am glad to see you," said a voice speaking
French. Kelly whirled, just as the Professor
touched him on the shoulder. The tall Russian
looked the agent over carefully. "You are at least
no worse," he said, sounding a little surprised.
"Except—your finger?"

"Cost of doing business," the agent said, glad
for the momentary pressure of the other's hand.
He switched to Russian and added, "I'm expecting
our papers to arrive in—" he checked— "half an
hour. The papers or God knows what. I'm
counting a lot on somebody I only knew six hours.
No trouble on your end?"

Vlasov shook his head. He was guiding Kelly
back to the corner from which he had spotted the
agent. "Your friends were honorable," he said.
"The gun would not have been of much use many
times, of course."

"Yeah, well," Kelly said. He was staring at his
hands, unconsciously curling the maimed,
bandaged finger out of sight. He looked up at
Vlasov. "Professor, do you know how we—how
everybody—intercepts microwave communications? I don't mean the signal, that's just a
matter of sticking up an antenna in the right place.
But how you get one phone call that you want out
of a million that're just garbage so far as in-

telligence value goes?"

Vlasov frowned. "No. . .," he said. Then, "This is important?"

"Professor, I—" Kelly said. "I don't know what's important." He shook his head, then continued. "Anyway, the trick is you run everything through a computer. The computer's programmed to kick out transmissions that have key words in them. 'Qadafi,' for example. Then a human being checks the few transmissions with the key word in them—and we get a tape of Qadafi telling a buddy in Ethiopia how he's going to go about killing the President of the United States."

"It still seems very burdensome," the Professor commented.

"Sure," Kelly agreed, "sure; there's still mostly garbage, and that's why the business costs the USG five, ten *billion* dollars a year. That's a fact. But it works, and my friend—" the agent gestured with his index finger— "I think your buddies on Dzerzhinsky Square have come up with a way to do the same thing with ordinary speech. I think they've been keying on your name since before you set foot in Algiers, trying to scope out the opposition."

Professor Vlasov was too much of a scientist to speak before he had done the math in his head. After he had done the math, he was also too much of a scientist not to blurt, "Why, that's absurd, *absurd*. Even if the KGB could *collect* conversations the way antennas do radio signals, the magnitude is—my name is not uncommon, surely you know?"

The agent nodded glumly. "Sure," he said, "in the right places it's like yelling 'Levy' in Brooklyn. But I'm telling you, Professor, they've been on top of us or just a step behind all along the way. The one place your technical people have had the jump on ours—our spooks—is in bugging devices." He spread his palms, flipped them an instant later to hide the bandage again. "As for impossible . . . if I read the background data right, there's about a hundred people on our side of the line who say what you claim to be able to do is impossible. *I've* met you, and I don't doubt you at all . . . but I've been picked up by the KGB too often on this run to doubt that something's up. And it's been okay since we've stopped using—that word."

Vlasov smiled sadly. "You believe that of human science," he said, "and still you refuse to believe that I might be correct—"

"I believe in AKs and BTR-60s and Mil helicopters," the American said in a rising voice. "*That's* what I've been seeing on this run. And if any of the bodies were green, I guess I missed them." His face and tone went neutral again. He added, "And I believe that's Don Marshal. Wait here a minute, Professor, while a friend and I make a little trip to the men's room."

The intervening years had been harder in some ways on the CIA operative than they had on Tom Kelly. Marhsal had been soft; now he was fat. The walk from the parking lot had beaded his face even in the dry Tunisian air. On the other hand, Marshal's suit fit him and he had not been prevented from shaving—as the agent had—by his scraped face.

The CIA man saw Kelly approaching and shifted the attache case to permit him to shake hands. His glance at the agent was an appraising one. If not warm, then it was at least less hostile than Kelly felt he deserved for clamping down on Marshal's guilt glands the way he had.

"This shouldn't take very long," Marshal muttered as he followed Kelly to the rest rooms.

"No problems, then?" the agent pressed.

"Only with my conscience," the other man said glumly. "And I suppose that was going to be a problem either way."

The CIA man took the first stall that came open. He locked the door behind him. Kelly waited for one of the adjacent stalls. He tapped on the partition as he seated himself in one of them. "Okay," he said.

Marshal passed a manila envelope under the partition. There were two worn-looking passports in the envelope—Austrian, which was a nice touch since Austria had business and refugee communities from all across Europe. The fuzzy photograph of 'Jean Gastineau' looked surprisingly like Professor Vlasov. That of 'Axel Brandt' did not look anything like Kelly, but neither did the photograph in Kelly's own real US passport.

"Fuckin' A," the agent murmured. "Snake, your people did a job to be proud of. I owe you one."

"Just don't saw off the branch behind me, you bastard," Marshal whispered back. "Here. And if anybody hears where you got this, I'll cut your balls off if I have to break into Lubyanka to find you."

The CIA man was passing another envelope under the partition. This envelope contained a gun.

General Electric had run off a batch of them under contract to the Department of Agriculture —a subterfuge which fooled only Congressional staff members who were trying to track down the billions of dollars spent annually on the intelligence establishment. The weapon was made entirely of a form of Lexan plastic. It was light amber to human eyes, and it was absolutely transparent to fluoroscopes and magnetic detectors.

That transparency extended to the ammunition. The gun had four barrels, stacked in pairs. Each barrel was sealed at the factory with a .60 caliber plastic bullet and a charge of black powder which was clearly visible through the wall of the tube. The lockwork was piezoelectrical, and the only

part of the system that would show up on an X-ray
was the tiny pellet of lead azide that primed each
load.

It wasn't a cannon. The plastic bullets shed
velocity like a suicide hitting the sidewalk, making
it a weapon for across the room at the farthest.
But as Kelly had said, he could not have taken a
Karl Gustaf sub-machine gun aboard the plane,
even if one were available. This would serve his
need—if it had to.

"Like I say, man," Kelly said, "I owe you and
Unk owes you—though he'll never know it. Hang
on a minute." The agent slipped the pistol into his
pocket. It was bulkier than a Chief's Special, but
its light weight kept it from significantly bulging
the coat. Kelly unclipped his little sheath knife
and passed it under the partition to Marshal.

"What the Hell is this for?" the operative demanded tensely.

"It's been a friend for a good long while," Kelly
explained quietly. "I ought to ash-can it right here,
since I can't take it on the plane this time,
but . . . look, snake, hold it a month for me. Open
letters with it or something. If you don't hear
anything by then, do what you please with it."

Across the thin panel, the CIA man muttered in
irritation. The knife was not merely fifty bucks
worth of double-edged steel to Kelly, however. For
five years, the agent had sunk himself in a world
without a human being to cherish. The human
emotions had spilled out onto objects. Understanding the phenomenon did not make it any the
less real to Kelly.

"Well," said the agent, "I'll be seeing you later."

"Hope to Hell you don't," Marshal snapped
back. But as Kelly started to open the door of his
stall, the operative added softly, "Keep your head
down, snake. And you don't owe me—we're even."

No one looked at Kelly with unusual interest as

he left the rest room. Professor Vlasov followed
the agent around to the Lufthansa ticket counter.
Kelly did not bother to watch for Marshal,
knowing that the CIA officer would wait a minute
or two before he exited. Kelly had never taken an
action simply because it would put someone else
in his debt. Certainly he had never risked his life
on the slim chance of a survivor's future
gratitude. But favors were like the clap: what goes
around, comes around. This one had come around
at a very good time.

Kelly paid for the round-trip tickets in American
dollars, took his change in Tunisian dinars. The
Tunisian dinars had been originally pegged to the
New Franc rather than the Old, so that it was even
now worth about ten times as much as an Algerian
dinar ... and all the currency he had in either
form was so much waste paper to Kelly now. He
had no intention of ever seeing the wrong side of a
North African border again, just in case somebody
figured out his responsibility for the previous
day's carnage in Algiers.

While the blonde female clerk made out the
tickets, Vlasov kept up his end of a conversation in
French about the one-day conference the two
would be attending in Frankfurt. There was
nothing illegal about travelling without luggage,
but it made the fugitives memorable. A bad story
was perhaps better than none at all, in case somebody checked passenger lists with the clerk.

It was nice to see a woman working again. Beyond
everything else, the Arab World would forever be
imprinted in Kelly's mind the same way South-
East Asia was. Blood, bodies, and a paranoia that
was not psychotic only because it was necessary.

"How are your instincts doing, Professor?" the
agent asked as they walked slowly toward the exit
control stations. They were clutching their
Austrian passports and the forged currency and
customs-control cards which Marshal had sup-

plied as a necessary part of the package.

"Instincts?" repeated the defector uncertainly. He had been glancing about the crowd with animation.

Kelly grinned. "When you figure things are about to go through the floor, you're jumpy as a frog on a hotplate. I figure things must be okay by you if you can stand and talk like a tourist, huh?"

Vlasov smiled back. "Yes," he said, "but you must also remember that I am insane and therefore untrustworthy, yes?"

Kelly began to laugh. But not immediately.

The short man watching the fugitives in the window's reflection had brown skin and wore a jellaba. Even a glance at the man's face would have displayed his Oriental features, the flat nose and the epicanthal folds at the corners of his eyes . . . but the watcher was a careful man. In any case, Kelly's perceptions had been whip-sawed to nothing by exhaustion and elation combined. The American had not noticed the watcher as a local, much less as the Cultural Attache of the Vietnamese Mission to Tunis.

As Kelly and the defector moved off to have their papers stamped, the Vietnamese turned to look at them directly for the first time. Then he strode briskly for the bank of pay phones in the lobby. His call was brief and simple.

It was the staff at the embassy proper, after all, who had the problem of relaying the information through an international operator.

XLIX

"Colonel," the voice whispered. "Colonel...."

Nguyen rolled upright. His right hand snaked under his pillow in a motion the embassy clerk did not recognize. The pistol was not needed here, of course. But Nguyen Van Minh had been back in the jungle while he slept, not in an office of the Paris Embassy of the Democratic Republic of Viet-Nam.

The clerk was holding out a phone. Beyond the blinds, rain was spattering the windows of the dark office. "It is Tunis," the functionary said. "You asked to be awakened...."

Nguyen took the phone. He waved the other man away. "Yes," he said, "Nguyen here."

"Colonel," said the thin voice on the other end of the line, "we have spotted them in Tunis-Carthage Airport. Their flight is Lufthansa 505, arriving Frankfurt at 18:32 local time. Today, that is."

Nguyen cursed under his breath. He had gambled that the fugitives would head directly to Paris. Well, Frankfurt was workable, the trains were fast and direct....

Anything was workable. Nguyen had a man to kill, and nothing would prevent him from doing so. Honor demanded it. He would describe the act to his superiors as a duty to the State when he finally made report; but the reality went much deeper. Headlines and the colonel's identification card had carried him through some obstacles. It was Nguyen's own personality, however, that had enabled him to run rough-shod over bureaucratic delays even before Hanoi cabled assent.

"You're sure of your identification?" the colonel asked. There had been no photographs available, and only Nguyen himself of the personnel in the West had seen either Vlasov or the American who had killed Hoang.

"There can be no question," the voice from Tunis insisted. "The Russian, Vlasov—tall, pale . . . his right arm missing? And he was in company with another European, not certain, of course, but he *could* be the man you described."

"Right," Nguyen said. "Well done." He hung up abruptly, staring for some minutes at the dial of the telephone.

"Is there anything else you need, sir?" asked the clerk who still stood near the door.

Nguyen looked up as sharply as a firing pin releasing. "Yes," he said, "a line to the Frankfurt Consulate. They should be expecting the call."

He would need someone to follow the fugitives from the airport, someone else to meet him at the train station and pass on the information. Simple enough, even for a three-man consulate which included only one intelligence officer.

The last of the work might be tricky, but that would be the colonel's pleasure to handle himself. It was work he did as well as any man alive.

Nguyen checked the magazine of his Tokarev by habit before he replaced the weapon in his holster.

7

"Come on, Professor," Kelly panted as he swung open the front door of the hotel, "you people are supposed to be used to *real* cold where you come from." The agent was tired, but he now had a loose sense of victory. Besides, he felt as if he were returning home after a long trip. Kelly always stayed at the Excelsior when he had an overnight in Frankfurt. Coming back to the hotel was a return to more than a building.

"Where I come from, we dress for the cold," Vlasov grumbled without bitterness. The agent's good humor was infectious, and the Russian, too, seemed to feel that they were at least in reach of safety. Like Kelly, he was damp from the drizzle. They had started to run the block from the train station to the hotel, but the events of previous days had simply not left either man enough strength or energy.

The desk clerk brightened as he saw the men. "Ah, Mr. Kelly," he said, "I had almost given up hope of you. Welcome."

"Emil," the agent said, "I almost gave up hope a time or two myself. Can you find a double room for my friend and me? Sorry I didn't phone ahead, but things got rushed. Oh—and our luggage is back in the airport somewhere. Do you suppose you could find a place to deliver a couple suits after hours? We'll pay what it takes to be able to change into something dry."

"Why yes, I can arrange that," said the clerk. He handed Kelly a registration card and a key with a long brass tag. "But I believe the lady said she had brought some luggage of yours along with her."

"The . . . lady?" repeated Kelly. He turned smoothly, his eyes wide open so that he had the full arc of peripheral vision that he might need. In front of him, the stairs; to the left, the front door and the rain-slicked dark beyond; to the right, the passage to the dining room and the tiny lobby beneath the stairwell. Kelly's lips smiled, and his right hand was firm on the butt of the gun in his pocket.

"What?" said the clerk. "Oh—"

"Good evening, Tom," said Annamaria Gordon. She walked from the lobby toward the reception desk. "I suppose I call you that here." Her smile was nervous, but when she stopped a pace from Kelly she stood with lady-like dignity.

Vlasov was puzzled but not concerned. He looked from the woman to Kelly and said, "I had not understood you would be meeting us here, madame."

"How?" Kelly mouthed. His hand was still in his pocket. His eyes were staring, trying to scan everything that might be a threat, a target.

Annamaria reached into her purse with a thumb and forefinger. She brought out Kelly's account book. "You left this in your luggage," she said. Her smile was suddenly brighter. "All I knew was that you were making up your route as you went along. You didn't have to come to Frankfurt, but it was logical, you know the city and you had to go somewhere you knew—" She riffled the pages of the spiral notebook. "You always stayed at the Excelsior when you came here. And Tom—I had to go somewhere."

"Mr. Kelly?" said the puzzled clerk.

The agent turned abruptly and completed the registration card. Over his shoulder he muttered, "I'd have come back." He looked up at the clerk. "Emil," he said, "we'll wait on the suits, thank you, until we sort things out." He started to take the room key in his right hand but stopped.

Holding the key in his left, Kelly led his companions to the stairs. His free hand hovered near the pocket of his coat.

Annamaria said in a low voice to the agent's back, "No, I had to leave. Buffy came and told me what . . . what Rufus had done. She had to talk to someone, poor thing. I . . . it was me by default, I suppose."

Kelly unlocked the door nearest the stairhead on the second floor. "If she told you that, I suppose you got a notion of what I did, too." He gestured the others past him with his left arm.

"You acted by the rules you lived by, Tom," the woman said as she entered the room. "Rufus acted by no rules at all, his or yours or anyone's. That makes him not a man but a bomb, ready to go off at random." She turned and smiled, at Vlasov and past him to Kelly. "If you get random, I'll leave you too, dear Angelo. But until then, I'll stay if you'll have me."

The agent shot the dead-bolt lock. Then he reached for Annamaria. Professor Vlasov smiled and edged aside, but Kelly stopped himself anyway.

"Oh, don't worry about me," the defector said. He looked around the room. It was plainly furnished with a desk, a pair of chairs, and two single beds with feather ticks. "I can—or there is another room, the one you have, madam?"

"No!" Kelly snapped. He took a deep breath and forced a smile. "First things first, Professor," he said. "You don't leave my sight until I put you in the hands of General Pedler or somebody I've met on his staff. We're not going anywhere near the Consulate-General here, either. There isn't anybody there at night who'd be able to figure out what I was talking about. And even in the morning—well, I trust Pedler, I don't trust a Consul General I've never met. Not to make decisions that might be your life and mine if they're wrong."

"I thought you might go straight to Paris instead

of—dodging again," Annamaria said. "Or Rome, or—but there aren't too many direct flights from North Africa. A friend in the Paris embassy would tell me if you were heard from there, and I—I thought I'd wait here for a few days, and then make plans if I had to."

"I've got visions of being tracked down by a world-wide network of embassy receptionists," Kelly said with a grin. He squeezed Annamaria's hand. "Anyhow, I'm glad that this time when I left clues, it was somebody I wanted to see who picked them up." He stepped over to the phone, taking off his damp jacket as he did so.

"Actually," the woman remarked with some asperity, "it wasn't a receptionist. In Paris, the Marines do that anyway. It was the Deputy Chief of Mission."

For the first time, Annamaria appeared to notice how wet both men's clothing was. "But here," she said in a cheerful voice again, "I really do have your suitcases in my room." She glanced at Vlasov. The Russian had seated himself on a corner of one of the beds. "At least you can sit in something dry, Professor," she added, "though I don't suppose it'll fit you any better than an outfit of mine would."

"Ah, take the key," the agent said. Looking at his own outstretched hand, he added, "That was a pretty dumb thing for me to say. I'll work on doing better."

Annamaria's touch and her smile were electric. Then the door clicked shut behind her.

Kelly dialed the desk. "Need to start the ball rolling," he remarked to Vlasov. As he waited with the phone to his ear, the agent noticed his coat on the bed where he had tossed it. He reached into the side pocket and brought out the pistol. "Suppose I'll have to deep-six this when you're clear," he said. "Tempted to keep it for a souvenir, but that wouldn't be fair to—"

"Yes?" said the phone.

"Emil," the agent said, "see if you can get the US Embassy in Paris for me—I don't have the number either. I need the Defense Attache's Office, General Pedler himself if he's around. I'll wait as long as it takes."

As the phone hissed, Kelly tucked the pistol back into the coat. He began to massage his scalp. "Never occurred to me I'd need to phone Pedler," he said to the Russian, filling the empty seconds, minutes. "Figure there'll be somebody there in the office who can raise him in an emergency. And he must have got enough word from Algiers already to know this is an emergency."

The defector was edging backward on the bed. His eyes flicked from the window to the door.

"What the Hell's the matter?" Kelly demanded tensely. "Professor?"

There was a sound in the hall. Kelly looked from Vlasov to the door, his scowl smoothing to greet Annamaria. The panel swung inward without a click from the latch. There were three men in black, filling the doorway. One held an open badge case. The other two pointed objects that looked less like guns as they stepped forward. The door swung shut behind them.

The phone in Kelly's hand made a sizzling sound. Then it went dead.

"Professor Evgeny Vlasov?" said the one with the badge. He spoke in Russian with neither accent nor tone. "We are from Section T of the Bundespolizei."

"What is Section T?" Kelly asked, putting the handset down very carefully without cradling it. He watched the intruders. The distance to his coat, to his pistol, he measured in his mind rather than with his eyes or his poised right hand.

It was too far.

The intruders did not respond to Kelly, though one of them kept his—gun—trained on the agent. "You must come with us, now, Professor Evgeny Vlasov," the middle one said.

Without changing expression, the third man in black turned. He was already raising his weapon when the hall door burst inward.

If the self-styled 'Federal Policeman' thought his gun was a magic wand, he reckoned without Nguyen Van Tanh. The Vietnamese colonel knew he had to kill everyone in the room; he started even as the door swung. The first five shots were so fast they could have come from an automatic weapon. Two through the torso of the man facing him, two through the spine of the man who had spoken to Vlasov. The 87-grain steel bullets howled through their initial targets, one of them shattering a window pane as it exited the room. All five shots ripped out in less than a quarter second. The last of them was kidney level through the intruder covering Kelly.

As it tore out of the body, the Tokarev bullet hit the man in black's gun. The narrow entryway dissolved in a white flash.

The muzzle blasts had been deafening in the confined space anyway, but even later the survivors were sure that the flash had been almost soundless. It was as dazzling as a magnesium flare, however, and it was by blind memory alone that Kelly dived for the coat and his pistol within it. He scrabbled to find the pocket.

Nguyen, blind as his opponent, caught the blur of motion and aimed for it by instinct. His trigger finger was as much a part of his pistol's lockwork as the firing pin itself. As it started to squeeze, Annamaria threw a jacket over Nguyen's head and jerked him backwards.

The Colonel's sixth shot cracked above Kelly's head. Kelly fired twice through the fabric of his coat. The plastic bullets smacked audibly as they hit. Nguyen thrust behind him with his left hand, weighted with a spare magazine. Annamaria caromed back into the hallway, tearing the blindfold from the Vietnamese even as Kelly shot him twice more—once in the center of mass, once behind the ear—and the Tokarev slipped from fingers which had already swung it on target one final time.

The pistol skidded on the carpet. Its owner did not. He sprawled instead like rice pouring from a fifty-kilo sack.

Kelly raised himself. His coat was smoldering, adding its fumes to those curling from the muzzles of his pistol. White sulphur smoke mixed in layers with the sweeter odor of nitro powder. The American stared at the fallen Tokarev. The pistol looked as worn and as deadly as a Marine sniper.

Annamaria was getting up. Kelly stepped to her, over Nguyen's body. "Are you all right?" the woman asked before the agent himself could speak.

"Bastard was better than me," said Kelly, tossing his own empty weapon to the nearer bed. Professor Vlasov had stood up also. There was an expression of hope dawning slowly over his face.

"Good thing I wasn't alone this time," the agent said. He drew Annamaria up with a controlled grace that belied the adrenalin tremors shaking all his muscles. "Best thing in the world that I'm not alone any more," he said.

"They can be defeated," the Professor said. "By guns, by my devices. By thousands of my devices above Earth."

Kelly released Annamaria. "It was the KGB," he said loudly. "It was the KGB, and one of them dropped a grenade!"

Doors were opening, spilling bursts of pop music and questions in a variety of languages. Wet air through the broken window swirled the powder smoke.

Professor Vlasov bent. The body of only one of the intruders remained after the blast, eyes staring upward. Vlasov ran the fingers of one hand over the floor. In the center of the area, the carpeting was gone and the hardwood surface beneath was charred through to the concrete base.

Inches further from the heart of the blast, the
nylon nap had melted and been drawn up in long
spikes toward a momentary vortex. Annamaria
knelt beside the defector.

There was a loud gasp from the hall. Emil stood
there, gaping into the room. Kelly could not be
sure whether the clerk was more horrified by the
dead bodies or the blast-eroded walls and floor.
"Mr. Kelly!" Emil said. "Mr. Kelly!"

Kelly nodded. "It'll be taken care of, Emil," he
said. "You know me. It'll be taken care of."

The clerk opened his mouth, but further words
would not come. He turned briskly and clattered
down several steps before he paused. "Oh, Mr.
Kelly," he said, a good servant even in the midst of
disaster, "there was a fault with the line, somewhere; but your call has been put through now."
He bounded down the rest of the steps to his desk.

The phone muttered. Kelly looked from Vlasov
to Annamaria. The woman was running her
fingers over the face of the man in black. Kelly
picked up the fallen handpiece. "Hello?" he said.

"Hello!" the phone repeated. "I said, this is
Major August Nassif. You'll have to state your
business to get through to the general, I don't care
who you are, and I'm not going to hold this line
much longer!"

"This is Tom Kelly," the agent replied. "I'm
about to be waist deep in Frankfurt cops." He
looked from the living humans to the body on the
floor. "I think General Pedler's looking for me.
Tell him my business is Skyripper."

Annamaria's hand gripped and tugged. The face
of the thing on the floor was the color of raw cinnabar.
The nose was a single slit, the mouth a round hole
with teeth like a lamprey's around the inner margin.
Fragments of the mask Annamaria had removed still
clung to the skin like tendrils of white gauze.

"Tell him," Annamaria said in a clear voice,
"that the business of the world is Skyripper."